Advance Praise for *Center*

"Timely and compelling, Waggoner's debut delivers a deft look at women and contemporary life, examining the choices we make and the decisions that define us."

—**Laura McNeil**, author of *Center of Gravity* and *Sister Dear*

"Nicole Waggoner is a fabulous writer, and the women of *Center Ring* are fully realized and completely captivating. Highly recommended."

—**Richard Fifield**, author of *The Flood Girls*

"*Center Ring* is a beautifully written, highly relatable novel about the balancing act that is modern womanhood. Waggoner treats her richly drawn, relatable characters with compassion and understanding."

—**Kristy Woodson Harvey**, author of *Dear Carolina*
and *Lies and Other Acts of Love*

"No matter what successes are achieved in life, missteps and self-doubt can make it nearly impossible to find balance. Nicole Waggoner's debut novel is an exemplary example of how five women, so different from one another, struggle with love, life, and identity. It is so much more than a story of friendship. It is a tale of endurance, hope, and determination. I want to jump into this book and become friends with all of these women. I am definitely looking forward to reading more from this author."

—**Whitney Dineen**, award-winning author of
The Reinvention of Mimi Finnegan

"Authentic, funny, and concerned with the things in life that matter most—friendship, motherhood, love, and, of course, flings with gorgeous Hollywood movie stars—*Center Ring* brings five unique women to life and tells their stories with compassion and charm."

—**Kamy Wicoff**, author of *Wishful Thinking*

Center Ring

Center Ring

Circus of Women | Volume One

Nicole Waggoner

SWP

SHE WRITES PRESS

Published 2016
Printed in the United States of America
ISBN: 978-1-63152-034-1 pbk
ISBN: 978-1-63152-076-1 ebk
Library of Congress Control Number: 2015955550

For information, address:
She Writes Press
1563 Solano Ave #546
Berkeley, CA 94707

She Writes Press is a division of SparkPoint Studio, LLC.

To Sister-Friends Everywhere

"No man can be happy without a friend, nor be sure of his friend until he is unhappy." —Thomas Fuller

Norah

*M*aybe she should have told her husband first. Then again, she knew emotional numbness was key in difficult conversations. A lashing from her girlfriends would help her field Matt objectively and possibly emerge from this fiasco with some shred of a support system.

Realizing the steering wheel was digging impressions into her uncharacteristically shaky fingers, Norah loosened her grip and attempted to script her confession.

"I need to tell you something, and I'd rather tell anyone but you."

"I hope you know how important you are to me."

Wistful for a traffic standstill, she eased into the trendy restaurant district and ignored the valet in hopes that parking blocks away would give her more time to think, or rather dwell, on her way to St. Peter's table.

"Reservation for Leila. Party of five, please."

Camille "Cami" Clark, 34,
Photojournalist; Creative Director, InFocus Productions

Cami

*F*ired? How? The conversation seemed to be on a constant loop in her mind, paired with equal parts embarrassment, self-loathing, and disbelief. Cami was as indignant about her stunned reaction to the words leaving her new boss's perfectly lined lips as she was about the ridiculous accusations themselves. This was why she'd always preferred working with men. Say what you will about workplace equality, but to Cami, the rules were simple: the more estrogen in the room, the more likely she was to be misunderstood. She'd caught more than one of her collaborators crying in the ladies' room after being asked a simple question such as "When will you be finished editing? Do you realize you've exceeded the hours you budgeted for this project? I assume you have a plan to make up these hours." Sure, most of the women she worked with thought she was a bitch. She'd made attempts over the years to soften her directness, but even when she could do it with a straight face, her tone always seemed condescending. Perhaps she could blame having grown up as the only girl among three rambunctious brothers, or the late physical development that had sent her running to sports fields, versus shopping malls. Whatever it was, she was tired of being a target of office gossip. Let them fail without her. No one dared deny that she had helped to make this company what it was.

A rogue tear ran down her cheek as she realized eleven and a half years of her life were now reduced to three cardboard boxes and two computers in her trunk. Cami slammed the door and tossed her keys to the valet at Cru.

Leila Oliver, 33, Ph.D.,
Professor of Humanities; Current Position: Stay-at-Home
Mother of Two

Leila

$\mathcal{L}$eila admired the soothing ambience of the restaurant feeling mutually grateful and guilty for the night out. Her days of taking uninterrupted adult conversation and eating a meal with two hands for granted had ended abruptly when her first child was born. She loved her daughters more than anything and felt blessed to be able to stay home with them, but tonight's break was just what she needed to recharge, wear real clothes, and feel like herself. Part of her yearned to return to the era of professional attire when her blow-dryer and flatiron left the drawer daily, instead of once every few weeks, and her racks of pumps didn't collect dust. She prided herself on making an effort to avoid the mom-jean stereotypes that dotted the punch lines of late-night-television hosts, but she was more than tired of her Casual Corner look. In her most honest moments with herself, she knew this inflated objection to her flats and leggings was misplaced resentment about the lack of balance in her life. Or, maybe that was the fatigue talking. Her oldest hadn't been sleeping well, and her youngest was going through an exhausting case of the twos. Wine and some laughs with the women she considered sister-friends would champion her into tomorrow. Didn't it always?

Ellie

"*Matchmaker* is such an archaic term, Ms. Lindsay. I prefer *connections coordinator*."

"Of course," Ellie said, stealing a glance at her watch.

"Moving on to the next question in my profile generator, I always like to know why my clients feel their last serious relationship ended—or, more directly, what traits their partners found difficult."

"I didn't like his girlfriend," Ellie quipped with a smile, fighting the urge to tap her foot. If there was one thing she could thank this sadistic industry for, it was teaching her grace under fire. Hiding her nervous "tells," as she referred to them, had become second nature after years of coaching clients to conceal signs of insecurity and deceit.

The "*matchmaker is an archaic term*" matchmaker smirked amusedly, and Ellie decided to cut to the chase. After all, if he expected her to pay his small fortune of a fee, she might as well be honest. "I agree compatibility is key to a successful relationship. That said, and in the interest of efficiency"—she gestured to his list of questions—"I'd like to give you a brief synopsis of what I'm looking for. And then we can fill in any leftover blanks in your"— she affected her best collaborative tone and sipped her sauvignon blanc—"inventory."

"I'm all ears," he said, not bothering to hide the condescension from his voice, and scribbled a note about her on his iPad.

Smooth, Ellie thought. She knew this game. After all, hadn't she used the same tactic just that morning with an arrogant journalist? She allowed him to direct the negotiation initially and then blatantly interrupted him to record a cryptic memo to her assistant about another offer concerning the client he was interested in. She'd wanted to remind him that she held the access to the information he needed, and thus the power, without giving him a tangible reason to lash out at her or her client. Some women danced backward in high heels; Ellie spun. She spun conversations and situations; she spun successes and failures; and, all too often in these days of camera phones and gossip rags, she spun scandals. She'd built her PR empire around dually boosting and salvaging clients' careers, regardless of their box-office bombs and personal missteps.

"I'm looking for someone who can handle the demands of my career," she said, with a grin bordering on smugness. "I have no interest in being someone's meal ticket, mind you, but I need to be with someone who understands what maintaining this level of success requires. It's not that I can't commit to a steady dating life or a vacation, but when I need to work, I need carte blanche to do so. I've been told many doctors work fewer hours. Also, children are a non-negotiable for me. I am not opposed to entering into a relationship with someone who has them, but I won't be having any of my own."

"Is that all?" His voice dripped with sarcasm. "And what would you say to those who characterize you as a workaholic? That you're selfish for not seeing children as a part of your life's plan?"

It was not lost on Ellie that he would benefit professionally by adding her to his repertoire of successful childless women. She knew this dance as well.

"I'd say that motherhood was once a dream of mine, but sometimes life interferes and you realize it's time to find a new dream." Ellie steadied her expression as she stifled a fidget. "My career will always be one of the great loves of my life. I'm asking if you can possibly find someone compatible with us."

"You can trust that I'll try," he said, fumbling to open his MacBook, and Ellie gave herself a tally mark in the win column that her poise and composure intimidated him. "Allow me to introduce you to a few profiles, and please be assured that you are even more impressive in person than on paper."

Ellie ignored his flattery, more certain than ever that there wasn't a man left in this town who didn't play games.

Kate, 34,
Exhausted New Mommy

Kate

Kate smiled as she heard the calendar notification ding. Tonight was her night. Most of the free world wouldn't consider an evening with friends anything to write home about, but a return to her weekly dinner with the girls was absolutely symbolic to her. She yawned as she unlatched two-month-old Liam from her nipple and transferred him gingerly into the co-sleeper, thinking sleep deprivation was a torture tactic regardless of what the Guantánamo headlines protested. She considered climbing into the bed next to her sweet boy, then shook her head and grinned at the prospect of being a free woman for the night. Was it wrong that she was excited to step out of her door sans an arsenal of baby gear? Of course it was. Maybe she just wasn't cut out for the mommy gig. It was so much harder than she'd ever imagined it could be.

Kate closed her heavy eyes, thinking Liam was, without contest, the best thing she had ever done and wishing he could tell her what she was doing wrong. Then he would know that she would do anything for him, that she was a better mommy when she wasn't running on fumes, and a better mommy when she laughed. She would know he knew how much she loved him.

As all new moms do, Kate reassured herself with the lie that things would get easier as he grew. *How does Leila manage to get out?* she thought, as she walked into the adjoining bathroom to apply makeup for the first time since Cami took the newborn photos. *She has two under five. What am I missing?*

Liam's trademark "I am about to projectile-vomit" cough sent Kate running back to their bed. She scooped him up onto her shoulder in a whirl of panic that he would choke on his reflux. *Breathe; just breathe*, she told herself. *All babies spit up.* Her phone chirped again.

New Text Msg: Ken Cell
I'm sorry, but I can't be home by 6:00. What is the latest we can leave for dinner?

We? Kate patted soft circles between Liam's shoulders. As if on cue, he sputtered and emptied the contents of his feeding into her hair and down her back. She shuddered, more at the realization that her only fashionable blouse was now unwearable than at the sour liquid oozing through the fabric. Four bars of Train's "Marry Me," Ken's ringtone, filled the room. That was never good news at this hour. A silent tear rolled down her cheek as she cleaned her baby and herself.

Thirty minutes later, Kate stood in her closest, still stinging from how cold she had been to Ken on the phone as she'd reminded him of how important tonight was to her, that it was the last thing they'd discussed when he left that morning, that she knew the entry had been on his calendar for weeks because she'd added it herself. He'd sworn he'd mistyped the text, but she knew better. He was fishing for permission to work late. Per usual.

The bra she'd bought mid-pregnancy hung snapped, albeit unflatteringly so, from her waist. Kate clenched her fists at the maze of clothes in front if her. She had exhausted all of her choices. This shirt fit but didn't work with that bra. That shirt nearly fit if she sat up straight, but it didn't cover the side fat that hung from her only choice of maternity jeans. She should just cancel. Cancel and climb into bed and pray for thirty minutes of sleep. If it weren't for her intense desire to see the girls, especially Leila, she would. Leila was the unwavering cheerleader of everyone she loved, and Kate knew she would encourage her and make her feel better. She pulled the best-worst-dressed candidate off of the closet floor and told herself tonight wasn't about how she looked. It was about seeing the women she considered sisters and proving to herself that she could find her center and still be *her*, despite being a stranger in this strange land of new parenthood.

Leila

$\mathcal{L}$eila smiled as she remembered Kate's scheming glance as they entered tonight's date on their phones weeks earlier.

"That's almost eight weeks after Liam arrives! We should be in a routine by then!" Kate gushed, and Leila forced a smile in return, hoping she looked convincing. At this point, Leila couldn't even write a card for a baby shower without feeling facetious. She wanted to say that the days were long and the years were short, but she had no idea where to start without sounding cynical. If more women could be honest with each other about how hard parenting was, instead of passing mommier-than-thou judgment as they jockeyed for the title of supermom, maybe she could. Leila sometimes thought the how-does-she-do-it-all supermom image was her generation's version of June Cleaver and Carol Brady and wished women everywhere could agree that all three, the supermom included, were fictional.

Leila hoped this restaurant would be as good as its hype. She knew one of their local GNO standbys would have been fine but felt insecure planning the same predictable dinner time after time as the others chatted about meetings, dates, and happy hours at new "it" places that had sprung up since her exit from the nightlife into the nightlight life. She knew it wasn't necessary, but she felt a misplaced need to stay relevant, despite the fact that she read far more *Curious George* than the *New Yorker* these days.

Pulling out her Kindle, Leila downloaded the latest novels from Pam Jenoff and Celine Keating she'd been dying to devour, then smirked at the thought of how much bathroom and elliptical reading she did. Thank God Kindle saved her place, or she'd never finish a book.

Just then, she heard Cami's unmistakable bark at the hostess stand. Her heart sank a small beat. She had really been hoping Norah or Ellie would arrive first. *Don't be passive-aggressive*, she admonished herself. *You've been friends for years. It's not her fault she communicates differently than you do. In fact, you should be more assertive and less fearful of confrontation. If you'd taken a page out of her book, you might have made a more effective case for the part-time position you proposed to the department before Clara was born.* Cami would never have smiled graciously through a goodbye party, accepting colleagues' compliments, just days after they'd told her she was one of their best but they couldn't create a place for her.

"Cami! I'm so glad you could come!" Leila rose to greet her and then thanked the hostess. She could tell immediately that something was off. Cami seemed as if she'd been punched. "Here, sit. How was your day? Did the Faces of Poverty campaign just love the portfolio? I thought it was simply beautiful," Leila said, and then chastened herself for her compulsion to fill the silence. *You are relevant to her, despite the lack of face-to-face time and telephone conversations. Don't ramble; trust your actions to show your investment in her life.* "I'm sorry," she went on. "I didn't mean to bombard you with questions right as you sat down. I'm just so happy to have a night to myself, you know?"

"Can I get a vodka soda with two limes?" Cami said, as she motioned to a bustling waitress. "I understand. I've been working twelve-hour days and crashing at nine o'clock every night. I missed a hair appointment and two personal-training sessions this week alone. But it's Friday and there is an eye mask in my future for tonight and tomorrow morning. How are the kids?"

"They're great. Listen, is everything okay? You seem distant, for lack of a better word."

Cami's jaw clenched, making Leila wish she had chattered about teething, tantrums, or anything else that would have given Cami a second to decompress from the stresses of her day until the others arrived.

"I'm not trying to be pushy, I just want you to know I care about you and that you're important to me. I also understand if you'd rather not talk about whatever it is," Leila stammered, and wished she could start the conversation over.

Norah

"Actually, I see my party." Norah attempted to politely dismiss the hostess. "I'm going to visit the ladies' room, and then I'll join them. Thank you." Her guilt intensified as she made a beeline for the bathroom. Maybe she wouldn't tell them. Why not leave her overly scheduled life up to chance, for once? If there was an opening, she would go for it. If not, she would remain in the isolation of her own creation. Norah had hoped Cami or Ellie would beat Leila to the restaurant so they could have a private moment. She loved Leila unconditionally, but she needed blatant honesty at the moment. Leila was too much of a nurturer to provide that. Ellie knew how to minimize damages and script a conversation. Cami wasn't distracted by emotion and could weigh in objectively. Plus, Leila was hard to disappoint. She had this uncanny knack for connecting with people and genuinely loving them for who they were, not who they should be or—as Norah feared she was about to learn at great personal cost—who she wanted them to be.

Kate

*W*here was Ken? She had hoped to slip out while Liam was sleeping. Instead, she was downing lactation tea to the tune of a Baby Einstein track while Liam stretched happily in his bouncer. As of now, she would be at least thirty minutes late. Why couldn't Leila have picked something closer? What was wrong with Zapata's? Close, reliable service, great salads, half-priced bottles of wine on Wednesdays. She was far too sleep deprived to navigate the expressway.

At last, she heard Ken's key in the lock and grabbed her purse.

"Hi, babe. Listen, I'm sorry I'm late. Jack came into my office at five forty, literally yelling about billings Accounts swears they never received. Just let me go to the bathroom, and the rest of the night is yours."

"Until I have to play milk cow, you mean," Kate's gaze was steel.

"Like I said, I didn't mean to be late. I'm sorry. Just let me go to the bathroom, and I'll take him for the rest of the night." Ken looked defeated as he shuffled down the hall into the bathroom. Was he seriously asking for a private moment after he'd shown up this late?

Kate fumed as she made her way down the hall. "I can't even *begin* to tell you how angry I am right now!" she shouted at the closed bathroom door, surprised by the intensity of her reaction. "Did you eat a complete meal today? Did you take a crap in private, or was someone screaming for you in the next room? Did you have three seconds to catch up on the news? Did you manage to go about your entire day without someone else's pee, poop, or puke somewhere on your body? Did you finish even *one* thing you started? And now *you're* asking *me* to wait while you go to the restroom in peace? Try breastfeeding and wiping your ass at the same time!" Kate turned on her heel and headed for the front door. "By the time I get there, it will be time to come home to feed Liam. I asked for three measly hours of downtime!"

Liam began to wail from his seat. In a fury of sensation, Kate felt overwhelmed by guilt, regret, fatigue, and the unmistakable tingle of milk letting down.

Norah

What in the world had they been talking about? Cami looked stressed to kill, and Leila was clearly wearing her poker face. Norah forced her best bedside calm as she headed toward their table.

"Norah!" Leila's easy smile and happy greeting seemed to twist the vise on her head more tightly. She returned her friend's embrace, perhaps sinking into it a bit too long.

"Cami." She nodded and smiled as a passing waiter paused to pull out her chair.

"Thank you. May I have a carafe of mineral water with lemons?" Thankful to be seated after ten hours in the office, she took a moment to enjoy the resounding tingle in her feet. Leila's eyes grew huge with excitement as she shot Cami a glance full of hope. Jeez. She should have known better. This was why she'd hoped Ellie or Cami would be first. They would simply assume she was on call or had an early surgery looming. Leila, on the other hand, knew her schedule better and was infinitely hopeful her battle with infertility would end any month now—despite five years sans the big announcement. Refusal of alcohol before a rare weekend off would only fuel her fervor.

"It looks like you're both set for drinks. I think I'll wait to see the wine list until Ellie gets here." Norah forced a smile as Leila looked away politely.

Ellie

"If there's anything else I need to know, anything at all, it's best you tell me now. Trust me. Embarrassment aside, you need to decide if you want me to handle it or the press. Something to think about. For the record, I'm sorry. You're definitely one of the most congenial, most humble clients I've ever worked with. We will bounce back from this. Let me make some calls, and we've found somewhere for you to lie low in the meantime. Do not tell anyone where you are. We want the media bored with this story before they have enough feed for a blurb, much less a segment. I've already put my team on high alert. Jess will be in touch with car information, et cetera, and I'll call later this evening once you're settled to update you on our progress. I'll be available by cell if you need me between now and then."

Ellie listened to the relief in the British lilt of her client's worried voice, reiterated that he would survive this, said goodbye, and walked into her dinner engagement forty minutes late.

As the hostess led her to the table, she wondered what she'd missed. Her friends' body language spoke volumes to someone in her profession. Leila sat straight, like a Stepford wife, while Cami brooded at the empty chairs. Norah surprised her most of all. She was usually calm personified, no doubt thanks in part to her surgical training, but tonight she seemed to be sitting on hot coals, even though her pager was noticeably absent from the table.

"Hello! Sorry I'm so late. I've been fighting fires from the car."

"No worries. Anything juicy?" Leila asked, grinning.

"Let's just say camera phones are a blessing and a curse for a certain heartthrob who took a recording artist who's not publicly separated from her husband on an Alpine holiday over the weekend. Another skier snapped a blurry pic of them kissing on the slopes, and it may or may not go viral if he manages to sell it to a gossip rag," Ellie exhaled for what felt like the first time in hours as she studied Norah out of the corner of her eye. "Nothing too terrible."

"Not for your client, anyway," Cami remarked.

"True, but considering the other camp is trading on a Cinderella marriage starring a virginal ingénue and looking for a scapegoat to save her brand, the odds aren't exactly stacked in my client's favor. Let's hope he can ride his five minutes of tween and cougar–induced adoration for a bit longer."

"I'll bet you're representing both of them by the end of it. That's happened before." Leila smiled as she passed Ellie the wine list. "Norah was waiting for you."

"Oh, I think tonight is a bottle-of-Hendrick's-and-a-straw kind of night, but thanks." Ellie wondered if Norah would take the bait. What in the world was she hiding? She thought things had been better with Matt lately.

"I'll split a bottle of cab with you, if you'd like," Leila offered. Ellie knew her intention was to be courteous, but if she'd waited two more seconds, Norah would have broken. Her lip twitch said as much.

"Twist my arm, then." Norah forced a smile. *Hardball*, Ellie thought, as the waiter returned with Cami's next drink and scurried away to fetch the bottle. The exasperated look on his face told her they'd better be prepared to leave a big tip.

Kate

*T*ears streamed down Kate's face as she looked up at Ken from the rocking chair. "I'm sorry. I didn't mean to be so angry. . . ." Her voice trailed off as she stifled a sob. "It's just, I miss my friends. I feel so incredibly lost right now. Liam is the best thing that's ever happened to me, to both of us, and I feel selfish beyond words for wanting a break, but I also feel like I'm drowning. I don't even know who I am anymore."

Ken wiped a tear from her cheek and kissed her head. "I know. I feel the same way. We'll get through this and look back on these days as a blur of joy and sorrow," he said, sounding more confident than she knew he actually was as he stroked her hair.

"Spoken like someone who's been to the real world and back today." She sniffed and smiled as her phone chirped. "I never finished my text! That's probably Leila!"

1 New Msg: Leila Cell
Where are u? Is everything ok? Let me know.

Norah

"She could have had the courtesy to call, or at least text. Totally inconsiderate. I had a shit day myself, but I'm here. Life doesn't stop for everyone else just because you have a baby," Cami said, as she grimaced and signaled the waiter.

"Actually, it kind of does. Life gets away from you for a while. I remember that feeling. You're so overwhelmed by the magnitude of everything changing. She doesn't mean to be hurtful." Leila shifted self-consciously at the thought of a confrontation with Cami.

Norah pressed her palm to the cool of her water glass and added, "I'm sure she didn't realize we were waiting to order. I'll stop by tomorrow. This is why I counsel my patients about PPD. Normal adjustment and stress can spiral quickly if no one is watching for the signs." Norah's voice was clinical, but her heart ached for Kate. She'd seen this all too often. Women felt so compelled to live a postpartum life worthy of a Hallmark card that they didn't pause to acknowledge or grieve for the unimaginable sacrifices motherhood required. Denial led to guilt, and guilt led to varying degrees of depression. She hated the stigma postpartum women felt when they admitted to feeling less than euphoric. She also knew that far too many in her profession rushed through the mandatory six-week postpartum exams, leaving their nurses to counsel patients about PPD after they finished the internal exam.

Norah's phone vibrated, ending her soapbox reverie.

Group Txt Msg (4 Recipients)
From: Kate Cell
I'm sorry. I typed this and never managed to send it.
Please forgive me, but I can't make it. I really did try.

"She could at least be honest about it," Cami said. "Admitting she forgot a dinner we mentioned weeks ago is more realistic than saying she tried to make it but failed. If she's not ready to leave Liam or she's just too tired, we would completely understand. I'd rather have honesty any day than a lie or an excuse."

Cami's indignation clearly came from a place of disappointment and missing Kate, but her words resonated with Norah. *Pull yourself together. This is why you came.*

"I have something to say." Norah's abrupt tone brought her to the center of her friends' rapt attention. She continued hurriedly before she lost her nerve. "Believe me, I'd rather tell anyone but you, but I don't feel deceit honors our friendship or all we've been through together. I'd like to preface this by saying that I don't expect your support or your forgiveness, immediate or otherwise." She took a sip of courage as Leila discreetly waved off the approaching waiter. "I've been having a relationship with someone from my past. It started two months ago, and it is either an epic mistake or a bridge to my future."

Norah's chest constricted with a mixture of guilt and anxiety as she looked at the astonished faces surrounding her. The tears moistening the brink of Leila's lashes were her breaking point. Taking the napkin from her lap, Norah blotted her own welling eyes and forbade herself to cry. *If you can take a woman's life in your hands, you can handle this. Get out of your head and analyze.*

"With who?" Cami asked bluntly. "And for God's sake, when?"

"Your schedule is unforgiving at best." Ellie said, stalling to her point. "Does Matt know?"

"I'm so sorry you're going through this." Leila tried but failed to stop the tear that trailed down her cheek as she reached for Norah's hand. "You must be a wreck inside. I'll—we'll—be there for you, regardless of the who, what, where."

"I appreciate that." Norah squeezed Leila's hand, reeling from the commotion in her head. She had been battling her conscience for weeks, but saying the words aloud brought every betrayal, every touch, and every second she had spent with him into a different realm of reality. She felt as if she could sleep for months.

"Well, you've gone public now," Ellie added, with a forced laugh. "That said, the real question is, where do you go from here? Better yet, where do you *want* to go from here?"

"I have no idea. I haven't told Matt yet. Honestly, I just keep expecting to wake up. I want to will everything away, press rewind, go back eight weeks and remind myself this is a bad idea. I want to survive this without hurting anyone, but I feel like I'm on some sort of precipice—damned if I do, damned if I don't." Norah said, somewhat relieved from sharing the weight of her secret.

"You still haven't told us who he is," Cami said in an oddly quiet voice.

"It started at the WHO conference." Norah sighed. "Matt was supposed to come, but we had a fight. Things haven't been good for quite a while—you know that—but we reached a new low. Between our hellish schedules, his disappointment at not making partner in the firm, and the fertility saga, things just dominoed into an ugly confrontation. We both said things we didn't mean—at least, I hope we didn't mean—and I flew to San Fran alone." Norah took another sip of wine. They might as well know it all. In for a penny, in for a pound. "I reconnected with a man named Enrique from my time ten years ago in Mumbai. He was the keynote speaker. My heart stopped when I saw his name in the program. I know it sounds crazy, but I felt younger just reading it. It was as if all the stress of the last seven years melted away. I don't know if it was the nostalgia or the fight or the fatigue, but I couldn't stop smiling. I felt"—she searched for the right word—"fearless, somehow. After his speech, I contrived an introduction during the physicians' reception. I know this sounds equally crazy, but his face lit up when he saw me. He looked years younger instantaneously."

Norah paused to survey her audience. Their faces were a tapestry of skepticism, heartache, concern, and shock. "We spent the rest of the reception reminiscing about our days at the fistula clinic. Lives saved. Communities educated. Days of purpose before the realities of drug reps and insurance premiums took hold. We relived an entire year of important work and liquor infused nights of dancing and passion. He invited me to dinner to discuss my India initiative, and we ended up flirting and laughing like teenagers until the restaurant closed. Somewhere between the champagne and the dessert, he reached for my hand, and it was electric. I was so consumed by the chemistry. He made me feel beautiful—desired. He made me laugh. I told myself it was just banter between old friends, but I knew it was more." Norah shook her head and added sarcastically, "Hell, he probably could have had me right there on the table if he'd asked. The connection was that intense. I had perma-grin leaving the restaurant. We went back to the hotel bar and"—she paused to gather her nerve—"and I asked him up to my room."

"Does he know you're married?" Ellie asked cautiously.

"Yes. We both are." Norah closed her eyes as the weight of her words hung heavily in the air.

"Are there children involved?"

"Yes. Three young girls." Leila looked wide-eyed and horrified as she withdrew her hand from Norah. "I'm so sorry. I didn't mean to hurt anyone. I don't know if I'm in lust or in love or in some hybrid of the two. It's something we want to pursue before we make any big decisions." Norah felt as if she'd swallowed a white-hot poker.

"Is there anything else?" Ellie's voice was deceptively calm.

"He lives here, in Pasadena. We took a suite at the Hilton for the next month. I've been with him almost every day since the conference, and it's been the best two months I've had in over a year. In the meantime, things are improving with Matt. I don't know if it's because I've been happier or trying harder, but they're better than they have been in a long time." Norah dropped her head into her hands as the jury of her peers cast their judgment.

Leila

*I*n the glow of the refrigerator light, Leila downed her fourth glass of water. She could already feel the dull headache coming on. The girls would be up in a few short hours, and she'd not yet been to bed. After the dinner, she'd gone to Kate's studio. She needed to talk to another mother, and she needed to check on her friend.

Kate

Kate scrambled egg whites absentmindedly, still reeling from Leila's retelling of the bombshell Norah had dropped at dinner and thinking she had certainly picked the wrong night to miss. Kate wanted to be there for her friend, but she couldn't stop thinking about the two families involved. Matt definitely wasn't her favorite of her friends' husbands, but he didn't deserve this. No one did. She wondered about Enrique as well. Was his wife standing in a kitchen somewhere, making breakfast for his children, while he and Norah made love in a hotel suite? Would she wonder if the physical changes three babies inevitably caused had driven him away? Norah was so toned and polished. Maybe it had to do with her confidence, but she was gorgeous even clean-faced, wearing scrubs. Maybe that was Kate projecting her own body issues onto a woman she'd never met. Maybe not. But she was absolutely certain of one thing: two families were on a collision course, and children would be hurt.

Ellie

As the car service pulled into the firm's parking garage, Ellie thought about how close she had come to being "the other woman" over the years. She was always attracted to the salt-and-pepper set, but they were rarely unattached. She'd seen too many lives damaged by adultery in this self-centered industry ever to consent to being someone's mistress.

She smoothed her charcoal pencil skirt and crisp white oxford. At thirty-six, she was proud of her trim figure and classic style. Spinning was, ironically, her exercise of choice. She attended a pre-dawn cycle class four mornings a week and was fiercely competitive with the other regulars. Her last serious relationship had been with Marcus, Cami's, and her, personal trainer. Eventually, she had rehired him as a trainer. She enjoyed the idea of being molded to physical perfection by someone who would never have her again. It was slow revenge for the embarrassment she had suffered at his hands.

Just then, Ellie's phone vibrated in an onslaught of incoming texts and red-flag e-mails. That only ever meant one thing. She dialed her first assistant.

"What are we in for, Jess? I'm on my way up from the garage."

"They found Patrick Grayson. We've gotten him into a car, but we don't have a destination."

"Send the driver here. Have the attendants move every available car to the street, and tell them to block the garage to badge only.

No exceptions. Send Pat's car to the service alley, and have a driver waiting in front and a car ready to close the gap between."

Ellie meant what she had said to Pat just before she walked into Cru. There was an honesty about him that was rare among most of the leading men she'd dealt with. At once ethereal and attainable, he had a boyish charm and a smooth London accent that had stolen the hearts of millions of women as he portrayed Lucas Lucien, a misunderstood fallen angel with a good heart, in a young adult trilogy turned blockbuster movie franchise called *Destiny*. The role might have skyrocketed him to the top of Hollywood's young heartthrobs, but Ellie knew he was desperate to prove himself as a serious actor.

14 New Text Msgs

Ellie climbed into the elevator and began doing what she did best. At moments like these, she wished she could see her own life with the same clarity she saw her clients' messes and successes.

Norah

Norah sank into the chair behind her desk. It had been a whirl-wind of a morning, and she hadn't slept in almost twenty-four hours. After she'd left Cru, she had met Enrique at their room. Matt was traveling, and she wanted to test a theory. She'd wanted to see if she still found him irresistible now that she'd shared her secret, or if the anonymity of the affair was to thank for the intoxication she felt near him.

Her mind wandered to their first night together. They lingered over jazz in the hotel bar, stealing touches, as flirtation evolved into intention. Enrique placed his hand on her thigh, sending waves of desire and a novel ache though her groin. Her breath hitched as she casually eased his hand higher, to the hem of her skirt, leaned in, and invited him to her bed.

Her knees quaked as they entered the elevator. Once they were alone, he pulled her close. It felt surreal to inhale the scent of another man after so many years of monogamy. She breathed deeply, want-ing to remember the smell of his cologne. His nose was in her hair. Was he doing the same?

Tilting her chin up so she was forced to meet his eyes, he whis-pered, "It's important to me that you know I've never done this before." Nor had she, she assured him, as their lips met. Burying his hands in her hair, he kissed her feverishly, his need for her resonat-ing through her body.

They moved quickly, shedding clothes and mirroring each other's intensity. She hovered above him, caressing his beautiful face, at once surrendering to the choice and languishing in the distraction from her internal monologue of responsibilities and constant worry. Every rise and fall of her hips reminded her what sex had once been like, before ovulation schedules and fertility treatments became ever present, ever expectant, guests in her bedroom. Forcing all thoughts from her mind, she sank more deeply onto him, focusing only on the rhythm of building sensation, then leaned back, pulling him up to her chest, so their bodies moved as one. In a frenzy of exquisite release and satisfaction, they climaxed within moments of each other.

Afterward, they stayed forehead to forehead for what seemed like an eternity. "Ladies first," he joked when they finally relaxed, still entwined in the crisp white sheets.

"Always the gentleman," she teased. "I'm guessing the condom was a happy coincidence?"

"I believe you're referring to the prophylactic of exponentially expensive proportions." He propped himself up on his elbow and smiled down at her mischievously. "While you were in the restroom, I told the bartender I'd pay him fifty dollars for every condom he could round up."

She threw her head back laughing—a release just as sweet as any other she'd experienced that night.

"Too bad he could only find the one." Enrique's eyes darted impishly as he traced her silhouette with his finger. Every nerve ending seemed to pulsate under his touch. Her brow furrowed in disappointment as she ached to have him again.

"We could call—"

"Or seven." He interrupted her, nibbling her ear before deftly shifting her to her belly and trailing kisses down her back.

"That should get us through the night." Her face lit up with giddy excitement as she clutched the pillow in anticipation.

"Dr. Meritt." The nurse-practitioner's voice brought Norah back to reality. "Room four is ready for you now."

"Thank you, Jillan." Norah smiled warmly at her trusted colleague while grimacing internally at the news she was about to deliver. Parts of this job would never get easier.

Ellie

"Ellison, here." She rubbed her temples as she listened to the words she'd suspected were coming. The Scarlett James camp was out for Patrick Grayson's blood and set to saturate the media in less than three hours. She, her team, and ultimately her client were their pawns.

Resigned to pragmatism, she attempted to assimilate the information she needed to construct a game plan to control damages. She could already picture the media hook—the blurry cell phone pic, refined and edited pixel by pixel, presented as a tell-all, and paired with a sixty-second sound bite while red-carpet pics, paparazzi shots, and past headlines peppered the screen. Images were the ultimate potter's clay in this age of twenty-four-hour media coverage. A simple digital collage, and Pat would be spun as the typical celebrity playboy. Ellie smirked at the irony of the same images inevitably being used when his career was on the upswing. She knew their camp was using her client to buy time as they readied for the imminent storm of Scarlett's contested divorce, no doubt preparing to present their client as the desperate ingénue, pushed to the breaking point and seduced into the solace of another man's arms. She only wondered what they had on Mrs. Platinum's producer husband. They must be under a gag order, or he would be the present target and her client would be sketched as the ultimate good guy, a perfect weekend fantasy for a woman on the mend.

Ellie knew better than to waste her team's energy delving into what had clearly been blocked by court order. "Thank you for letting me know. I won't forget this favor." She took a moment to collect herself, then buzzed her first assistant. Jess smiled nonchalantly behind her as she closed the door. Ellie had taught her well. Give nothing away.

"I've just spoken to Mr. Grayson's team. He's extremely anxious." Jess took a seat and prepared to take notes.

"Where do we sit getting Pat—Mr. Grayson, rather—out of the public eye?" Ellie fought the urge to glance away or fidget at her unprofessional slip. "As I'm sure you've realized, we're essentially chum in the water."

"I understand. I've contacted all of our go-to hideaways, but the press is already staked out. I have several flight options, but there's word that foreign paparazzi is hovering as well."

"Where do we sit regarding the garage?"

"Fourteen to twenty-four photographers are waiting between the second and third levels of the Shank's parking garage across the street. As usual, the building manager has no interest in working with us."

"Call Tim. Tell him Mr. Grayson will speak in forty-five minutes. He'll leak it to the networks, and the leeches will follow the microphones. Have maintenance take a podium to the north lawn. Whil they're scrambling for position, I want Mr. Grayson taken down t service elevator to my car. You're to drive him to my house. F Stacie notify the beach guard and Malibu PD. I don't want surprised if you're followed. Stacie should contact the gatek well. I want the code changed every half hour for the ne four hours. I'll be in touch about where we go from t' fumbled through her desk for an antacid as Jess rose t make sure he's wearing a hat. He doesn't always thin'

Ellie tapped her fingers nervously as her phone e of the *Friends* theme song she'd programmed for '

New Text: Leila Cell
I saw the Pat Grayson/Scarlett James pic at the gym.
Good luck, Ginger!

Ellie smiled briefly at the screen and checked her reflection in the mirror as she prepared mentally for the lion's den that awaited her. This noise could not have happened at a less opportune time for him career-wise. He was set to start a national media tour for his latest film, *Life of Us*, in five days. The role was edgy—an intentional deviation designed to shake his typecasting. In the film, he portrayed a thirty-two-year-old man who, having been diagnosed with ALS, dedicated the remaining years of his life to leaving video diaries for his husband and children. Critics were hailing it as Oscar worthy and it had taken the Jury Prize at Cannes; however, Ellie knew the press tour would now revolve around his Alpine tryst with Scarlett, instead of increasing demand for an independent film in limited release. She would require rote questions about the role but knew those would be delegated either to the final minute of each interview or to the cutting-room floor.

Cami

*C*ami blinked suddenly as she awoke from her Ambien- and vodka–induced hiatus. The last two days had been her first sans employment in over twenty years. She scrolled through her phone to see what she'd missed. She was surprised by the mass of e-mails from her coworkers. Now former coworkers. What did they expect from her? High fives and butt slaps on her way out the door? She opened her CareerConnect app and changed her status to "looking." She'd been headhunted in the past; surely a decade of loyalty to InFocus hadn't made her unmarketable. Her so-called "generous" $20K severance barely covered an eighth of the business she'd brought in during this quarter alone. *Generous, my ass*, she thought, as she made her way to her closet. Several minutes passed while she stared blankly into her rows of slacks and suits. What did she wear on Monday now? An immense feeling of emptiness engulfed her and turned her throat to lava. Gym clothes. That was the answer. She'd see if Marcus was available for a session. A little eye candy and a workout always lifted her spirits.

Leila

*L*eila smiled as she unloaded the week's groceries into the pantry, thankful her children would never know real hunger. She would never forget what it was like to truly starve. How it felt to choke down a spoonful of Crisco while her mother slept on the sofa. She would coat it in the pastel rainbow of sugar, Equal, and Sweet & Low packets she pocketed from school and call it ice cream for the younger ones. A wave of gratitude washed over her as she remembered how far she'd come and recommitted to not taking her blessings for granted. Escaping that life and its cycles had been equal parts miracle, determination, and luck. Where would she be without the teachers and mentors who'd convinced her she had control over her destiny? Without the crossing guard who passed down socks and underwear to her from a—as Leila later learned—fictitious niece? Without the librarian who always packed too much lunch for one person?

She now believed that cycles could be broken to her very core. She must make time to take the girls to visit Mrs. Lenore later this week. Of all her benefactors, Leila felt she owed the most to sweet Mrs. Lenore. A veritable Mother Teresa, Mrs. Lenore had headed an urban outreach effort from the Methodist church. She drove a van that stopped at trailer parks and HUD developments to bring hot meals, clothing donations, and Scholastic books to the children. She'd taken a particular interest in Leila after seeing her divide her biscuit into four portions, eat one, and save the rest to give to her siblings the next time the cabinets were bare. After that, Mrs. Lenore drove miles out of her way every Sunday to bring the family canned goods and homemade bread. Eventually, Leila began to accompany her to church after the delivery. There, she learned that being poor wasn't a sin, and that there was a greater power who loved the little children. She learned that love could be unconditional, that struggles could lead to greatness, that there was often darkness before the dawn, and that kindness itself was an admirable goal.

Mrs. Lenore was also the reason Leila developed the confidence to believe education was her ticket away from the cycles of poverty and neglect she lived every day. It was Mrs. Lenore who first suspected her dyslexia and worked with the school to help her get the literacy support she needed. Leila would never forget the moment letters turned into words on a page. She became an avid reader— learning about the world vicariously, devouring the escape from her hardships. She spent almost every lunch and recess period in the library. Initially, she preferred to spend her breaks there because she could rinse her siblings' underwear in the hot water of the relatively quiet bathroom, and also because she didn't own a coat. But, as her skill set grew, she began to crave the knowledge offered between its walls. She loved the predictability of the card catalog and the unending answers to her questions. She studied everything from how to end the life cycle of the head lice that tormented her, to oceanography, to the realities of animal testing and cruelty. When they called her name at sixth-grade graduation, she'd climbed from the bottom of her class to the top. She might have been the only student who didn't have family in the audience, but she was also the student who beamed the brightest when she saw Mrs. Lenore and her beloved librarian in the front row. Later, they gave her a bouquet of white daisies—still her favorite flowers—and a wrapped copy of *The Giving Tree*. It was dog-eared from years of use in the school's library, but Leila had never loved anything more. That night, she stood it upright on the cardboard box she used as a dresser and smiled giddily at the sheer joy of owning a book. Her very own book. Leigh Anne now owned a book. She just might be on her way.

Ellie

*E*llie took a deep breath, allowing herself one smoothing of her skirt, before ascending the stairs and preparing for the blinding flashes.

"Good afternoon. Thank you for coming. I will take questions post-statements." She paused for the predictable roar of discontent as they realized the man of the hour would not be making his own statement. When the volume dropped to a low grumble, she continued, "I will be speaking on behalf of Patrick Grayson this afternoon. He asks for your respect of his privacy during this difficult time. He also wishes to thank his fans for their outcry of love and support. Mr. Grayson knows he is not the first"—she paused for effect, then smiled conspiratorially—"nor will he be the last to be deceived by half truths and mis-intentions." She kept her gaze steady as she scanned the crowd for her preferred reporters. "To the best of Mr. Grayson's knowledge, Mrs. James is separated from her husband and in the process of finalizing their divorce. I'll take questions now." A garble of voices filled the air as she signaled to a well-positioned mic. "Tim, from *Huffington*."

"Where is Pat Grayson, and why is he hiding if he's done nothing to be ashamed of? Are they still together?"

"Ignorance is bliss, as they say." She smiled again. "But Mr. Grayson takes marital vows seriously and has ended the relationship. He feels responsible for any disrespect shown to the families involved, regardless of Scarlett James's deceit. He is taking time to gather himself in preparation for the premiere of his latest work, *Life of Us*, a role he hopes will be inspirational to husbands and fathers." The crowd erupted in a blinding series of shouts and flashbulbs. "That will be all for today." Ellie descended the stairs to a cascade of homophobic expletives and disgust. Vultures with a sudden onset of moral convictions. Masochistic, but fitting.

Kate

*W*ho knew navigating a trip to pick up the dry cleaning, refill prescriptions, and replenish the diaper-wine-produce supply at Costco would ever feel like an epic accomplishment? Kate was proud she'd finished three of her four errands. Who needed a sexy trainer like Ellie's Marcus? She would have killer arms in no time from lifting the twenty-plus-pound combo of Liam and his car seat–stroller. Kate smiled as she remembered her BC—before childbirth—concept of full hands.

Cami

*C*ami felt self-conscious walking into the gym during the middle of the workday. Was it an obvious sign that she'd been fired? *Pull yourself together*, she chided herself. *For all they know, you've taken the day off.* She headed directly to the free weights and began stretching. Scanning the area for familiar faces, she noticed Marcus working with a client on the mat. He was demonstrating proper lunge technique while the Oompa Loompa-colored woman gazed on. Cami loved to watch him move. Every sinew in his legs looked as if it had been carved to perfection as he coiled across the room. Hard work always paid off, she thought, as she continued stretching. While she could stare at him all day, she would never be able to fathom how Ellie saw anything serious with him. Moreover, she would never understand how Ellie had missed so many red flags during their relationship. Ellie would protest the fact to her grave, but Cami knew she was a romantic at heart. She wondered if her friend would ever really trust a man again, much less accept another ring. Then she wondered if *she* would.

Norah

"I'm thankful to have been a part of it." Norah smiled as she sewed fine plastic-surgery sutures to repair the patient's tear. Theses stitches took twice as long but healed seamlessly. "I read a study once, in a medical psych course, about a group of researchers who interviewed one hundred women the day after they gave birth. Then, they interviewed the same group of women twenty years later and compared the two accounts. The stories were almost identical, despite being told decades apart. It's a day you will remember forever. I am so glad you had the birth you wanted, and that we were able to be a part of your story." Norah posed for the standard photos before leaving the room to check the progress in the next room. Her heart sank as she pulled out her phone.

4 New Text Msgs (from Matt Cell)
3 Missed Calls (from Matt Cell)
(1) At the restaurant. 6:45
(2) Do you want me to get a table? 7:20
(3) I'm guessing you got a call? Haven't seen you in 4 days. 7:45
(4) Jon is meeting clients downtown. I bowed out so WE could have dinner. I'm going to head there now. Salvage some of my time. 8:30

Shit. She'd completely forgotten about their dinner. She hastily typed a reply as her pager vibrated.

Reply
I'm sorry. I've been bouncing between 5 rooms, 3 of my patients and 2 of a partner who's in emergency surgery. I'm likely here for the night.

1 New Text (from Matt Cell)
Last time I checked, nurses knew how to text. I'll see you tomorrow. Maybe I should make an appointment.

Reply
It's out of my control now. I'm sorry. Cafeteria coffee date?

1 New Text (Matt Cell)
Happy anniversary.

He might as well have slapped her in the face. *You pick tonight to suddenly care about anniversaries? How convenient,* Norah fumed, as she made her way to the nurses' station. *How easily you forget the times I've eaten alone on "date night" when you were tied up in court preps or with clients. I was a doctor when you married me. Remember? Or is that fact only convenient when I'm paying your law school loans?*

Cami

"*D*iaphragm in. Engage your core to stabilize. Good. Give me two more, and we'll hit the showers." Marcus grinned as she pushed through her last set.

"Is that an invitation?" Cami grunted as she released the weights.

"Standing." He grinned again as he rubbed her shoulders with a towel. "Pun intended."

"You're ridiculous." Cami said stretching her neck. "One of these days, I'm going to put that bravado to the test."

"Mine or yours?"

"Cute." Cami flashed her most sarcastic smile. Being the only girl among three athletic brothers definitely served her well when it came to dealing with cocky men like Marcus—in the office or otherwise. Too bad she couldn't say the same for her dealings with other women. She would never be the communicator Kate was or the empathetic confidant Leila was. She was, however, fiercely protective of her "sister-friends," as Ellie called their group. It was she who'd been the rock during the ups and downs of the last decade. She'd packed and cleared Ellie's boxes after the Marcus fiasco, even negotiated the property settlement. She'd played liaison between Leila and her mom at their lowest and taken Kate to meetings when no one else knew she needed them. There was little she wouldn't do for these special women—the only women who saw her true colors. Year by year, she learned from them. Their strengths no doubt completed her, yet she couldn't bring herself to share her embarrassing termination. She didn't have the resolve to listen to Ellie spin it as an opportunity or to hear Leila's rendition of her marketability. Aside from that, Norah and Kate needed to take center ring now.

Norah

1 New Text—(from Ken Cell)
Just FYI—I'm getting worried. How quickly should a
nursing mother lose pregnancy weight? Kate swears
she's eating.

Reply
At this point, no more than 1–2 pounds every 2 weeks.
Does her sponsor know?

1 New Text—(Ken Cell)
No. She's even more defensive about it than usual.

Reply
Let's get her in for a blood draw. We'll be discreet.

Norah had suspected this might happen. Kate had gained steadily
during her pregnancy—dutifully, even. They all should have been
watching her more closely postpartum. The hormones and sleep
deprivation were likely wreaking havoc on her psyche. She'd come
so far in the last five years. Norah didn't want to see that progress
collapse now.

The next text she sent was to her partner, Kate's doctor, explaining her suspicions and asking that Kate be scheduled for additional
postpartum labs. She hated herself for having been too self-involved
to notice Kate's spiral. She owed her sweet friend better than that.

Ellie

"Jess and crew will be out shortly. Thank you." Ellie subtly checked her reflection in a mirror app before she got out of the car, hoping she didn't look as frazzled as she felt. This wasn't the first time she'd hidden a client at her home, but it was definitely the first time she'd returned there while doing so. If she were followed, her property was guaranteed to be teeming with cameras every time one of the firm's high-interest clients made the news. To Ellie, her Malibu condo was as indicative of her success as it was symbolic of her dedication to the ups and downs in the unforgiving profession she happened to love. It was definitely not the grandest home in the development, but it was her perfect fit, her soft place to land. After the split with Marcus, she had needed a new vibe. Her motto was "New home. New start. New dream." She had fallen in love with the property immediately. Its Tuscan-inspired stucco and red tile roof reminded her of Cinque Terre, her favorite place in the world. It had two living areas, the upstairs of which was floor-to-ceiling beveled glass with panoramic ocean views of the development's private beach. Ellie had hired Kate as her designer and given her carte blanche to make the place a home. Kate, in turn, had paired Ellie's love of clean lines and functional pieces with well-mingled color palettes to create densely detailed rooms worthy of a magazine spread.

Of all the beauty Kate had brought to her home, Ellie's favorite was the miracle she'd worked on the lower balcony. Kate had completely redesigned the space to bring the "indoors out," as she called it, metamorphosing what had once been a blasé collection of waterlogged decking, faded lounge chairs, and a broken hot tub into an oasis enviable of the finer resorts Ellie had visited over the years. She had meticulously overseen every aspect of the transformation, replacing the worn originals with beautiful eco-planks and flagstone, and had scoured the city for vintage furniture finds she could upcycle with weatherproof fabrics and pops of coral and turquoise. Her *pièces de résistance* were the lighted pergola and recessed positioning of the hot tub.

Ellie could not believe her eyes the first time she saw the finished project. Kate had taken her vision of a waterfront paradise and multiplied it by ten. Ellie would never forget exploring the deck on her first night in her new home, trying desperately not to imagine how romantic the moment could have been if Marcus hadn't betrayed her. Just as a pang of sadness at building a home for one versus a home with someone had pierced her throat, she'd spotted an iridescent glow in the center of a potted palm. It was a pearlescent picture frame enclosing a note in Kate's elegant script: *New home. New dream. Same beautiful you. Love, Kate.*

Ellie made a mental note to call Kate in the morning and schedule a lunch, or at least a happy hour. Taking a moment to realize what this home meant to her, and hoping it could remain so, she punched the security code on her side door, thought better of not covering the pad, then changed the code from the other side. Ellie entered her mudroom to a wave of uneasiness in her gut. She hated feeling as if she were being watched. This was a risk. She should have known better.

"Ellison." Jess rose from her seat when Ellie entered the room. "Good evening. I've settled Mr. Grayson in the upstairs guest room. He's there now."

"Thank you. Has he eaten?"

"He insisted you not go to any trouble."

"Okay. I think that will be all for this evening. It's been a long day for all of us, and I'm sure you're more than ready to be home. Thank you for your work today."

"Of course." Jess nodded. "As far as we know, no one has found him. I'll do my best to keep it that way." Jess signaled her assistants, and the trio left in tandem.

Once alone, Ellie walked out onto the deck and sank into her favorite chaise lounge. She prayed she wasn't making a catastrophic mistake. What was it about the lens of a camera that emboldened the paparazzi? Was it greed? Was it the same high that made people act like fools in hotel rooms? Sure, the ski-slope picture had sold for fifteen grand, but what kind of vulture lived his life scavenging for pictures? Patrick Grayson was a person after all. Better than most, from what she'd seen.

Just then, the patio door slid open, making her jump.

"Oh!" Ellie clutched her chest. "Pat! It's just you. You scared me." She shifted embarrassedly in her seat and hoped he couldn't see her flush. The soft glow of the living room lights framed him, and Ellie couldn't help but notice how handsome he looked with the hint of stubble and tousled hair indicative of his castaway state.

"I'm sorry. I"—he cleared his throat and stepped into the light of the deck—"just wanted to thank you for . . . well, for, everything." He ran his hand through his auburn waves. "I know this is a risk for you. For your privacy, and, well, what I'm trying to say is . . ." He grinned and ducked his head. "Hell, I've made a mess of saying thank you, now, haven't I?" Ellie watched him shift his weight from one leg to the other, still nervously smoothing his hair.

"It's fine and you're welcome. Come, have a seat. Can I get you anything?"

"No, you've already done too much," he said. A long moment passed; then he perched on the chair beside her, still visibly shaken from the day's events.

"I was just about to open some wine. Would you like a glass?" she asked, as she walked to the outdoor wet bar. What was it with women and British accents? She swore she could listen to him read from the phone book for hours. "This is usually the best part of my day. I never get tired of the waves." Ellie felt him watching her move and was suddenly desperate to fill the silence. "They're my constant." She quickly opened the bottle and grabbed two glasses.

"Hmm." He smiled, staring at the moon. "Much better than my constant. If I never see another flashbulb, it will be too soon."

"I'm with you there. Did you see the press conference?"

"Stacie showed it to me. It already has fifty thousand hits on YouTube." He swirled the wine in his glass, before taking a long drink. "You were great. I don't think I could have faced them." His brow furrowed as he stared into the waves. "For what it's worth, she said they separated last year and are in the final phase of divorce. We've been seeing each other on and off for the last four months. I'm just"—he ran his hands through his hair again—"dumbfounded. I would have told your team if I thought it mattered. She kept it all so private, and I thought I was honoring that somehow. I would never—"

"I understand." Ellie steadied her voice. "And if it makes you feel better, I've been there. Betrayal like that hurts. It's a deep pain that pierces to the core."

"Exactly. I get that it's not so much her as it is her handlers and her team, but I . . . I just don't fancy being used. She knows how much *Life of Us* means to me and what a scandal like this could do to all of that." Finishing his glass in a single drink, he continued, "It's as if I have no one to trust. Everyone wants either a piece of me or a piece of the pie. Even my family's gone bat-shit crazy. It wasn't so bad in the beginning, but these days, every time I bloody turn round, one of them has sold a picture to the papers of me as a skinny kid with specs, kicking the football the wrong direction or scratching my balls in the middle of a primer concert."

Ellie laughed, picturing a younger version of the star fumbling on a soccer field. She refilled their glasses, wishing she knew what to say. It would only get worse from here, and he hadn't had nearly enough media training for the storm that was sure to follow.

"Well, as they say, you can never go home again. If I were you, I would decide what you want from *this* life. Your film is fantastic—I think it will speak for itself—and the attention can only help. Plus, the film took the Jury Prize from Cannes, so that on its own should bring the artsy demo. The trick is bringing the work to the center. You're going to be asked about Scarlett, and of course about the photo, ad nauseam—that's a given—but we can always spin it. I'll demand scripted questions, and we'll get you ready." Ellie made a mental note to veto questions about whether he would be reprising his role as Lucas in the *Destiny* prequel.

"Thank you. Part of me just wants to take the money and run, you know? Buy some land somewhere, have ten kids, and live in whatever semblance of normalcy I can. If that makes any sense."

"It makes more sense than you can imagine," Ellie had gone off the grid once herself. It hadn't helped. "You've lost your center is all. Either you'll find it again or you'll find a new dream. Just remember, you're not alone in this."

"I know, and I'm grateful to have someone I can, er, confide in." He reached over and squeezed her arm affectionately. Ellie loved the way his eyes shone when he smiled and crinkled when he laughed. She must remember to keep her guard up. He was a client, a lonely one at that—nothing more.

Kate

*K*ate only allowed herself to step on the scale once per hour. It read 127.4—still high, but better. She was starting to feel normal again.

Ellie

Two bottles of wine and three sandwiches later, Ellie and Pat stood laughing in her kitchen. He was sitting cross-legged on her island while she put the remnants of their late-night snack back into the refrigerator. She couldn't believe how much they'd shared during the last three hours. Somewhere between the wine and the cold cuts, their energy had shifted from professional to personal. Their conversation had flowed as freely as the grapes as they discussed everything from politics to disastrous fashion choices to losing their virginities to a mutual hatred of raisins and sun-dried tomatoes. Ellie understood Norah's predicament a bit better now. It was as if she were intoxicated by his charisma and their easy banter. Things felt so effortless with him. Her own conscience was screaming that this was a bad idea—a gray area professionally—but she couldn't help herself. She hadn't felt this comfortable with a man since the early days with Marcus.

"So, when do I get to know the rest of your story? Why hasn't anyone snatched you up yet?" His eyes danced as he laughed.

Ellie's voice went instantly to ice, her blue eyes wide and stinging. "Ah. The classic 'why are you still single' conundrum."

"That's not what I meant." He hopped down from the island as she looked away from him. "I just meant you're beautiful, successful; you've built a lovely home, so—"

"So what's wrong with me? Right?" Ellie forced herself to meet his gaze as a crushing sensation of insecurity burned in her chest. She knew he hadn't meant to hurt her, but maybe this was the sign she needed to remind herself she was treading on thin ice.

He crossed the distance between them in a single stride, sending the unwelcome realization that she loved the way he moved coursing through her mind.

"I only meant"—he reached for her arm, pulling her gently toward him—"that I think you're phenomenal, and you should be made to laugh like you did tonight every day." His eyes were pleading and sincere. "Every single day." She wanted so badly to lean into his chest. To give in to the connection she had felt just minutes earlier and let him lead her up the staircase.

"I understand. It's late. We should say goodnight." Ellie pulled away from him, then, softening, added, "Thank you for tonight. It's been a long time since I've enjoyed a man's company so much. There was someone," she added hesitantly, "but for a long time there's been no one."

Perhaps he could be her favorite mistake? Ellie shook the thought from her mind before she told him goodnight.

Leila

Still glowing from her orgasm, Leila snuggled into the crook of Wes's shoulder as he scrolled through the DVR. She still loved being in his arms, even after all of these years.

"Jon Stewart?" he asked, smoothing her hair.

"Perfect." She smiled up at him, before falling asleep to the opening credits.

Norah

Norah's pager vibrated, waking her with a start in the on-call room. She swore she hadn't known what three consecutive nights of sleep felt like in the last seven years. She stretched and prepared to go live, as Ellie called it. Checking her phone, she realized that, in her three hours of sleep, she'd missed an apology text from Matt, two calls from Ken worried about Kate, and a pharmacy notification that her Clomid refill was overdue. Between her office hours, her nights on call, and her ovulation calendar, she felt as if her sun rose and set around windows and days, not hours. She knew she, of all people, especially considering her current situation with Enrique, shouldn't hold on to her anger at Matt, but she was still hurt by his "appointment" text. Why was she always his whipping post? He seemed to hold her continually responsible for his insecurity. Things went further downhill for them every time he didn't make partner at his firm. Norah knew he was deeply sensitive about being the oldest associate, and that he thought he deserved partnership after his years of service and loyalty. It didn't help his ego that without that promotion, she would continue to make twice the money he did, nor that they had been unable to conceive. He had apologized numerous times early in their relationship for not taking better care of her. Had his stringent upbringing in the Midwest ingrained this pressure in him to be her provider? Norah often thought he might have been happier if he'd followed in his parents' footsteps by marrying straight out of high school and starting a family in his early twenties.

A smirk crossed her face as she remembered meeting her in-laws-to-be for the first time. An emergency C-section hadn't left her time to change into anything more presentable than clean scrubs, so she'd gone to the restaurant straight from the hospital. She would never forget the disappointment on his mother's face as they were introduced. She'd stared at Norah as if she were some kind of alien, sneaking furtive glances at her pocket badge and pager all evening. Matt, on the other hand, had beamed with pride, chattering obliviously through the dinner about Norah's work in India and her ideas for the fistula initiative she hoped to launch there one day. During dessert, Norah fell further from grace in her future mother-in-law's eyes after mentioning their visit to a Bed and Breakfast in the Redwoods during her last weekend off. Matt had warned her they were conservative, but she had no idea they believed their twenty-six-year-old son was still a virgin. His mother had been horrified at the idea of their spending the night together in a hotel, blinking back tears as she glared at Norah, while his outraged father staunchly reminded him that this was not how he had been raised. Did they think she was his first? Hardly. That she had seduced him? Norah had been so taken aback that she'd all but choked on her wine—no doubt committing another sin with every sip in their eyes.

It was also not lost on her that Matt's family believed their current struggle with infertility was due to her demanding career. She could not remember a Christmas or Thanksgiving when his mother or perpetually pregnant sister, Faith, hadn't loudly recommended she take time off to *really focus* on starting a family. Norah often joked to the girls that she should start wearing ankle-length denim skirts and holiday sweaters if she had any chance of connecting with those two women. Matt had come to her rescue more than once when his family teased her about ticking biological clocks, insisting that if anyone understood ovulation cycles and female anatomy in the room, it was Norah, and forcefully reiterating that their family planning was private, not up for open discussion at the dinner table. She loved him for that. She also knew that no matter how hard she tried or how happy she made Matt, his family would never accept her. They would never see her career as anything but a distraction from the role they felt she should be playing—a role that, in their eyes, would never be compatible with medicine.

This sudden clarity prompted a flood of images in her mind. She could picture Faith holding her and Matt's baby and telling them how "nice" it must be to have a nanny, how she would gladly trade her mommy on-call schedule for Norah's hours at the office and hospital. Although Norah knew Faith's barbs came from a place of insecurity and a need for fulfillment, she could picture snide jab after jab, no matter how happy she and Matt managed to be, or how devoted she was to their marriage. In Norah's world, her love for Matt and her love for her practice were not exclusive of each other. She thought her commitment to hard work and compassion served her well in both, but, on the other hand, perhaps that was the central problem in their relationship. Did Matt feel as if he was in constant competition with her professionally and in constant competition for her attentions personally? Was that what fed the tension between them? Did he see starting a family as bringing balance to their roles, and their fertility struggles only magnified that discrepancy? Where was the man who'd been so incredibly proud of her at that dinner years ago? Was Faith right that her "type" of woman could never make him happy?

She hated the idea that women picked teams against each other. Didn't they all have enough strife, no matter what their roles?

Leaving the on-call room, she texted him:

I forgive you. We need to talk.

Ellie

Pat kissed her neck as the water and steam cascaded around them. She turned to face him, desire and anticipation playing a tantric duet in her body. Pressing her chest to his, she traced the line of his collarbone with her lips, slowly guiding him backward toward the shower ledge, eager for . . .

Ellie bolted upright in her bed, both relieved and disappointed to find she was alone. What was wrong with her? She was dreaming about him now? Seriously? She had worked too hard to risk everything for a crush on a client and a fling. Why was she giving the physical effect he had on her so much power? She was a modern woman—solely in control of her career, her finances, and her personal life. Her sexuality should be no different.

Fishing through the top drawer of her nightstand, Ellie pulled out a black satin case and headed to the shower.

Kate

Scraping the cold egg whites into the trash, Kate made a silent promise to eat nine almonds in an hour or so. This didn't mean anything. No one liked cold eggs. She knew Ken was watching her like a hawk these days, but he also worked fifty hours a week and got home well past the dinner hour. The way she saw it, something had to go. If she couldn't control when she slept or showered these days, how could she possibly find time to practice her recovery principles? Eat seated? Eat at scheduled times? Eat balanced meals? What new mom had time for that—much less one who wasn't cooking for a family, or even for another adult? Sure, she'd powered a few pounds off. No biggie. Just a few more, and she would be happy again. She'd have clothes that fit and wouldn't feel like such a slob. Besides, it wasn't like she wasn't eating at all; she was just eating when she could. She may have gotten distracted from her eggs this morning, but she would make up for it at lunch. Leila had invited her and Liam over for a "mommy date," as she called it. That meant the kids would play and she and Leila would get to catch up, uninterrupted, when they napped.

Leila

Leila's phone erupted for the seventh time in two hours with "In Another Life," her mother's assigned ringtone.

"Mommy! Can we sing that song together? It's so pretty!" Clara said, running through the kitchen. Leila scooped up her oldest daughter and danced a few beats in the kitchen.

"I love you, sweet girl," she said, giving Clara a twirl before setting her on her feet. "Now, please go play with Julia, and we'll all have a tea party when Ms. Kate gets here. Mommy is getting our feast ready." As Clara ran off to join her sister, Leila considered ignoring this call as well. She knew better than to answer, but Darla was clearly on one of her reconnection binges. She would likely call all day and all night, leaving tearful voice mails on both Leila's and Wes's phones. Leila had become a pro at ignoring her mother's cellular assaults, but she knew they bothered Wes to no end, especially when he was at work.

Leila grimaced, wishing she could give both her girls and her husband better. They certainly deserved better. They deserved involved, supportive in-laws and grandparents, the type Leila felt so envious of any time her playgroup began to talk about date nights and dentist appointments sans babysitter money. His family visited regularly but lived on the East Coast. She and Wes had no one local to speak of. In fact, they'd had to split time between Kate and a babysitter just to deliver Julia by planned induction. She and Wes had come home from the hospital alone, for the second time, and

Leila had wondered wistfully what it would be like to snuggle her newborn in bed while she recovered from delivery and a family member helped with Clara. Wes worked from home the first few days, but that was all his position could spare.

She allowed herself a moment of closed eyes and gritted teeth in which she tried to remember what she was and was not accountable for, and what had made her stronger. After all, wasn't forgiveness giving up on the hope that things could have been different? Centering, Leila willed herself to remember Wes's mantra about her family. "I don't love you in spite of your past; I love you because of it. Without those hardships, you wouldn't be who you are today. You'll always be my Leila. Nothing your train wreck of a mother does can change that." He was her ever-patient champion, never wavering in her sight, but she knew her past placed stressors on him, and she hated herself for it. It had been seven weeks since she'd spoken to Darla, and Leila could gladly go seven more. Long ago, she had sentenced the woman who gave her life to the harshest consequence a mother can endure—that of being unneeded by and inconsequential to her child. No hope of parole.

"Hello," Leila answered, resigned to get it over with.

"Well, hi. It took you long enough, Leigh Anne," her mother said, as the strike of a cigarette lighter echoed in the background.

"How are you?" Leila asked, thinking that clicking lighters and the snap of a belt were equal candidates for the signature sound of her childhood.

"Worried about my daughter, but that's nothing new. What are my grandbabies doing these days?" she asked, before breaking into a coughing fit.

"Right now, they're getting ready for some company. My friend Kate and her son are coming over for lunch." Leila busied herself tossing the salad and checking the soup on the stove.

"Which one's that? You know I can never keep your friends straight."

"Kate was the one you met when you and Randall came through on your way to the races."

"I think you mean your daddy. One of these days, you're going to get tired of being so pissed and cut the man who took you in some slack." She coughed again. "You know he didn't have to."

"I really don't think we need to revisit that conversation. I am not angry. I wish things could have been different, but I refuse to spend my life dwelling on that. I'm focusing on living life in the present," she rushed, "and, on a happier note, Julia will turn three in two weeks. Do you think you can make it over to meet her before then?" Leila asked, brushing olive oil on crostini as she watched the girls building Lego towers in the living room.

"Ain't that convenient. That baby's almost three before her own grandmother gets to meet her."

"You know you're always welcome."

"It don't feel that way. Are you inviting me now so you ain't embarrassed by us at the birthday party in front of those rich friends of yours? Can't have the white trash cluttering up the place while you're puttin' on airs, can ya?"

Leila knew there was truth in her words, but she forbade herself to be incited into an ugly argument. "Mom, you know if you'd like to see her now, tomorrow, at the party, whenever, I'll send a cab for you. That's always been on the table. Aside from that, I feel like you're trying to pick a fight, and I'm not interested."

"Them roads go both ways, last time I checked. I got to see what your daddy's got going on and let you know." The lighter flicked again. "Days off ain't exactly plentiful with our bills."

"I understand," she said absentmindedly, as the girls ran squealing down the hallway. "I'm sorry, but I need to hang up now so I can check on the girls and finish making lunch."

"I guess that's all the time you got for me. I love you, baby girl. Bye." Leila heard her choke back a sob but didn't know if it was real or fabricated. The woman was a pro at playing the victim and twisting history into her own version of reality. In her mind, she was as devoted to her daughter and granddaughters as her circumstances allowed. Of course, she didn't see them more than once a year and hadn't even met Julia, but she had as many excuses as complaints for not having done so. She was constantly disappointed in Leila, insisting over and over again that she couldn't believe a daughter she had raised could have grown up to be so selfish, to make all the time in the world for her friends but none for her blood. Leila wasn't in close contact with any of her half siblings, but she knew they felt the same way. Two of the four were doing well for themselves, with steady jobs in the service industries and children of their own. The other two were slaves to vicious cycles of addiction and incarceration and contacted Leila only when they needed money. She and Wes had offered to fund their rehabs but refused to enable them financially.

Leila rubbed her temples as the girls squabbled over a toy in the living room. She was proud of all she'd overcome to be living *this* life. She'd left her first life behind her so long ago, but at moments like these, she knew the stain and stench of the trailer park would never vanish entirely. Part of her would always be Leigh Anne—the lonely, scared little girl who wanted to be anywhere but home.

Ellie

Ellie stared absently out of her office window, still thinking about the note Pat had left on her bedroom door.

> *Ellie,*
> *I'm sorry I was an arse tonight. It was wonderful until I went and ruined it. I meant what I said. You deserve to be made to laugh every single day like we did together.*
> *Apologies,*
> *He who should have his ears boxed*

He was asleep when she left for work, but she had given Stacie, the associate Jess had assigned to be "monitor," strict instructions that he was to be treated as if he were on a true hiatus. He was available to his team by phone and e-mail, but his location was not to be disclosed to anyone under any circumstances, unless it was cleared with her directly. Ellie suspected his agent might have something to do with the sale of the photo. She knew the greedy bastard cared only about his cut and would gladly see Pat spend the remainder of his career in one cookie-cutter romantic comedy after another, rather than allow him to take the risks necessary to grow his craft.

Reaching for her phone, she texted her houseguest.

Text: To Patrick Grayson Cell
Good morning. Thank you for your note. I had a lovely

evening with you as well. Laughing is cheaper than therapy, after all. The refrigerator has been restocked. Consider yourself on vacation. Use the next few days to energize for the promotional tour. Jess will be by in an hour or so for a media training session; then the rest of the day is yours. Please don't hesitate to ask Stacie if you need anything to make your stay more enjoyable. She can make arrangements for you.

1 New Text: from Patrick Grayson Cell
Will u be home tonight?

Ellie stared at the little blue screen.

Reply
Possibly.

Cami

*C*ami thumbed through her portfolio nervously as the elevator rose to the seventh floor. This was her first job interview in over ten years. Were they allowed to ask her why she'd left InFocus? She hoped not. Snapping the leather case closed and returning it to her messenger bag, she reminded herself that *confidence* was the word of the day. *Confidence* and *experience*.

The elevator opened into a sleek waiting room, full of minimalist black furniture and galleries of stunning black-and-white photographs. Cami stood tall and walked to the receptionist's desk.

"Can I help you?"

"Yes. I'm Camille Clark; I have a one thirty meeting with Dean Gatz."

"I'll let him know you're here. Please have a seat." She smiled politely and motioned to one of the sofas. Cami forced a smile in return, realizing she must be aging more quickly than she thought. The girl looked like she was barely out of high school. Cami glanced around the room, wondering if any of the people waiting were her competition. They, too, looked terribly young. Maybe they were intern candidates? She wondered what they were thinking about her—probably that she was a client, judging from her Kate Spade case and tailored pantsuit. After all, it hadn't been that long ago that she had been the one waiting in a lobby on pins and needles to be called for her first interview after college graduation. She had been as uncomfortable in her seat as she'd been in the skirt and pumps Kate had insisted she wear.

She and Kate had attended the same design school. They'd met freshman year, after being assigned as roommates. Having grown up in an all-male household, Cami had found in Kate her first female role model to speak of. They'd bonded initially after Cami offered to take the dresser and give Kate the closet. As she watched Kate hang outfit after outfit, she felt suddenly sheepish about having brought nothing but Umbro shorts, jeans, and T-shirts. Kate politely offered her borrowing rights to anything in her wardrobe, but Cami declined, saying she was studying to be a photographer in the field, so how could she possibly work wearing heels and short skirts? Kate would later tell her how much this comment hurt her feelings.

Cami stiffened at the memory of that tearful tequila induced confession. Kate had sat on the edge of her bed, crying after having been dumped by that month's Prince Charming, saying no one in her life, Cami included, took her seriously. She had become angry and defensive, demanding to know why dressing nicely and wearing makeup made her any less serious about design than Cami was about photography.

Cami had refused to apologize, shouting that if Kate looked less like Career Barbie and more like a serious designer, people might respect her for her talent. She'd stormed out of their room, furious. Kate had been cold to her for weeks after that, and Cami had been lost about why she was still mad. Had she not apologized at least three times, saying she was sorry about the "Barbie" comment? She wished she could go back to the easy days of fighting with her brothers. Those fights were like fireworks in the sky—an eruption of emotion but with few to no lasting consequences. The fight with Kate was different. It was as if her anger were a blister, slow to form, painful when it burst, and raw to the touch long after the cause was gone.

Cami shook her head and made a note to thank Kate for not writing her off as a bitchy tomboy during those early days. Essentially, she owed her relationships with Ellie, Norah, and Leila all to Kate.

Cami's thoughts shifted as the young woman across from her

loudly answered her cell phone. "I can let you know by early next week. I have a few more offers to consider. I'm truly hoping to land in a creative direction role." Pausing, she added, "No, thank *you* for your time."

Creative direction? That was the position Cami had been called to interview for. There was no way the girl had more than three years' professional experience at her age. Cami took in the well-dressed twentysomething, wondering if students today simply walked into their dream jobs, no grueling apprenticeships required.

Just then, the lobby door opened and an assistant called her name. As Cami stood, the young woman she'd been watching looked up from her iPad, raised her eyebrows, and smirked at her. Caught off-guard by the arrogant disdain in her expression, Cami hastily shrugged her bag onto her shoulder and gathered her portfolio. The weight of the heavy case shifted as she bent, causing her to stumble awkwardly on her heels. The girl snickered under her breath, and Cami felt her cheeks flush with anger and embarrassment. She turned, looked directly into the girl's eyes, and said, "I'm glad you found that funny. The thing about cases is they get heavier the longer you work. Clearly, you believe you're on your way up in this business. If that's true, our paths will inevitably cross again, and when they do, I can assure you your portfolio will not gain any more weight. I'd hate for you to embarrass yourself"—Cami narrowed her eyes—"further, that is." She turned on her heel and walked confidently toward the open door.

Kate

"That's mine!" Clara protested, as Julia snatched a piece of pasta from her plate and chewed happily on its end. "Mommy! That was my favorite one!" She whined and crossed her arms with a pout. "I was saving it!"

"Clara, please control your voice. I know you're disappointed, and that's okay, but let's try to love our sister more than we love ourselves. Look in my eyes and hear Mommy's words. She doesn't understand that you were saving it. She just thinks the coolest person in her world must have the coolest pasta in the world." Leila reached over to pat her shoulder. "It's pretty nice to have someone love you so, so, so much that even your spaghetti is more fantastic just for being yours. What do you think?"

"Okay, Mommy, she can love me and my noodles, but I wish she'd love my broccoli a little more." Clara smiled as she offered Julia her last bite of green tree. "Want to eat Sister's colors?" Julia giggled and happily took the broccoli out of Clara's hand.

Kate loved to listen to Leila talk to her children. She was so direct, but tactful. She seemed to honor their feelings while teaching them empathy for those around them. It was the polar opposite of anything Kate had ever known. She had grown up in a house full of WASPs, picture perfect in so many ways and severely lacking in others. Manners were a given. Etiquette was expected, drilled, demanded, but the reasons behind it were never, ever explained.

On paper and in photographs, her family's life had been idyllic.

Kate and her older brother, Cameron, had it all: the best private schools, exclusive summer camps, elaborate birthday parties, dream vacations, and lessons of every kind. They had also known their nannies better than their parents, known not to speak unless spoken to, known there were harsh punishments for social missteps, known they were their grandparents' puppets, known what it was like to live through a vicious public scandal, and known—with absolute certainty—that a gilded cage was still a cage. Cameron had beaten his wings against its bars until they broke, and Kate had followed suit in her own way.

She could picture her mother's gallery of carefully posed family shots. Here they were in Hawaii for Cameron's tenth birthday; here they were at the Olympic Village; here they were in Africa; here they were in Aspen at Christmas. The list went on. A flood of plastered smiles and breaking hearts filled Kate's mind. She wished she could make her own additions to the gallery. She would love to see her mother's and grandmother's faces if that wall were to truly reflect those trips and milestones. Here they were, building sandcastles with the nanny while their parents fought in the cabana. Here they were, sneaking into the laundry to smell the perfume on their father's suit jackets to guess which "friend" had accompanied him on his business trip. Here they were, visiting Cameron at drug rehab. Here was Kate at ninety-three pounds. Her mother should have been on Ellie's payroll. She certainly knew how to build, brand, and, most importantly, *protect* an image at any cost.

Kate looked down at her plate. Leila had made tomato-basil soup and bruschetta, two of her favorites. She savored the smell of the rich soup in her bowl and took a bite of broccoli.

"Okay, sweet girls, go wash up and call Mommy when you've picked a book and are ready for stories." Leila winked at Kate and mouthed "almost time," with a big grin and a glance at a fictitious watch. Kate smiled back and pretended to clap her hands. She was grateful Liam was still sleeping contentedly in his car seat. She cut her remaining piece of bruschetta in half and scraped the cheese to the side before taking a bite from her empty fork.

Leila returned a few minutes later with a broad smile on her face. "Three resting babies? I think this deserves a toast."

"Definitely." Kate smiled as Leila took two glasses out of the cabinet and a bottle of wine from the chiller, feeling grateful to have a mommy friend she could relate to.

"All right." Leila filled the glasses and handed her one. "Here's to two mommies on a time-out."

"Amen. I'll cheers to that!" Kate laughed and sipped her wine.

"So, what've I missed since the last time we talked? Is Ken still working crazy hours?"

"He is. In fact, would you mind if I took the rest of my soup home so I don't have to cook tonight? It's such a pain for just one person."

"Not at all. I'm glad you liked it enough to eat it"—she paused, noticing how little was gone from Kate's bowl, and added awkwardly—"twice in the same day."

Kate shifted uncomfortably. "I think I ate too much salad and bread waiting for it to cool off. You know I love bruschetta." She picked up her fork and took a bite to prove her point.

"That heats up well, too. I'll send a few pieces of it home with the soup."

"Thank you, and"—she reached for Leila's hand—"I appreciate that you made my favorites. I've sat too many times at this table without appreciating how much planning it takes to make and serve a nice meal with two children underfoot and then clean it all up." She laughed, hoping to lighten the concern on Leila's face. "Liam isn't even mobile yet, and I'm doing well to get cereal on the table."

"You're welcome." Leila patted Kate's hand. "And it gets easier. Mostly, you just have to accept that nothing, not a single task or part of your day, will ever be uninterrupted again, and that some things will get harder just as other things get easier. You'll look up in a few weeks and be grateful he can finally sit in the high chair while you cook and babble with him; then you will wonder how you'll ever be able to take your eyes off a lightning-fast crawler." She took another sip and added, "I couldn't have managed this meal when Clara was Liam's age. You just learn to juggle. One ball in the air at a time."

"There's something *What to Expect* forgot to mention." Kate smiled. "I was always so organized at work, constantly multitasking and managing different projects at the same time. I don't know why my days fly by now, full of the sweetest snuggles and firsts and moments, then end with me frantically scratching things off my to-do list while he's asleep or after the nighttime feedings." She took a sip of wine. "And it's never enough."

"Kate, no one ever learned to juggle by tossing ten balls in the air at once. You're expecting perfection before you've had enough practice. Give yourself some time."

"That definitely makes me feel better. Maybe there's hope for me yet." Kate felt a flicker of relief at Leila's words. She would learn to be a master juggler, or else she would learn which balls were important enough to keep in the air and which ones to let fall.

Cami

As Cami entered his office, Dean Gatz crossed the room to shake her hand. She was surprised by how young he was, only a few years older than she was.

"It's a pleasure to meet you, Ms. Clark."

"Thank you. It's a pleasure to be here." She lied thinking she shouldn't have been fired and shouldn't need to be here.

"Please, sit. I must say, I have been a fan of your work for quite some time."

Cami sat, feeling more at ease knowing that her reputation preceded her.

"I'm flattered. Thank you, um, again," she stammered, and opened her portfolio, adding, "I love what I do."

"That much is evident." He leaned back in his chair, completely at ease. Cami felt slightly irritated by his casual pose. Was he taking this meeting as seriously as she was?

"I've brought some sample projects I feel represent my strengths as a creative director."

Reaching across the desk in a fluid motion, he closed her case. "Let me be frank. Your work speaks for itself. I am confident you can fulfill my vision for this company creatively."

She was really at a loss now. What was he implying? "I'm familiar with your performance at InFocus. By familiar, I mean impressed. This position is very similar, with a few additional responsibilities."

"I am proud of my time at InFocus as well. I feel I made lasting contributions to its growth and success." The sting of having been fired pierced her chest again as she said the words. "I must say that creative direction alone was a sixty-hour-a-week position. Can you clarify what you mean by 'added responsibilities'?"

"I can. And I appreciate your asking, by the way." He smiled, and Cami cocked her head trying to gauge his intent. "I've worked hard to brand this company as hip and modern—cutting-edge, if you will. In order to keep it that way, I require a steady stream of young blood and fresh talent. I scour publications and independents for their best and brightest and pay them moderately to grow their craft here, under experienced directors. They're arrogant pains in the ass to work with after the first year or so, but that's a price I'm willing to pay to stay competitive. They keep my thumb on the pulse of emerging markets, and that is what keeps us relevant, keeps us growing." His voice was determined, verging on passionate, as he described the company's model. "That said, I need a director who can see both sides of this coin. On one side, the art is the product; on the other side, the product is a business and must be run on deadlines and within budgets. Where do you see yourself in that framework, Ms. Clark?" He leaned forward in his chair, and Cami noticed a glint of humor in his eyes. He must have spoken to someone at InFocus. She definitely had a rep for riding people hard when it came to budgets and schedules.

Cami turned up one side of her mouth in a wry smile. "I'm sure my reputation precedes me on that note as well. Anyone who's ever worked under me can tell you that I demand we work as a team to reach project goals. Art needing more time to develop is one matter, but distraction and poor management of time and resources are unacceptable in my eyes if you share my team's vision for the project. It's akin to life on the baseball diamond. The shortstop can't be working his tail off to win games while third base stands there, spitting chew and scratching his—" She cut herself off before she went too far. "My point is that if you're wanting a photojournalist by craft with a head for the game, then I'm your pick. You won't find better."

Cami felt a fire for her profession rekindle as she talked to him about his model and the double-edged sword that was art and industry. She relaxed her shoulders for what felt like the first time in days.

She was surprised when he broke into a wide grin across the desk. "I must say, that's exactly what I hoped to hear from you. I need a bulldog with the eyes of a dog-show judge to fill this role." He chuckled, and she stared at him skeptically, not sure if she'd just been insulted or hired.

"I'm hoping you meant that as a compliment?"

"Damn right, Clark. The job is yours for the taking." He drummed the desk playfully. "Now, what do you say we go grab a drink and talk numbers?"

"I have previous plans until eight, but I can meet you after," Cami said, determined to keep her poker face on until after she'd seen the salary.

"Let's say Bogart's at nine o'clock. My niece is in the office, interviewing with marketing, and I told her we'd have dinner. You may have seen her in the lobby. Early twenties, jet-black hair? She's a bit of a spitfire, but her talent's unmatched. I'll shake her before nine so we can talk hardball." He opened the door for her, and a receptionist waited on the other side. Cami told him goodbye and smiled broadly as soon as her back was to him. She thanked the receptionist as she held the door for Cami to exit into the lobby.

"Ms. Gatz, they're ready for you now."

Cami's heart sank as the young girl she'd exchanged words with stood and gathered her things.

Ellie

Ellie swirled her martini as she scrolled through her e-mail. She was grateful Norah and Cami were running late. Pat's case had her undivided attention at the moment, and she needed to make sure her teams were on top of the firm's other clients. She was reviewing activity reports, contact logs, and promotional agendas. She knew most of her managers resented filing these reports and considered them her way of micromanaging their authority. Ellie's rote answer for these complaints was that, at the end of the day, it was her name that signed clients, her reputation that kept them, and her name on the door. She owed it to everyone she employed and everyone she represented to stay involved in each team's campaigns.

Satisfied all but a few fires could wait until Monday, she closed her Mac and attempted to focus her thoughts on her friends, instead of on her houseguest and his problems. She wasn't sure why she felt so anxious. It wasn't the girls. She had shared hundreds of dilemmas with them. It couldn't be work. As far as that was concerned, this was the same old, tired happy hour, the same carousel of stressors, just wearing different clients' faces week after week. Was it Pat? The secret of hiding him at her home? Did she want to be somewhere else? Her mind had wandered off and on all day to their chemistry on her balcony and their banter gone wrong in the kitchen, to her dream and his note. She had already made a reservation to stay downtown tonight. It was the right thing to do professionally. She could not risk losing control with him and certainly did not need a repeat reminder of what it meant to fall for someone you could never truly have.

Just then, a light tap on her shoulder made her jump. She whipped around to see Norah smiling beside her as the hostess pulled out her chair.

"Hi. I'm glad you could come." She relaxed and patted her hand.

"Me too. It's been a hell of a week." Norah settled into the chair across from her and reached for the wine list.

"Tell me about it. It must be in the water." She smiled.

"So, patients in three out of my four rooms today were reading magazines covered with pictures of Scarlett James and Patrick Grayson. You've always spoken so highly of him. How's he holding up?"

"Well, it's complicated. My hands were tied this time. Scarlett was cheating on her husband, and either she or her husband or she *and* her husband are using Pat as a pawn in their pending divorce. I believe him when he says she told him they'd been separated for months. He's . . . he's just different from most of my client-turned-adulterer campaigns. There's something about him that tells me he would never compromise a family or a marriage knowingly." Ellie finished her drink and continued, "Hiding him has been hell. I knew it would be, but it's what he needed. The paparazzi found our first place and staked out every other feasible location in a heart-beat, or, rather, a tweet. The exclusives and special editions the magazines are running are all compilations of old paparazzi pics of him on vacation and catalogued shots of him on set and location. Of course, we've given nothing more than variations on the press conference statements I made." The muscles in her shoulders drew tighter, and she realized how much tension she was carrying. "I'm sorry. You know I'm not prone to panicked preambles like that. I'm just a little . . ." She paused. "No, I'm *very* scared of repercussions right now."

Ellie was surprised to see Norah's eyes widen with hurt. She recapped everything she'd just said and realized how insensitive she'd been. "Norah, I know what you're thinking. I'm sorry. That's not what I meant. Pat's case is totally different. You're not using anyone. You're simply too good to do that. Like Pat. Please understand, I don't think your situation has anything to do with the Scarlett fiasco."

Norah rose to leave, saying, "Except that innocent people are being hurt. Whether they know it or not."

Ellie felt as if her heart was in her throat. "Norah, please don't leave. Let me explain."

"I'm not interested in your spin." She turned to go, and Ellie stood, touching her arm.

"No spin. Something's happened. I need to talk to someone as badly as you must. Please, just sit. We're too good of friends not to be here for each other right now. I'm sorry I was so selfish just then. I didn't choose my words wisely, and you don't know the whole story." Norah's posture softened, and Ellie hugged her.

"Okay. I'm sensitive to the point of irrational these days, so I probably owe you an apology as well." Norah fidgeted and avoided Ellie's eyes. A waitress approached and offered to refresh Ellie's drink. She selected Norah's favorite cab from the menu instead and joked it was probably wise to switch to vino, based upon her ill-timed rant. "Thank you. So, what's going on with you that I don't know?" She smiled. "This might be the closest I ever come to classified information, aside from medical charts."

"I don't even know where to begin. I had to make a snap decision about where to send Pat once he was found. His car was being followed, so I had him driven to our building. I blocked all the viable entrances, exits, et cetera, as usual. Our building has been completely surrounded before, but we've never had an issue getting clients in and out discreetly with a blocked garage. Anyway, I'm rambling. Long story short, I had Jess drive him to my house." Ellie sipped her water and took a breath. Norah looked stunned.

The waitress returned with their bottle, and they went through the awkward motions of smelling and tasting the selection.

Once she was gone, Ellie kidded, "Can we say 'comic relief'?" Thankfully, Norah laughed and seemed to soften.

Glancing humbly at her phone, she added, "All I can say is that the hardest part of my job is making real-time decisions under great stress. We both have lives in our hands, hundreds of variables to balance. Having the choice between a rock and a hard place is sometimes the best outcome you can hope for in high-pressure moments like those."

"Isn't that the truth. I still stand by my decision to take him home—I mean, send him to my house—but what happened next is a gray area." Ellie studied Norah's face for signs of judgment and, finding none, continued. "I came home late and dismissed Jess and her assistants. They said he was settled for the night, so I went out on the deck to decompress. You know that's my norm. I was staring at the waves, chastising myself about the huge risk that lay in returning home while he was there, when Pat opened the patio door and I all but jumped out of my skin."

Norah laughed. "Oh, to be a fly on your deck. Then what happened?"

"I poured some wine and we talked. At first, it centered around work and his predicament. Then we just talked like equals, or like friends, rather. And I know it sounds silly, but the best way to describe the rest of it is that we laughed . . . and laughed. I don't know what came over me, but I told him things I've never told anyone but my sister-friends. Things I haven't told any man I've ever loved, Marcus included. He brought my guard down somehow. I never wanted the night to end. It was as if I were getting to know him in a safe little world with no expectations or spin, just two real people, versus the facades of a life lived in pictures and a life built on the careers of others." Ellie looked into her friend's eyes surprised by the brooding intensity she saw.

"It's a bubble. You've gotten to know each other in the safety of a bubble. It's the same with Enrique and me. We have this ridiculous connection, but it's safe to explore only within the confines of our room. If we go public, we have to make decisions. What's worse is, neither of us is completely out of love with our spouse. My biggest fear is that I want the bubble, but I want it with Matt. Then I spend another tray of room service and another night with Enrique, and I realize he appreciates what I do—how hard it is. He knows what my work in India could mean. We talk about a life and practicing together. I know it sounds crazy, but he's the first person I want to call when something good happens and the first person I want to tell about my day. I want Matt to be that person. Like he used to be."

Norah looked down at her lap, and Ellie realized she was beginning to feel that way about Pat. Even now, she was wondering if he was lonely and if he thought she was still angry with him. Did he have someone else waiting in the wings? Probably. How could he not? Ellie felt suddenly embarrassed about gushing over their night to Norah. Pat could have anyone he wanted. Of course it wouldn't be her. She didn't want that anyway. She couldn't want it. She'd worked too hard to blow it all on a misguided fling with a client.

"Here you are." The hostess broke her reverie as she led Cami to the table.

"Sorry I'm so late. I was across town. Did I miss anything?" Norah and Ellie both laughed at the irony. Cami seemed flustered as she poured herself a glass of wine.

"You have no idea," Norah said, glancing at Ellie.

"Seriously? What's going on? What did I miss?"

"In a nutshell?" Ellie half spoke and half laughed the words. "Bubbles."

"Yes, glorious secret bubbles," Norah added, her voice trailing off into an infectious giggle that made Ellie snort.

"What? Are you talking about champagne? Is this your first bottle?" They laughed again as Cami lifted the wine to see how much was left. "Is that some sort of secret joke?"

"Oh, I think we're all keeping secrets these days." Norah smiled at Cami. "So, what's yours? Spill it."

"How did you find out? Did Marcus tell you?" Cami looked stunned and skeptical at the same time.

"What do you mean by Marcus? Did Marcus tell me what?" Ellie's voice was instantly sober. Were they together? She knew he had always been attracted to Cami. He flirted with her constantly, even while they were engaged.

"Tell you I was fired." Cami looked hurt, and Ellie felt instantly guilty about jumping to such a harsh conclusion. "I've had nothing to do during the days since but work out, so I thought he might have mentioned it."

"No. I haven't had any sessions this week." She changed the subject quickly. "How on earth were you fired? You practically built InFocus from the ground up."

"I'd tell you if I knew. They cited 'creative differences' as their reason in the paperwork."

"Cami." Norah had whiplashed from jovial to concerned the second Marcus was mentioned. "I'm sorry. I know how much you invested in that company. Your work is top notch. It really is their loss."

"Thank you. I'm sorry for killing the mood." Cami took a nervous sip of water and smirked. "Soooooo, what did I miss?" Ellie and Norah laughed at the sarcasm dripping from her voice.

"Well, I'm still meeting Enrique anytime I can. Things are getting serious. We're starting to talk about making a life outside of our protective bubble—i.e., the hotel suite. Selfishly, I wish we could just extend it. I'm not sure I'm ready for the next steps—whatever they might be—with him or with Matt." Norah shook her head and refilled her glass.

"Isn't that the thing about bubbles?" Cami seemed to be choosing her words more intentionally than usual. "Aren't they magical for a moment, until they bust? They can't be permanent. It's impossible."

"Which brings us to Ellie's bubble." Norah smiled warmly at her friends as Ellie laughed and retold the story of how her beachfront sanctuary had become her and Pat's bubble. She told them about her overreaction in the kitchen, about her dream, and about his note. Over dinner and the rest of the wine, they shared their fears for their futures and their worries about Kate. Ellie made a point to memorize this moment. She knew their group was different and the same all at once. She also knew that part of her anxiety stemmed from the realization that they were all sitting on a precipice of some kind. New paths would be forged, and none of them would ever be the same.

Norah's phone vibrated on the table. Glancing at the screen, she drummed her fingers nervously before passing her phone to Ellie.

Leila Cell
Group Txt Msg (2 Recipients): Norah Cell, Cami Cell
I had Kate over for lunch today. I'm worried.

"I just got the same text." Cami frowned. "When she slips into old patterns, she avoids me like the plague. I haven't seen her in weeks, and she won't accept any of my invitations for coffee, drinks, a massage, or even a run."

"Has anyone talked to Ken?" Ellie asked delicately.

"He's watching her. He messaged me and I had her called back in for labs. Her blood is clean."

"That's because she's nursing." Cami tapped her index finger against her thumb absentmindedly. "She'd never risk pills while Liam's health is tied to hers."

"That's true, but her supply will start to diminish as her body's resources decline. She'll move to formula, and then what?" Norah's phone vibrated again, and a millisecond of excitement broke the concentration on her face.

"Very true. I guess your only choice is to act quickly, while she still has self-imposed limits. The best-case scenario is that she will recognize the signs and accept help developing new mommy-friendly coping skills," Ellie said, seeing Kate's predicament in a PR framework of timed actions, risks, and advocacy.

"True. I'm meeting someone after this, or I'd insist on popping over to Kate's tonight with a movie and a hummus platter." Cami's eyes shifted nervously to Ellie.

"I agree," Ellie said, forbidding herself to jump to the conclusion that it could be Marcus. Wasn't Cami always private about her personal life? "Let's get plans on the calendar with her." She continued resolutely. "Maybe that's all she needs to stabilize. She may just feel isolated, like she's lost her identity and been thrust into an alien role." Ellie refilled her glass to avoid Cami's eyes and looked at Norah.

"I agree." Norah smiled at her friends, and Ellie knew she was wondering whether they'd had similar conversations about her. "But, as much as I hate to admit it, there's little to nothing we can do tonight except to send her a casual text that we're thinking about her, or make a point to each call her tomorrow." She paused to meet their eyes warmly and raised her glass. "We'll get her through this." Taking a distracted sip, she added, "So, where are you ladies off to for the rest of the evening?" Norah's phone vibrated again, and Ellie smiled as her friend stared entranced at the screen. If only bubbles could last forever.

Norah

Norah was almost ecstatic as she slid the hotel keycard into the pad. She wished she still felt this way going into her real home. Enrique looked up from his laptop as she entered the suite, his white grin glowing against the tanned lines of his cheekbones and dimples. He closed the computer quickly and rose to help her with her jacket. Her skin pricked into goose bumps at his touch. She smiled over her shoulder at him, sinking back against his chest. His hands automatically began massaging her shoulders.

"You're even tenser than usual tonight," he whispered into her hair.

"I know." She sank more deeply into the kneading pressure of his fingers.

"Would you like to take a shower? I can rub out that knot while I tell you about the partners' meeting I had today."

"That sounds nice." Norah wanted to discuss some things with him as well: the end of their bubble, for one, and, secondly, the possibility of going away together for a few days to test-drive their connection in public.

Ellie

"One moment, please." Ellie closed her eyes and took a breath. She was standing, overnight bag in hand, in the atrium of the Four Seasons. Her driver patiently acknowledged her as he sat her suitcase on its end. She felt eerily unbalanced, as if she'd lived this scene a million times. Lonely beds in posh hotels might as well be part of her job description. What if she gave in to her whim and went home? How detrimental could one more platonic night laughing with Pat be? Ellie felt suddenly envious that Norah was probably in Enrique's arms right now. Her excitement had been as tangible as her anxiety when she talked about their decision to extend the affair beyond the conference, regardless of the risks. She clearly knew the potential damages to her marriage but believed their connection outweighed every other factor and deserved to be explored.

As for Ellie, empty, solitary luxury waited upstairs. At home, familiar and unfamiliar territory echoed promises and warnings. Couldn't she just enjoy going home to someone waiting for her? She might as well be standing in quicksand. She'd been down this path before with Marcus. The chance she'd taken on chemistry and attraction then had almost cost her everything. Getting back on her feet had been like trying to skip rocks on the ocean. On the other hand, despite that lapse in judgment, she still trusted her instincts about Pat.

That settled it. She would spend tonight here.

Just as she turned to dismiss her driver, her phone vibrated with incoming text messages.

3 New Texts from (Patrick Grayson Cell)
(1) Two blokes walk into a bar. The third one ducks.
(2) A PA shows up late for work, and his boss yells, "You were supposed to be here at 8:00!" The PA replies, "Why? What happened at 8:00?!"
(3) I just wanted to make sure you had a laugh tonight.

Ellie's hand curled around her phone, and her cheeks flushed against her will. Just seeing his name on her screen made her beam. Who else in her life could instantly lift her spirits like that? There was no denying it now; she was enamored by him.

She quickly typed a reply:

Thank you, Pat. I needed that. In fact, I need more energy like yours in my life.

1 New Text from (Patrick Grayson Cell)
Then what are you doing downtown? Take a chance on me. Come back. I promise to be a lamb.

Ellie could picture his face staring hopefully at his phone, waiting for her reply. She knew what he needed from her. He was aching for someone he could trust. He lived a larger-than-life existence and wanted someone who genuinely cared about him, not just about the idea of him. She knew what she should do but didn't have the heart to hurt him more by staying away.

Reply—To (Patrick Grayson Cell)
A lamb, eh?
1 New Text (from Patrick Grayson Cell)
On my honour.

Ellie grinned broadly at the screen and crossed the lobby to her driver. She was gifting herself another night in the bubble. It was temporary, after all. Pat would be whisked away on the media tour in a few days, and she would be returning home alone once again. He would need her support out there, and developing their friendship would allow her to be there for him personally, as well as professionally. She toasted mentally to new friendships and tapped her foot as her car sped down the expressway.

1 New Text (from Patrick Grayson Cell)
If you're indeed coming home, the lamb would like you to release his babysitter, aka Stacie. He promises not to open the door to strangers and not to play with matches.

Reply—To Patrick Grayson Cell
Done. But if you don't answer your phone, I'll have no choice but to assume you're on hold with Poison Control. :)

1 New Text (From Patrick Grayson Cell)
No worries about that. If I don't answer it's bc I've popped round to the Starbucks. I promise to wear a hat.

Reply—To (Patrick Grayson Cell)
LOL. Or you've just gone for a quick dip in the ocean.

1 New Text (From Patrick Grayson Cell)
Brilliant idea! Can I grab your mail while I'm out?

Ellie laughed as she dialed Jess and asked her to dismiss Stacie. Jess sounded surprised at her request but did not question it. They spent the remainder of her commute scrutinizing Pat's promotional agenda and responding to interview requests. Ellie felt protective of him and wanted to do everything possible to cushion the interviews.

As her car entered the gated division, she shut down her computer and attempted to relax her neck and shoulders. The driver pulled up at the side entrance of her condo, and Ellie thanked him for his time as he opened her door. Refusing help with her suitcase, she purposely stalled at the keypad until his lights faded in the distance. Satisfied she wasn't being watched, she entered the code and stepped into the mudroom. Coming home felt oddly different tonight. It was refreshing to enter her kitchen to warm air and the smell of popcorn.

"Honey, I'm home!" she called sarcastically, dropping her bags and laying her briefcase on the counter.

"It's about time," Pat mocked, in a false soprano. "You never take me out anymore."

"Funny," she joked, opening the refrigerator absentmindedly. It was odd seeing it stocked with real food instead of her normal staples of vitamin waters and single serving quinoa. "So, what have you been up to today?"

"You know. This and that. Interview preps, then talking my mother off a ledge. She can't stand not knowing where I am. She says they're harassing her even more than usual."

"I'm sorry. She doesn't deserve that. No one does."

"It goes deeper than that for her." He casually hopped up on the island. "You see, she had an affair with one of my father's associates nearly thirty-five years ago. She and my dad separated over it, then reconciled a year or so later. They got pregnant with me on a second honeymoon shortly after and have been happy since. Apparently, neither knew what they had until they'd lost it."

"So the presses are running stories about her affair?" Ellie was confused.

"Worse. They're fabricating all kinds of pictures and scenarios questioning my paternity. Even running headlines declaring cheaters' genes don't skip a generation and the like."

Ellie made a note to assign more monitoring to the international papers and tabloids. She had focused her team's energies primarily on the US publications because the upcoming tour would be national. "Here, have a look." He hopped down from the island and scrolled through several screen shots of tabloid covers. The headlines were vicious, calling for "*PATernity*" screenings and such. They'd morphed images of his mother and father to create the illusion they were fighting publicly. Another cover showed Pat with his head buried in his hands and claimed he'd just been told. The next cover was his father leaving a liquor store and sources reporting he was bingeing and suicidal.

"I don't think I'll ever get used to the leeches," Pat said.

"And you shouldn't have to." She stood on tiptoe to reach the wine rack. "I owe you and your family an apology. My team should have been more on top of the UK publications. I'll handle that."

"No worries." He ran his hand through his hair. "I look at a girl twice, and we're engaged a week later. My mum knows their game." Ellie knew he was merely being polite.

"Thank you for being understanding. I would fix this tonight if I could." She rummaged nervously for the corkscrew.

"Don't do that." He caught her wrist. "Seriously, Ellie. This isn't your fault."

"My fault or not, consider it handled." The abject honesty in his eyes derailed her train of thought. "Thank you for, um, persuading me," she added softly, and poured two glasses. "I don't think I've ever come home to the smell of popcorn here before."

"I sent Stacie on a fool's errand for organic blue kernels to get some peace."

"Clever." Ellie laughed. "Would you like to go out on the deck?"

"That sounds lovely." He shuffled to gather their glasses and the bowl of popcorn as Ellie made her way through the living room toward the back door. She stood up straighter, suspecting he was watching her from behind. She glanced over her shoulder and smiled when he looked away a second too late, embarrassed at being caught. Ellie thanked herself sarcastically for sticking with Marcus's grueling regimen of lunges and wall squats.

"It's getting colder; let me grab a few blankets and turn on the heaters." Ellie bustled around as he put their glasses and the popcorn on an ottoman table and settled onto one of the chaise lounges.

"It's so peaceful here," he murmured contentedly, and stared out at the sea. Ellie took the chaise next to him, following his gaze over the waves and into the moonlight. She closed her eyes and listened to the steady rhythm of the water, oblivious to the fact that Pat was staring directly at her as he said, "So beautiful—so very, very beautiful."

Cami

Cami sat across the high-top table from Dean Gatz, feeling as if there was an elephant in the room. There was no chance his niece had spent an entire dinner with him and not mentioned her altercation with Cami. Should she address it? Ellie had suggested she ignore it, table the issue, until she knew whether she'd be working with the girl or not.

"Well, Clark." He finished his brandy in a practiced motion. "I don't know about you, but I'm going to call this meeting a success. You drive one helluva bargain, but I think we can make you happy salary-wise."

"Thank you." She smiled. "I look forward to joining the team."

"Understand, the board may have my head come Monday, but I believe you're worth it."

"Not only am I worth it, but you can trust I'll work every day to grow and market the art that pays that salary." Cami looked directly into his eyes, knowing her security was at stake. "And a year from now, you can march confidently into the boardroom with our profits and tell them how worth it you knew I was."

"When I'm clearing your raise, you mean." His eyes glinted with excitement, and Cami smiled. His no-frills approach was absolutely refreshing.

Kate

*K*ate felt both contented and productive as she closed her sketch-book and paused the James Taylor album she'd been listening to. After Liam's arrival, she had begun to love quiet evenings like these. The nights when bedtime went well, Ken was out, and she could sketch and design in peace seemed to recharge her patience and energy for the next day. Leila had asked her to brainstorm some ideas for her and Wes's bedroom, declaring an end to their white duvets and beige walls. Kate was envisioning a spa-inspired theme centering on green bamboo, smooth aspen, and river rocks as the palette. Tomorrow she would take Liam to find fabric swatches and paint samples. She smiled inside, so happy to have a project, and took another bite of the apple she'd been eating for dinner.

Ellie

"Come on, give it another go," Pat mustered, trying to contain his laughing fit.

"One more," Ellie warned, playfully and feigned exasperation. "I'm glad I amuse you." She pursed her lips together and tried her best to push air through them into anything but spittle.

"You really can't whistle, can you?" He threw his head back laughing, and Ellie chucked a piece of popcorn in his general direction. It missed him by a foot, bringing on more hysterical laughter. "But look at that arm—clearly, the Yankees can use you this year!" He pitched himself completely flat on the chaise lounge, clutching his belly to catch his breath.

"You're awful." She laughed again and threw a whole handful of popcorn at him. "What am I going to do with you?" Ellie collapsed back on her chair, smiling from ear to ear and still unable to fathom how he'd crossed the line from client to friend.

"Send me to my room, I guess."

"Yes, and order Stacie back to keep you in line."

"Anything but that!" he said, melodramatically.

Ellie sat up on the chaise and noticed a strange shape bobbing on the shoreline. It was a boat, completely darkened. That was odd at this hour. Surely it was coincidental.

"Pat, look." She sank lower in her seat and pointed at the boat. "Do you see it?"

"I do." He paused, suddenly serious. "You don't think it's paparazzi, do you?"

"I don't know. Let's hope not." She stood and walked to the railing. "I'm going to let them see me make a call. Do you think you can get back inside without standing up?"

"It's certainly not so difficult as whistling, but I'll try." He grinned nervously and rolled off the chair. Ellie dialed the condo's security officer and asked him to check out the boat immediately and give her a report. She watched anxiously for the next several minutes until she saw the flashlights on the sand. Paparazzi were one thing, but what if she had compromised his safety and hers? What if some deranged fan was plotting a kidnapping, or worse? Her phone rang, and she answered it within the first beat of the ringtone.

"Ms. Lindsay?" the officer asked.

"Yes. This is Ellison Lindsay."

"This is Officer Martin. It looks like we have nothing more than a very lost fisherman on our hands."

"I understand. Thank you for your prompt response. If you don't mind, I would like you to check the boat for high-powered cameras. I have cause to believe I may have been photographed, and I'd like to file charges if so."

"Yes, ma'am." Officer Martin kept his voice professional, but Ellie sensed he was irked at her extending what should have been an open-and-shut report into a possible harassment investigation.

"Thank you. Please call me directly if you find anything."

"Yes, ma'am. We'll keep you posted."

"I appreciate it. Good night." Ellie ended the call and turned to go inside. Tomorrow she would arrange for Dominic, the bodyguard Pat used when he made public appearances, to join them.

Pat was sitting in a chair away from the window. He stood as she entered. "What's the verdict?"

"They said it's a lost fisherman. I asked them to check for cameras, and they're searching the vessel now." She said, realizing that if their bubble hadn't already been compromised, it would be soon. She felt suddenly vulnerable and swallowed hard to control the wave of emotion burning in her throat. How could she have been so reckless with his safety, much less with her own?

"Ellie, are you okay?" Pat crossed the room to stand behind her. "Please, talk to me." He put his hand on her shoulder. "Listen, I'm sorry I've put you at risk. You're in this situation because of me."

"No." She turned to face him. "It just hit me how naive we've been. I . . . We . . ." Tears welled in the back of her eyes and she choked them back. "It could've been . . ." She stopped to gather her breath and voice.

"Stop. You're trying to find a reason to blame yourself." Pat pulled her close to his chest. "This is my life. You know that. You could've had a veritable legion of security here, and it wouldn't have made a bit of difference." He slid his hands to her elbows and held her at arm's length. "You have to hear me, Ellie."

"I just feel like I've failed you somehow. I've been in this business too long to—"

"To think you could have done anything more." He interrupted her, and she looked up into his pleading eyes. "The way I see it, we dodged a bullet just now. Obsessing over it won't help either of us." He gently squeezed her arms, and she felt her cheeks flush.

"I know, but—"

"But nothing." He released one of her arms and ran his hand anxiously through his hair. "I don't know how to describe it, exactly, but the time I've spent here with you has been the freest, and most rewarding, two days I've had in . . . in longer than I can remember. I will always be grateful to you for giving me a refuge when I needed it most. And at great personal risk." He wiped the tear she was unable to stop with the pad of his thumb, sending a jolt of electricity down her spine.

"I'll never be absolutely sure I made the right decision hiding you here, but I want you to know I will never regret one single second we've spent together." His eyes were wet and piercing, as if he were weighing her words for spin. "I'm sorry—my words are failing me. What I'm trying to say is that I didn't know how terribly lonely I'd been until we spent the first night together. I knew I'd put up walls since Marc—uh, since my ex—but I didn't realize how guarded I had become. How cold." She closed her eyes, thinking her soul felt reignited somehow, and allowed him to fold her into his arms. Her heart was pounding as she pressed her cheek into the soft fabric of his shirt. She could feel his racing pulse as he held her closer. The electricity between them sent her mind swirling in a flurry of scenarios. A simple advance, and he would be hers. She could feel it.

"All I can say is, I'm glad you let me in. I don't know the whole story, but there's no fault in protecting yourself. I've seen how giving you are of yourself and how loyal you are to those you love. I can't imagine you were any different with him." He cupped her chin and gently tilted her face so he could find her eyes. "You're so much to so many"—he grinned—"how can you possibly be the 'bastard whisperer' as well? Give yourself some grace." He smiled down at her mischievously, and Ellie snorted at his witty insult. "And you snort when you laugh unexpectedly? On top of your many other talents? I was right indeed. Definitely no room in the repertoire for jerk whispering." He leaned into her and put his lips on her forehead. Ellie closed her eyes, determined to live in this moment, however fragile and fleeting it might be.

"Thank you." She relaxed and reached down to clasp his hand. "Pat! You're so cold."

"I know. That would be Patrick Grayson fun fact number eighty-six: my hands turn frigid when I'm nervous." He tucked them into his pockets. "My last co-star actually requested I hold a heating pad before we filmed our love scenes." His expression was a mixture of amusement and embarrassment. "Sex on film—every bit as romantic as it looks, you know. So long as the boom doesn't knock you in the head or the crew didn't gorge themselves on breakfast tacos or chili fries at craft services beforehand."

"Hot." Ellie laughed. "Let's go upstairs."

"Perfect. I'm still too wired to even attempt sleep." He looked anxious as his eyes shifted to the staircase. "Besides, I believe you owe me a few fun facts."

"Oh, I think you've had enough for one evening. You might never come back if you know it all." Ellie headed toward the stairs, in awe that he could bring out her playful side even in a moment like this. She realized now that this part of her had also been dormant for far too long.

"Try me." He grinned, all charisma, and she reminded herself he was off limits.

Norah

Norah woke with a start at the obnoxious buzz of the pager. She slapped the nightstand, eyes still closed, searching for it. *Please, please, let it be nothing.*

"Norah." Enrique's voice brought her fully into consciousness. "Shh . . . You can go back to sleep." He stroked her hair and guided her back onto her pillow. "I'm sorry."

"It's fine." She blinked groggily. "It's just a reflex. Even when I'm not on call." She felt uneasy but added, "I'm also not used to there being more than one pager in the room."

"Of course." He was already inching toward the edge of the bed, his mind clearly on the call. Norah grimaced, realizing how often she had done the same to Matt. Her pager woke him at ungodly hours, and she apologized, with varying degrees of sincerity as the years passed, and got ready quietly in the dark of their bedroom and bathroom, turning on as few lights as possible. This might be the guiltiest she'd felt during the entire affair. Was she available to Matt only in intervals? Blocks of her days and nights were clearly off limits, given her job, so what did that leave? Add in his travel and hours, and how could they be anything but stressed? She resolved to talk to him about balance. They'd re-centered before. It was worth another shot.

Norah had hardly finished her thought before the welcome black shroud of sleep saved her from her self-imposed inquisition.

Enrique left the room in silence, pulling out his phone to text his wife. He paused to take in sleeping, naked Norah, surprised he could feel so strongly about two women at once. If someone had told him six months ago he would be in this position, he would have called them a fool. He and his wife might have serious problems, but he loved her. He loved their girls. And he loved Norah.

Leila

Leila knew she should go to bed. After all, the girls had no concept of Saturday morning. She sank more deeply into the sofa and selected the next episode of *The Late Show with Stan Goldberg* on the DVR. She loved the nights when Wes crashed early and she was alone with her wine and her favorite shows. In a previous life, she would have scoffed at such a mundane Friday night. These days, however, a few hours of uninterrupted couch time felt like a mini-vacation. She would be tired the next day, but it would be worth it. Any bit of downtime in her, and every mother's, world was always short-lived. She loved this life, as demanding as it was, and was happy to create her own little reprieve when she needed it. Leila smiled at her sleeping blessings and pressed PLAY. These were good problems to have.

Norah

Somewhere between medical school, internships, Mumbai, and establishing her practice, Norah had created categories for her different levels of fatigue: mild, moderate, non-imperative, functioning, etc. She blinked, thankful her five blessed hours of sleep had put her back into the moderate range, and also thankful for the opportunity to roll over beneath the warm duvet without the looming threat of an alarm clock. In her dream, she and Matt were back in their first apartment. She was working the graveyard stint of residency then, and he insisted that her morning was his morning. No matter what the time, she would get dressed and come out to find him smiling in the tiny kitchen, with her coffee in hand. "Your morning is my morning. We both knew we'd have to carve out time to be together."

They had been so happy then. So in love with each other. They were constantly touching, cuddling, making love. Norah cringed as she realized how far they had drifted from those days. Even their hours were reversed. She was now more available at night than ever before, and Matt was constantly traveling to meet with clients. It was her turn to carve out the time, to be flexible. She had a new understanding of why Matt thought he had an open license to take on unpredictable hours in pursuit of making partner. It was because she had. Her hours were unforgiving, and he was tired of waiting for her. Things were also coming to a head with Enrique. She had to make a decision, and soon.

Norah's phone vibrated on the nightstand and she reached for it.

1 New Text—From Matt Cell
Where are you?

Norah absentmindedly typed a return, her mind on ending things with Enrique.

Reply
I slept in. I'm still in our room.

1 New Text—From Matt Cell
WTF, Norah!!! I'm in our room. I caught an early flight.

Norah's heart raked against her breastbone. *What had she done?* Her hands began to shake violently as her mouth filled with bile. She threw the duvet off and ran to the toilet. Her stomach lurched, and she vomited through her fingers. Holding the cold porcelain, she alternated between gasps and dry heaves. *What had she done? What had she done?* It was over. She had ruined them.

She could hear her phone ringing incessantly and vibrating with incoming messages. She scraped herself off of the floor and walked on wobbly legs back to the bed to find the traitorous device.

1 New Text—From Matt Cell
Find My iPhone says you're at the Hilton?!?

Norah typed as fast as her weak arms and shaky hands would let her.

Reply
Meet me somewhere. Let's talk. Please.

Her mouth was parched, acidic from the vomit, and her raw throat ached with strain. Tears flowed unwiped into the corners of her mouth as she stared at the screen.

1 New Text—From Matt Cell
Go to hell.

I'm already there, Norah thought, as she sat naked, cold, and crying in the shattered remains of their bubble. She stared at her phone without blinking as if it could give her answers.

Ellie

The sun beamed through the living room windows. Ellie woke slowly and snuggled more closely into the warmth of Pat's arms. The night before had been as surreally chaste as it had been intimate. She closed her eyes, wanting to relive everything that had happened after they'd come upstairs.

She ducked into her bedroom to change, and he went to start the kettle for tea. When she came out of her room, he was standing behind the wet bar, wearing a makeshift apron he'd fashioned out of a bathroom towel, and began to impersonate a chef célèbre filming a cooking show. She smiled at how ridiculous he looked as he told her to sit.

"There, there, lovelies. While we were on break, I just moseyed out to my garden to harvest the wheat for today's biscuits," he crowed, exaggerating his accent in an octave above that of his normal voice. "Now, remember, if you don't have fresh wheat on hand or your scythe is out being sharpened—don't you just hate it when that happens?—store-bought will do in a pinch." He smirked sarcastically. "But don't be surprised if your more discriminating guests can tell the difference." He arched a brow at the fictitious camera, and Ellie laughed. "Through the magic of the telly, I happen to have a batch ready to go." With a flourish, he whipped out a box of Trader Joe's Banana Crisps from under the cabinet. "How easy was that?" Pat reached down again and tossed a plate into the air, catching it with his other hand. "Of course, there's always time for plating." He plopped the cookies, still in the box, onto the plate with a grand gesture. "And, voilà!" Breaking character, he winked at her. "I'm afraid we're all out of time for today, but I do hope you'll tune in next week. This has been *From the Store, Just Like Mum Made!*"

"You're ridiculous." Ellie laughed as the kettle whistled.

"Now, now, there's no reason to be snarky. You're just jealous because the kettle and I can whistle and you can't." He whistled the theme from *The Andy Griffith Show* as he poured the water and carried their steaming mugs to the sofa.

"Well, speaking strictly as your publicist, it's good to know we can always market you to the foodies if you ever get tired of the acting scene." Ellie tucked her legs underneath her as he sprawled out beside her.

"You mean when I've gained forty pounds and squandered all of my money on fast cars and starlets?"

"Exactly." They both laughed, and Ellie grew pensive. "You know," she paused, "you're really good at that."

"At what? Embracing my inner Julia Child?"

"Obviously, but I was talking about the way you have of putting people at ease. When I saw that boat, every muscle in my body tensed up. If you'd told me anyone would be able to make me relax after that, much less laugh, I would have called you crazy. If I hadn't come back and I'd gotten that call from Stacie, I would never have forgiven myself. Especially if—"

"Ellie, don't. Don't ruin this by wishing it over before it has to be."

"I'm not, Pat." She shifted onto her knees so they were at eye level and took his hands in hers. "I just think you have a remarkable effect on the people around you. On me."

"Then let's not talk about the what-ifs anymore. We both know I leave for the press tour in three days. Until then, no matter what hell may come, let's just be us. Privately, between these walls. Let's treat this time for what it is—a gift." He moved his hands to her shoulders and pressed his forehead to hers. "It will never be like this again. I want to know you better, to know you *this* way before it changes."

He looked down solemnly and then met her eyes. "And I hope you feel the same."

He was right. Ellie was borrowing trouble, protecting herself because she knew this peace couldn't last. She could continue treating their time here like the fragile bubble it was, guarding against the inevitable fallout, or she could surrender control. Resolved to live in the simple magic of this moment, she put her hands on either side of his face and whispered, "I do. More than you can know."

His face burst into a huge grin as he pushed himself to standing. "Then come." He pulled her hand, leading her to the center of the room. "Stand here and close your eyes." She stood there, feeling at once silly and excited as she listened to him shuffling back and forth around her living area and into the guest room. Another minute passed, and Ellie heard the whir of the electric skylight panel retract.

"Okay. You can open them now."

She wasn't quite sure what to think as she took in the scene he'd prepared. The lights were turned to dim, and he'd arranged a pallet under the skylight out of the down comforters and pillows he'd gathered from the upstairs guestrooms. "It's nothing grand, not what you deserve by any means, but it's my way of continuing what we started." Nervous, he shoved his hands into his pockets. "Getting to know each other, that is. It seems we've had our best talks under the stars." Pat sat in the middle of the fluff and reached for her hand.

"It's perfect." She took his hand and smiled as he led her down to lie beside him. In less than two minutes, he'd managed to create the most sincere romantic expression she'd ever seen. Every other evening she'd ever spent with a man, regardless of expense and candlelight, suddenly paled in comparison with this moment. How she wished it could last forever. Pat's face was bright and youthful as she nestled into the pallet beside him. He was staring up at the stars, searching for something.

"Are you ready for Ellison Lindsay fun fact number seventy-eight?"

"Perpetually."

"In middle school, I pretended to be an astronomy buff just to convince the boy I liked to invite me over to see the telescope he'd gotten for Christmas."

"And how did that work out for you?" Pat's eyes shimmered with amusement.

"Well, it didn't take me long to embarrass myself by confusing Orion's Belt with the Big Dipper, and he all but laughed me out of his backyard."

"Oh yeah? I find it hard to believe any red-blooded American boy would've been that dense."

"Yup. Scarred me for life. Think thirteen-year-old me sitting on a curb, bawling my eyes out, until my older sister came to pick me up," she joked, and stared up at the sky. She would give anything to talk to Sheridan right now. "And I still can't find either constellation."

"So, aside from your passion for astronomy, what were you like as a kid?"

"It took me a long time to find my niche. I was the youngest, and I wanted to be just like my older sister. Too bad we weren't good at any of the same things." She smiled and rolled over to lie on his chest. "Sherri was something special. She was good at everything she ever tried: sports, art, band."

"The kayak?" Pat smiled.

"Everything. She had this crazy knack for connecting with people, and our house was always full of her friends and clubs. I swear she never met a stranger." Pat tugged at the collar of his T-shirt, and Ellie could tell he'd picked up on her use of the past tense. "Our parents divorced when I was twelve and Sherri was sixteen. It was ugly, to say the least. She was my rock through it all, even though she was hurting, too. That year, I joined Speech and Debate. Sherri thought it would be a good outlet for me emotionally, and she was right." Ellie blinked twice and centered herself. "I had a phenomenal teacher who taught me the true power of language and spoken communication. I learned how to use my words to express, to persuade, to collaborate. I learned that the right clarity could help defuse any storm and bring you to your goal. I went to the national championships the next year in the Lincoln-Douglass and Impromptu divisions."

"So you were ordinary until you were a prodigy." He eased up on his elbow, and she propped herself up to face him.

"I think you're being generous, but thank you. From then on, I was active in every speech, Cross-X debate, and drama forum I could join. I even led a campus march on the school board to protest the firing of our beloved theater teacher after he was called out for participating in a rally to protest "don't ask, don't tell." I majored in communications in college and in PR in grad school. Throw in a few hellish internships and entry-level positions, plus seven years with Camelot before I started my firm, and you have my résumé in a nutshell." She looked away from his beautiful eyes and laid her head back on the pillows to take in the starscape above her.

"I'm afraid I'll come off a bit dull after that." He tucked a stray piece of hair behind her ear and lingered to touch her cheek.

"Don't worry. *Yaaaahh.*" She pretended to yawn and stretch. "I'll just head to bed now and catch it all on the next *E! True Hollywood Story.* Good night." Ellie pushed herself up from his chest as he laughed and pulled her back down.

"Fair enough. What if I told you the only reason I'm where I am today is because I ducked into the school auditorium to get away from a bully?" His face was taut, and she knew it wasn't something he liked to relive. He tugged at the collar of his shirt, and she cupped his hand.

"Pat, that's awful."

"It was. He was a kid named Greg. He and his friends called me Patsy for two years straight. They made it a mission to give me a weekly dose of trashed knapsacks and faces full of urine during the bulk of middle school." His tone trailed off and Ellie moved to lie on his heart. "Greg carried a paring knife to school every day inside the elastic of his boxer shorts. At least I assumed, as he wanted me to, that he carried it every day. You see, I threatened to tell once, and he shoved it into my face. He swore he'd carve the letters *P-a-t-s-y* into my forehead if I ever uttered a word. I believed him and kept my mouth shut." He closed his eyes, and Ellie sat up, pursing her lips at the thought of a young, skinny, wide-eyed, beautiful Pat being bullied.

"So, he was the person you were running from?"

"Yes. But I wasn't the one who told." He reached for his tea to avoid her eyes. Ellie could see Jess's media training was working. "I also wasn't his only target. Long story short, I was leaving the"— he cleared his throat awkwardly and lay back down—"no lies, the astronomy club, and he chased me through the building. I knew I couldn't outrun him, so I sprinted and ducked into the first crowded place I saw. It was an audition for *You Can't Take It with You*. I signed up to be on the set crew and wound up auditioning for the next production. I've never shared that part of my story publicly."

He shifted his weight to his side and gently moved his arm behind her head. She was surprised to see him close his eyes again. Immediately, she understood. That story was part of his secret self. Keeping it personal was a coping mechanism people at his level of exposure developed to deal with the world's belief that it knew everything about them. He'd just shared something very few knew with someone who could potentially exploit it.

"Don't you see," Ellie rushed, "that's what makes you so personable, so *you*? You've never forgotten what it felt like to be victimized, to feel exposed and vulnerable. That's why you're able to tolerate this life in the spotlight and to appreciate it for what it is."

"Or maybe I'm just no stranger to being bullied." He looked dark, and she knew his mind was on mobs of flashbulbs and microphones.

"Possibly." Ellie reached up to stroke his cheek. "Or maybe you're just exceptionally full of grace." He looked away, turning his upper body slightly with his eyes. Ellie sat up, unsure of what she should do. "Hey." She turned his face from the stars in the night sky to hers. "It's my turn to ask you not to ruin this. You wanted to be real, right? This is us; this is us being real. Tell me the rest."

"You're right." He chastely kissed her forehead again. "I'm sorry. I get awfully sensitive on that topic." He softened his posture and lay back on the pallet.

"I understand. Angst is angst." Ellie gave him the space he needed and forced her own demons from her mind as she relaxed into the warmth of his chest. She listened to the rest of his story and tried not to flag the different ways she could win the Trevor Project campaign with his story onboard. A few minutes later, he pointed out a series of stars above the skylight and talked about his fascination with the night sky as a kid. He'd had his first kiss at space camp, with a girl who would later marry his younger brother. Ellie told him more about her college days with News 9 and a short-lived wild streak in which she took up smoking and dated her Modern Art professor. Pat laughed and whistled "Hot for Teacher."

Sprawled out on her lap an hour later, he confessed how worried he was about the upcoming release of *Life of Us*. He knew half of the world was waiting for him to fail and slink back to playing heartthrobs and rom-com leads. In a solemn moment, they talked about going off the grid. Ellie told him about her time in Cinque Terre. She'd rented a villa and all but run away shortly after Marcus destroyed her. Looking back on that time, she now realized running only gave more power to the person who hurt you. Pat understood. They both knew he'd been crushed publicly and privately when his long-term girlfriend and *Destiny* costar, Blythe Barrett, was photographed kissing another cast member in a hotel elevator. If the press's lampooning every detail of the split hadn't been painful enough, Blythe had gone on to guzzle champagne in Oprah's green room, then admit on national television that she'd wanted to split months before but stayed with him because she couldn't risk alienating his fan base.

"Some things never change," he said, only half joking. They both knew Blythe's publicist's botched handling of that debacle was part of what had brought the pair to Ellie's firm. "Speaking of which, I can still find Orion. I'll show you for the small fee of a few more Ellison Lindsay fun facts."

"What else would you like to know?" Ellie tapped him on the nose playfully, her words followed by a yawn.

"Nothing in particular. I just want to know everything that makes you, well, *you*." He stroked her hair into patterns on the pillowcase. "Like, how are you possibly not jaded after so many years in the business? I feel like I'm lied to, on average, fifty times a day. I don't have many people in my life who know the real me, or who care to, if I'm absolutely honest with myself. I'm constantly waiting to be betrayed. Like the mess I'm in now with Scarlett. She said she wanted to keep us private so we could make a real go at a relationship, spouted all kinds of nonsense about being broken from her failed marriage. I think back to that day on the slopes, and I realize she was using me to pump up her image. She wanted us to be photographed. I didn't see it then, but looking back, I realize how she posed us and just waited to be caught. Once we hit the mountain, she couldn't stop kissing me at every bend."

"I suspected as much." Ellie lightly traced the line of his arm with her fingers. "All I can say is, I know what it feels like to be used. Publicly. I haven't told you much about my ex." She sighed and sat up. "To this day, I'm still not sure whether I loved him or just loved the way he lied. My friend Kate summed it up that way once." Pat leaned back on his elbows, face full of empathy. Ellie swallowed hard. "You're the first person, aside from my sister-friends, I've ever told the entire story. He was a personal trainer named Marcus. At first it was refreshing to be with someone whose job was so much less demanding than mine, someone who just wanted to have fun and wasn't consumed by ambition. I see that for the lie it was now. He was constantly available to me, never balking at the hours I worked or the time I spent on the road. I'll admit I took advantage of that. When his lease came due, he asked if we could move in together. I said yes, mostly because I felt guilty that he still paid rent on an apartment he rarely used. He moved in and asked me to marry him that Valentine's Day. As clichéd as the whole thing was, I agreed." Ellie saw the surprise on Pat's face as she continued. "I said yes because I didn't think anyone else would put up with being ignored every time my phone chirped or my e-mail dinged. Case in point, my phone rang minutes later with news that one of my Major League Baseball clients was being arrested after busting a stripper's implant. As if that weren't bad enough, our firm was sponsoring an event the next day in which he'd pledged to wear pink and swing for breast cancer awareness. I spent the rest of the night in the office, feeling terrible. Marcus knocked on the door around 1:00 a.m., said all the right things, and gave an Oscar-worthy performance of accepting that as the norm that came with loving me."

"Ellie." Pat shook his head. "I get it. You let him in because he felt safe, and then—"

"Then it happened. My financial advisor contacted me to say we needed to meet urgently. Marcus was stealing from me, wiring five hundred dollars here, nine hundred dollars there, into his private accounts. The first transfer was dated one month into our relationship. I'd never given him access to any of my finances."

"Ellie—"

"It gets worse. Much worse. I started losing clients left and right. I was the director for Camelot PR at the time, and my boss called me in to discuss abuse of power. Marcus had gone through my contact list to recruit celebrity clients. He contacted their agents on behalf of the firm, claiming he was a business partner opening a high-end gym, with plans to market a home exercise DVD featuring celebrities doing his circuit workout. Then I found out he had been reading my e-mail and selling private information about clients' projects, travel schedules, and so on, to a gossip columnist. He also sold photographs he took from my marketing files. The board forced me to resign, and I was mortified. I came home from that meeting to confront Marcus and found him in bed with my personal assistant. She was in on all of it."

Ellie paused, ashamed. "Let's just say the fallout wasn't pretty. I saw their clothes—pants, bra, underwear, skirt, et cetera—in the hallway before I got to the bedroom. I threw them off of the balcony, and then

I threw her and Marcus, naked and clutching the sheets from my bed, out of the apartment. I couldn't bear to stay in that space anymore, so I put it on the market, fully furnished, the next day."

He reached for her hand, and she silently hoped her story hadn't lessened his opinion of her. Their palms kissed, and he traced her knuckles with his thumb. "Now, that must have been a sight." To her relief, he seemed entertained instead of alarmed.

"It was. My neighbors were less than impressed, but I was too furious to care. I figured a jury of my peers would never convict me."

"Hell hath no fury." Pat smiled mischievously. "Note to self: stash extra clothes in bushes."

"Ha ha. Let that be a warning to you, Mr. Grayson." She pushed him back playfully onto the pillows.

"Lucky for you, I happen to find Mad Ellie adorable." He crossed his arms casually behind his head. "I felt terrible for hurting your feelings that first night in the kitchen, but it was also all I could do not to kiss you and whisk you up the stairs. All mad and huffy, you looked irresistible." Pat blushed slightly, and her heart raced as she looked down on him. His tousled auburn hair and blue eyes were still spectacular, even in the dim light.

"Oh yeah? Well, I must find Apologetic Pat equally irresistible, because I almost made you my favorite mistake that night," she teased.

"Mistake, huh?" He smiled. "It looks like we're both becoming experts in self-control." Pat grinned and pressed her hand to his lips. "Isn't it exhausting?" He turned her palm in his and stroked the sensitive underside of her wrist. His touch sent electric pulses down her spine. It was exhausting indeed. They were balancing on the excruciating ledge between physical and emotional intimacy, the gravity of which was becoming too much to bear for either of them. Ellie was beginning not to care how brief their time together might be. She wanted to fall into him completely. She felt herself waking up inside again and wanted to be his in this moment, before it was too late. She pulled his hand to her heart.

"Ellison Lindsay fun fact number one: I am falling head over heels for Patrick Grayson." She looked up into his beaming face, and their eyes locked. In the beat of a breath, their unblinking gazes told them it was time. Ellie moved his hand to her cheek and closed her eyes. She never wanted to forget this moment.

Cupping her face in his hands, he brought his lips millimeters from hers. "To beginnings and foundations. To the 'us' we're building." He hungrily took her lips in his. The kiss was raw and tender, mirroring the emotions of everything they'd shared that night. He crushed her to his chest, and they sank into each other, kissing and pressing their bodies together. "Ellie." He broke their kiss, his voice a hoarse whisper. "This is me promising to honor the risks you're taking by letting me in every day we're together, no matter what."

They stayed in each other's arms, kissing and caressing, until Ellie eventually fell asleep on his shoulder. It had been simply wonderful. She snuggled deeper into his chest and attempted to memorize this moment. He would be gone all too soon, and she wanted to remember how he felt beneath her.

Just then, the click of a lens jerked her from her peace. She sat up quickly and looked around the room, but they were alone. She was hearing phantom cameras.

Kate

*K*ate grimaced as Ken pulled out of her. At least one of them had enjoyed it. They'd definitely been in a rut since Liam was born. Not only did she look and feel different physically, but her sex drive was virtually nonexistent. The last thing she wanted to do when she finally made it to bed was to pretend to be interested in Ken's climbing on top of her for bad sex. Lately, he was going through the motions as much as she was. Kate longed for the days when they took their time enjoying each other, instead of rushing into the finale. For the most part, she just lay there, willing the baby monitor to wail and counting Ken's rabbit-like thrusts. It usually took him twelve. Then he would thank her and she would go to the restroom to wash and weigh herself.

Kate took her phone from the nightstand and texted Leila.

1 New Text—To Leila Cell
Just tell me the sex gets better. I haven't come anywhere close to the big O since I was still preggers.

Kate smiled as her phone sounded the Mary Tyler Moore theme she'd assigned to Leila's texts so long ago. Her sweetest friend truly did turn the world on with her smile and had this talent for making people feel like they were, without question, going to make it after all.

1 New Text From: Leila Cell
LOL! It does. Wes and I have been there. Norah's
advice was "inebriate and lubricate"!

Kate laughed as Liam began to stir over the monitor. Yawning,
Ken swung his legs over the side of the bed.

"Let me get him. Why don't you sleep in this morning? Little
guy and I will run out to the farmers' market, and I'll make you
breakfast."

Now, that's foreplay, Kate thought, smiling. Having a baby did
indeed change everything. She closed her eyes and debated whether
she should sleep or take a leisurely shower.

Ellie

*P*at stirred beneath her, and she watched him slowly come into consciousness. Ellie ran her fingers through his hair, happy to be the first thing he would see this morning.

"Now, there's a happy face," he said sleepily, and kissed her fingertips.

"It definitely is. How could I not be after last night?"

"Agreed." He flashed the dimpled, boyish grin that had made his face a name and added, "One doesn't usually expect so much from waking up on the floor wearing last night's clothes."

"True story." Ellie laughed and pushed herself up from his chest. There was still so much left to do. She needed to call Jess in to make arrangements for the security team, and to touch base with producers to obstinately reiterate that what he would and would not discuss during the interviews was directly related to each outlet's relationship to her clients. She didn't throw the weight of her name around often, but she knew she was the only one who could be sure the scripted questions she had written were not only included but also factored into the Monday-morning meetings.

"Hey. Where did you go just now? You were a million miles away in a heartbeat."

Ellie's attention snapped back to him. "I'm sorry. I was thinking about what I need to accomplish this morning. I need to work for a bit, and then the rest of the afternoon is ours. What do you have today?" She snuggled back into him in an attempt to reassure them both that she was not preoccupied. Then there were the passes. She hoped Jess didn't need a reminder about who was blacklisted. Surely she had pulled the files.

"Well, I was hoping to ask you in." Folding her more closely into his arms, he pulled them both to sitting.

"In? I don't understand?" She tucked her legs around him and searched his eyes for what she had missed.

"Given that I can't ask you *out*, per se, I thought I'd ask you in." He took her hand to his lips. "I've been told I'm one hell of a cook."

"Oh yeah?" She pulled him to her so their lips were all but touching. "My place or yours?" Her eyes danced as he laughed and kissed her.

"Maybe a test run first." He hopped to his feet, and Ellie stood up with him. "To the breakfast table, Ms. Lindsay," He faked a bow, and she laughed. He was quite possibly the most beautiful creature she'd ever seen. She would miss this when the bubble burst. Women all over the world would give anything to be standing in her place right now, and she would give anything not to share him. Ellie put his hand in hers and headed for the stairs. They took them two at a time, slowing their pace on the landing to kiss against the wall. Pat put his hands on her hips, pressing her to him with the most excruciating tease. She moved her attentions to his neck, shudders of anticipation coursing through her. His hands were in her hair, and it was all she could do not to drag him back up the stairs to her bed. He broke their kiss, eyes shining, and bolted down the remaining stairs. How was his mind possibly on breakfast? Then again, how could she feel anything but overjoyed that he was making such a tender effort to court her? She was still lost about how he had possibly managed to date her in her own home, and under house arrest, no less. She smiled as her mind wandered to images of Leila and Wes eating in the Costco food court every Valentine's Day as an homage to their humble beginnings. This was how it should be. True and right and real. Building your foundation into something more.

Cami

*C*ami wiped her face with a towel as she cooled down from her run. Considering all she'd had to drink the previous night, she needed a good sweat. The treadmill slowed to the final phase of her cooldown, and she looked at the women walking and reading on either side of her. Reading at the gym was the ultimate irony, in her opinion. If you could turn a page, you weren't working hard enough. The woman in front of her was a prime example. She was glued to the *People* magazine she'd spread out on the machine, barely breaking a sweat, and looking up only to point out pictures to her friend.

"Have you seen this?" Cami eavesdropped, willing the clock on the display to tick more quickly so she could hit the sauna. "It's a whole spread on Pat Grayson." The woman held up the magazine, and Cami rolled her eyes at the glossy headline: "Where in the World Is PatSon? And with Who?" The page and the one adjacent to it were packed with pictures of the star on beaches and red carpets, all with high-profile women. *I'll tell you where he is,* Cami thought. *He's taking advantage of my romantically deluded friend.*

"Wherever he is, you know he's not sleeping alone." The woman laughed. "And if he is, I'd fix that problem for him in a heartbeat."

"Get in line!" The other woman snorted.

Cami had held her tongue during the happy hour, but she thought Ellie was making the biggest mistake of her life. She had worked like a dog to build her firm; how could she possibly compromise that by getting involved with a client to begin with, much less with one who was clearly some sort of sexy playboy? She'd fallen from the top once before; couldn't she see how much further this drop would be? Cami couldn't help but be entertained by the paradox that the friend who should be at home was probably waking up in a hotel, and the friend who should be at a hotel had most likely gone home.

As the timer hit zero, Cami turned off the machine and fought the urge to give the women gawking at Patrick Grayson a second glance.

"Hey." She'd been so lost in thought, she almost hadn't seen Marcus approaching. "You finished already?"

"Six miles after a hard day's night is about all I've got today. I'm headed to the sauna now."

"Perfect. I'll join you. There's something I want to know."

"No, it doesn't happen to every guy," Cami cracked, as they headed toward the locker room and he swatted her bottom playfully with his towel.

"No charge for that." He grinned, and she rolled her eyes.

Norah

*N*orah sat broken and frozen, phone in hand, staring blankly at the texts on the screen. Isolation and exposure pierced her soul as she crumbled under the sheer magnitude of what had happened. Her life had changed forever in a single, careless keystroke. Norah began to shake violently as she tried to bring herself to call Enrique. Could he possibly forgive how incredibly stupid she had been this morning? Where would she even begin? Her stomach turned again, and she stumbled to the bathroom. As she thrust her head into the toilet, a fresh wave of heaves ripped through her body. She was as empty as she could physically be, but still the spasms did not relent. Norah doubled over in agony as the acid sloshed into her throat and a series of blinding cramps seized her bowels.

"Norah, are you in here?" Enrique's voice caught her by surprise, and she frantically pulled a towel from the rack, not wanting him to see her like this. "Norah?" His voice was confused and concerned as he opened the bathroom door. She looked up at him from her perch in front of the toilet, her face glowing with sweat and stained with trails of tears.

"I'm so sorry" was all she could choke out.

"Oh, baby." He wet a washcloth in the sink and knelt beside her. "Shh . . . here." He placed it across her neck and began to rub her back. After a few more minutes, her nausea subsided slightly and he helped her into a robe. "Why didn't you tell me you were sick?"

"I . . . I didn't know you were coming back." Norah sat on the edge of the cool bathtub, feeling weak and pathetic.

"Deanna's flight was delayed, so I thought I'd shower here, rather than at the hospital." She'd forgotten he was picking up his wife today.

"Drink this." He handed her a ginger ale from the minibar. "Your blood sugar is low." Norah looked at her shaking hands and wished that were the only reason.

"Enrique, I don't know how to tell you this." Her voice cracked, and she thought she might vomit again. "I've made a big mistake."

"No! Norah, don't do this. Not when we've only just begun." He sat beside her, flustered, and took her hand. "We'll make more time to be together. Please."

"It's not that." She did her best to conceal her surprise at his reaction. "Matt knows about us." Norah looked down, ashamed.

"Shit." Enrique stood up and paced across to the sink. "How?" He leaned on the counter, head in his hands, his reflection volatile.

"Please don't be angry." Her stomach twisted. "I misread a text from him asking where I was. I thought it was you and responded that I was in our room." Norah swallowed hard as bile threatened to rise in her throat. "He's home a day early and was standing in *our* room."

"Just tell him autocorrect or a nurse messed up the text and you were in the OR." Enrique's eyes were frantic.

"It won't work." She braced herself to tell him the rest. "He used the Find My iPhone app. He knows I'm here." She wiped her eyes and added, "He told me to go to hell."

"I can't believe this, Norah! What were you thinking?" He slammed his hand down on the granite countertop. "How could you be so—"

"So *what*?" She erupted with rage and hurt. "Would you care to finish that sentence?"

"Stupid, Norah. How could you be so stupid! Do you have any idea what you've done to us?"

"It was a mistake!" She narrowed her eyes at him as her heart wrenched. "Possibly not my biggest one." Norah sandwiched the inside of her bottom lip between her teeth to fight back the tears that pricked her eyes. Enrique softened, humbled by her words. He moved to stand in front of her, and she pulled away from him. He put his arms around her anyway.

"Listen, I was wrong just then. I shouldn't have lost my temper. The worst part about it is, I don't even have time to stay with you and work this out, because I have to get to the airport." *To get his wife.* He would leave her here alone, shivering and vomiting in the middle of her crisis. The reality of those words was her undoing. The toilet was suddenly miles out of reach. Norah slumped over the side of the bathtub as her spirit emptied its pain in a deluge of tears, sobs, and ginger ale. Enrique stayed behind her, caressing and trying to offer comfort for the remaining minutes he could spare. He begged her to let him call someone for her, but she insisted she was fine and that she would call her friend Leila if she continued to vomit.

When he was gone, Norah pushed herself up from the cold porcelain and trembled to the sink to wash her face. "Pull yourself together," she ordered the wan, haunted reflection that stared back at her. "You cannot just sit here and fall apart."

Leila

1 New Text—*Unknown Number*
This is Dr. Orlando. I am a friend of Dr. Merrit's. She
has promised to call you if she gets worse, but right
now she is at a hotel near Mercy Hospital, fighting a
stomach virus. I wanted to make sure someone other
than me was checking on her. Thank you.

Leila shifted Julia to her other hip as she reread the text. It had
to be from Enrique. Did he not know Norah at all? She would be on
her deathbed before she called anyone for help.

Reply
Thank you for letting me know. I assume you mean the
Hilton. Can you please send me the room number?

Leila almost pressed SEND but hesitated. She deleted the portion
about the Hilton from the message, deciding it was her passive-
aggressive stab at Enrique for being cryptic about whether or not
her friend needed help. She also didn't want to put Norah in a com-
promising position if he didn't know that she'd confided in the girls
about their affair.

Leila walked into the family room to find Wes. He was reading
a book while Clara watched television. Julia scooted down from her
hip to join her big sister on the rug. "Can I talk to you for a minute?"

Seeing the concern on her face, Wes closed his book and followed her to the kitchen. "Is everything okay?"

"I'm not sure. It's Norah. She's sick, and I need to go pick her up."

"Oh, okay. I thought it was something serious. Your face . . ." He paused, and she felt grateful he knew her so well.

"I'm sure she'll be fine. I'll be back as soon as I can." *Please don't ask where she is*, Leila silently prayed, as the girls squabbled over the book.

"Of course. Is she at the hospital?"

"Or near there. I'm waiting to hear for sure." She hated being dishonest with him.

"Okay. Take your time. You're a good friend, Leila." Wes crossed the kitchen and hugged her, intensifying her guilt. The expression in his eyes gave her an uneasy feeling that he was hiding something as well. Did he know something about all of this? She leaned up to kiss his cheek as her phone vibrated.

"I love you. I'll see you soon." She walked into their bedroom before she opened the text. Leila was not used to hiding things from him.

1 New Text—*Unknown Number*
The Hilton, room 1159. Thank you.

"You're welcome, jackass," she muttered and began to get presentable to leave the house. A few minutes later, she was in her car, headed down the expressway. Leila smiled as she noticed she had driven halfway downtown without realizing she was still listening to Disney XM. She changed the station to NPR and tried to center her thoughts on how she could best support Norah right now. Of course, she would have no idea what her friend really needed until she knew exactly what was going on. At the moment, the best she could offer was the Ziploc baggie full of assorted "shi-barf-its" remedies she had on hand. For Norah's sake, she hoped carob tea, baby wipes, and diaper-rash cream were all that was in order, but Leila's

gut told her they weren't. She would always love Norah unconditionally, like a sister, but she had struggled not to allow this affair
to strain their relationship. In all honesty, every time Leila thought
about the affair, she thought about Enrique's wife, about Matt, and
about the children involved. She worried Norah would be unfairly
characterized as the villain when it ended. Reckless behavior like
this was simply not like her. Until this moment, Norah had lived the
life of a humanitarian in action. She gave of herself, of her money,
and, most importantly, of her time. Had she entered this affair as a
reaction to living selflessly in every other area of her life? Was she
compensating because Matt refused to be happy unless he had her
undivided attention? He hadn't always been that way. Leila knew
this because she had met Norah shortly after Matt had met Norah.
She knew firsthand how devoted to each other they'd been. Leila
and Norah had struck an instant bond during an event to promote
HIV prevention in Africa. Norah was nearing the end of a grueling residency, and Leila was working sunup to sundown to finish
her dissertation, teach her classes, and make time for this wonderful guy, named Wes, she'd just met. The two had laughed during
the speakers' reception at how willing the silver-headed set among
them was to write checks yet how unwilling they were to hear about
the important work those checks would support.

"Enter the tax-deductible donation powered by an open bar,"
Norah joked, and Leila agreed, telling her another VIP guest, in his
forties, had loudly proclaimed that there were enough people looking for a handout in the United States and that he didn't see the need
to contribute to greedy hands abroad. He had challenged his table
to look around the room and find one person who had benefited
from a handout in this country before they emptied their pockets
for ingrates an ocean away. Leila was in deep conversation with a
group of professors when she heard his rant but felt compelled to
mutually exclude herself from one conversation and introduce herself to another. She began by apologizing for eavesdropping but said
she would like to offer the insight he'd requested.

Leila relived what it was like to be Leigh Anne for a moment and took the ultimate vindication in having become her own advocate. At the end of her story, the gentleman apologized and offered to write two checks—one for that night's benefit, and one for the educational-intervention charity Leila's benefactor had begun. Leila thanked him, but not before suggesting he spend a little more time considering the impact one life changed could make on future generations, regardless of the continent.

A few hours later, she sent a colleague over to talk to him about an initiative in which fourth-, fifth-, and sixth-grade at-risk girls were recruited into an after-school program that offered homework support and taught leadership, self-esteem, positive peer pressure, and life skills, like financial planning, social etiquette, and interview prep. The clubs also stressed that the girls educate themselves about sexual health—the hard fact being that contraception was every woman's responsibility if she hoped to break the cycles of poverty and unwanted pregnancy.

In Leila's eyes, she was where she was today because someone had pulled her up and given her the tools she needed to succeed. Without that, she would not have been "the exception," as so many claimed about lives they couldn't understand. After she recognized the cycle that could hold her in the trailer park for what it was, all Leila wanted to do was break it. She knew, because of Mrs. Lenore's constant preaching and an intense desire not to become her mother, that the worst thing she could ever do was get pregnant. Leila spent years wishing she could impart that knowledge to her peers as they became teenage mothers and fathers. For these reasons, coupled with a sheer loathing for the men her mother and Randall brought into her life, Leila's longing for acceptance ended when it came to the opposite sex. She was seventeen before she dated anyone seriously and in her sophomore year of college before she went to bed with a man she loved.

After the benefit, Norah invited her out to a bar near campus, and they closed it down, talking and becoming fast friends. Over the next year, they were joined at the hip whenever their schedules would allow and eventually rented an apartment together. Their relationships with Wes and Matt grew in tandem, creating tight bonds within the foursome that continued today. Until this moment, Leila hadn't given any thought to what this affair might mean in Matt and Wes's relationship. Would Wes choose sides? Would Matt demand it? Leila shook her head and forbade herself to stress about things out of her control. No matter if, when, or how this ended, Leila would support Norah. Their bond would survive this. She channeled her thoughts toward the positive and exited toward the hospital.

Ellie

Ellie struggled to keep her mind on the work at hand. She stared at the clock, anxious to get home. Any reservation in any city in the world could be theirs, yet he had made even the most exotic locales pale in comparison with her own condo. If that wasn't a true beginning, how could anything else be?

"Ellison?" Jess looked irritated.

"I'm sorry." She shook her head. "What was that, again?"

"For the premiere. You still haven't given any okays on who he should take. I was thinking Shanyn Clift. Platonically. She is a new client who also has an indie film releasing soon. They worked together two years ago, and there are at least twenty press snippets of her referring to him as a mentor and praising his humility on set. She knows how to work the camera, and her team assures me she'll be impeccably styled. It would be good for him."

"I agree." Ellie looked at the pictures of Shanyn and pictured Pat on her arm. "It's important he doesn't go alone. Triple-emphasize the platonic element. I want to exhaust the angle before the Scarlett James camp can exploit it."

"So Shanyn it is?"

"Yes." If they were to build a relationship, Ellie knew she could not let the role of girlfriend compromise the role of publicist. It was in his best interest to take a date to the premiere. They needed to connect his name with someone new.

"And, last on the docket, how would you like to address the protests? Demonstrations are expected at every venue."

"We don't. Let them wave their signs and look ignorant. The film speaks on its own for marriage equality as a civil right. Let's not cheapen it by engaging them."

"I'll chalk it up to free publicity." Jess laughed, and Ellie agreed. The film would be the talk of the conservative networks thanks to those protestors and the twenty-four-hour news cycle's advertisement of their shameless stunts.

Leila

Using the key Enrique had left at the front desk for her, Leila opened the door to room 1159. Norah was asleep, curled tightly into the fetal position. As Leila approached the bed, she felt nothing but love and empathy for her friend. Even in sleep, she looked shaken and miserable. Her hair was plastered to her head by her own sweat, and her face was red and tear-stained. The pillow was wet as well. Had she cried herself to sleep? Leila looked around the room, half wishing the walls could talk and half afraid of what they might say if they could. Norah could never truly love someone who would leave her like this. Leila prayed he hadn't simply shoved a trash can by the bed and gone home.

Just then, her phone sang "Wedding Dress," her text tone for Wes, and she silenced it as quickly as possible.

1 New Text—Wes Cell
Matt called. We're going for a beer in about an hour. Tori is available for the girls. Take your time, and bring her here if you need to. I'm not sure what to think. I love you.

Norah tossed restlessly in her sleep, and Leila smoothed her hair. She was relieved that Wes didn't seem angry. She hadn't given enough weight to the idea that he loved Norah, too. In fact, it had been he who had suggested they ask Norah to be in the delivery room when Clara was born. Wes had feared Leila might need more support than he could provide. He'd also known that she ached for a mother or a sister to call on. To this day, Leila was thankful Norah had been in the room as her advocate. She had pushed for hours, fully dilated but still unable to move Clara down the birth canal. At 2:00 a.m., her doctor, Norah's former partner, suggested a C-section, based on Leila's level of fatigue and failure to progress. Norah asked to see him in the hall, then reported back that the nurse would "supervise pushing" while Norah took over as birth coach. Leila believed she could finish, but she was also exhausted from the labor, worried about her baby, and in no state of mind to make decisions. Wes, worried about his wife, asked Norah if a cesarean would be safer, easier. Norah smiled and asked them to trust her. She pushed the mirror from the rocking suite to the end of Leila's bed.

"No." Leila was adamant. "Absolutely not. I have no desire to see this, and Wes is on a need-to-know basis. I would like to have a sex life again eventually. I don't see how this will help any of our goals."

"Just trust me. I've never had a patient regret seeing her child come into the world. They always object, and I always insist. You are about to perform a miracle. Every intern and support staff in the room will see it. Why would you miss that in favor of a misguided notion of modesty? If men did this, it would be a spectator sport and there would be medals. Trust me. You are pushing like a champ, but not effectively, because you can't feel your pelvis. The epidural causes a disconnect of sorts. The mirror will fix that. Your body knows what to do. Give it the visual connection and see what happens. I promise."

Norah was right. The mirror made all the difference, and Norah's partner delivered Clara an hour and a half later. Not a day went by when Leila wasn't grateful she had watched her babies come into the world. She left the deliveries with a newfound awe at what her body was capable of, what she was capable of. It gave her a special breed of confidence that if she could conquer childbirth, she could conquer the craziness that was new parenthood.

Norah stirred in her sleep, reaching for what Leila assumed was Enrique's side of the bed. Her hand searched the sheets, and her eyes fluttered awake. Leila reached to hold her hand and waited for her to come fully into consciousness.

"Shh . . . it's just me." She smiled down gently at her friend. Norah blinked, confused, and looked around the room.

"How . . ."

"He texted me."

"I'm just so . . ."

"Shh . . . it's going to be okay." Leila squeezed her hand. "Let's get you out of here." Norah sat up and silently nodded her head. Leila, trying to reserve judgment, gathered her friend's things: makeup bag, shampoo, a few sets of scrubs, nothing that indicated anything more than a lengthy overnight trip had occurred in this room. Nothing, that was, except for the box of condoms that sat on the bathroom counter beside a shaving kit. Leila stilled her face and went back into the main room. Norah had changed from the robe into the slacks and sweater she'd worn the night before. She was pale against the cream-colored cashmere, almost ghostlike.

"Matt knows. I'm not sure where to go. I can't stay here, and I can't exactly go home."

"You'll stay with us." Leila forced a smile. "One step at a time. Let's get you well and rested; then you can decide what you want from there."

"Thank you." Norah's lip trembled. "For everything."

"No worries." Leila's heart broke to see her strong friend reduced to this fragile shell of herself.

Cami

Cami sat across from Marcus, surrounded by the cleansing heat. She closed her eyes and enjoyed feeling the toxins draining out of her pores. When she opened her eyes, he was shirtless.

"Your turn." He flexed, and she shocked him by taking off her tank top.

"Nice." He grinned at her sports bra and pretended to slip off his shorts. Cami laughed. He was like being around a bratty sibling.

"Cute." She rolled her eyes as he pulled his shorts back up over his hipbones. "So, aside from a peep show, what do you want?"

"I want to get into fitness modeling, and I need to have some pictures taken for my portfolio."

"So you want me to be the photographer?"

"I thought we could swap"—he winked—"services."

"I'll get you some names." Cami laughed. "You can't afford me."

"This is true. Besides, I think I've had my fill of older women."

"Oh yeah?" She wiped the sweat from her neck and chest with her shirt. "Well, there is a difference. Girls will put up with cute boys who treat them badly. Women know those are the boys you take home, not the ones you take *home* for the holidays."

"Ouch. Nice kitty." He smiled and she laughed.

"Sometimes that's a perk," she said, stretching her hamstring. "These days, I don't like to share a bed any longer than it takes me to have an orgasm. All of the fun and no commitment." That was how Cami liked her lovers. She didn't do clingy. Candlelight and rose petals were just not her thing. She liked men who challenged her and who had their own lives. She didn't need someone to offer her his world. She had her own.

Ellie

$\mathcal{E}$llie thought her heart might jump out of her chest as her car pulled into the drive. The anticipation of a night "in" with Pat had her tingling. Thanking her driver, she smoothed her skirt and fought the urge to rush to the door. Her heels clicked on the pavers, ticking away the seconds until she would see him. She punched the entry code and relished the sensation of coming home to someone she cared about.

"Wherefore art thou, Romeo?" Ellie laughed as she walked into her kitchen and set her bag on the counter. A single glass of champagne gleamed on the island. Propped against it sat a handwritten card marked with her name.

> *Ellison,*
> *No day or night with you will ever be long enough. This is me asking you "in," not because I can't ask you out, but because there's nowhere in the world I'd rather be than with the woman who has enamored me like never before. This is me asking you into my life and into my heart. This is me asking myself into yours.*
> *Patrick, aka the Lamb*

His words touched her heart. *Enamored* might be the best term for the way she felt as well. She had never fallen for anyone so hard or so quickly. It was as much out of her character as it was exhilarating.

She was sipping her champagne and rereading his note when Pat stepped around the corner, dressed in a flawlessly tailored suit. He smiled, blushing slightly. Ellie held his note to her heart and said, "Thank you. This means—" He crossed the space in an easy movement, and she took him in her arms—"so much to me."

His smile crinkled his eyes as he gently cupped her cheek. "I know what the press is saying about my past relationships." His expression was desperate. "It's important to me that you know this isn't some sort of elaborate one-night stand for me."

"I know. And for what it's worth"—she pulled him closer to her—"I've never felt more at home here, or anywhere, than I have over the last few days with you. I want to be in your life, this way, and I want you to be in mine." She raised her glass in a mock toast with her free hand, before kissing him. "To standing on the edge of the 'us' we both want." Pat gave her a smile she couldn't read as the sounds of Christina Perri's "Arms" filled the space.

Ellie kissed him more deeply, moved that he had been able to predict the perfect ballad to express her feelings. "You put your arms around me, and I'm home," the artist's soulful voice sang, as Pat began to sway them from side to side. Ellie moved her arms down his back, memorizing the curves of his muscles and the enchantment she felt. She realized she was every bit as off-limits to him as he was to her, but he was letting her in, despite what she could do to his career and what he could potentially lose. He had seen through her walls and believed in their connection. He had let her in. His openness and sincerity gave her the strength to trust again, to consider sharing her life and loving unguarded.

His face was all mischief and excitement as he pulled away from her gently, letting his fingertips slide slowly over her chin and cheeks. "Come, I've a surprise for you on the upper deck."

Ellie laughed as she trailed behind him up the stairs and out onto the balcony. The salty breeze felt refreshing as she stepped out onto the smooth wood. Her eyes scanned the empty shoreline.

"It's been clear all day," Pat said, following her gaze. "Come, we'll be careful." Ellie hesitated, looking farther down the beach. "I know you've got some poor bloke frittering his weekend away, monitoring the leeches and glued to the Twitter boards. Let him do the worrying. Relax." This was true. Jess had assigned that task to Stacie and another junior associate. Ellie forbade herself to waste their precious time together being paranoid. Fewer than a dozen people in the world knew where he was, and only Norah and Cami knew they were becoming involved. It would never be safer than it was right now.

"You're right. Just let me . . ." Ellie was about to add that she should go get her phone, in case that "bloke" alerted Jess to something, when Pat opened his jacket and patted the inside pocket. Her phone peeked out over its edge. She laughed, shocked again that he knew her so well. "Well played, Mr. Grayson." She grinned, wondering when he had swiped it from the counter.

"Why, thank you." He tipped a fictitious hat to her, and she reached for his tie. Pulling his mouth inches from hers, she twirled the silk around her finger and smiled broadly, saying, "Patrick Grayson fun fact number three hundred forty-seven: the day you have to work this hard for a one-nighter is the day you know it's time to call the Food Network."

He laughed loudly and lifted her off her feet so she was pressed to his chest. He kissed her again, before covering her eyes and leading her down to the recessed level of the deck. When she opened her eyes, she was surprised to see the tiki torches were lit and the hot tub was uncovered. Champagne sat in an ice bucket on its ledge, beside a bottle of massage oil and two towels. He grinned broadly, eyes wild, as he studied her reaction.

"Surprise. I thought we might enjoy watching the sunset this way." He looked her up and down. "I've no doubt the view is rather fantastic." A tug of his collar revealed his nerves, and Ellie laughed at his coy double entendre.

"Oh, I'm sure it will be." She stared back and gestured to his chest. He shrugged off his jacket and began to loosen his tie. Surely he wasn't going to strip naked right here on her balcony. His grin grew more and more taunting with each button he unfastened. Ellie's eyes popped, and her cheeks flushed. She squinted down the coast, torn about whether to stop him. Before she could say a word, he unfastened his belt and dropped his pants.

"Disappointed?" He smirked. Instead of underwear, he was wearing a pair of nautical red swim trunks.

"Hardly." Ellie grinned, taking in the gorgeous curves of his body as he slipped out of his shoes and laid her phone and his shirt on the table beside them.

"Your turn." His eyes were bright as he stepped into the hot tub.

Leila

The house was quiet as Leila settled Norah in the upstairs guest room and went downstairs to make her some toast and broth. She was thankful Tori, the neighbor's nanny, had taken the girls to the park and out for ice cream.

> 1 New Text—*Unknown Number*
> How is Dr. Merritt? Does she want me to call in a script?

As if you're the only person in her life with access to a prescription pad? Leila thought sarcastically, plucking the white paper pharmacy bag from her purse. She wondered if Wes was getting an angry earful from Matt right now. She must make a point to keep all of this separate from her own marriage. Wes was entitled to his opinion and had every right to support both friends however he saw fit. Leila arranged the food and pharmacy bag on the tray, tucked a bottle of wine under her arm, and made her way back upstairs.

Norah sat nestled into the corner of the sectional, freshly showered, wearing one of Leila's yoga outfits. Her hair hung in dark, wet waves tucked loosely behind her ears, instead of in her signature sleek twist. Even pale from stress and fatigue, she still had a certain polish to her features that made her naturally stunning.

"You look like you're feeling a little better." Leila smiled and sat the tray on the coffee table.

"Yes. Never underestimate the modern miracle that is hot running water." Her green eyes were rimmed in red as she forced a smile. "This smells good." Norah reached for her soup and took a small sip. Her phone vibrated, and Leila looked discreetly away as her friend read the screen and pressed IGNORE. During the drive from the Hilton, Norah had told her about the mistaken text and subsequent fights with Matt and Enrique. Leila uncorked the wine and poured herself a glass. A quiet moment to herself was something to celebrate, even if it wasn't under the best of circumstances. "That's the second time Enrique has called. I know he wants to apologize, but I just need some space."

"I think that's reasonable. Have you told him that?"

"No. I'll send him a message later, when I gather my thoughts." She took another small sip of broth.

"Well, I hope it goes without saying that you're welcome here for as long as you'd like. Wes agrees."

"Thank you. I am so torn about what I even want out of this. Part of me wants to beg Matt to give us one last shot, to try couples' counseling because I owe it to him. Another part wants to call Enrique and say I still believe we have something together. And the biggest part just wants to sleep. My personal life isn't the only mountain standing in front of me right now. Monday is the beginning of two weeks on after-hours/weekend call. I have fourteen patients at full term, and my partners have another twenty-two between them. My day-surgery board is packed as well." She laughed and added, "Maybe I should list Mercy as my temporary address until I find my way through this mess."

Leila grinned. "I swear, in any other profession except for teaching and medicine, that amount of time spent after-hours in a public place is called squatting." She took a long drink of wine and missed her professorial days. It had been over three years since she had resigned from the university, and the ache of that loss had yet to ease. Perhaps it was time she revisited the idea of going back. Then again, she would never have a second chance at this time with the girls. She was lucky to have the choice to be home with them; was she even entitled to want both? Thousands of working moms without that luxury would gladly trade her.

"Leila." Norah touched her knee. "Are you okay?"

"I'm sorry. I was thinking about teaching. I miss it every day." She pressed her lips together. "It's not that I don't love *this* life, because I do, it's just sometimes I feel like I've let go of something I spent the better part of my youth and twenties striving to achieve. It's as if there's this bitter irony to working that hard to succeed in a profession, only to set it aside after you become a parent. It was such a large part of my identity." She looked into her friend's supportive eyes. "And now, even though it's still who I am, I feel disconnected from that part of myself." She tucked her legs underneath her, hoping she didn't sound horribly ungrateful for all she had. "First-world problems," Leila said, with a forced smile, and swirled her wine.

"That's not selfish at all. Believe me, I understand. It's a question of identity. We are who we are because of what we've done and where we've been, so how do we assimilate those core qualities and experiences when it's time to move on to a new phase of life? What do we keep, and what do we leave behind to meet the new stage, to become something more, without sacrificing what already defines us?" Norah gripped her water glass more tightly at the timeliness of their conversation.

"Exactly. It's like walking a tightrope. If you lean too much on work and ambition, your relationships with your spouse, family, and friends suffer. Then, if you compensate by directing more energy toward the people in your life, your career stagnates. And all the while, you have to move either forward or backward with both feet, or the rope will dip and you'll fall." She shrugged her shoulders. "At the end of the day, it's all about balance. We're all living in some sort of crazy, beautiful circus. We balance on these tightropes of expectations and juggle our needs with our desires, our achievements with our failures, our relationships with our families and careers, our chances with our choices, and our demons with our joys—fully aware that success is never permanent and failure is never final." Leila, surprised by the detail in her own words, suddenly realized how important the idea of a balanced identity was to her. She resolved to find a professional outlet that would mesh with her family priorities. There had to be a median.

"These are true words, friend." Norah knitted her fingers together. "At the end of the act, if you're standing on the rope, keeping all of those proverbial balls in the air, and you still know who you are, you've become a master juggler." She smiled wryly.

"Until life throws you the next ball, that is." They both nodded, knowing it was true. You could never control the rope.

Ellie

The last bit of light split the sky into an explosive array of pinks and lavenders. Ellie leaned against Pat's chest as he massaged the aromatic oil into her neck and shoulders. The combination of the gorgeous canvas above them, the steamy water, and his kneading fingers made her feel at once relaxed and invigorated. "That feels wonderful." She sank more deeply into his hands. "Is it strange that part of me keeps expecting to wake up and realize the last few days have all been a daydream?"

He laughed and softly pressed his lips to the back of her head. "For a full year or so after the first *Destiny* film released, every morning when I woke up, I would have this split second in which I questioned whether or not it had all actually happened. The lights and flashbulbs made everything seem like a dream." He gathered her hair and swept it over the front of her shoulder. "Then I'd thank my lucky stars for this extraordinary life and pray for the strength to survive it." He brushed his lips across the ridge of her shoulder and up her neck, sending delicious shivers of excitement down her back. When he made it to her ear, he lowered his voice to a whisper. "Then I would hope beyond hope that there was someone out there crazy enough not only to understand life in this industry but to love me in spite of it." His lips grazed her ear softly, and she twisted to face him. "I'm still working on that last bit." Pat's eyes were bright as he teased her. "If you know anyone who's looking, too, that is." He ducked his head, as if he were afraid she would hit him. Ellie laughed and moved her legs to either side of his.

"I'll be on the lookout," she said, as she lowered herself onto his lap and began to kiss him softly. Pat dropped his hands to her hips, looping his fingers through the ties of her bikini. Ellie buried her hands in his hair as he tilted his pelvis so that their hips moved up and down together in the most exquisite rehearsal. Ellie knew they wouldn't make love here, not for the first time. That wasn't his style. Pat slowed the rhythm and lifted her to the side, never breaking their kiss. He hovered over her, caressing her arms and legs beneath the water, before gently pulling back.

"Are you ready to continue our evening inside?" he asked, eyes twinkling.

"If you insist." Ellie laughed, trying to ignore the butterflies that suddenly filled her stomach. Pat offered her his hand, and they stepped out of the hot tub. Wrapped in towels, they walked into the living area. Ellie excused herself into the half bath off the kitchen to change and promised to meet him upstairs for a drink in a few minutes. She barely recognized the borderline giddy face in the mirror as she combed her blond hair to the side in a loose ponytail. Who was that ridiculously happy woman? Could she be trusted, or was she in fact making the biggest mistake of her career? He was a *client*, and an important one at that. Then again, that definition no longer seemed to apply. Did she trust herself to fix the fallout for the firm if this ended badly? Her mind began to spiral between spinning the conflicts of interest and alerting legal to the necessary proactive measures. What would happen if the relationship progressed? She could always delegate his management to another team and privately monitor that their decisions were in his best interest.

Dark images of the last risk she had let herself take taunted her psyche, fresh humiliation lapping at the edges of her mind. *Get it together*, she chided herself. *You are not defined by your mistake. You've done more than enough penance for that lapse of judgment. Being fooled once shouldn't make everything you might feel for someone after artificial. Pat is different. Clearly, he's earned your trust. Listen to your mind. And listen to your heart.*

Ellie centered on the words and looked up at her reflection, determined—decision made. She slipped into a pair of white linen pants and a fitted, dark-blue V-neck. Satisfied with her "night in" attire, she opened the door. The living area was darkened, with the exception of a glowing strand of white Christmas lights on the floor. "Pat?" she called, oddly unable to shake her nerves as she followed the winding strand of lights to the staircase. Norah Jones's tender voice began to sing "Come Away with Me," and she stopped on the landing. He had planned this as well. Her hand brushed over a piece of card stock tied to the strand of lights. It read:

This is me vowing never to forget how it felt to wait for you at the top of these stairs,

She held the note, tracing the soft glow of the path with her eyes. Three steps ahead, another card was illuminated by the strand.

Knowing it was a once-in-a-lifetime moment.

And wanting nothing more than to take you in my arms and make love to you.

Her heart raced as she stepped up to the last card:

This is me knowing no relationship of mine will ever be simple and asking you to brave that with me.

Ellie followed the strand to the top chewing on his words. Pat stood on the last step, beaming as he took her hand and pulled her into his arms.

"Ellie, this is me promising always to remember how I feel right now when life gets in our way. I know we'll have to leave the shelter of this safe little world far too soon, and I'm promising to keep everything we've built and shared here in the forefront of my mind when things get difficult. To keep the outside world separate from you and me. Can you do the same?"

Ellie smiled, eased that he recognized their time here was a bubble and forbade herself to further question the decisions that had brought her here.

"Yes, I can. I can promise to remember what led us to this moment, and, most of all, to honor that when we're tested."

His face radiated relief. Without speaking, he moved her arms around his neck and pressed her closer to him. Their eyes locked together, and ever so slowly he began to move them to the music. Ellie gave herself completely to the electrified feeling of her body as it moved with his, to the moment he had created for her, feeling as though he'd already been making love to her all evening. Pat moved one hand to her cheek and kissed her deeply; the other spread on her lower back, gently pushing her forward as he walked backward toward her room. He moaned softly at her touch on his bare skin as she slid her hands from his waist to underneath his shirt. She stopped her caress above his heart and pressed her palm over its rhythm. He took his hand from her back and cupped it over her fingers, squeezing gently in time with the beat. At that moment, she knew what was happening was right for both of them. She moved her lips to his neck, trailing tender kisses across his collarbone to the base of his throat. Ellie squeezed him closer to her, before turning her body so that she walked in front of him, leading him the rest of the way to her bedroom.

Norah

5 New Text Msgs
3 Missed Calls (Dr. Orlando, E. Cell)

Dr. Orlando, E. Cell (1/5)
(1) I hope you know how sorry I am for losing my temper this morning. I was overcome by it all. I don't want to lose you. 11:15
(2) I texted your friend. I was discreet. Please don't be angry. I am sorry it's not me there with you. 11:45
(3) Do you need a script? 1:30
(4) Please let me know you're okay. I'm worried. 2:45
(5) Can you meet me tomorrow? We should talk about this. 5:45

1 New Text—(From Matt Cell)
I'll be on travel for three days beginning tomorrow evening. If you need anything from OUR room, get it then.

1 New Text—(From Jillan Channels Cell)
Can you possibly meet me at the office tomorrow? I'm speaking at a doula class and was hoping to grab the cervix and dilation models. I can ask Petra if you're busy.

There was only one person in that strand she could answer easily. She heard Leila's footsteps on the stairs and felt grateful she wasn't alone tonight.

Leila smiled at her as she rounded the banister. "Here's your tea." Norah reached for the mug and grimaced as a wave of nausea gripped her stomach. "Are you sure I can't get you anything else? Maybe some crackers?"

"No, but thank you. I think I will have a Zofran chaser for my tea, though."

Leila's brow furrowed, and Norah followed her gaze to the pages of cautionary material stapled to the Ambien bag in front of her. Knowing Leila never took so much as an aspirin if she could avoid it, Norah found her friend's reaction endearing. "I know having a houseguest wasn't on the family agenda when you woke up this morning, but I'm grateful to be here."

"It's really no problem. Besides, I know you'd do the same for me." Her voice seemed distracted. Norah hoped Wes hadn't come home angry after Matt's inevitable rant. The last thing she wanted to do was strain her sweet friends' marriage, along with her own.

"You're sure it's okay? If not, I've grown quite used to the hotel life over the last two months." She smiled wryly, knowing the joke was ill timed. Leila laughed but still seemed worried, as if she were choosing her words.

"Listen, I hesitate to even bring this up, so please forgive me in advance if I insult you professionally or personally." She paused, and Norah knew what was coming. "Do you think you could possibly be pregnant? I'm not trying to be callous, but I'm looking at these drug facts, and I'm wondering, *What if . . . ?*" She knitted her fingers together and studied Norah's reaction.

"It's unlikely, but it's definitely crossed my mind. Enrique and I used a condom every single time. They're not foolproof, of course, but it was my non-negotiable. As for Matt and me, there was an overlap when things were getting better between us, and we were together twice. Again, unlikely, given the timing and our fertility history, but I plan to take a test in the office on Monday, as a precaution."

"Well, if you want to know tonight, before you take anything else, or just to be safe, I have a test left over from our Christmas scare." The last thing Norah wanted to do was get up and continue the unrewarding hobby that had become testing herself for pregnancy over the years. Then again, she knew she should take the advice she would give her patients in this situation.

"Okay, I'll drag myself off this couch to pee on a stick, but only because I know you'll worry if I wait until Monday. Then I'm going to bed for a year or two."

"Thank you." Leila smiled and headed to the bathroom. "You won't have to drag yourself far. I keep all of the extra tampons and stuff up here because the girls are constantly unloading the cabinets in the downstairs bathrooms. Child locks have nothing on those two. I'll set it out for you."

Norah couldn't help but smile as she listened to her friend, ever the caretaker, rummage around in the bathroom cabinets. She was about to say as much, when she heard Wes call from downstairs.

"Wes is calling for you. Something about a sippy-cup lid."

"Duty beckons." Leila rolled her eyes. "I'll be back up with some extra pillows and water in a minute."

Norah thanked her again and stepped into the toilet cabinet. As she willed herself to urinate, she wondered what the best response to Matt's text would be. Perhaps she would ask Ellie to help her choose the right words. Placing the test to the side of the sink, she washed her hands and walked groggily back to the sofa. One minute more, and she could go to bed. A check of her phone later, her heavy head found its way to her shoulder and her eyes fluttered shut, despite her brain's efforts to keep them open.

Leila

*O*n her way upstairs, Leila did a mental happy dance that both girls were almost asleep before eight o'clock. While their nighttime routine worked five out of seven nights, she greeted each successful seven thirty bedtime with a sigh of relief that she and Wes would have a few hours of television and adult conversation together at the end of a long day. Those hours were the only time she was conscious *and* off the clock. Leila smiled at the heap of sleeping Norah as she rounded the banister. She eased her down onto a pillow and covered her with the blanket. Confident her friend would sleep comfortably, Leila walked to the bathroom to turn off the light and make sure there was ample toilet paper. The white pregnancy test glared against the dark granite counter. She picked it up, and the world froze within the width of a pale pink line.

Barely breathing, she stood motionless, fixated on the line. Her instincts told her Norah hadn't seen it. Leila blinked again, assuring herself her eyes weren't deceiving her, and looked at her sleeping friend's peaceful reflection. Hot tears pricked the backs of her eyes as the irony of the situation darkened her heart. A baby now? After all this time? And what if her marriage didn't survive? What if it wasn't his? She debated waking Norah and then decided her knowing tonight wouldn't help or change anything. She couldn't spare her friend any of the stressors dawn would bring, but she could at least give her one more night of innocence.

Ellie

Ellie shuddered in sheer anticipation as Pat lingered and teased beneath the thin piece of lace. It was the last thing that separated them. His other hand massaged her breast, threading her nipple between his fingers. As he began to make slow circles under the fabric, she gasped, pressed against him, and kissed a line from his ear to his neck and across his collarbone. Every shiver of his body excited her further. He kissed her hungrily, never breaking the rhythm of his hands.

"Lie back," he whispered, and guided her onto the sheets. He hovered above her, nipping and nuzzling her neck until she moaned, before turning his salacious attentions from one breast to the other. Heart pounding, she arched against the tantalizing motion of his hands. He moved the hand from her breast to her face and kissed her tenderly, slowing his strokes in time with their mouths, until both hands were on her hips, stilling them. She quivered at the tickle of the lace slipping past her ankles. He worked his way to her navel, then kissed lower and lower, from one hipbone to the other, until his mouth replaced the lace in a burst of warmth and desire.

Ellie's arms stretched above her head to clutch the mahogany bedpost as her throbbing muscles drove her closer and closer to the edge. Wave after wave of euphoric sensation coursed through her. His pulsing, relentlessly delicate rhythm continued until her legs stiffened and her body shattered into a million fragments of sweet release.

Pat grinned like a Cheshire cat as he surrendered her hips and watched her come down from the height of her orgasm. He pulled her, breathless, into his arms, and she rested her head on his shoulder, spent but aching for him.

"You're so beautiful, Ellie," he whispered into her hair.

She flushed, pushing herself back to look at him. She would never again see those blue eyes and trademark bedhead hairstyle in pictures without thinking of this moment. Tousled and mussed definitely suited him.

"Thank you." She began to kiss his shoulder. "That was—"

"Only the beginning." He took her face in his hand, stroking her cheek with his thumb, and guided her down again onto the pillows. Ellie's hands glided over his back, tracing the chiseled curves of his pelvis as their hips rolled in unison. His hands slid into her hair, and he pressed her breasts against his chest, elongating the moment in which he made them one for the first time. Her name escaped his lips as he sank fully into her. She drew a sharp breath at the throbbing fullness and buried her hands in his hair. Her muscles clenched deliciously as she curled her leg around him and began to move her hips in time with his.

They made love late into the night, without rush or distraction, neither wanting it to end. Finally sated, they fell asleep entwined in each other's arms, sharing an intimacy just as real as any other they'd experienced that night. Pat woke her again in the wee hours of the morning, and she him just after dawn. The clock ticked, ever present and ever ignored.

Kate

$\mathcal{P}$encils flying, the colors and lines leaped from Kate's mind to the page. The familiar whoosh of the shading pencil was soothing to her soul. Everything was coming together beautifully, as if the room had a life of its own and she was merely the creative vehicle. An artistic night in her studio was the very best medicine after the ego blow she'd taken that afternoon. Join a moms' group, Ken had suggested. It might be fun for you to meet other new moms and for Liam to grow up with other babies. Judging from the flier, she should have found her place. Moms for Moms: A Community of Support, it had said. From minute one, she felt as if she'd stumbled, uninvited, into some sort of a sorority meeting. The well-dressed women made polite, noncommittal eye contact with her, while the ladies in bare faces and ponytails studied her skeptically from head to ballet flat. She could still feel them exchanging glances as she took an empty seat on the bench lining the play area.

Several minutes of uneasy silence passed as she struggled to convince herself Liam would survive rocking in a swing that was certainly a petri dish of childhood diseases. Kate eventually struck up a conversation with the woman next to her, who was using the *more* sign with her baby. To Kate's surprise, the woman's daughter was five weeks older than Liam and could already clap her hands. The lady beamed at Kate's acknowledgment and insisted baby sign language classes were behind most of her daughter's advanced development in gross motor areas. Leila's girls had signed, and Kate was trying to learn all she could about it. Communicating with Liam in a new way excited her. Another woman chimed in that her six-month-old was up to twenty-four signs and five spoken words. Kate was slightly suspicious but impressed.

As the introductions were made, she found it odd to be introduced as "Liam's mom" by "Sophie's mom" to "Aiden's mom." Didn't they want to know her first name? Aiden's mom and Sophie's mom were soon joined by "the twins' mom," and Kate quickly lost interest when the three began to compare their dizzying weekly schedules of story time, signing time, developmental yoga, and baby gymnastics. She had no desire to fill Liam's days rushing to classes and appointments. Instead, her motivation to take this time away from work had been to actually *be* with him. She loved their tummy time and their snuggle time. Couldn't that be enough, or didn't it count without an instructor? Weren't their walks to the farmers' market and the duck pond quality time? What about the time they spent reading board books and swaying to Bob Marley and James Taylor? She just didn't see how $75 a month in Signing Time class tuition could do more than the *Baby Signs* book Leila had passed on to her.

The twins' mom contritely asked if Kate had an opinion about swim lessons. Kate smiled and admitted she did not, resisting the urge to ask whether there was a "sleep through the night" class she and Liam could join. Maybe she was reacting to her own childhood of ignored excess, but she was determined to be a different kind of parent. Liam would grow up knowing he was loved unconditionally and that his parents would support all of his interests, not feeling as if he were being pruned and branded into perfection as he bounced from one lesson to another. Was all of this talk about activities and schedules purely for bragging rights in mommydom?

Another woman joined the conversation, claiming signing was a good beginning but Kindermusik was the trick to preparing kids for preschool interviews and elementary mathematics. Speaking of preschool, a different mom countered that her ten-month-old had finally cracked the top twenty of two private-school waiting lists and that she would never forgive herself for not having applied earlier. Kate congratulated her on the heels of the others, feeling sheepish that she and Ken hadn't even considered selecting a school this early.

Their conversations splintered into separate groups, and at various moments Kate wondered if she was watching some sort of bizarre draft pick. The women seemed intent on sharing their "stats" and having them properly recorded: who had pushed the longest, who had gone natural, who did not poop on the table, who was still breastfeeding, whose fertility battle had been the most brutal, who had gotten pregnant simply by sharing the same soap with her husband, whose baby was sleeping through the night in its own room, who made her own baby food, who was ready to "try" again. The sign language aficionado continued to caution Kate about waiting too long to start the program, mentioning her graduate degree in early childhood development for the fourth time.

Liam began to wail from the swing, and Kate scooped him up. He was hungry. *Please not now.* She had no desire to feed him in front of this audience. It would be awkward to leave, and more than awkward to stay. She fumbled in the diaper bag for her nursing cover. By the time she was settled and had him in position, he was kicking and red faced. He thrashed beneath the cover as she tried desperately to convince him to latch. Her heart rate escalated in time with his screams. Various women paused their conversations to glance at her. She smiled and switched sides. The breast he'd refused began to leak, and she moved him back, hoping he would latch and soothe. Instead, he clamped his gums down on her nipple and she cried out in pain.

Kate felt the room's attention shift to her. "Did he bite you?" So-and-So's mom left a separate conversation to ask, bringing Kate to the collective center of that group of women as well.

"That's why the signing is so helpful. It gives them a way to communicate before they're verbal. You'll see," What's-His-Name's mom said.

"Try it without the cover. Nobody wants to feel trapped while they're trying to eat."

"It's the position. Look at the way she's holding him. Try something besides the football hold."

"I was a fly's fart away from weaning Maddox when he went through that stage. I'm so glad my La Leche sponsor talked me through it," said a mom Kate hadn't met.

"You're braver than I am. When Guy bit me for the first time, he drew blood and I invented a new definition of the word *wean*. Truth be told, I was beyond ready to stop weeks before that."

"I totally feel you there. Three months was long enough for me. Eventually, you just want to stop feeling like your body is on loan."

"There's no way Aiden and I could still be nursing. We're just too active and involved in activities. My sister is going on seventeen months, but she's one of those women who will whip it out anywhere—no cover or anything."

"You mean she'll feed her baby anywhere? How horrid." The woman rolled her eyes while Aiden's mom nodded obliviously.

Kate slipped now-irate Liam out from under the nursing cover and struggled to reposition her breast in her bra.

"I'm sorry—I'm just not very comfortable nursing in public. I think I'll just . . ." Liam arched his back, limbs flailing, as she fumbled through the diaper bag for the formula wheel and bottle.

"Brody bit me so many times that I started calling him my vampire baby. We still finished the year, though. I just turned every feeding into a learning opportunity."

Kate jostled Liam to her shoulder. She would have given anything for someone to stop giving notes and pour the warm water from the thermos into the bottle for her. The women, most of whom she still hadn't met, continued to talk over and around each other until she felt surrounded by a whirlwind of questions and criticisms.

"Is it your supply?"

"That's what it was when Maddy acted that way. I just wasn't producing enough."

"I've been supplementing lately, just until my body can catch up," Kate said, while hastily unscrewing and filling the bottle.

"Catch up? That's ridiculous." *Tactful*, Kate thought, stinging.

"Who in the world told you to do that?" She had no idea whose mom this woman was.

"She's right. That really is the worst thing you can ever do as a new mom." *Ever? This was the worst thing she could ever do? One could only hope.*

"It makes it too easy on them, and they won't take the breast. A bottle is instant gratification, and—"

"You're lucky he'll take it from you," another mom interrupted. "None one of my three would look at a bottle from me. I couldn't even be in the room if my husband or mother had any chance of feeding them. I guess we were too bonded or something." *What the hell did that mean? Am I really destroying my bond with Liam?* Kate loved him too much to risk that.

"Well, I would have stopped a long time before I did if organic formula were more trustworthy and less expensive. I know the breast is best, but I am exhausted. I want to quit every single day." The woman laughed nervously, and Kate instantly related to the guilt.

"I hear you. Kudos to all of you marathon nursers, but after being pregnant for ten months and nursing for six, I am ecstatic to wean Ben and have my body back."

"I could never do that." Someone's mom glanced smugly at her formula wheel. "The research against FF is just too powerful. Human milk for human babies."

"She's right. Just keep telling yourself you're doing what's best for your baby. He'll thank you for it in the long run." *So, we're back to me. Fantastic.*

"Were you watching for early hunger cues? Crying is one of the last signs. Did you wait too long to feed him?"

"Hungry babies aren't exactly known for their patience." The women laughed, and Kate's cheeks burned with heat. Liam grabbed at the bottle before the lid was secure, spilling a quarter of the liquid onto the bench.

"Is that bottle green plastic? I don't think that brand is BPA free. Glass is the safest bet." *Is my baby sucking on poison? It was a shower gift. I have no idea.*

"Have you seen an LC? Maybe your mechanics are just off."

"No, I haven't." Kate answered quietly, embarrassed.

"Have you tried anything at all?"

"You know about the tea, right?"

"The tea doesn't work for everyone. The herbs are a sure bet; just make sure you—"

"You're so tiny—are you eating enough?" *Can they tell? Is it that obvious?*

"I was just wandering the same thing! Are you getting your extra three hundred calories a day?" *Yes, 1,450 on the nose, every day.* That was supposed to be enough, based on research she wasn't proud of.

"You must tell us your secret for bouncing back so quickly." Aiden's mom laughed.

Kate forced a smile and joked that she clearly didn't have any answers, while Liam sucked contentedly on his bottle.

"Yes! In fact, you're so thin that I wondered if he was adopted when you walked in."

"Me too!"

"I wondered, too, but only because he doesn't look like you. Then I saw your face putting him in the swing, and I knew you were just freaked because he's obviously your first." *What if he was adopted? How would you be making an adoptive mom feel right now?* Kate locked eyes with Liam, trying desperately to disengage herself from the center of attention. Her heart was racing. Two more ounces, and they could make an exit.

"I'm on baby number three, and I still boil binkies. I've been told more than once to step away from the bleach during cold and flu season."

"Ahhh . . . I never worry about any of that, and my kids are never sick."

"That's because you breastfeed. I'm terrified of this flu season. It will be the first one when Finn doesn't have my antibodies. I'd still be nursing if I could, but he won't. And you know how I feel about vaccines."

"Pump and tell him it's juice."

"You don't give him juice, do you?"

"My pediatrician says juice is trainer Sprite."

"No sugar water for my kids, either. We're all green smoothies at my house. You should see how much we spend on organic spinach."

"Just wait until baby number two comes. You can't keep up the no-sweets, no-treats lifestyle as long with the second one."

"Just watch me."

"She's right. You can if your first one never leaves it. They don't exactly discover doughnuts on their own."

"Exactly. Is it any wonder we have so many obese kids in this country? We start them out on powdered animal milk that's designed to grow a newborn calf into a two-hundred-fifty-pound cow, then pump them full of rice cereal and juice, give them handfuls of corn 'puffs' for finger food, and finish it off with a big ole slice of cake at their first birthday party."

"Let me know how that works out for you. I'm not saying you can't keep a healthy lifestyle. I'm just saying that sometimes foods are harder to completely control. You'll see."

When Liam finished his bottle, Kate reloaded the diaper bag as quickly as possible, hoping to slip out unnoticed. Just before she stood, the twins' mom tapped her on the shoulder.

"I'll walk out with you."

"I know my way to the parking garage, but thank you." Kate knew she must be veritably crimson by this point.

"If you insist. I was going to tell you privately, but you should know today's open play is the exception. This playgroup is by invitation only. If you'd like to be considered for a trial membership, you need to go to the website and complete the application. Honestly, I can't say that I would bother." The woman gestured to the playground's exit gate. Kate stared at the woman as she processed her words. Speechless, she stood tall, planted a soft kiss on Liam's head, and left the room in a wake of hushed whispers. She was failing him in every area, and he deserved so much better. How could she have neglected to find him a school in the same instant in which she had failed to keep up his food supply? The cold truth was, she didn't deserve him.

The pencil in her hand and the Zen of her studio quieted the world for a few blissful moments. This was beauty. If only she could paint him a beautiful life.

Leila

Leila looked from her reflection in the mirror to sleeping Norah, feeling her friend's peace slip away like sand through an hourglass. She would wake, still weary from the unsolved problems of yesterday, to face even bigger obstacles today. As she put the pregnancy test back on the counter, Matt 2.0 came to mind. She and Wes had taken to distinguishing between the happy, exuberant Matt they used to know, Matt 1.0, and today's Matt—the jealous, angry person who was getting harder and harder to love.

She closed her eyes as a wave of gratitude washed over her. Wes just might be her greatest blessing. In the last ten years, not a day had gone by when he hadn't made her feel loved unconditionally. Even now, when every wrinkle, every roll, and every pore glared back at her under the bathroom lights, she knew she was beautiful to him. He told her every day, but, more importantly, he made her feel it.

She turned off the light and headed to the stairs. How could she possibly want more than she already had in this very moment? She padded down the steps, ticking off her blessings in her mind. Healthy children, a husband who adored her, food in the pantry, and an education no one could take from her. It was almost overwhelming in contrast with where she'd started. Add the weekly cleaning service and consistent orgasms, and she really did have it all. Somewhere in the middle of her ordinary life, she had begun to live a fairy tale.

Wes was lying in their bed, scrolling on his iPad and watching

Chelsea Lately, when she opened the door to their room. With a gesture so practiced it had become automatic, he looked up, paused the television, and smiled at her. How could she possibly ask for anything more? She returned his smile and lifted her shirt over her head. The pudge and grayish streaks that hung over her jeans made her reach for the light switch.

"Don't." He smiled again and flipped the comforter to the side. "You're beautiful." The growing bulge in his boxers made her smile. She took her hand from the switch, happy she still had that effect on him after so many years. What if he worried about his body the way she worried about hers? Would she want to go to bed with someone obsessed with how much his hair was fading? Or with someone who dwelled on every single mole and patch of back hair? He was the most beautiful man in the world to her. Nothing would ever change that.

For the first time, she fully understood how he saw her. She unsnapped her bra and flung it to the side. He sat up straighter in the bed and put his computer on the nightstand. She locked the bedroom door, and stepped out of her jeans. She slipped her underwear down to her ankles and kicked it to the side. His eyes shone as she slid into bed beside him and worked her hand up his thigh to the elastic of his boxers. Her fingers dipped under the waistband, grazing the familiar.

"I love you. Thank you for always seeing the best in me."

"I love you, too." He moved his hand to her breast, sending a chill down her spine. She leaned into him, kissing and nuzzling a line from his neck down to his navel. He arched his pelvis, and she pulled his boxers down to his ankles. In another practiced motion, he flicked his leg and they joined her panties on the floor. She took him in her hand, caressing his length, then retracing the motion with her mouth. Tonight would be for him.

Ellie

$\mathcal{E}$llie sipped tea as Pat whisked eggs and chatted about the weeks of in-room dining that awaited him on the road.

"Bloody hell." He broke her reverie as he held out his now-eggy T-shirt. "I swear that's never happened before."

"That's what they all say." She laughed and reached for the hem of his shirt. "Only one thing to do now." She pulled it up, grinning at the thought of him making breakfast shirtless in her kitchen.

"Ellison Lindsay." He feigned insult and took three steps back. "I am a gentleman."

"Clearly." She laughed and released his shirt. "Apologies."

"Apology accepted." He beamed, then took off his shirt in a single motion. Ellie blushed as he walked to her, watching her take him in. She had never wanted to be in anyone's arms so badly. Pat kissed her softly, then lifted her onto the island. She wrapped her legs around him and traced the line of his breastbone. Desire flamed through her as he simultaneously kneaded her shoulders and intensified their kiss.

She hooked her fingers into the loops of his jeans and pressed herself to him. She could feel he wanted her just as badly. Ellie was seconds from taking her shirt off as well, when the clearing of a throat destroyed the moment. She whipped her head around to see Stacie standing in the doorway to the kitchen.

"Ms. Lindsay, I'm . . . uh . . . I'm sorry. Jess didn't tell me not to come in. I . . . I can just go upstairs to the office." Ellie glared at her as she scurried out of the room. Pat put his forehead to hers, and she searched his eyes.

"So it begins." His voice was defeated. Ellie didn't know what to do except hold him and promise they were in this together.

Her phone rang incessantly on the counter. She looked over his shoulder, trying to decipher the text on the screen. All she could make out was Jess Cell and the code 911. *Please don't let this be the end.*

"Why do I feel like the second I let go of you, things will never be the same?" he whispered, as her phone threatened to vibrate itself off the counter and onto the floor.

"It might be about another client, or one of our interests." She whispered the lie, pressing her forehead closer to his, desperate to give them another moment of blissful ignorance.

"And when it's not?"

"Then we deal with it. You and me." She tilted his chin so he was forced to meet her eyes. "With a slight assist from the best PR team money can buy."

He laughed, brushing her lips with his. "Thank you, Ellie." Pat shrugged, and added sheepishly, "I'd best go put on a shirt." He turned to go, and Ellie slipped off the island. In an exact reversal of the roles they'd played the night she'd seen the boat, she reached for his hand and pulled him back to her.

"Trust me," she said, with far more confidence than she felt, and squeezed his hand. "We've got this." He folded her into his arms and kissed her hungrily. She opened her eyes to study his face, surprised by how absolutely pained he looked. He broke the kiss, ran his thumb over her cheek, and walked dejectedly from the kitchen.

As soon as he was out of earshot, she dove for her phone. Why had she let herself get so distracted? She must have left it here when she'd come down to start the Keurig before she went back upstairs to join Pat in the shower. She shook her head in disgust with herself, thinking of all of this happening while they leisurely made love against the steamy glass, then again, spread out on fluffy towels, before dressing and coming down to make breakfast. Her heart pounded as she calculated that the phone had now been out of her sight for an unprecedented two hours.

9 Missed Calls
14 New Voice Mail Msgs
11 New Text Msgs

Rather than waste time listening to what could by now be outdated information, Ellie immediately called Jess. Jess answered on the first ring and asked her to please hold. That was never good.

"I apologize for being out of touch this morning. What's happening, and what are we doing about it?"

"Essentially, around five o'clock this morning, Scarlett James was photographed buying a pregnancy test." Jess paused, and Ellie knew that was the least of their worries. "She's been egging the paparazzi to follow her nonstop since the press conference, so this is likely a stunt. We all know she could have acquired a test discreetly if she wanted to avoid the spotlight."

"Of course. If that's all we're dealing with, why the 911?"

"It gets worse. The photographers outside the drugstore mobbed her, asking about her divorce, how long she and Pat had been having weekend rendezvous, and where her good-girl image had gone. She dumped the pregnancy test out of the plastic bag, then crumpled on the pavement, tucked her chin to her knees, and sobbed. A million flashes caught her tears, and a million more caught her thong. When her handlers found her, she pointed to the EPT box on the curb and yelled, 'That's on him. That's why he's hiding. And that's why he's the biggest fraud who ever lived.' The audio and print visuals have been viral for the last hour. I sent Stacie when I couldn't contact you. It's up to you where we go from here, but a typically reliable source tells me Scarlett has been hospitalized for exhaustion, and that her labs were indeed positive for pregnancy."

"Do we have any reason to believe he's been found?" Ellie tapped her fingers on the counter, hoping Stacie hadn't come from the office and had taken precautions not to be followed if she had.

"As of now, no. But we both know if there ever were a three-million-dollar shot to be made, this is it. They're everywhere he frequents, even the farmer's market. I can't be certain they won't trace the gag order to you and circle your house from there. You should know his team is very frustrated. They think he's in the UK, but they're blaming us for all of this."

"Thank you, Jess. Let me discuss our options with him, and I'll be in touch. In the meantime, I will coordinate his team. As for hers, do nothing. Keep our gag order in place, and let them look the fool. I don't care to speculate why she wants to prolong this attention, but I won't feed into the inferno of free publicity they're trying to create for her."

"Ellison, may I speak frankly?"

"What would you like to say?"

"With all due respect, I disagree with you. I think we let her live the image she's created. She wants to be the jilted lover? Fine. So be it. She's making a hell of her own creation. When we ignore it, we feed into it. Our silence gives her team power to keep branding her as the damaged ingénue. She's clearly grasping at straws here. Why should we be one of those? They know he'll speak at every national venue come Monday regardless, so why shouldn't we make a statement now, instead of giving her and her team an open stage to paint him as the villain until then?"

"Jess." Ellie paused. "First, I'd like to compliment you on your astuteness. However, I stand by the decision not to speak or release a statement until he's asked about it during the interviews. Our resources are better spent preparing him to represent his side of the story during the tour than trying to deny her claims. The media will pit them against each other at all costs, no matter what. Any statement we make now only gives them more material for the cycles. After he makes the LA rounds on Monday, they'll saturate the print markets with those statements. Hopefully in context."

"I respect your decision, but I still worry they have the upper hand here. Has he given any indication this is a possibility?"

"True or not, our position stays the same. I will speak to Mr. Grayson about how he would like it addressed." Ellie rubbed her temple with her free hand.

"There's one more thing."

"Yes?"

"She says they've been engaged secretly for the last two months."

Ellie, taken aback by the words, pushed her emotions deep into her throat.

"Thank you. I won't be out of touch again. Please keep me apprised of developments, important or not. Also, I'm sending Stacie back to the office. I need you to call in someone from legal. I want a new NDA drafted for her. It should include any and all of my private affairs, and it needs to be signed today."

Norah

$\mathcal{N}$orah pulled the blanket more tightly around her body and willed herself to retreat back into the blissful black nothingness. The quiet house and the sun streaming through the windows told her it must be midmorning. As she blinked the Ambien fuzz from her brain, the events of the weekend flooded her mind and she wished she were still dreaming. No such luck. She was indeed waking up at Leila's. The family was at church, and she'd been caught. Matt truly hated her now, and she didn't blame him. Enrique's texts still sat unanswered on her phone. He certainly didn't hate her, but he wasn't exactly free to love her, either.

One thing at a time. A challenge is only a crisis when interventions fail. She stood and walked into the bathroom. Her face was pale. She needed to make a point to get some biotin and probiotics in her system before her on-call marathon further weakened her immune system and wreaked havoc on her skin.

The pregnancy test sat, expired, on the counter. The dried parchment beneath the display window faded to show both the control and the indicator lines. She rolled her eyes at the pale streaks bleeding together through the membrane under the display, before tossing it into the trash. She would take a fresh test at the office. The clothes she'd worn the day before sat laundered and folded on the countertop. Leila had come through again. She must find a way to thank her.

A quick shower later, Norah was wearing the only clean clothes she had to her name. It was time to make a plan. She would meet Jillan at the office, prefill some paperwork to make the week easier, and then gather some things from the house. Somehow, she needed to convince Matt to talk to her. Her stomach turned at the thought. Lately, he was like a toddler in the midst of a temper tantrum when he was angry. He raged more and more loudly until he got the attention he wanted from her. She usually refused to acknowledge him until he was calm, but that didn't keep him from banging his head on the floor. Could she let her silence speak for her until he was ready to talk? No. That was the prideful way out. Regardless of the ways he'd hurt her over the years, she'd broken a vow and he deserved an apology for that. Was there a chance he would ever accept that she had acted impulsively in San Francisco? That she hadn't intended for things to snowball into a full-blown affair? How would she ever explain what had happened next, when she still wasn't sure herself? Was it a reaction to stress? She spent her days, and often her nights and dawns, calculating the decisions she made for other people. Every day, she strove to give the women in her rooms one hundred percent. She'd spent years earning the privilege to wear that coat, and they deserved nothing less than her absolute best. She listened to them, to the point where she was always running late to the next room. They understood, knowing in turn she wouldn't rush through their appointment. She learned their names, provided solutions to their pain, cared about what kind of births they wanted, believed in them, and trusted their bodies.

Norah looked at her reflection in the mirror and told herself that, whatever trespasses she had committed in her marriage, being good at her job wasn't one of them. Matt had known this career was part of her future when he asked her to be a part of his. There were times when she didn't even want to open the door to her own home after work because she knew she was walking into some sort of bizarre competition between their days. He tested her all the time to acknowledge the hours he worked and the ways he took care of them financially—and no matter how many times she passed those tests or told him she was proud of him, it was never enough. He was intimidated by her success and took out his insecurity on her by resenting the hours she worked.

Then there was Enrique. Being with him was like coming in out of a blizzard. She suddenly didn't have to weigh every word she said against whatever version of Matt happened to call or predict how he would interpret each syllable based upon the day he'd had.

It hadn't always been this way. There was a time when Matt loved to hear about her patients and was excited when a few extra hours on her part avoided a C-section or when she caught something invaluable in a patient's labs. There was a time when she loved to hear about his briefs and strategies. Was he even that person anymore? Was she? Or was she merely holding on to the idea of the man she'd fallen in love with?

Norah admonished herself for letting her mind wander. First things first. She needed a ride to the hotel.

Group Text (To Cami, Kate, Ellie)
If you're free this morning, I could use a friend and a ride. I'm at L's. I don't want to bother her further.

Reply—Kate Cell
Ken is on a run. He should be back in 30, and I can take you. If you need to go now, I can be there in 20, screaming baby in tow. I hope you're okay. LMK.

Reply—Ellie (2)
(1) My bubble popped in a very public way this morning. I can send a driver, but I can't get away from mission control today. Let me know.
(2) And I'm sorry. I'm here to talk if you need me.

Norah looked at Ellie's response and hoped she was okay. Lately, she'd had such a glow about her—a glow Norah didn't want to see vanish in the whirl of a public scandal. She hoped Patrick knew how much Ellie must care for him to risk her privacy.

Her phone vibrated again, and Kate was on her way. Good—their relationship had been strained since Norah had confessed about Enrique. Maybe this was the first fence she could mend.

(1) New Text To Dr. Orlando, E. Cell
I will be at Mercy in 2.5 if you're free for a consult.

From the beginning, they had agreed to text each other using only professional codes, out of fear their spouses or nurses might stumble upon the messages. A new wave of guilt clenched her stomach. She had never felt more like "the other woman" than she did right now.

Ellie

Ellie pressed her palms into the cool granite and squeezed her eyes closed. Her heart screamed it wasn't true, but her head was frantically constructing every piece of information she had about his relationship with Scarlett into a sadistic puzzle. Had she been so incredibly naive that she'd fallen for a pretty face and a line? No. She refused to spiral into a brutal self-interrogation based on a pop tart's desperate attempt to save her image. She would simply ask him. Whatever his reply, she held the power. Worst-case scenario, it leaked and she laughed it off as a steamy weekend with one of *People's* Sexiest Men Alive. No one had to know how deep things had really been.

"Ellie."

She snapped her eyes open at the sound of his voice. He stood in the doorway of the kitchen, holding his phone and looking panicked. His disheveled hair and the strained elastic of his shirt collar told her he'd been pulling at both.

"Stop," she said, as he took a step toward her. She gestured to the phone in his hand. "Is there anything else I need to know? Do you remember when I asked you that? I am balls to the wall now and asking you—*again*—if there's anything else I need to know."

"I just read everything they're saying. Who gives a flying flip about all that? It's bollocks, Ellie!" He took another step toward her, but her arctic gaze stopped him in his tracks. "Tell me you know that! As long as we know the truth, the rest of the world can scream and believe whatever crazy lie they fancy. I'm talking about you and me—the only goddamn 'us' in this whole circus! I'm asking my bloody girlfriend to have a little faith in me."

"Right now, Mr. Grayson, your *bloody* girlfriend is not at liberty to flit around in denial. She has a job to do."

"It's a crock, Ellie! You'd know that immediately if you weren't so scared of how you feel for me. You're looking for something to hide behind."

"Your girlfriend wants nothing more than to believe you, to believe she isn't some elaborate one-night stand. But your publicist is asking you if you gave Scarlett a ring!"

"Yes, but I can explain."

"I'm sure you can. Don't worry. You'll have seventeen national opportunities to do so come tomorrow morning." Ellie turned her back to him and forced her heart to settle into an acceptable rhythm. His hand was between her shoulders in an instant.

"It's not what you think." He rubbed her back hesitantly. "Let me explain." She heard him swallow hard. "Look at me. Please."

This was her Rubicon. She could walk away right now, relatively unscathed, but to go forward was dangerous. She felt her heart growing hard, shutting out everything she had felt for him just minutes before. It would build new defenses, and she would be just fine.

"It's true. I gave her a ring. It was a birthday present. She was giving a concert in Toronto, and I was shooting *Life of Us*. I was supposed to meet her backstage after her show. I canceled because the director changed his vision and called a reshoot. We were on a roll. Her assistant texted that she was very upset and asked if I knew it was her birthday. I didn't. I asked if she could have something delivered, then sent a birthday card with a messenger to accompany it. I didn't even know it was a ring until Scarlett called to thank me. It wasn't an engagement ring; it was a birthday present. She knew that. I have the picture she sent to my phone. It's a simple lattice band with an opal on top. Her birthstone."

He kissed the back of her head and turned to leave the kitchen.

Ellie both knew and didn't know what to think. She had every reason to question him, but her heart told her not to. Trust was everything to her. Did that make all of this more real? If she trusted him now, in the midst of all of this doubt, did that mean what they had was strong? Or was she a fool?

The easy decision was to let him go and release herself from all this. She could be back on her patio, relaxing from the stresses of his campaign, tomorrow. Did she want to give up everything she had invested in this place? It was only a matter of time now.

Ellie took a long breath and turned to face him. After all, she had never been afraid of tests. "I believe you," she whispered, looking down.

"Thank you. There is definitely something else you need to know." He ran his hand through his hair, and Ellie steeled herself for whatever he might say next. "I can be absolutely certain the baby she says she's carrying isn't mine."

"How?" She searched his eyes for clues of deceit.

"Because we've never been to bed together." He tugged at his collar and smiled. "As you may have noticed, that's not something I take, um, lightly."

Cami

*C*ami stacked her now-empty boxes against the wall. It was hard to believe the next chapter of her professional life would begin tomorrow. Behind her, an entertainment network blared the fiftieth account of the Scarlett-Patrick scandal to break in the last two hours. She'd tuned in to the channel after reading Ellie's response to the group text. They were calling it Scargate.

Image after image of Scarlett filled her screen. Unseen sources "close to her" reported they'd watched her struggle in a miserable marriage and had never seen her so happy as she'd been after she and Patrick Grayson had begun their affair, that she couldn't wait to announce their engagement once her first marriage was behind her, that the two had wanted to start a family quickly and were currently debating where they should live. Their blurbs were dotted with pictures of Pat's London apartment, his vacation house in Montana, and Scarlett's mansion in the Hamptons. Cami wondered how much of America realized this was merely speculation paired with stock pictures of them and their real estate. The only photo they were actually in together was the now-infamous picture of them kissing in Aspen. The rest were pictures of Scarlett on tour and at various events with her husband. Then, of course, there were pictures of Patrick grinning with one beautiful woman after another. If making a dollar were this easy, Cami was working way too hard in the medium she'd chosen. She had shot enough artists and celebrities at home over the years to know that if you owned the rights to your photos, they could never be warped like this. She smirked, thinking if she got bored when she retired, she might take a job making seventeen-second photo-video mash-ups a few times a week. The stories went on to quote "intimate" friends' accounts that the two had fought in Aspen when Scarlett admitted she still wasn't legally separated from her husband. They reported that Pat had asked for his ring back and left in a rage.

After what seemed like the millionth rephrasing that Scarlett was not only depressed, abandoned, and pregnant but now on suicide watch according to a "source," Cami looked for the remote. She hoped her friend had kicked the idiot to the curb. But, knowing Ellie, she would probably proclaim whatever Shetland pony he was sitting on at the moment a white horse, then fix this mess for him. When the scandal cleared, he would move on to the next bed and the rest of them would be left to watch a devastated Ellie shrink away into herself, just as she had after the Marcus debacle. Unfortunately, Kate and Norah were busy putting their own fragments back together. That would leave only Cami and Leila. Leila would know what to say, and Cami would be there to handle everything else. She looked at the roll of tape in her hand and remembered the days she'd spent packing Ellie's downtown loft while she was licking her wounds in Cinque Terre. Sure, she could have hired movers to pack, but it somehow seemed too personal to be left to strangers. She owed this and so much more to Ellie. Cami tried not to need her often, but there were still days. Unless you'd lived through grief like that, you just couldn't relate. Kate and Ellie knew her pain. They had lived it every day alongside her. The faces they missed might be different, but the cutting pain of a life cut too short was the same for all of them.

Cami taped the last box shut and told herself not to go down the road of what could have been if he'd lived. Not today. Her phone chirped, and she welcomed the distraction.

1 New Text—Kate Cell
BC I don't want there to be another elephant in the room, I want you to know that I've been distant bc I'm struggling at the moment. I also want you to know I'm working on it. Please don't worry. I'm picking Norah up now, and then I would love a GNO. I have no idea what's going on with Ellie after all this, but Norah and Leila are in for tonight. Zapata's at 6:30.

Finally. Cami smiled at her phone. She'd missed Kate, and this was a good sign. She wasn't sure how far she'd relapsed into her disease, but at least she was acknowledging it. That was new and promising. Maybe this time would be different.

Reply
Sounds good. I'm proud of u and I'll meet u there.

Kate

"And that's when I left. It was awful. I felt like I'd been convicted of negligence by some bizarre jury of my peers. I just keep wondering when I'll know that I'm doing it right—parenting, that is. Every time I turn around, I see all these other women doing it with ease, like they were born to this role. I feel like I'm driving myself nuts trying to read all these books about scheduling, and signing, and growing happy children, just to be constantly reminded I'm doing it wrong. Part of me is terrified I must be missing a gene. Lord knows I don't come from a line of great examples."

She checked her side mirror as they merged onto the freeway. Norah laughed, and Kate felt her shoulders ease a bit. She had been anxious about seeing Norah for the first time since she'd learned about the affair. Kate thought about Norah every day and wanted to call, but as soon as she found a quiet moment to pick up the phone, her mind fixated on Enrique's wife and daughters. Maybe she was reacting to the disaster her father's scandalous affairs had wrought in her adolescence, but she just didn't see how Norah could sleep with a married father of three. Of all people, she should understand the consequences of that. She'd lived it, too.

"So what if you're not the BABY ON BOARD bumper sticker type? There's nothing wrong with that." Norah's words brought her back to the moment. "There isn't a singular way to 'do it right.' Don't you think parenting is almost like design in that way? Beautiful spaces and places are made from combinations of ideas and qualities. So are phenomenal families. You need to give yourself some credit. No one who matters thinks you're doing this badly but you."

"I want so badly to do this well, but it feels like a project that's spun out of control. I'm making mistakes I don't even know are mistakes at every turn. Does that make sense? It's as if the big moments build on each other from the second you find out you're pregnant. From that moment on, you're not you anymore. You're *pregnant*. You're *due*. It starts with the announcements to family and close friends— *we're having a baby!* Then the excitement of making it FBO. After that, every milestone is like a mini-celebration. *It kicked! It's a boy! We've chosen a name!* At work, people watch you like you're carrying a time bomb and preparing to exit the building before it explodes. They ask you every day what you plan to do *after*. You're passed over for one assignment after another, under the assumption that you cannot possibly commit to both. You don't even realize they're expecting you to make a choice, because you're riding this euphoric wave of congratulations and milestones. Then, after the showers and nursery decor, it all climaxes with the newborn excitement. The first pictures, the Facebook post, the birth announcements. Then what? You go home, and it's like you rode the biggest ride at the park and no one prepared you for the exit. How do you say it's fantastic but exhausting?" She paused, suddenly aware that she was rambling. "Anyway, I'm sorry to chatter at you like this. It's just been so long."

"I know it's been hard." Norah shifted in her seat. "And I'm sorry. I've been a lousy friend lately. I should have been there for you."

"I don't think you've been a lousy friend. If I'm honest, I have essentially barricaded myself in the apartment since Liam was born. Aside from running errands and the occasional night in my studio, I haven't been out much. I'm just a little lost right now." Kate took advantage of the stalled traffic in front of her to touch Norah's arm. "But I'm on my way back."

Norah squeezed her hand. "I'm glad. You've been missed." She paused with a grimace and took a sip from her water bottle. "And I want you to know that I understand my situation hits close to home for you. I can't tell you how much your support means to me right now. That's not to say that I expect Enrique to leave his wife, et cetera, but I want you to know that this was about a connection and about feeling alive again, not about sex or a thrill. I almost wish it had been that simple, or that I did it merely to hurt Matt."

Kate's throat went dry as she tried to form the words to apologize for her quiet judgment of Norah.

Ellie

*F*our blue eyes stared at one another. Ellie released the breath she hadn't realized she was holding and let herself return Pat's embrace. She was grateful there was a clear answer to at least two of her questions. With a start, she realized that Jess was right. She searched his eyes, asked him to trust her, and made the call. Her team would release a statement that he had been briefly, but was no longer, in a relationship with Scarlett James and was definitively, by abstinence, not the father of her child; he maintained that he believed she was separated and wished her well in all future endeavors, including repairing her marriage. The rest could be handled in the interviews.

While Jess attended an emergency conference call Pat's manager had requested to coordinate their teams with the security team, Ellie spent the next hour calling in favors with her network and press contacts. During the last of those calls, Pat stepped out on the balcony to phone his mother. Ellie watched him walk away, anxious to finish her conversation so they could enjoy their last minutes alone together. When she finally finished, she walked to the glass door and smiled, remembering how he had made her jump when he opened it that first night.

Pat was sitting on one of the chaise lounges, staring pensively out over the water. She took a moment to simply stare at him. He was wearing a loose, long-sleeved white shirt and tan cargo pants. With the breeze gently blowing his hair and his profile backlit by the sun, he looked as if he'd been posed for a magazine shoot.

She sat beside him, and he put his arm around her. "I'm not ready for this to end." He said as she laid her head on his shoulder. What she wouldn't give to have more time with him before they were engulfed in the whirlwind tomorrow would bring. It all started with a 6:00 a.m. fitting for his parade of appearances.

"I know." She curled more tightly against him. His heart was pounding through his shirt.

"I want to thank you for . . . well, for trusting me and, um, for everything." His words brought a tingle to her skin as she remembered how he'd fumbled to say thank you on the first night. He was nervous. He shifted to look at her, and she noticed his eyes were moist. "I . . . I know this is a risk for you, and I want you to know that I understand if you want to end it here. For a moment in the kitchen, when you were angry, I was afraid that you wouldn't believe I hadn't proposed to Scarlett. I was afraid I'd lost your trust. My first thought was, *God, please don't let her end it now.* Then I came out here and I listened to my mum sob into the phone that my dad is drinking again and that the police had to escort her to her car after church because of the paparazzi, and I thought maybe I'm being extraordinarily selfish and irresponsible even to consider asking you to be with me. Why would I subject anyone or anything I love to this life?"

His eyes were piercing, and Ellie fought the urge to look away. She was nervous, too. In the flash of a camera, her life might never be the same. She could be followed and harassed. She could be forever defined in the public eye as his current or former girlfriend. Pat blinked, pained at her silence, and she reached up to touch his cheek.

"I guess I could say the same thing to you. If anyone has been irresponsible, it's me. If I hadn't crossed a professional line, you would only be dealing with the Scarlett fallout, not worried about us or my privacy." She looked out over the waves and then back into his eyes.

He closed them tightly for a long moment and pressed his cheek more deeply into her hand.

"I'd give anything for more time with you before—"

"Shh . . . no more 'before,' no more 'when.' Just now. Just us. The rest will come, and we'll face it."

She moved her hand to his heart and stared into his eyes.. He slipped his arms around her, and she was finally home.

Norah

Norah looked at her beautiful friend and wished she could give her any of the answers she needed. How could Kate see the possibilities in flawed remnants of fabric and castoff pieces of furniture but accept nothing but perfection in herself?

"Thanks for listening. I'm sorry for the diatribe. I might have been a little overexcited at the idea of adult conversation and a captive audience."

"Not a problem. It was nice to hear. I like knowing what's going on with you." Norah patted her knee. "I'll see you at Zapata's later. Enjoy your day. You've definitely earned it." She released her seat belt and opened the door.

"Norah?"

"Yes?"

"There's one more thing I wanted to tell you." Kate glanced from Norah to the Hilton sign. "I'm . . . I'm sorry for being so angry. I realize I've been less than supportive, and I will try my best to separate my feelings about, um, all of *this*"—she gestured to the sign—"from my relationship with you."

"Thank you." Norah forced a smile to hide the pricking pain behind her eyes. "And for what it's worth, I'm sorry. I never meant to hurt anyone. You included."

Kate nodded, and Norah shut the door. As she walked away, a tear fell from her eye and her shoulders felt like they were carrying her weight in stones.

Leila

The joy on her girls' faces had been worth the $80 a head, plus parking, but *The Wiggles, Live!* had nothing on the madness that was her attempt to leave the event-center parking lot. After her fifth K turn, she was finally in the "right" lane.

"I'm *soooooooooooo* hungry! Mommy! When are we going to *eeeeeeeeeaaaaaatttt*?"

"Clara, speak kindly. That tone does not tell Mommy that you are grateful. Didn't we just have a wonderful time at *The Wiggles*? Why don't you sing about the big red car instead? Julia knows the words, too."

"I 'ant 'ome 'ockolat mook!" Julia screamed, and threw the pacifier she was too old to have.

"Girls!" Leila cringed at her own angry tone and lowered her voice. "Mommy loves you very much, but I need you to be on my team right now. We are leaving this parking lot. I am hungry, just like you, and I promise we will eat soon. Right now, I need you both to grab a book out of your cubbies and look at it. Julia, please help Sister." Leila's fingers were white on the wheel. Sometimes she wondered if she said, 'Mommy loves you very much' only to buy herself cooldown time. Hopefully, her girls would remember their favorite show come to life, and not her tirade trying to leave the parking lot.

Sheesh. Why was she such an idiot when it came to directions, and why had she lost her temper? They deserved so much more. This day was supposed to be magical for them, and she'd just ruined it. So much for buying tickets six months in advance so she could give Julia an experience, versus a toy, for her birthday. At least there would be wine and girl talk tonight.

Norah

Norah shook her head, determined to focus on the job at hand. She would get her car and drive to the office. That was simple. One of her best friends was on the road to forgiving her. That alone should be enough to salvage this weekend. She was not a common whore, no matter how it felt to wait for her car at the valet wearing the same clothes she'd been in when they'd parked it.

Mercifully, her phone beeped.

1 New Text—(From Jillan Cell)
I'm at the office. No rush :) I'll just be studying until you get here.

Norah punched a reply that she was on her way, and then cringed at the recognition that her last, distracted reply had brought her here. What did she even want from this? Did she love Enrique? Actually, she did. She could fall for him completely if he were in a position to truly love her. At this point, that was all she wanted. When she was with Enrique, she felt like she was with a partner. She loved opening the door to their room and knowing that he would be ecstatic to see her. She loved being able to rattle off the stats of her day and knowing he would understand when she just wanted to take a shower or sleep for an hour or two. She missed that with Matt. He had been anything but happy to see her lately. It was just so easy with Enrique.

Then again, she'd been right when she'd labeled it a bubble. It had popped before they'd been able to take it public. If she was honest with herself, she didn't want to force Enrique into any decisions about his marriage. Could what she and Enrique had even last in the midst of on-call schedules and demands out of their control? Could it last when they weren't making a conscious effort to see each other? In the real world, their connection would be tested. There would be children in the mix, child care for them when they were both on call at different hospitals, divorces, property settlements, and the powers that were solely their exes' to wield. Did she really want him, or did she just want a connection? When she was with Matt, she wanted to be alone.

She shook her head again, thinking she was borrowing trouble before she'd talked to either man. Still, she needed to take a hard look at her feelings. These last few months might have made her feel whole again, but at what cost? Was she simply bucking for control against what was missing in her life with Matt?

The attendant brought her sedan to the podium, and she fished a few bills out of her wallet.

"Thank you, ma'am." He opened her door and added, "I'll see you tonight."

"You're welcome," she mumbled quickly, embarrassed that she had become a regular. *Pull yourself together,* she told herself. *We're taking today one step at a time.*

Ellie

$\mathcal{P}$at stepped in front of her to open the patio door, and she smiled, remembering how his elegant manners had impressed her and her staff the first time they'd met with him and his manager to discuss working together. She turned to tell him so, when the sound of footsteps coming down the stairs in double time stopped them both in their tracks. Pat instinctively pulled her back, just as Stacie rounded the corner of the first landing. Ellie pulled her hand from his and glared up at her. Jess had called her to the office well over two hours earlier. What the hell was she still doing here?

"Um, hello." Stacie shifted her eyes from Ellie to Pat to where they'd been sitting outside on the patio. "I was just on my way out. I had some urgent e-mails to attend to before I headed back." Ellie nodded, counting her blinks and watching her shift the computer satchel on her shoulder nervously. She was lying.

"I wasn't expecting you to still be here. I'm sure you have a weekend you'd like to go enjoy." Ellie intentionally clipped her words and motioned to the kitchen. "Thank you for your time today."

"Of course." Stacie flushed and fumbled down the remaining stairs, her eyes still on Pat. Ellie didn't say another word to her as she hurried to the kitchen and exited through the mudroom door. She had little patience for junior associates who overstepped their positions, and even less tolerance for those who abused their proximity to clients. "Have, uh, have a good evening." Ellie nodded in response and walked toward the stairs.

"Ellie?" Pat was behind her in an instant.

"I'm sorry. I just need to check something upstairs in the office."

"Is everything okay?" His voice was tense as he kept pace with her on the stairs.

"She's lying. I can feel it."

Ellie punched the code to the office door and pushed it open. The room looked absolutely untouched, but her gut told her she wasn't being paranoid. Taking out her phone, she typed a text to Jess.

> New Msg—To: Jess Cell
> Stacie is just leaving my home office. I need someone to check that the read and sent receipts on her last e-mails match that time stamp. Copy me when you find out. I need her new NDA signed and filed w/ a copy on my desk. 911. Thank you. Your hours this weekend will not be forgotten next quarter when we discuss bonuses.

She steeled her face and looked back at Pat. He was confused, probably worried she was creating a reason to freak out and end them. Didn't he see that she—that they—had enough real reasons to run screaming from each other into their professional corners without adding imaginary ones?

"Is anything, um, out of order?"

"No." She told her face to soften and crossed the room to him. "But you were right, in the kitchen, when you said I was scared of how I feel for you." Ellie took his hand, wishing she could control her mind as easily as she could her expressions. "I am." His eyes dimmed, and he looked away from her. "But that doesn't mean I've forgotten our promise. This is me knowing it won't be easy."

"So, this wasn't—"

"This was just one of the many times to come when I'll need you to understand when I say I have to work for a minute. It's not always this pressing, but when things are heated, it can be. It's the price I come with."

"I think I can handle that." Pat grinned, and she felt her shoulders relax. "In fact, it sounds like a bargain, comparatively."

"True story." Ellie laughed, despite the visions of flashbulbs that flooded her mind.

Norah

*J*illan closed the heavy textbook she was poring over as Norah approached. Simply seeing the warmth in her emerald-green eyes lifted Norah's spirits. She swore Jillan had a God-given gift for making those around her feel calm and capable. It was one of the many reasons she was so incredibly popular with their patients.

"Hello, gorgeous!" Jillan laughed and pushed a strand of fiery-red hair behind her ear.

"You're kind." Norah rolled her eyes, knowing she looked terrible. "So, are you ready for hell week? I was glad to see you're doubling at Mercy." Norah scanned her badge and held the door open.

"As ready as I'll ever be. Should we make a bet on how many purple pushers Dr. Blieger will leave us?" Jillan laughed again, and Norah smiled, thinking the hearty sound was a balm for her tired mind.

"If it's fewer than eight, drinks are on me."

"Scratch that—if we're drinking, I'm buying after this favor. I've been so crazed lately that I almost forgot I was teaching at the midwifery center tonight, much less that I needed props."

"No problem. Help yourself. I'm going to do a little raiding of ye olde supply closet myself and then hit the charts."

"Good luck." Jillan winked, knowing Norah was going to test her urine for HCG, as she had done so often over the last two years.

"Thanks." Norah said trying to shake the overwhelming feeling of regret weighing on her heart. As she headed to the restroom, her phone vibrated in her pocket.

1 New Text—Dr. Orlando, E. Cell
I'm sorry for the late response. Today is Alianna's
birthday, and I'm unavailable. I do have a block of
time available tomorrow after 5:00. I would like to
weigh in before you make any decisions.

Norah dismissed the wave of jealousy she felt reading his message as she filled the dropper with her urine sample and dripped it onto the kit's pH window. She discreetly wrapped the cup in a paper towel before putting it in the wastebasket. Seeing it would only give the office staff something more to gossip about the next morning.

She put the test on the counter and walked to her office. Jillan's boisterous laugh filled the quiet hallway as she chatted with her husband on the phone. Norah couldn't remember the last time she'd laughed with Matt that way. She perched on the chair behind her desk and wished Ellie could script the conversation she was about to have. A framed picture of her and Matt on the beach, smiling, with their arms around each other, glared at her mockingly. That trip seemed like a million years ago. She turned it away from her and picked up the phone. She would call from her desk so he knew she was at the office, not lying naked in a hotel bed, making fun of him with her lover, as he was probably suspecting.

A young female voice answered on the second ring. The hole in her heart ripped wider as she forced out her request: "I'm calling for my husband, Matt Merrit."

"I'm sorry"—the girl giggled—"he's a bit, um, how shall I put this . . . *preoccupied* at the moment." The once-familiar, now-foreign sound of Matt's laughter was her undoing. She started to slam the phone down on the receiver, then stopped herself. She wouldn't give them that satisfaction.

As one hand managed to end the call while her forehead sank into the other, the door to her office burst open.

"Congratulations!" Jillan shouted, and beamed, tossing the kit onto her desk. "Oh my God! Can you believe—" She stopped short as Norah's eyes traveled, horrified, from the phone on the receiver to the cell phone on her desk to the small blue circles on the test strip. Her lungs fought for air, and a million shards of glass pierced her failing heart. "I'm so sorry. I didn't mean to overstep. I shouldn't have—"

"You're fine. Um, it's fine." Norah choked on the garble of words as her throat blazed and hot tears began to roll down her cheeks. "I'm . . . I just . . . I don't know what to think right now."

"Oh, honey." Jillan walked to her desk and put a maternal arm around her. "Just thank the good Lord even crazy dreams come true. Isn't this what you've been waiting for? It's your own little miracle."

Norah's stomach turned, and she heard her own voice say, "There's something I need to tell you."

Kate

Kate looked around the circle of faces. She could do this. She *had* to do this. It wasn't just about her anymore, or even just about her and Ken.

"My name is Kate. I . . . I haven't been to a meeting in a while. The last time was in the final weeks of my pregnancy. At that meeting, I felt like I'd finally overcome this disease. Something about growing such an innocent little life inside me, and having to eat so he could grow strong, made everything so much easier. I thought I could carry that determination with me after he was born, to think of myself as this little baby I could hurt or nurture through my diet, but it's not working. Instead, I'm struggling to find the time to even practice my recovery principles, much less make time to journal my challenges. I feel like I'm holding on to a slippery slope with nothing but my fingernails. I need to find a handhold. I can't deny that anymore. This week, my breaking point was my milk supply. I am not producing enough to meet all of his needs, and I'm afraid there's no going back now, no matter how many calories I consume."

"Thank you, Kate. We're glad you're here." The group leader smiled affectionately. "And your weight today?"

"One hundred and fourteen pounds." She looked down at her lap, knowing she was one of the biggest in the room.

"Would anyone like to offer Kate a comment or a connection?" the leader asked.

"I would." A pretty blonde in the middle raised her hand. "I think it took a lot of courage to come back here on your own. I can speak only for myself, but I've never been able to do that. When I think I have things under control, I stop going to meetings. Things will be going great for a while, once for almost a year, and then something triggers me more than usual and I give in just a little bit. It usually takes four or five months for anyone close to me, usually my mom, to notice, but by the time they do, I'm . . . well, I fight them because I still think I'm in control. I always have to hit epic lows before I learn."

Kate nodded, wanting to say something but too caught up in the emotion the girl's story stirred inside her. She looked up for the first time, surprised to see how many more hands were in the air. She was struck by the varying degrees of confidence with which people raised them. Some signaled the leader indirectly, while others held their hands in the air eagerly.

The leader gave the girl three seats down from Kate a nod. "Your story gives me hope. I know that's not what you came here to do, but when I listened to you talk about your son and your husband, I kept thinking that maybe one day I'll be able to police myself. I want to be aware of when I'm being a pain in the ass to others and making them worry." Nervous laughter lilted through the circle.

"Thank you," Kate said. "This is the first time I've ever recognized my own spiral."

"What do you think was different this time?" the counselor asked with a steady tone.

"Honestly," Kate said, stalling, "I don't know."

"There must be something. Did anything stand out when you realized you were relapsing?"

"I looked at my calendar, and I realized I hadn't made or kept plans with anyone except for the pediatrician in weeks. My friend Leila texted me a Groupon for massages and asked if I'd like to make plans for a day out. I looked at the expiration date, and my first thought was how many more inches I could lose before the masseuse saw the fat on my back. I knew I couldn't do it in time on my own. Then I thought about the pills." She closed her eyes, and images of the blue bottles in every grocery store and pharmacy filled her mind. "I told her no and then scraped the rest of the granola I was eating for lunch into the trash." Kate uncrossed, then re-crossed, her legs. "That's when I knew."

The counselor nodded, and the circle began to clap. Kate looked down at her hands as the corners of her mouth turned slightly upward. Maybe she could do this.

Norah

Norah drove as if on autopilot through the familiar exits and streets from her office to their house. She didn't care if the girl was still there. She was going to get the things she needed for the week and then check into a room. She would have Petra scan her tomorrow, and when she knew the gestational age of the fetus, she would begin to make decisions. One step at a time.

She pulled into the driveway, heart pounding. Her hand hovered over the garage door remote as if she were holding a scalpel and debating an incision point. When she pushed the button, there would be no going back. This would all become part of her story. No, it would become part of their story.. *Their story?* Did that mean she and Matt, she and the baby, or she and Enrique? She couldn't shake the feeling that she was coming home as an entirely different person. She would open the same door, walk down the same hallway, but nothing would be the same. And she didn't want it to be. She didn't want to walk through that door into her broken marriage. She wanted to walk through that door and into who she and Matt had been four years ago. She took her phone from her bag and typed a text.

New Text—To Leila Cell
Just tell me you remember when things were good. I'm about to walk into my new normal. Send Zen vibes.

Norah opened the door and, out of sheer habit, hung her keys on the hook. She cleared her throat as she walked into the kitchen. If Matt and the girl were here, she wanted them to hear her. Their island and countertops were full of empty beer bottles and wine coolers. Who in the world had he brought home? Had he picked her up at some sort of prom?

"Matt?" she called, unsure of whether she wanted him to answer. She walked into the living room, thinking their house looked like frat boys had robbed them. There were clothes strewn everywhere, and the stale smell of tobacco hung in the air. She looked at the staircase, wondering if she should walk up to their bedroom. She could picture Cami smirking and asking her if she was seriously worried about protocol at this moment. She could visualize Ellie raising an eyebrow and saying, *One does not simply knock on her own bedroom door. She opens it and deals with what's behind it.* Leila would tell her to leave now, and Kate would insist there wasn't a single thing she needed from this place that couldn't be bought over the next few days. Norah told herself to focus and made her choice. This was her house, after all. Matt never let her forget that. His credit score had been too low for them to qualify for the interest rate they wanted, so they had put everything in her name. At the time, he had been embarrassed but also desperate to call himself a homeowner. Norah hadn't shared his urgency to move, but had eventually given in because they wanted to start a family. The house had happened because Matt wanted it. Never mind that buying it added thirty-five minutes to her daily commute and more nights spent in the on-call room because going home would cost her two hours of precious sleep. He didn't care about that.

Norah shook her head and noted that there was a certain kind of grace in clarity. No matter what happened from this point on, she would not be controlled by fear and guilt. She knew now that she had settled not for the wrong man but for his crumbs. In a way, Matt had done the same thing. He wanted a dutiful wife and white picket fences, and he was content to tolerate her hours as long as that life was on the horizon. Unfortunately, she couldn't give that to him. Maybe that was why she'd agreed to the house and to the commute that would further extend the time they spent apart. Or maybe he had simply chosen the wrong woman.

When they met, she didn't have any secrets. She was who she was. She was on fire for medicine and for becoming the physician she wanted to be, regardless of the obstacles. Then, over the years, something changed.

Norah walked to her bedroom door and raised her fist to knock, then stopped and pulled the handle. This was *her* house. The room was empty, but she could hear the shower running. She told herself not to look at the bed, but she couldn't resist. The white duvet was slung to the bottom, and the Egyptian sheets she loved so much were a tangled mess in the middle. Foil packets littered the ground around Matt's side of the bed. A dark voice reminded her it didn't look all that different from the way she'd left the bed at the Hilton all those times.

Norah walked to the bathroom. She stopped at the doorway, staring at the steam on the glass.

"Matt, I'm here." Norah cleared her throat. "I don't know if you're alone or not, but I'm going to get some things from our room and wait downstairs for you. We need to talk."

"I don't have anything to say." She knew then that he was alone. He would have put on some form of bravado if not.

"Then I'll talk. I have things to say that you need to hear." Norah clenched her eyes at the broken chords that were his voice. Was he standing under the steam, trying to scrub the guilt away, as she had done after the first night with Enrique? "I'm going now. I'll see you in a few minutes, or whenever you're ready." Matt didn't answer, and she walked to their closet. She grabbed a suitcase from the top shelf and began to pack. A series of loud coughs followed, and she knew he didn't want her to hear him cry. He always did that.

Norah took all the clean scrubs she could find, two sets of slacks and three white shirts that would work with all of them. She shook her head, reached into her pocket, and placed her ring on the dresser for perhaps the last time. The water pelted on and she noted that she could barely feel her legs moving beneath her as she walked downstairs not knowing how she would ever make it through the next two weeks on call. She was already exhausted and not fully recovered from the virus.

Norah looked around the kitchen, disgusted by the pans on the stove and the dishes on the table. Seeing the crepe skillet in the sink was like a dagger to her heart. Matt had made her crepes for breakfast the morning after they'd spent their first night together. After that, it was their tradition. He made them for her on every birthday and every anniversary after. The funny thing was, she hated crepes. She didn't tell him that first morning, and there was no going back after. He was so proud of himself when he set the plate on the nightstand. Then again, a different man had made these crepes for a different woman.

His feet pounded down the stairs, and she recommitted to not letting his dramatics distract her. She propped the handle of her suitcase against the wall. He was dressed in a J. Crew T-shirt and Puma sweats that reminded her how much she hated seeing his shopping excursions on their—rather, *her*—credit card statements.

She debated speaking first, then decided to put the burden of the silence on him. He scowled at her, walked to the fridge, and jerked a bottle of beer from the door.

"Want one?" he asked, more out of habit than to be considerate.

"No."

"Are you working?" He sneered, making a show of putting the second beer back in the refrigerator. Before she could answer, he added, "Remember when we used to have fun? Do you remember that? You and me, we didn't used to be like this."

"Yes. I . . . I want to talk to you about that." His body language told her he was poised for a fight. "Do you mind if I sit?" She made her way to the counter barstools, hoping he would join her. He stood, propped against the island still glaring at her. Thank God he wasn't a prosecuting attorney, or she would feel like she was on the witness stand.

"Honestly, I don't care what you do." He took a long draw on his beer. She had hurt him so badly. Before this, he had been a strictly after-five kind of person.

"If you don't want to talk today, that's fine. I understand your needing time." She told herself that the seventy-six ways in which he'd hurt her in the last twenty minutes were not irrelevant, but they were also not important right now.

"So, if you're not going to work and you're not coming home, what are you doing tonight?" His eyes darted everywhere except for hers, and she wondered if he was hiding something else as well.

"If you're asking what I'm doing tonight, that's an easy question." She stopped, realizing she was engaging him. "But I think what you really want to know is where I am going from here."

"I can't believe that's what you think I want to know. I am not even thinking about our future right now!" He slammed the bottle on the counter, sloshing suds over the sides. "I want to know where the *fuck* you're going *to* when you leave here! I want to know who you're screwing! I want to know long has this been going on! I want to know why my wife is wrecking my life!"

Norah tried to hold back her temper. She reminded herself she didn't want to close the door on them out of anger. Some part of him had to feel the same way. If that were true, they could possibly come to terms on the rest. The conception-date calculations in her mind wielded their weight, and her throat went white hot. It was not lost on her that Matt could never accept that. He had been vehemently against adoption from the beginning of their fertility issues.

1 New Text—(From Leila Cell)
I do remember the good days. I remember them all too well. I hope you're okay and that you're still coming tonight. I'm here if you need to talk.

"Tell me he didn't just text you." Matt's face burned red, and Norah forced herself to channel the part of her that still wanted them to work.

"It was Leila. We're having dinner tonight." Her voice sounded tiny and foreign. She sat up straighter on the barstool.

"Of course you are. You always did have time for them, didn't you? All the while, there I was in the back of the line. Behind your job, behind your friends, behind your mother. Just once, you could have made me a priority."

"Matt, none of this is about them. It's about us and"—she gestured to the trashed kitchen and up the stairs—"all of this. I'm so sorry that I hurt you. We're broken. We need help. Can't you see that?"

"Oh, I see it! I'm not blind. I look back now, and I have no idea how I ever fell in love with such a selfish woman." He shook his head. "I don't think you ever knew what love was, Norah. All I've done for the last seven years is love and support you, and all you've done is hold me back and tear me down!" He threw his hands up in the air. That was her undoing.

"Don't you dare call this *love*! We both know it's anything but!" She swung her feet to the ground and shoved the stool behind her. The grating sound of the metal legs scraping across the travertine made her wince. "Love isn't competitive. When you love someone, you don't envy them. You don't let some twisted notion of masculinity test them until they break and start resenting their own success!" She paused, unable to lower her voice and daring him to interrupt her. "What we once had, that was love. Remember that? Do you remember when we were proud of each other? There was a day when I would have done anything to spend the rest of my life with you. I miss what we used to have every day, and I know you do, too." He shrugged, and she felt as if he'd slapped her. "Now"—she narrowed her eyes at him—"when I see your name on my phone, I cringe and the word *bastard* is on the tip of my tongue." He stared back at her, stunned. "Believe me, I don't want to be that person any more than you want to be married to her." She turned her back to him and walked to her suitcase. A single tear rolled down her cheek as a cramp pierced her lower abdomen, stopping her in her tracks.

"Do you know where I could be by now if I had anyone giving me half as much time and support as I've given you over the last five years?" he yelled at her from the kitchen. Her head whipped around to face him, and she barely recognized the livid sound that was her own voice.

"Aren't you tired of singing the same old song yet, Matt? Because I know I'm tired of hearing it! You tell me how your career would have been different if I'd been here waiting on you every night? Tell me again, how did I cost you a promotion? How did my medical license ruin your life? One of these days, you'll stop blaming other people and start asking yourself the hard questions about what you're doing wrong." She popped the handle of the suitcase and began to roll it to the door.

"See! That's what I'm talking about! You always assume it's me who's doing something wrong, not measuring up."

"That's not true! What do I always tell you? How many times have I said, 'So what if you haven't made partner yet? That doesn't mean you're not on your way'? Instead, you'd rather pout and point fingers at me."

"I'm standing here, looking at my wife, who's been screwing someone else for God knows how long, and you have the nerve to suggest I ask myself what *I'm* doing wrong? Who is he, Norah? What does he have that I don't? He's a doctor, isn't he? I know you enough to know that. Does he"—Matt rolled his eyes and thrust his fingers into quotation marks—"*understand* you?"

Norah shuddered as he spit out the words. *How dare he mock me, when he brought someone else home to our bed just hours ago?* Another pinching sensation shot through her abdomen as she struggled to control her rage.

"Couldn't I ask you the same questions?" she yelled. "At this point, it's not the who; it's the why! I know why I cheated, and call me the biggest fool who ever lived, but I am going to walk out that door and hope that you will do some soul searching. I'm not ready to throw us away." She looked up the stairs and then back at him. "Even after this. Not without doing everything we can to save it. I want us to get some help."

He braced his palms against the counter and stared blankly down at them. "You should go. She'll be back soon."

Norah knew then that he wasn't sorry. It was conclusive. He wanted this. She walked slowly to the door, followed only by the sound of her suitcase rolling on the tile.

Cami

*C*ami arrived thirty minutes early to make sure their table was in order. The last thing Kate needed was a hectic hostess fumbling over a reservation she'd arranged for her friends. In Cami's mind, Zapata's was mediocre, but Kate and Leila loved it. The hostess returned, saying the reservation wasn't in the book. She apologized and offered to pencil their group in at eight o'clock. Cami slipped her a $50 bill and was seated in the next ten minutes. This was Kate's night, and Cami wouldn't have it ruined.

Leila

Leila sat in the restaurant parking lot, listening to the voicemail from the university for the third time. She was equal parts happy and apprehensive. Wes would tell her to go for it. She imagined his proud face and told herself to reflect. If she really wanted this, she would find a way to make it happen. She would need child care she could trust. Clara was slated to start full-day Montessori preschool in the fall, but Julia was Mother's Day Out–bound for the next two years. Those four short hours wouldn't be sufficient for a working mom. Then again, they were offering her a part-time position. Maybe it could work?

Leila closed her eyes for a second and tried to imagine the juggling involved. Would she have all of the same demands of a full-time position, with half as much time to deal with them? She immediately imagined dropping both girls off at separate schools and heading to the university. Could she even hope to thrive in this role? The thought of teaching again was more tempting than the bread and gelato she was about to try to avoid. There were so many things to think about before she even considered it. Her girls were her primary goal. She wanted to give them everything they deserved, but most of all, she wanted them to remember a present, committed mother. Then again, she wanted them to know she was as strong as their father was. Every time one of them rocked a baby doll, pretending to be Mommy and waiting on Daddy, she wondered if she was inadvertently teaching them that being a mother was exclusive of being independent. If so, she had failed them horribly.

No. She would return to teaching when they were older and they would have plenty of time to internalize their mother as a professional. Leila looked at her phone and reminded herself she didn't have to make a hard-and-fast decision tonight. At times like these, she felt like finding a plaid unicorn might be easier than finding balance in her life. Thank goodness she was married to a man like Wes and the girls would grow up with their relationship as an example. He loved her unconditionally. That would never change, regardless of her decision. More important, he would let it be her decision. In that sense, her and Norah's marriages were polar opposites. Leila understood Norah and Matt's relationship better than anyone. After all, she had known them since the beginning. She'd watched them fall in love and watched them grow apart over the years. In the early days, Matt always joked that law and medicine were jealous bedmates but that he and Norah would find a way. And for the first four years, they did. It was as if they had a unique brand of determination to find time to be with each other.

In those days, Leila and Wes had been touched by how much Matt relished his time with Norah. Leila often left their weekly ladies' happy hour feeling drab about her passion for Wes after seeing Norah just off three days on call, gush about her pending weekend with Matt. The two were always planning day trips and excursions, while she and Wes seemed to repeat the same combination of dinners, drinks, plays, movies, and Costco. She'd been so worried she and Wes were petrifying that she'd surprised him the next Friday night with lingerie and candlelight. He'd dropped his briefcase as soon as he saw her, and dinner had been served two hours later, cold, on the couch while they watched *The West Wing*.

Leila smiled as she remembered the best part of that night. Wes had untied the knot that that secured her robe and told her the lingerie and prime rib didn't hold a candle to this moment. Her shoulders had relaxed as she realized they weren't petrifying, they were evolving. That was the night they began to discuss starting a family. Wes came from such strong roots that he couldn't imagine life without children. Leila, in stark contrast, had grown up knowing that a pregnancy was the fastest way back to the trailer park. She never developed the romanticized notion of babies that so many of her peers held.

Her heart skipped a beat as she realized that was why she was so concerned about the girls' perception of motherhood. It wasn't about them. These were her demons. She was terrified they would throw away their chances prematurely in favor of a Gerber commercial. She sent up a prayer of gratitude that they would grow up completely differently than she had. They would have Wes's view of life: education, career, marriage, family.

She chuckled, thinking that imparting to her daughters her phobia of having sex before attaining a degree might not be such a bad thing. She prayed they would wait until they met someone who loved them as much as Wes loved her. Someone who fell in love with them for who they were as young women, like their father had their mother, and who loved them only more over time, despite the ups and downs. Wes wasn't the first man she'd ever loved, but he was the first one she'd ever trusted completely. There was a difference between loving someone and baring your soul.

Leila stepped out of her car, wondering whether Ellie knew that. She had been all but destroyed after Marcus. It wasn't the failed relationship that tortured her most, but the damage her reputation and hard-won career had sustained in its wake. It had torn her in two. Leila hoped her ever-in-control friend could ignore the shoulds and coulds for ten seconds and let Pat have a chance. Leila remembered the happy hour after Ellie's firm had finally signed him following brutal contract negations and meetings between their teams. It had been clear to Leila from the beginning that Ellie was invested in him differently than she was in her other high-profile clients. He had impressed her. That wasn't easy to do. Leila smiled, remembering how Ellie seemed oddly flustered when she described his manners and lack of ego. She wondered how Pat managed to bring Ellie's guard down and hoped he could keep it that way.

1 New Text (Wes Cell)
Have fun tonight, beautiful.

She grinned at the screen. There was something to be said for the passion of a new relationship, the steamy nights and endless discoveries about each other, like the evening Ellie was likely having right now, but she loved these everyday moments with Wes. After two children and a decade together, they were closer now than they'd ever been. She texted him that she loved him, and recommitted mentally to always being honest with him, to holding on to what worked and letting go of what didn't. If she was lucky, they would do 'old and gray' together.

Ellie

"I held her hand until the end. From the beginning, I promised her I wouldn't leave. And I never did." Ellie paused as memories of forging her parents' signatures on the forms required to "home-school" herself for the remainder of Sherri's last year filled her mind. "Her favorite nurse, Jackie, sat with me for three hours after they removed the tubes, and for another five hours past her shift, but I still couldn't let go. I realized the time eventually and told her to go home." Ellie shook her head. "It was a lifetime ago now, but the memories are still crystal clear."

"Maybe that's what's so hard about it." Pat cupped some of the warm bathwater in his hand and poured it over her shoulder. "The clarity, that is." She pressed her back closer to his chest. Ellie shut her eyes and committed the way this moment felt to memory. It was almost therapeutic to believe in a man again. She was about to tell him that Marcus was the only other man she'd ever shared this part of her story with, when he broke the silence.

"I feel the same way almost every day." He paused, and she felt his body tense behind her as he caressed her thigh beneath the water. She squeezed his hand and told herself not to speak—to give him the time he needed. "My grandfather passed away the night before the LA premiere of the first *Destiny* film. It was crushing. I loved him. In many ways, he was the strongest and wisest man I've ever known." His voice dropped, and she interlaced her fingers with his and began to make soothing circles with her thumb. "Understand, he supported my acting only as a way to pay for university. He and my mother kept meticulous records of the earnings I made from every commercial and every piece of print work. When my jobs became more lucrative, they began to make investments on my behalf. Oxford was their dream for me. The assumption was that I would quit acting after my gap year and focus all of my energies on my studies. I always knew I wouldn't quit, but I had no idea how to tell them without disappointing them.

"You should have seen their faces when my acceptance letter arrived. My mother cried, saying it was a dream come true. They were so proud to have an Oxford man in the family. I can still hear the pride in my grandfather's voice as he clasped my shoulders and asked if I truly knew what it meant for the country that someone from modest stock like ours, the son of an ordinary bookkeeper and a secretary, could make it to Oxford with enough diligence and hard work. Then he passed the sherry he'd been saving for the very moment. I'll never forget looking around the room and thinking I'd never seen them so happy together. But I was miserable. Somewhere along the way, Oxford had taken a back seat to theater. I spent my gap year auditioning for anything and everything that came my way. I'd never worked so much. Then, midsummer, I went to the open call for the Lucas Lucien role in *Destiny*. The director wanted a fresh face and an authentic accent. I told myself this was my shot. I'd never wanted anything more.

"The next five weeks were grueling. They would call me back, pass me on, change their minds, and then call again. Finally, I was passed on to LA with ten others to read with Blythe. The audition date fell during mandatory fresher, or freshman as you would say, orientation and registration. I can still see the shock on my grandfather's face and hear the fury in his voice when I told him my plan. He had no concept that this could be my big break. He knew the *Destiny* books were wildly popular, but he had no idea how iconic the Lucas character was. He erupted that I'd lost sight of who I was, of everything we'd all been working and sacrificing for. He fished a tabloid full of photos proposing that Princess Di's death was a hoax from his post sack and said I was chasing a life that no sane person should want. He thrust it at me, said to look around at everyone on the streets, watch how they walk about and buy the *Star* today like it had nothing to do with the demise of a wonderful soul they'd idolized. Then he waved it in the air and said, 'You watch how fast that changes when the anniversary of the accident comes round next week. They'll be scrambling over each other for a spot on the memorial, fighting to throw themselves on the pyre they themselves just remembered to be outraged enough to light.' He asked whether that was what I wanted for myself, much less for my family. He told me not be stupid, to see Oxford as my big break to pursue the sciences I'd loved since I was a child, and to see the audition as giving all of that up for a hobby.

"I told him he was wrong, and he fumed that even if I did make it, I would be a slave to a cannibalistic industry that would devour my values. I told him he couldn't understand, because he wasn't a dreamer."

Pat drew back, and she knew he was fighting his emotions for control. "That was the first time I ever saw him cry. I understand why now. You see, I was his dream. And I destroyed it. He was frigid when I landed the role and colder when I left for filming. I thought he'd come around when he saw what a phenomenon the film would be, but that never happened." Pat ran his hand through his wet hair. "Like I said before, he carried the post. He carried it for almost forty-five years and was due to retire one week after he died." Pat cleared his throat and continued, "He had a massive heart attack and collapsed on the sidewalk during his route."

Ellie reached for Pat's hand as her heart made its way to her throat. She didn't want him to be in this club. There was nothing quite like losing someone you loved on the brink of the best part of their life. "The woman who found him said he had her copy of *Us* clutched to his chest. Blythe and I were on the cover, posed as Lucas and Aria, kissing bare chest to bare chest. His last words were

'I don't know why.'" Pat cleared his throat again, and she pressed herself closer to his body. "I'm not dense enough to think seeing the cover of the magazine caused the attack, mind you, but I hate that the last image of me he ever saw was one designed to amp up the sex appeal of a PG-13 film."

"Pat, I—"

"It gets worse. I didn't go home for the funeral, because of the premiere." She turned to face him. "I'd like to say I was following my team's advice, but that's just not what happened. I didn't go because I knew it would be detrimental to my career not to be photographed on the carpet with Blythe and the others. I felt like I was on the verge of my break, and I wasn't willing to lose that." He shut his eyes in shame, and she slid her hand behind his hair. "I felt like that was death and this was life. I felt as if I couldn't change anything by grieving with my family, but I could be in control of my"—he shook his head at the irony—"own destiny." Ellie looked into his eyes with a newfound hope that he could understand the rest of her. "The British paparazzi flocked to the funeral anyway and my family blamed me for the harassment. I started a charity in his name to support science education in public primer schools and have tried to make amends, but I'll never truly make it right with all of them. They think I care only about the fame and money. And they resent me."

Ellie took a centering breath and released it slowly. "I understand." He met her words with an embarrassed shrug. "Before you ask yourself how I could possibly relate, it's important that you know this part of my story." Ellie reminded herself she trusted him as her mind revolted against what she was about to say. She would share part and keep the rest for another day. "I've never been to my sister's grave."

He stiffened, and she pulled away. "That can't be all," he said. His eyes were skeptical, and she knew he deserved the truth.

"After the ceremony, it was just overwhelming. Looking at all of the pictures on the screen and watching her deteriorate from that awful disease all over again didn't feel like we were honoring her. It broke my heart to watch her friends, the other popular girls, flip their hair and take pictures next to her memorial sign, each one out-crying the last, and to watch our broken family hug each other and pretend they weren't still at each other's throats over the divorce, like they hadn't refused to be in the same room together when the priest gathered us for her last rites. They'd all hurt her so much when she was alive. I didn't feel her in that space, and I knew I wouldn't feel her in the cemetery. So I left. I drove myself to the library and wrote the speech that would eventually take me to the debate nationals." She shuddered at the memory of her family's outrage. "Half of them hadn't spent any more time than it took to drop off flowers in her room after the surgeries were over. They hadn't held her trash can or scrubbed in to hold her hand during the spinal taps. In all honesty, Sherri would've been worse off if they had." She shuddered at the memories. "I . . . I'll tell you the rest soon, but I think that's all I can bear tonight."

"I understand." He poured more water over her back and pressed his lips to her forehead. "I could go on and on as well. The good news is that we've only begun to know each other's stories." Selfishly, Ellie was glad he had more to tell and allowed herself to sink a little further into their relationship. They were both complicated and hurting in their own ways.

"It's not that I don't want to know all of your story—believe me, I do; it's just that my life is far too complicated to love anyone simple."

"Isn't that the bloody truth?" She smiled at him, trying to ignore the nagging itinerary that was preventing her from enjoying the next part of their evening.

"So"—Pat grinned down at her—"Ms. Free Spirit, I know you prefer to bash about your days with little to no schedule, but I clearly need a plan for after I leave California." His voice dripped with play-ful sarcasm. "Turns out, I'm very busy and important."

"I think I recall something about a film." She laughed and dipped her hand below the bubbles to rest on his hip. "While you're on the

LA circuit, I'll meet you at the Mandarin. The penthouse is reserved for you and your teams. It's going to be mission control for mine as well over the next thirty-six hours. When our teams are finished hashing it out, and you're finished with the radio parade and the syndicated interviews and"—she smirked—"are dressed for the next twelve appearances . . ." He rolled his eyes and splashed her playfully. It was common knowledge that he was happiest in Hanes T-shirts and jeans. She continued, "Maybe we can slip into a conference room for lunch before it's time to leave for *Goldberg*."

"Are you going to be there?"

"I'll be at the *Goldberg* appearance." She felt him draw back and looked up at him. "That's what I had planned professionally before . . . before all of this." She pulled his hands to her heart. "It doesn't mean I can't meet you on the road. It just means you're assigned to one of my top-notch teams and I hadn't planned to supervise the appearances personally."

"No, it's not that. I understand." His brow furrowed. "I just thought you might want to be with me through all of this."

"Of course I want to be with you; it's just that I didn't plan for the travel and time away." He looked to the side, and she turned his face back toward her. "Pat, if we're going to make this work, we have to be real with each other. We're going to have to get used to wearing different hats when we're together. Professionally and personally, I mean."

"I know that. I'm just starting to get nervous."

"I promise you're in good hands. Jess will be with you on the tour, and I'll be watching everything closely."

"I know that, but it would be nice to know someone who genuinely cared for me was by my side. I'm sure it's just my nerves, but I feel like I'm walking into a media shit storm. I wish there were another way. In fact, if it weren't for the extraordinary story this film has to tell, and all the work everyone else has put into it, I'd say the hell with all of it and spend the next six months in Montana. In many ways, I feel like I'm letting them all down. If I hadn't taken the role as my shot at breaking into real film, this ridiculous scandal wouldn't have compromised their work."

"It can still be that for you. That's our angle." She pressed her forehead to his.

"I'm not talking about angles, Ellie." He brushed her cheek with his thumb, and his voice fell to a whisper. "I'm talking about how the whole damn world identifies me." Pat closed his eyes, and Ellie understood this was about him, not his image. "I've waited for what feels like an eternity to do real work, to do something brave, and in the blink of an eye, I'm back to being an object. No matter what I do from here on out, I'll never be able to separate myself from Lucas Lucien."

"The way I see it, that's a gift." She stroked his thighs. "You've made enough money to take risks and to seek whatever roles you want to play. Take them and know you'll always be able to trade on the *Destiny* fame. We, my firm and I, will keep you relevant. If there's one thing you can trust about your fans, it's their loyalty. Just ask the Goldberg security team. They supposedly don't need this many precautions and barricades when presidents visit. Five hundred people are camped out already."

Pat laughed and reached for his glass on the edge of the tub. "To *Destiny*."

Ellie reached for hers and added, "To trending on Twitter."

Norah

1 New Text (From Leila Cell)
Did you take another test?

Reply (To Leila Cell)
Yes.

1 New Text (From Leila Cell)
I just want you to know I'm here for you. I saw the first
test last night when I came upstairs with your water.

Reply (To Leila Cell)
That means a lot to me. Thank you. Please keep this
to yourself. I need more information before I make
decisions.

1 New Text (From Leila Cell)
Of course.

Kate

Kate looked around the table, feeling overwhelmed, as their conversations braided together into some alien sense of cohesion. She had missed so much. Ellie was dating a client? How had that even happened? Leila might be going back to the university? She especially hated being the last to know Cami had been fired and hired. Norah's hand gently squeezed her leg as they listened to Leila talk excitedly about an arts festival she wanted them to make plans for. Kate knew they were all watching her. She took a bite of the crab dip to make them happy and tried not to think about the buttered bread crumbs and gorgonzola cream. Leila's hand found hers briefly under the table and she felt stronger.

"I just don't know what she's thinking. It's a huge risk." Cami's words were blunt, but Kate understood she was just worried about having to pack up another apartment for Ellie if she lost it again. Norah scrolled through her phone, and Kate noticed Leila watching every keystroke she made. Were they texting about her? "From what I understand," Cami continued, "I couldn't care less that most of what they say are lies, but I still don't think Ellie has any business being with some sort of teen heartthrob turned cougar bait."

"I think she really believes in him." Leila shifted her glass from one hand to the other. "When have we ever heard her speak so highly of a huge star before, much less of an independent film? I think she's hoping to rebrand his next chapter."

"Ellie has her blinders on. She's seeing what she wants to see right now." Cami swished the ice in her glass. "So what if his film is brilliant? And so what if it's not? Ellie thinks she's saving him. Somehow she's twisted representing him as an actor into reinventing his identity. Not wise. Look at Clooney. He's been nominated time after time for an Oscar, but what's the first thing that comes to your mind when you see him?" Cami looked around the table, and Kate shifted uncomfortably in her chair. She needed to speak soon. "That he's a sex symbol."

"Sure." Kate sipped her wine. "In my mind, he's always going to be the pediatrician I wished I'd met on *ER*, but that doesn't necessarily define what I think about his art. If anything, when I see the new Clooney movie with Oscar buzz, I assume I'll get to look at something pretty, even if the film is terrible."

"I see your point," Cami conceded, but Kate knew it was mostly out of gratitude, not out of agreement, that she had joined the conversation.

"I could see Patrick Grayson's career headed in that direction," Leila added. "He's been consistently good in every role he's played, even in the big-budget features that have flopped."

"Well, I'm not worried about his career. What's the worst thing that can happen to him? He has to pay a few million in child support and sign on for the fourth *Destiny* film? He'll be fine. I'm worried about Ellie." Cami said reaching for the bread basket.

"I'm not." Norah broke her silence for the first time in minutes. "I'm sorry, Cami. Call me a romantic, but I was excited for her when she described the way he makes her feel. I know what it's like to be in a bubble, to know it will end but to go for it anyway. All I can say is, I'm glad she isn't leaving that bubble questioning what could have been if she'd taken a chance on happiness. I don't know whether I'm glad I did or not yet, but I'm glad I'm not still questioning what if I had."

"Sometimes," Kate stammered, "sometimes it takes having everything you thought you wanted to realize what you really can't live without." Her words seemed to hang in the air for a moment as their truth registered on each face.

Cami

_C_ami stared at the dim glow of the alarm and tried to ignore the hole that was burning in her chest: 3:55, 3:57, 4:00. She hated mornings like these. It had been almost eleven years, but the pain was as fresh as it had been the morning she'd answered the call. When she concentrated, she could still feel his arms around her and hear his laugh. Of all days, she'd hoped not to start the first day on her new job feeling haunted. She shook her head and reminded herself that this pain was nothing new and would never go away. Reliving it on an important day like today wouldn't help or honor anyone, her included.

There would be no going back to sleep now, so she might as well get up and attack the day in a way that would make them both proud. Cami rubbed her temples and swung her legs over the side of the bed. She was nervous. If Blane were here, he'd grab their shoes and take her to "run it out." He would want her to be on her best game today. She rolled her stiff neck and walked into her closet. She ran for a lot of reasons, but his memory was the biggest of them. When she ran their paths, she could feel him beside her. She could picture his gait so clearly, hear his measured breaths, and all but see his huge, goofy grin when they cleared the first mile she always hated. When her pace dropped at the fifth mile, he would lengthen his stride to challenge her, then turn around, trotting backward, teasing and egging her on. "Come on, babe! You got this! Push!"

She threw a tank top over her sports bra and grabbed some Under Armour pants. She reached for her shoes on the rack and ran her hand over a well-worn pair of gray Nikes with neon yellow shocks. She knew they were an odd thing to keep, but they were him. She'd been through countless pairs of running shoes since he died, but each new pair sat by his. Besides, they were definitely less creepy than an urn.

Cami strapped on her shoes, grabbed some water, and headed out the front door. She inhaled deeply, then stopped short at the smell of fresh rain on the pavement. She could push past a lot of memories, but not this one. Not today. She sat down on the front step and let the cool air wash over her. The smell of the rain that morning had burned itself into her memory. It should be one of her happiest, not one of her most painful. She and Blane had been dating for almost two years at that point. She'd met him the same way she'd made most of her social connections in college—through Kate. He was Kate's brother, Cameron's, best friend and roommate. They met over Memorial Day when Kate and Cameron invited fifty of their closest friends to their family's beach house for the long weekend. At the time, they were both dating other people—he seriously, and she merely for the convenience of not having to go to every party alone in popular, pretty Kate's shadow.

The night they were introduced redefined everything she thought she wanted in her future. He was different than anyone she'd ever known. From second one, she couldn't stop smiling when he did. That was, at best, unnatural for her. The light in his eyes warmed her somehow. He was captivating and honest to a fault, all at the same time. They sat on a porch swing and talked for hours while Cameron and his other jock friends pounded beers around the bonfire and Kate and her band of beauties giggled and lounged nearby. Cami loved the way he walked so gracefully in the sand, even though he kept his hands shoved nervously into his pockets. He was attending school on a track scholarship, and had big dreams of coaching high school students to excellence. He told her he came from a long line of teachers and was excited to join the "family business." Cami told him about her dreams of becoming a photojournalist and snapping of-the-moment pictures that documented living history. She mentioned she was struggling to find the right project for her Fluid Movement final, and he invited her to photograph the recreational soccer team he coached on Saturdays. Cami agreed and went to the field the next weekend.

To her surprise, she found herself focusing her lens on the children's faces, instead of on their movements. She was struck by how they responded to him. Blane had such an easy way of connecting with them. She shot it all—their looks when he corrected them, the goals they made, their misses and falls, the bad calls, and the loss by one in overtime. When she developed the film, what struck her most was that when the kids looked at him, they saw themselves as successes. She broke up with her boyfriend that afternoon and was at every game for the rest of the season. Blane was conveniently single a week or so after that, and they began to date. She knew he was her match less than a month into the relationship. She loved that he challenged her even more than she challenged herself—something she hadn't thought was possible, given how doggedly competitive she was in everything she did. They trained together, studied together, played together, but, most important, they didn't accept anything less than each other's best. He was the first man who ever made her want to talk to work things out. Their mutual stubbornness and quick tempers gave them plenty of opportunities for that.

Regardless, they were inseparable. He took her home to meet his family almost immediately. Cami was nervous, but Carolyn, his mother, welcomed her with open arms, insisting anyone who made her son this happy was already like a daughter to her. His father patted her back and said he heard she was one hell of a math tutor and an even better forward on the basketball court. Blane blushed bright red and shoved his hands in his pockets. She fell in love with him a little more over that weekend. His home really was a family. She loved how down to earth each of them was. They were loud and full of anecdotes about their lives. They were quick to laugh, quick to tease, and even quicker to forgive. His mother got distracted chatting with Cami and torched the lasagna she was baking. As the smoke detector blared, the whole family laughed and yelled dinner was ready. One Chinese-food delivery later, they finished the evening kicking the soccer ball in the front yard with his sisters while his parents sipped sweet tea in lawn chairs on the porch. It was perfect.

Later, they all crammed onto a saggy sofa in the den to watch *The Cutting Edge*, a family favorite. Blane put his arm around her during the opening credits, and his sisters giggled. Cami blushed, noticing that they had the same shiny brown hair and smattering of freckles that he did, and shrugged his arm away.

Later that semester, Cami traveled with the track team whenever she could, and they spent the off-season weekends camping and hiking together. It was the best year of her life. After graduation, Kate was planning to move to New York to attend graduate school, and Cameron was taking a sales internship in Philadelphia. That left both of them with apartments they couldn't afford alone. In fact, Kate's father covered far more than Kate and Cameron's portions of the rent, in exchange for the good influence he felt the pair was on his children. Cami paid a mere $100 a month, and Blane $150. After weeks of searching, they finally found a small space they could afford together on her measly intern earnings and his first-year-teacher's salary. They didn't have much in the way of extravagances, but they had second-hand furniture, a washer and dryer, and each other. That was all they needed. Then came the rain.

Ellie

Ellie stared through the darkness at the sleeping man beside her. He looked peaceful with his arm stretched around her pillow and his chest rising and falling in a gentle steady rhythm. His eyelids fluttered, and a smile touched his lips. He was so beautiful. Ellie tried to chase the anxiety about the day's events from her mind and live in this moment. She wanted nothing more than to snuggle back into his arms and make love to him again, but there wasn't time. The day was breaking, and they would have to go. They had both known this moment would come.

She reached up to push a stray piece of hair from his forehead. He smiled again in his sleep and shifted closer to her. She wished she could pinpoint what it was about him that made her feel whole again. Her phone vibrated on the nightstand, and she reached for it instinctively. It was a message from Jess that the penthouse was in order and security would be ready for them by seven thirty. She looked from her phone to the alarm clock as the realization washed over her that they were living the last three hours of their bubble. It wasn't quite four o'clock. She knew she should sleep, but she didn't want to miss a moment. What if they couldn't survive the next part and this all became a memory? Everything else could wait for the next hour. Ellie ran her fingers from Pat's hair to his cheek and down his chest. He stirred beneath her touch as she followed the line of her hand with soft kisses over his neck.

"Mmmmmm," he murmured sleepily, and opened his eyes.

"Good morning." She tucked her hair behind her ear and smiled down at him.

"It's definitely off to a good start." He grinned, and she leaned to return her phone to the nightstand then shifted her knees to either side of his body. His eyes crinkled mischievously. "I thought you'd be all business this morning, Ms. Lindsay."

"Me too." She smiled. "But it turns out I have a highly capable team for that. I'm on a break at the moment."

Kate

$\mathcal{K}$ate cringed as she listened to her mother's voice mail.

"Hello, Katherine. It's Mother. I have decided to make a visit for Cameron's birthday. Don't worry, dear, I will stay at the Wilshire. I don't want to, um, crowd you and Kenneth. Also, I am bringing your grandmother with me. She wants to meet her great-grandson. I've told her you call him William, so please refrain from using that awful nickname in her presence. In fact, I've done a bit of research and it's still not too late to change it on the poor dear's birth certificate. We'll talk more when I arrive. Goodbye, darling."

She rolled her eyes and ran her hand over nursing Liam's wispy blond hair. A visit from her mother alone left her and Ken feeling as if they were stranded in a hurricane. Add her grandmother, and they might as well be weathering a tsunami. Kate looked down at her running shoes, feeling good about making a healthy choice to deal with last night's binge. She and Liam would use the jogging stroller for the first time. Then she would make herself lunch. Thirty minutes later, Liam was burped, changed, and cooing happily at the toys she'd hung over the stroller. Maybe this could be their new morning ritual. If he insisted on having her up at four forty-five every morning on the dot, they might as well be running by five thirty. Kate smiled as the elevator hit the lobby and she made her way to the intricately carved oak and glass doors.

"Good morning, Mrs. Stone!" The doorman smiled brightly. "Good morning, little Liam man!"

"Thank you, Jacob." She returned his warm smile and maneuvered through the door. The smell of rain fresh on the pavement hit her like a ton of bricks, and she stopped short before trotting on to avoid looking awkward. She prayed Cami hadn't gone for a run this morning, and then realized how ridiculous that prayer was. Of course she had. Kate could picture Cami waking up nervous about her first day and deciding to run one of her favorite paths. She could see her clipping in her earbuds and walking out of the door into the smell of rain. Why did it have to rain today, of all days? She wondered if Cami had powered through, or if she was in pain. Kate began to jog, and Liam cooed happily at the vibrations of the stroller. The wind felt cool and refreshing on her face as she picked up her pace. She wondered if she would ever become centered enough to focus solely on the joy that morning had brought, not on the immeasurable pain. She kicked her pace up another notch thinking about how much scheming Blane had done to surprise Cami on a seemingly ordinary Thursday morning. She would never forget his call weeks before, saying he'd asked his mother for his grandmother's ring and was going to propose to Cami. He wanted her to be there, as a surprise. Kate had squealed in excitement and booked a ticket back to LA within the hour. Blane had meticulously planned everything down to the last second. She and Cameron would hide around the bend of Cami's favorite trail. Blane would sprint ahead just before the curve and be waiting there, on bended knee, when Cami turned the corner. Kate would man the camera, and Cameron would toss Blane the ring as soon as he was in position.

It had gone off perfectly, except for the early-morning rain that glistened over the road and trees. Cami rounded the bend, pushing herself full throttle, only to stop abruptly at the sight of Blane kneeling, ring in hand, fifty feet in front of her. Kate remembered how striking the pictures were when Cami turned them to black and white. His brown bangs clung to his forehead with sweat, and his cheeks and freckles were flushed with exertion and excitement. Kate would never forget his humongous grin, or how shocked Cami had been. She had snapped what felt like a thousand pictures of the moment, but the words had been Blane's and Cami's alone to know. To this day, Kate didn't know what he'd said, but it was the first time she'd ever seen a tear run down Cami's cheek or heard her voice quiver.

Liam began to fuss, and she slowed to a stop. She doubled over in front of the stroller and put her hands on her knees to catch her breath. As she rearranged the blanket around him and fished a teething toy from the stroller pocket, she admonished herself for being so out of shape. Once he was content, Kate unzipped the pocket that held her phone and texted Cami before turning the stroller back toward the apartment.

1 New Text (To Cami Cell)
Thinking of you this morning. I'm here if you need me.
I know you will do great today in spite of the rain.

The proposal came two days before Cameron's twenty-fourth birthday. He had invited Blane and three other friends to spend the weekend in Malibu, riding Jet Skis and soaking up the local nightlife. Even before the proposal brought her to town a few days early, Kate and Cami had planned to spend the weekend together, catching up in Cami and Blane's cozy, albeit tiny, apartment while the boys were away. It was wonderful. Kate's father took them to dinner; then they sat up until 3:00 a.m. watching reruns of *The Golden Girls*, swapping stories, and laughing hysterically, just like in the old days. They both fell asleep on the couch, with the television blaring an old episode of *Friends*, around four.

The call came at six o'clock. Kate's phone buzzed on her knee, and she glared at it through the slit of an eyelid. It was her mother. When would she learn not to call before eight? Kate swore she called this early only to scan Kate's voice for hungover hoarseness, or to listen for signs that her boyfriend had spent the night, or for some other juicy disappointment she could chew on until Kate was forced to visit at Christmas.

She ignored her call and unkinked her neck from the no-longer-comfortable position it had been in when she had fallen asleep on the couch cushion.

"Are you going to answer that?" Cami grumbled, as Kate's phone rang again.

"Sorry—it's just my mother," she whispered, before flipping it open and pulling up the antenna. Cami grunted in annoyance and flopped over onto her other side. "Hello, Mom," Kate said hurriedly, hoping her mother could hear her over the beep of the low battery echoing down the line.

"Katherine. I've been trying to reach you." The phone beeped again. "Surely you did not forget to charge your cellular phone while traveling. Seriously, Katherine, if you're going to treat that phone as a plaything, your grandmother and I won't pay for it any longer." Kate went into Cami's room and began to dig through her suitcase for the charger.

"I'm sorry I missed your calls, Mother. I was in the shower. I did forget to charge it last night, but I will plug it in this morning."

"None of that matters now. I've been trying to reach you because something terribly unfortunate has happened involving your brother."

Kate's heart stopped as she crammed the charger's plug into the outlet. "Is everything okay?"

"Yes, everything is going to be fine. There was an accident involving Jet Skis. Cameron was thrown into the shore and sustained a concussion and a broken elbow. He was taken to the hospital, but he's going to be fine. The boy who was driving sustained the brunt of the crash, and far greater injuries. I'm telling you all of this because I don't want you to worry if people begin to talk. We're told there was some ugliness with the beach guard and a few local officers, but our lawyer assures us that the charges will be dropped and nothing will hit the papers."

"Who was driving?" Kate asked frantically, as a thousand scenarios involving Zac, Blane, and Harry tearing across the waves ripped through her mind.

"Harold's mother's heard from him and says he wasn't involved at all, and Zachary's mother is refusing to give the lawyers any details. As far as I'm concerned, she can pay her own legal bills if she wants to behave that way. Not that she can afford them now that Tom's left her. I've also uninvited them to the opening at the Greek."

"*Mother!* Who was driving? Was it Blane? Is he hurt?"

"Don't take that tone with me, Katherine Annette Grace! As if he even has any connections I could call. I'm telling you, everything is going to be fine! Your *fa-mi-ly* is going to be fine. Frankly, I'm disappointed in you. Why in the world would you go into some sort of tirade about Camille's live-in boyfriend when your own blood is lying in a hospital bed as well? You know how I feel about that." Kate's ears narrowed in on Cami's startled voice in the living room as her mother went on for the millionth time about how natural it was that graduate school had put some much-needed distance between her and the ill-mannered, poorly spoken Camille before she could hold Kate back further from her prospects.

Cami was on the phone . . . with Carolyn. Kate pressed the END button abruptly and flung open the bedroom door. Cami was ghost white, and the receiver was shaking in her hand, dial tone blaring. Kate didn't know what to do except go to her and hold her.

"What did she say?" Kate whispered, and smoothed Cami's hair. Cami opened her mouth to speak, but no sound came out. "Shh . . . it's going to be okay." Kate turned her gently toward the sofa and told her to sit.

"It's Blane. He's . . . he's in a coma. She . . ." Cami's voice was broken and tiny as she stared at nothing. "She said they're asking the family to say their goodbyes." Kate crushed her friend into the tightest hug she would allow and went to find her car keys. *Goddamn you, Cameron*, she thought, as she pushed her pain deep into the pit of her stomach.

Ellie

Ellie smiled at Pat as she watched his fingers move furiously. Her phone buzzed for the thirtieth time, and she typed a reply. They both stared intently at their screens, answering messages and responding to the business of the morning, while their car sped down the expressway. The driver stopped fourteen blocks before the Mandarin, and Ellie reached for Pat's hand. He pressed her wrist to his lips one last time before she lowered the privacy screen and slipped seamlessly into the waiting cab. Her phone screeched for her attention, and she answered it. Minutes later, she and Pat stood reunited at the garage-level service elevator, escorted by suited security. When they reached the penthouse, Pat asked the gentlemen to give them a private moment. The pair exchanged skeptical looks but stepped out of the elevator. As soon as the door closed behind them, Pat tugged at his collar and stumbled over his words.

"I just need a moment." He looked flustered as he pushed his hand through his hair. "I'm not ready for this."

"Pat." Ellie shifted her bag to her other shoulder and reached out to touch his sleeve. "There's no shame in being afraid. We'll get through this."

"It's not that." He stared at her, eyes pleading. "It's us. I'm not ready to let you go. It will never be like this again." He shut his eyes but didn't reach for her.

"I know." She shifted her bag again. She wanted nothing more than to press him against the wall and kiss him. "For what it's worth, I'm a little scared, too."

The head security guard tapped his fist to the elevator door just as she shifted her bag to pull him close. Pat pressed the button, and the door opened into the lower level of the penthouse.. *So it begins*, Ellie thought, as plastered smiles and fourteen pairs of eyes prepared to pounce.

Cami

$\mathcal{C}$ami walked into the sleek office and hoped she wasn't inheriting her predecessor's secretary. Experience told her that wouldn't end well. She settled into the black leather chair behind her new desk and looked at the gallery of framed awards and accolades she'd hung over the weekend. They looked foreign on this wall, and she wandered if they would bring her respect or date her in front of the young team she was about to meet.

A tap of knuckles on her door, followed by Dean Gatz's booming voice, brought her back to reality. "Beating the boss in on your first day? Good form, Clark." His face broke into a mischievous grin as he leaned casually against the door frame. She wondered how much effort it took to maintain that designer stubble.

"Thank you. I plan to make it a habit." She smiled as he stepped fluidly to the chair in front of her desk and took a seat.

"Good. That'll give the kids something to look up to." He crossed one long leg over the other and brushed a manicured hand across the breast of his suit. "Half of them come straggling in around ten o'clock, and the rest of them show up with varying degrees of hangovers around eleven. Drives me bat-shit crazy, but it's not a battle worth fighting. When I pitch a fit and demand creative meetings start at eight, the idiots are half-asleep and ridiculously unproductive. I've found it's more effective to let them show up when they're"— he stopped to roll his eyes—"*ready* and let them work into the wee hours than to force more traditional schedules on them."

"I understand. You should know I'm willing to stay late when needed, but I don't plan to work regularly into the night unless it's absolutely necessary." She crossed her legs to match his stance and gave him a wry grin. "That's what project managers are for."

Dean slapped his knee and proclaimed that they would get along beautifully.

Leila

Just breathe. You're here because of where you've been. They will stare at you through their designer glasses, but that's the point. You have the same pair. That's also why you're here. Smile, give your speech, and thank the Lord that even impossible dreams can come true with enough hard work. Do not confuse being accepted with being successful. You will never be one of them, and you never want to be. You want to be who you were with nothing when you have everything. Relax.

Leila fidgeted in her seat, trying to discreetly work her thong into a more comfortable position. If she'd been more on top of the laundry this week, she would've had comfy, functional, seamless underwear to wear so they wouldn't ride up when she climbed the stairs to the podium. She smiled a bit inside as the presenter who would ultimately call her name was introduced. If fighting the urge to pick her underwear out of her ass was the worst part of her day, this was a good day.

She blushed as he listed her accolades and tried to fight the indignation that her successes had to come before her story for this crowd to truly listen. She adjusted her glasses, knowing this wasn't the audience that had saved her but that they had the pocketbooks to fund the programs that had.

Photos of children in the reading programs and leadership academies the organization funded flashed across the screen. Their smiling faces reminded her she needed to be convincing. A particularly powerful montage of pictures followed a series of children from first grade, listing the services they received from Faces of Poverty and affiliates through their high school graduations. Under each cap-and-gown photo, the students' GPAs, awards, and college acceptance letters beamed. These young people were on their way to bringing better opportunities to future generations. They could very well be sitting in this chair one day, feeling grateful someone who'd never met them happened to believe in a cause that could change lives. After all, a benefit just like this one had funded Lenore's work after the fourth year of her mission, when the families she and the church served had begun to exceed the funds. An organization had shown her the light, but an individual had saved her.

Leila's name was called, and she wished she could evict the blush from her cheeks. She approached the podium and told herself she'd done this a hundred times before in her classroom. Cami and Norah would tell her that donors were donors and that they didn't matter. The place cards on the tables would change, but Faces of Poverty's goals wouldn't. Ellie would tell her not to give them the power to make her nervous, that she had earned the right to be among them and had earned the right to say no to them. She had earned that right with blood, sweat, and tears. Leila's heart began to race as she climbed the steps to the podium. "Good morning, and thank you for being here today," she began. "As Mr. Brackeen said, I serve on the governing board of the Faces of Poverty organization as a professor." She flashed a panoramic smile. "I could stand here and speak about teaching for hours, but I don't think there are enough mimosas in the beverage cart for that." A ripple of laughter went through the audience, and she relaxed into the story she'd told a thousand times. She told them about her childhood, about where she would be statistically if it hadn't been for the interventions Mrs. Lenore had set in place. She talked to them about the success stories in the making their donations were currently funding. A well-dressed man in the middle section yawned and tapped his watch at the man sitting across from him. She paused intentionally and waited to catch his eye. Maybe her classroom management wasn't that rusty after all.

"We're all here because someone took a chance on a dream. At one point in all of our family stories, there is an immigrant who was brave enough to lose sight of the shore, or an ordinary student who found his passion, or a tinkerer with a big idea. Regardless of the specifics, we are all here today because someone in our past wanted more and saw a path to achieve his or her dreams. If there weren't, our stories, even those of the wealthiest among us, would end where they began, and the majority of us would still be carrying European passports." The crowd chuckled again. "This organization does not find the dreamers among the masses. We teach the masses to dream and then show them the way out through education. We teach them to hold on to their dreams with what can best be described as stick-to-itiveness. We teach them that cycles can be broken. We pair them with role models in their communities and with "big brothers and sisters" in the program grades above them to serve as mentors and watchdogs. We create positive peer pressure and ingrain the need to give back early on. If we're honest with ourselves, we all know there's a block in every town that no one talks about. What many don't realize is that the children who live there believe their stories have already been written. Unlike your children and my children, they don't have that innate belief that their dreams will come true. They have only to look around them to know they rarely do, to know they're not getting very far."

She took a piece of construction paper cut into the shape of cloud from her folder and slid it under the document camera. The photo stream of children the organization currently served paused, and the childish handwriting on the cloud came into focus.

My name is *Annabelle*.
I am in *2nd grade.*
Today, my dream is *to have my own vacuum.*
This dream will come true when I *clean houses.*

"They have no idea they can start again and become the authors of their own life stories. When it comes to control, they have none. Let's give it to them. Education has to be a tangible way out if we want to make a difference. As of now, let's become advocates and break these cycles. It only takes one. Trust me. I know. And they need to know they can rewrite their endings just like I rewrote mine."

Leila surveyed the faces in the crowd as they stared up at the screen. "In closing, I would like to introduce you to a remarkably driven young woman." She looked to the side of the stage and nodded to a smartly clad twenty-two-year-old she'd had the pleasure of teaching. "Annabelle was referred to our program by her second-grade teacher. What you see on the screen was the first of what we call 'dream clouds' she filled out for us. She has been involved in the academic, leadership, and after-school outreach programs funded by Faces of Poverty since that year. She graduated from high school with honors and earned a scholarship from the Department of Mathematics at UCLA. This May, she will be the first in her family to graduate from college and has already been accepted into the university's MBA program. She is currently mentoring teenage girls in our middle and high school leadership programs. Annabelle is here today to explain how she plans to give back to her community via the programs you've funded, and to extend her own financial support upon graduation, in hopes of helping others. Please join me in welcoming Annabelle Chen."

Norah

*N*orah smiled as the whoosh of the fetal heartbeat filled the room. It didn't matter that this was likely the ten thousandth time she'd heard the sound—its magic never faded. There was nothing that quite compared to the hope and anticipation wrapped up in that steady beat. It was the sound of life surrounded by warmth, and of innocence cushioned and protected from the inside out.

The young father's eyes danced as he beamed down at his pretty wife. "Can you believe that's our daughter's heartbeat?" She looked from him to Norah, her face full of joy.

"Amazing, isn't it?" Norah held the Doppler in place for a few more seconds before wiping the sono-gel from her abdomen. Sharing this moment with her patients was her favorite part of every prenatal visit. Norah pushed the call button for Kelly, one of her nurses, then answered their remaining questions and emphasized how important the gestational diabetes test she would administer during the next visit was, given the patient's medical history. She bid them a warm goodbye as Kelly entered the room, carrying the neon-orange glucose solution, ready to explain the instructions for their next appointment.

Norah's phone buzzed in the pocket of her lab coat as she headed to the next room. She paused in the hallway to read the screen.

1 New Text (Jillan Cell)
Petra is set to scan you during lunch. Would u like me to be there?

Norah reached for the iChart by the door with a motion so practiced it had become automatic and typed a reply on her phone.

Ellie

*J*ess and Kipton, the head media liaison, were seated at the end of a large conference table, staring intently at a MacBook screen. Ellie stood behind them, nodding intermittently and scribbling notes onto a tablet with her stylus. Across the large room, Pat was standing on a block, his back to her, facing a three-paneled mirror. His arms were outstretched in what could best be described as a crucifixion position, while three sets of heads and hands tugged at the hem of his pants. He caught her eye in the reflection and flapped his arms like a bird, mouthing, *Caw, caw*. A laugh escaped Ellie's lips, and Jess's head whipped around to face her, then snapped toward Pat's reflection. He blushed, breaking into a giant grin, then lost his balance and almost fell from his perch.

Turning her back to Jess, she crossed the room to the large bay windows. The penthouse balcony prevented her from seeing the sidewalk below, but she knew it was overrun with fans and photographers. Attempting to keep their location under wraps was moot, given the number of lighting and technical crews who had been in and out of the hotel since early morning, preparing the interview spaces, and the cameramen and reporters who would be arriving over the next three hours to interview Pat and his castmates about *Life of Us*. The LAPD would keep the entrances and exits clear, but the hotel would remain surrounded until Pat's departure for the rest of the tour on Wednesday. The leeches were there, hoping to get "the shot," or any shot, of him, but they would settle for a candid of his costars. At the moment, everyone else in the film was a no-name. Come tomorrow, the leeches would have propelled them from obscure to little-known to up-and-coming.

Ellie gritted her teeth, knowing how much worse things could get if the interviews didn't go well, or if she and Pat were discovered. In the same instant, she chastised herself for not having assigned recruiters to the other *Life of Us* talents. Smaller firms surely had. Then again, it might not be too late. A short-term investment and a little vulturing on her part could pay big dividends if they rode Pat's coattails to . . .

"Ellison?" Ellie jumped at the sound of Jess's voice behind her. She must get her nerves under control. "May I have a private moment?"

"Of course." Ellie gave her a nod and smoothed her skirt. "We can slip into the dining room off of the main suite." Jess nodded and turned on her heel in that direction. Once they were in the room, Ellie motioned for her to sit. Something in Jess's demeanor this morning made her feel uneasy. She would remain standing and keep her authority.

"As you know, we've been keeping close tabs on the networks, social media, print media, et cetera, since the photo went viral. I feel we've been as proactive as possible, especially in regard to the alleged engagement and pregnancy, but it hasn't been as effective as we'd like."

"Are we talking damage control?" Ellie asked pointedly, and leaned purposely against the table behind her. "Define *effective*."

"Yes. Scarlett's team is fanning the fire from all sides that he used and exploited her. They're saying he lured her into an affair, convinced her to separate from her husband with a proposal, then ultimately destroyed her marriage, before refusing responsibility for the child. In fact, there's a picture of him and Scarlett at the last *Destiny* film premiere that's set to hit this afternoon. It's just a rope shot of the cast and everyone involved in the soundtrack, but his arm is around her and they've edited the background, along with everyone else, out of the shot. You know how they'll spin it. On top of that, pictures of the ring, on her left ring finger, have dominated the entertainment networks for the last thirty-six hours, despite our best efforts. Whoever is running her media camp is pitting her fans against Pat's all over the blogosphere, literally drawing teams."

"Do we know who it is?"

"No." Jess uncrossed and re-crossed her legs. "Believe me, I've tried to find out. I want him or her working for us."

Ellie stared harder into Jess's eyes, at once glad and apprehensive that she could predict her thoughts. "So, you're telling me our efforts haven't triggered the waves we want. Your reports tell me they've been successful, so my question is, where do we stand?"

"The entertainment networks are having a field day with the fan face-off. It's getting ugly. Then, of course, there's Camp *Destiny*." Jess paused, and they exchanged a knowing look. "They've been vicious in protecting Pat and antagonizing Scarlett's followers. Their loyalty is unmatched, but for every five"—she rolled her eyes and lifted her fingers into air quotes—"*Pat*riots, there's a tech-savvy goon who utterly detests all things related to Patrick Grayson and the *Destiny* franchise trolling up negativity all over the Web. It goes without saying that we would normally ignore all of this, but the memes and YouTube spin-offs are starting to compromise our goals."

"I see. Our best bet is to handle this the same way we would a bad *SNL* skit. His fans know he can laugh at himself. If anything, he's been in the hot seat for poking too much fun at Lucas Lucien and the *Destiny* films during interviews. Once they see that, they should lay off and let it blow over. Our goal is not to alienate that fan base. We need to bring them into this film, and into his future work."

"Of course." Jess's voice was steady, but her pursed lips gave her away.

"Is there anything else I need to know?" Ellie fought the urge to tap her foot and narrowed her eyes.

"Yes. There is." Jess's voice quivered for a half a beat. "And I'm afraid it's my fault." Ellie steadied herself for whatever she was about to say. "Stacie refused to sign the new NDA."

Ellie's eyes widened as images of the kiss Stacie had interrupted flashed through her head—shirtless Pat, the island, and her legs around his back—not to mention what she had likely seen from the office window when they were on the balcony. "When she returned to the office that afternoon, I told her she was to meet with Frank from legal and then to report to my office. I didn't confirm with Frank before I met with her. When she came to me, I told her I was reassigning her to another team, as a probationary measure, and that she would be fired if she disobeyed my instructions again. I admit I was harsher than was probably necessary."

"And what did she say?" Ellie's stomach wrenched at the effort it took to maintain control of her voice.

"She was smug and cryptic. She said she had decided to pursue a change of industry. Into *insurance*. The way she smiled when she said it . . . I don't know what happened. My instincts went haywire. Then she quit."

Norah

"Thank you, but I'm fine. I'll grab something at the hospital later." Norah smiled and thanked Molly for her offer as she reached for the chart. The day had been typical, calmer than most, even, but she was already tired. She blinked and swiped the iChart open. Forcing the cobwebs of fatigue from her mind, she banished the feeling that her life at the moment was just like these rooms—a revolving door of different faces and different problems waiting on her to answer them and make decisions. Her stomach growled in answer, and she ignored it.

"Hi, Dr. Merritt!" Janie's face lit up, and Norah smiled back at her. Janie would always be one of her favorite patients. Here she was, beaming, three days past her due date with baby number four and waiting on a cervical check. She had come to Norah via a referral from another patient after being told her second child was unviable. She'd followed her instincts, canceled her D&C, and sought a second opinion. Norah would never forget reading the scan. It was cloudy at best and could easily have been mistaken for a molar with a quick look at the markers, but she simply wasn't sure. The IUD was still in place, but the labs were unsubstantial. Norah would forever cherish the expression on Janie's face when she told her that she disagreed with her previous physician and that the TVU she'd ordered confirmed she was merely in the earliest stages of pregnancy. Janie had cried happy tears, and Norah had put her hand on her shoulder, explaining that miscarrying was still a heightened threat in this situation, but the embryo was healthy at five weeks' gestation. The IUD removal had been successful, and Baby Caden was now four.

The sound of the fetal heartbeat filled the room again, and Janie closed her eyes. She looked so centered and serene.

"This really is our last baby, so I'm trying to soak up that sound while I can."

"There's nothing quite like it, is there?" Norah smiled, noted the calculation, and pressed the call button. A minute later, Jillan was in the room.

"Hello, lovely! I was hoping to see you today."

"Well, there's a lot of me to see," Janie joked, and patted her round belly.

"You definitely wear it well," Norah said sincerely, and stretched a glove onto her hand.

"At this point, I am considering having business cards drawn up that say PROFESSIONAL PREGGO AND LACTATOR."

Norah laughed. "I'd add AND EFFORTLESSLY FABULOUS to that. You know the drill. Heels together, knees apart."

"You're sweet, Dr. Merrit. I've been really uncomfortable this morning. Here's hoping he's on his way. If he waits much longer, he'll be able to walk himself to the nursery from labor and delivery."

"Come on, sweet baby number four." Jillan grinned and blew on fictitious dice as Norah finished the exam.

"Jillan's magic works again. You're at five centimeters, ninety-five percent effaced, zero station." Norah beamed at the mixture of surprise and delight on Janie's face. "Let's send you over and get ready to meet this baby today."

Minutes later, Janie was on her way to the hospital. Norah and Jillan stepped into the quiet that was the hallway during the lunch hour.

"I guess you're up next, Doc," Jillan said, in an uncharacteristically hushed voice. Norah looked into her eyes and nodded, feeling as if she were free-falling from her professional life into her personal life without a parachute. She forced herself to breathe steadily and turned her head toward the ultrasound suite. That door might as well be a threshold between the hell of isolation she was living and the aftermath of all she'd done. She looked back at Jillan, feeling the blood rising in her cheeks as the realization that she didn't want to be alone during the scan, much less in any of this, hit home. Her heart was pounding.

"Still want to be my stirrup buddy?"

"You know it." Jillan's eyes crinkled, and something in her face made Norah almost believe everything was going to be fine. Almost.

Ellie

$\mathcal{P}$ATSON IS A DILF!!!!! Ellie stared through the tinted windows at the mob of screaming fans holding a rainbow of neon posterboard. LET ME BE YOUR SCARLETT LETTER!! She'd been to this set at least a hundred times, with clients who were higher profile than Pat, but she'd never seen anything quite like this. Not here. This was a veritable madhouse. I'M YOUR *DESTINY*, PAT!

"Not acceptable." Jess spoke into her Bluetooth and jotted a note on her phone. Ellie knew she was working even more diligently than usual. Part of her wanted to be furious that Jess had allowed things to escalate so far with Stacie, but the bigger part of her understood why she had. Ellie knew what it was like to work yourself to the bone, to go above and beyond your position to prove yourself, only to think you've made it and then have it all end in a simple mistake with your name on the line. She could have easily fired Jess for this misstep, but she would rather keep her on as the hardworking apprentice she already was and benefit from the newfound gratitude that would keep her in the firm longer. Jess was constantly headhunted, and it was only a matter of time before someone would woo her. Ellie chuckled inside, thinking it would not be the money that cost her Jess, but the power. She didn't have much further to climb at EP.

Her phone buzzed with a text from Pat, and she tilted the screen from Jess's view.

1 New Text—Patrick Grayson Cell
Tell me I'm ready for this. I can't remember being this nervous before an interview since the hand double who played guitar for me in *Destiny* posed as me rolling a joint in that video that went viral.

Reply—
That should have been your publicist's problem. You're ready. Trust me and stick to the script.

1 New Text—Patrick Grayson Cell
Thank you. I will.

The curtness of his digital words took her away from her e-mail and back to this moment. She shook her head, realizing that even though his car was barreling a mere one thousand feet in front of hers, full of a team of "frenemies" standing to make a buck, he felt alone. She had failed to really read his words. Sure, he needed her professional assurance that he was ready for tonight, but he also needed her support as his girlfriend. He needed her, not her position. She would see him soon, but there wouldn't be a private moment to make it right.

1 New Text—To—Patrick Grayson Cell
I'm sorry. Yes, you're ready. You'll be fine. They're good at following our script, but even when they aren't, they keep it light. It's the reason they get so many of my first interviews. I miss you, and I promise this isn't my favorite thing to do.

1 New Text-Patrick Grayson Cell
1/2 Good to know :) All of it, that is.
2/2 And what is your favorite thing to do. For the record?

Ellie smiled briefly at his reply and turned her phone facedown on her knee as she finished composing an e-mail to her lawyer. She closed her eyes for a moment and hoped she was preventing, rather than creating, heartache for the people close to her.

1 New Text—To -Patrick Grayson Cell
I thought you knew. My favorite thing to do is you. For the record.

1 New Text—From-Patrick Grayson Cell
Likewise. Should I mention that tonight?

1 New Text—Patrick Grayson Cell
Patrick Grayson fun fact #654: clowns and marionettes give me the creeps. This is me.

Ellie laughed inside and tapped a reply.

1 New Text—To-Patrick Grayson Cell
You should know I shave my arms. This is me.

Ellie proofed her e-mail, flagged it as urgent, and set read receipts to notify her when her attorney read it. Meanwhile, a million different scenarios and consequences swirled through her mind.

Norah

"Exciting times, Dr. Merritt." Petra grinned and closed the door behind her. Norah slipped off her scrub bottoms and underwear and slid onto the table. It was her turn under the paper drape. A moment later, Petra knocked on the door out of habit and stepped into the room, followed by Jillan.

"Thank you for staying through lunch." Norah forced her calmest voice and knitted her fingers together. "I'll owe you both a proper sit-down meal soon."

Petra's perky voice was almost a singsong as she typed Norah's name and LMP into the query boxes on the screen and rolled the condom onto the ultrasound wand. Norah had had at least five TVUs during her and Matt's struggle with infertility, but she couldn't shake the surreal feeling that she would never be the same after this one. "Honestly, I was so excited when Jillan asked me to stay. I am just thrilled for you and Matt."

"Thank you," Norah said, and Jillan shot her a cautious look.

"Is he coming? Should I wait?" Petra smiled and gestured with her free hand.

"No, he can't make this one," Jillan answered graciously, and stepped closer to the table.

"No problem. Dr. Merritt, you know the drill." Norah scooted toward the end of the table and put her feet in the stirrups.

"Are you ready?" Petra asked.

"Yes." Norah answered absentmindedly, as her eyes focused on the monitor.

"Here we go." Petra inserted the probe into her vagina, and Norah wiggled her toes for distraction at the pressure. The screen turned from black to shades of gray. Her eyes searched the images, scanning every inch like an eagle scouting its prey. Her left ovary had clearly ovulated. Petra chattered lightly, all the while taking the routine pictures and measurements. Normal size. No enlargement. No fibroids. *Angle the wand*, Norah pleaded silently, until, at last, she centered on a clump of tissue. Petra smiled and toggled the volume button. In an instant, the steady heartbeat filed the room. Jillan's hand found hers as she stared speechlessly at the screen. At the tiny clump of cells that had just changed her life. At the heartbeat she had heard, loved, and delivered a thousand times. Her own heart pounded as her eyes grew wider and wider at the data Petra was gathering. CRL-22mm. Her mind panicked through the gestational age calculation $GA=-0.0007(CRL)2 +.1584 (CRL)+5.2876$, as Petra sang, "Gestational age: ten weeks, three days!" and typed *B-A-B-Y!!!!* in all caps next to the embryonic sack.

The overlap. She had conceived during the overlap.

"Breathe." Jillan's voice shook her from her focus. "Just listen to the heart." Her chest wrenched at the rhythmic sound, and she knew, no matter what happened next, she was changed forever.

Ellie

*E*llie stared at the monitor in the green room. All was going well so far, excepting a gag in the opening monologue when Stan Goldberg announced that Patrick Grayson was this evening's guest, then fanned open his suit jacket to reveal a line of blue and pink bubblegum cigars in the breast pocket. Ellie hoped that was the only surprise in store.

Monologue and second commercial insert finished, Goldberg bowed theatrically and jogged from his seat to the interview table. "Nation, please join me in welcoming the little-known Patrick Grayson to the show." Laughter mixed with prompted applause filled the studio, and Pat reached to shake his hand. The crowd quieted on cue, and Goldberg cleared his throat. "All right. I'm just going to come right out and say it. You, sir, have made my show's LA Vacay a living hell." He gestured to the screen behind them as it morphed from the show's logo into a live feed of the crowds gathered behind the barricades. "At first, I thought I'd pissed Jay Leno off."

Pat drug his hand through his hair and said, "Yeah, I'm, er, sorry about that." The dimpled grin that had made him famous crossed his face as he shifted in his seat. Ellie smirked and thanked God he was somehow even more charismatic when he was nervous. It was endearing. Too bad she couldn't say the same for all of her clients when they found themselves in the hot seat.

"This is probably just a normal day for you, isn't it?" The camera feed panned over the mob, stopping on a group of perfectly tanned blondes wearing Lucas Lucien bikinis. "And if so, can I be your best friend? Pretty please?" The audience laughed and catcalled.

"Sure." Pat's smile crinkled his eyes. "We can form some sort of duo. Fight crime and the like." He grinned again at the ever-in-character Goldberg.

"Hmm. A gorgeous, chiseled, glasses-wearing reporter by day, and a caped hero by night." Goldberg raised an eyebrow at the camera and stroked his chin as the audience tittered. "It seems like it's been done before."

Pat chuckled. "True, but that was a one-man show. Not a duo." Ellie willed them to get back on script. Getting carried away in an interview on the heels of a scandal rarely ended well.

"Ah! And they shall call us GolPat, cleaning up the streets with superhuman charm. And"—Goldberg put his hand to the side of his face in a faux aside—"what exactly is your superpower?"

Pat shifted and pushed the rolled sleeve of his dress shirt farther up his forearm. Ellie would need a drink after this one. "Hell if I know. Smoldering, perhaps?" he said, and shrugged his shoulders self-deprecatingly.

"I suppose if that doesn't work, we can always take down the barricades and release the mob of Pat-riots." The audience roared with laughter.

"Indeed." Pat reached for his mug.

Do not insult your fans. Do not insult your fans, Ellie willed silently.

"Flying monkey–style."

"Fuck." Jess whispered.

"Combine them with Goldberg Nation, and we'll be unstoppable." Pat smiled and held out his balled hand for a bump. Goldberg's fist crossed the desk toward Pat's, all but touching it, before he drew it back to smooth his hair in an exaggerated gesture. He looked straight at the camera, sucked a prolonged breath through clenched teeth, and said, "Yeah, I'm gonna have to pass. Turns out I have my own Super PAC." The audience laughed again as he re-extended his fist. "No hard feelings?"

"None taken." Pat said jovially as the lights came up signaling a short production break. Goldberg leaned in, covered the mic on his lapel, and whispered something into Pat's ear.

"Should one of us go out there during the break?" Jess asked.

"No. Not here," Ellie answered, without taking her eyes from the screen. She sensed Jess disagreed but was still too cautious from the morning's events to argue. Ellie knew this in-studio audience was probably the most diverse, and the least loyal, Pat would see on the first leg of the tour. A publicist speaking in his ear now would be the kiss of death on the Internet. She could see the captions now. "We're better off just letting it play out." So far, as much as she hated the deviation from her script, he wasn't doing terribly. They could spin this. The *Destiny* fan base had forgiven him for poking fun at the fanatical following of the franchise, and at his character, several times before. As long as he didn't completely alienate them or totally botch the next two and a half minutes, he might even earn a few new fans and some new respect.

The lights flickered, and the camera feed re-centered on Goldberg and Pat. The audience clapped and chanted, "Stanley, Stanley," before subsiding at the lighted cue and Goldberg's raised hand.

"Welcome back, Nation. Patrick Grayson is our guest tonight." Goldberg swiveled in his chair and pretended to crack his knuckles. "Now that we're bros, I feel like we can get—as your people would say—down to the nitty-gritty. In English, we say *to the point*." The audience laughed, and the screen behind them came to life again. This time, it was a picture of Pat and another of the *Destiny* leading men, signing autographs and pushing through a mob of clothes-ripping fans as they left a Manhattan restaurant. "It appears you are a reincarnation of some sort. Perhaps a Beatle?" Goldberg raised an eyebrow emphatically. "Or"—he swiveled again—"cue it!" A collage of all the starlets Pat had been linked to over the years filled the screen. "Perhaps you're Prince Charming, endlessly trying on fair maiden after fair maiden, looking for the right, shall we say, fit?"

Ellie looked at Jess, who went promptly to the wet bar and poured them each a glass of vodka over ice.

"That's quite nice. Mind if I use that?" Pat quipped, and the audience laughed. "The truth is—"

"Wait, wait! This just in." Goldberg held his other hand to his ear, as if tuning in to a headset. "'PatSon gives exclusive interview to Stanley Goldberg.'"

Pat laughed again. "The truth is I'm not your typical Hollywood playboy, regardless of what the papers want you to believe."

"Newspapers are inanimate, Bro. They are incapable of lying."

"That's true." Pat shifted with a laugh and continued. "But their editors, or their pocketbooks, love the idea of me bashing around the globe with a different woman in every time zone when the truth is, I'm actually terribly boring in that respect."

Ellie allowed her shoulders to relax by a modicum. This was somewhat on script. Her fingers tightened around the cold glass as she tried to ignore the irony of the situation. For once, she was selling who a client really was, yet here she stood, terrified of what he might say.

Goldberg gestured to the screen and shrugged his shoulders. "Oh, really?" He craned his neck toward the collage as the image changed to one of Pat lying beside a bronzed beauty on a beach, then to one of him and another actress, dressed to the nines, posing on the red carpet. "You don't seem to look lonely there, or there, or definitely not with your hand there." The audience roared at a shot of Pat sitting courtside at a Nicks game with his arm draped around Blythe Barrett, his fingertips dangling dangerously close to the bottom of the low-cut V-neck dress she was wearing.

Pat blushed and put his hand to his forehead, covering his face in a mixture of laughter and embarrassment. The audience *awwww*ed, but Ellie knew the sarcastic undertone and pseudofandom could go either way.

"All right, bro." Pat gave a forced but convincing smile. "I say this to you now, not because I'm in a heap of shit." He tugged at his collar and added, "Can I say that?"

"Fuck if I know," Goldberg countered into the camera. Jess grinned, and Ellie shot her a death ray.

"Agreed." Pat laughed again. "Not because I'm in a heap of shit over my recent, um, skiing holiday, but because I feel young girls make up a good chunk of my fan base, and if I could tell them one thing . . ." He looked into the camera. "Girls?" His eyes darted to the side of the set, toward the exit to the green rooms. Ellie and Jess held their thumbs posed over their phones, ready for damage control in the tense air. There was no way he could get back on script now. "It's to have a ridiculous amount of fun falling in love. Fall in love over and over again, get carried away, shout it from the bloody rooftops."

Ellie hit the group-message button on her phone and typed "911."

"But don't give your body away as often as your heart. I promise I certainly don't. All of the beautiful women you see here can attest to that fact. Wait. Be courted. Then wait a moment more. Give the nice guys like me a chance not to finish last, for a change."

Goldberg grinned and put his hand to his forehead. "On behalf of dads of daughters everywhere, I offer you a tip o' my hat, good sir."

"Bro, rather." Pat extended his fist and smiled.

"Right." Goldberg grinned and bumped his knuckles. "So, you're telling me I won't be needing these?" He opened his jacket and ran a pink bubblegum cigar under his nose.

"Not so much. Well, not for me, anyway." Pat's cheeks flushed in an instant, and Goldberg transitioned seamlessly into a plug for *Life of Us* before ending the interview. Ellie's thumb hovered, paralyzed, over her message. She had spent so much time and energy trying to spin him out of an adultery scandal, when she should have been spinning who he really was.

Norah

Norah shut the door to her office and walked to her chair. Holding the ultrasound film in one hand and her phone in the other, she tried not to think about how different this moment should have been. How different it could have been. Here she sat, on the heels of the news she'd waited years to hear, staring at her phone and trying to decide whom to disappoint first. She would give herself a minute to sit and reflect, and then she would make a plan.

Outside her door, the hallway was slowly coming to life as the nurses and staff filed in from lunch. The next block of patients would be in rooms soon, and then she would be at the hospital. Norah rubbed her temples and visualized the tiny blurb on the ultrasound picture. A soft knock at the door brought her back to reality.

"Come in." She smoothed her hair and sat up straighter.

"It's just me." Jillan opened the door and stepped into the room. She smiled as she pulled it closed behind her. "I won't interrupt for long, but can I throw in my two cents?"

"Of course."

"Take my advice with a grain of salt, but I couldn't walk by your door, knowing you were in here alone, and not say it. I can only imagine how difficult this all must be, but what if, just for the next few minutes, you lived *this* moment like you always wanted it to be? Obligations aside. Let it be just about you for a second. Pick up your phone and call someone who you know will be over the moon at the news, no matter what the circumstances. You deserve it. The rest can wait."

"Thank you, Jillan." Norah stared back at her. "I needed to hear that."

"No charge for this session."

Norah picked up her phone again and took a picture of the ultrasound film.

Text—To Leila Cell-
A pic from my lunch break. I hope you like it.

Norah imagined the look on Leila's face when she opened the picture. If she listened closely, she might even hear her squeal from across town. The ultrasound stared back at her as the hallway outside her door began to bustle with assorted voices. Her lips crept into a smile as she turned the picture facedown and stood from her chair.

Text—To Mom Cell
Can you meet me tonight? More than likely at Mercy or near there. I have good news, but it's complicated.

Cami

Cami sat at the head of the conference table and surveyed the faces around her. This must be the hipster trend she kept hearing about. They all seemed to have dragged a stylist and a tailor to the Goodwill.

"Good morning. It looks like most of us are here, so let's get started." Dean smiled and shot Cami a sarcastic look. "I'd like to introduce you to our new creative director. This is Camille Clark. I've recruited her from InFocus, our primary competitor in the current markets. My expectation is that she drive you hard to meet our deadlines and expand our business. If you're compliant and committed to being part of the team, you'll stay. If not, she has my permission to clean house." He met every eye around the table and grinned. "Let me pass on a piece of advice from my divorce attorney: choose your battles and your enemies wisely."

Cami was surprised by how unaffected their young faces seemed. At their age, in an entry- to mid-level position, she could not have jumped high enough for her bosses. And she never would have shown up to work in jeans and Converse. As Kate always said, never dress for the position you have; dress for the position you want. Dean gestured to her, and she stood.

"Thank you. It's a pleasure to be joining Gatz, Ferris, and Heart. The binders in front of you contain my plans and a projected schedule for the remainder of the art campaigns currently in progress." Her words were met with rolled eyes and slouched shoulders.

"Well, I'll leave you to it, then." Dean gave her a look that said, *I told you so*, and left the conference room. A shaggy-haired boy drummed the fingers of one hand on the cover of the folder in front of him and took out his phone with the other. Cami looked from him to the empty chairs of the three photogs who hadn't even bothered to show up.

"Good—you're ready to take notes." His eyes met hers for the first time. "I was just about to ask someone to take the meeting's minutes for the absentees."

"No, thanks." He blew his bangs up in protest and raised an eyebrow. "I'm not a secretary."

"No, you're not. They work far harder." She narrowed her eyes at him, and the young woman next to him chuckled. "For future reference, if everyone is here, no one will need to record the minutes. Peer pressure—use it for good, not evil. Now, where were we? Please turn to the budget graphs on page two."

Kate

Kate was on air when she carried Liam into the now-spotless apartment. She'd taken a hiatus from their cleaning service after deciding to stay home with him. She laughed, thinking how logical the decision had seemed before he was born. *Ken, let's put what we're paying the maid service into a vacation fund. I'll be home and can clean while he naps. It shouldn't take more than an hour or so a day to keep clean.* How very, very wrong she'd been. Norah's text about sending her housekeeper for the day had come at just the right time, when Kate had been mid-panic about getting the place ready for her mother and grandmother's visit in less than twenty-four hours. No matter how early she woke up or how late she stayed awake, she could never seem to get on top of everything. There simply weren't enough hours in the day. Now that the house was clean, maybe she and Ken could have date night in. She could use a good back rub before stress knots one and two arrived, and before she had to see the tortured shell of Cameron.

Leila

*L*eila's heart skipped a beat at the picture of Norah's sonogram. She beamed down at the tiny blurb, thinking how blessed it would be to have Norah as a mother, no matter what the future brought. She typed a text and then decided a voice mail was in order.

"Hi, Norah. Please don't think I expected you to answer this call, but a text just wasn't enough. I want you to know I am so happy for you. Thank you for sharing such a special moment with me. I realize how complicated things must be right now, but just remember, this isn't the first plot twist we've been through together. The next chapter will be amazing, regardless of the cast."

> 1 New Text—To Kate Cell
> Norah's text about sending Veronica to clean for you made me smile. I'd like to add to it. The girls and I will be by to watch Liam at 5:00. Ken is expecting you at Zapata's. Happy Kate Day!

Leila pressed SEND and smiled. Kate and Ken deserved a break. If nothing else, maybe it would take their minds off the impending visit. Her own mother was certainly no picnic, but Kate's mom was absolutely brutal. Every time she left, Kate struggled, Cameron had episodes, and Ken vented to Wes. The woman was the only thing that could make the anniversary of Blane's death worse for Kate, Cami, and everyone who loved them.

Norah

1 Missed Call (Leila Cell)
1 New VM (Leila Cell)

1 New Text (Kate Cell)
I cannot tell you how much of a blessing Veronica was this morning. Thank you x 1 million for sending her!!! The house might actually be ready for the firing squad now!

Norah slipped her phone back into her coat and walked toward the break room to raid the fruit basket for a quick eat on her way to the hospital. Truth be told, she owed Kate twice as much as a day of housekeeping, given what an absent friend she had been to her lately. Besides, it was high time Matt began cleaning up his own messes. If he and the girl didn't want to live in the filth they'd created, he could always hire someone himself.

"Caffeine break?" Deidre smiled and held the door for her.

"You know it." Norah raised her eyebrows and ducked into the room. The acrid smell of Mexican to-go boxes and microwave dinners slammed into her nose as if she'd sprinted face-first into a brick wall. Water and bile sloshed against her teeth, and she knew there was no containing it. She doubled over the trash can just inside the door as Meagan, her partner's nurse, stopped in her tracks, half-eaten paleo canned chicken in hand.

"Dr. Merrit! Are you okay?"

"Yes. I'm fine. I apologize for ruining your lunch." She stood up straight and held her hand under the sanitizer knob on the wall. Three minutes and a trip to the restroom later, her mouth was rinsed and she was en route to Mercy. The office rumors would be flying now.

Ellie

"The Mandarin, please." Ellie climbed into a cab forty-five minutes after Pat left the studio. Jess would counsel him in the morning, on the way to Ellen's set, about what could have gone better. She would fight the urge to mention any of that tonight. If this was going to work, they would both have to learn to balance their personal and professional roles in each other's lives. The cab ride was short but gave her the time to argue with her attorney about serving Stacie the NDA papers.

1 New Text, From Patrick Grayson Cell
Missing you tonight. Wishing I were in your arms, waterfront.

Text—To Patrick Grayson
Are you sure you're not just lonely?

1 New Text, Patrick Grayson Cell
Positive. That's not how I roll. Remember? LOL.

Ellie smiled at the thought of surprising him. He wasn't expecting her. The screen flashed again, this time with a confirmation that Anne, her personal assistant, had scheduled a delivery for Cami in the morning. She couldn't believe another year had gone by. Ellie usually requested that Anne send something fitness related, like a BodyBugg or a gift certificate to the most popular marathon du jour, but this year she had simply sent a bottle of scotch that was old enough to buy its own scotch.

Blane would have been thirty-four, and they would have been married ten years. Ellie might not have had the pleasure of meeting Blane, but she would never forget the first day she'd met Cami, and later Kate.

It had been nine years now, but the words *Stephen's Ministry* on a dry-erase board in the community meeting room of the YMCA still lived in her memory. They had both come to listen, not to share, but the room's energy compelled Ellie otherwise. During the coffee break, she gravitated toward Cami. Grief was grief, but they were definitely among the youngest in the room of parents and widowers. Over the next few weeks, they began to meet up for drinks and lunches. Cami understood why Ellie was working like a dog to climb the ladder in the world of PR. Everything she had done since Sherri's death was meant as her own tribute to a life cut short. Cami was doing the same thing.

Months later, Cami introduced her to Kate and Ellie knew it was a sign of trust. Kate meant the world to Cami. Their bond was as strong as that of any set of biological sisters, maybe even stronger, given that they'd consciously chosen each other. She stared at the concrete jungle passing by her window, trying not to think about who Sherri would have been today. Would she be living in Manhattan, like she'd always planned? Ellie did her best to brush aside the burning pain that her question would never be answered. Years ago, a grief counselor had warned her that every day would be hard in its own way, but the hardest part of losing someone so young often came when the living ran out of predictable coming-of-age milestones, like an eighteenth birthday or high school graduation, and could no longer connect to where the person would have been in life. Moments like these held a sadness all their own.

Ellie remembered how much harder her grief journey had become the second May after Sherri's death. It was the summer she would have graduated from Stanford. Ellie winced at the memory of sitting stone-faced during the commencement until her name was called to accept the honorary degree being conferred on Sherri. She would never forget mustering every ounce of strength her eighteen-year-old soul was capable of to walk across that stage with her head held high. In the moment when she crossed the podium, her forced smile became genuine and finally touched her eyes. For a few, brief seconds, she swore she could feel Sherri walking beside her. The thousands of eyes watching her, pitying the family, and thanking God it hadn't been their child melted away, and a soothing warmth washed over her. Something in the fibers of her soul told her they had walked the stage together.

Ellie closed her eyes and tried to relive the warmth that had engulfed her that day. There was nothing she wouldn't give to be able to talk to Sherri right now. To call and tell her about the entire Pat situation. Ellie knew Sherri would listen without judgment. She cringed again imagining Sherri as a mother. She would be like Leila, lending an ear to the little stuff about ladybugs and dragons and imagined boo-boos, regardless of how trivial or inconvenient the complaint, and knowing that those bonds would one day help her children to discuss the hard stuff when their problems got bigger.

Ellie checked the clock on her phone. The last eighteen, adrenaline-fueled hours were starting to take their toll on her nerves. The cab driver honked and weaved through the congested traffic surrounding the hotel, and she wished she were going home to her quiet little piece of paradise.

1 New Text—From Patrick Grayson Cell
Turns out you can hear the ocean from here too. LOL. I believe the kids call this a selfie.

Ellie enlarged the picture attached to the text and laughed. He had taken a photo of himself in the bathroom mirror, holding a sea-shell-shaped soap to his ear. She began typing a sarcastic comment about the toilet seat being left up in the background, when another text lit up her screen.

1 New Text—Marcus Cell
Hey. Sorry to be a pain, but you're PA won't give me a straight answer. Do u want you're sessions next week or can I fill them?

You're—you are. Ellie exited out of the message, irritated he had texted her personally, instead of waiting for an answer from her PA. Her private and public lives might as well be teetering between the front and back burners of a stove at the moment, and she had no idea what the next week's out-of-office commitments would be. It had taken ten e-mails between her admin and her PA just to get a haircut and a session with her stylist on the books for next week.

1 New Text—To Marcus Cell
Fill them.

Then again, maybe it was a sign. Here she was, for the second time, allowing her personal life to threaten all she'd built, and now rebuilt, professionally. The cabbie honked again and slid into the line of cars waiting to drop their guests in front of the hotel atrium. She packed her electronics and brushed away the fact that she'd referred to this building as the "heartbreak hotel" during the first few days after Marcus betrayed her.

"Have a good evening." She handed the driver his fare and tip as a porter opened the door and asked if she had any bags. "No, but thank you." Ellie nodded and walked toward the beautiful wrought-iron doors. She'd worked with clients and their teams here a hundred times since the week after Marcus, but the déjà vu of walking into this place, worried about how another man could wreck her life, was eerie.

Her cheeks flushed as the embarrassment of how weak she'd

been that night cut anew. Even though she'd thrown him out with dramatics worthy of a made-for-TV movie and purged the space she loved of everything he owned, the rooms felt haunted. There hadn't been enough Lysol, penicillin, or holy water in the world to keep her there. His plotting, the lies, the cheating, and the theft were devastating enough, but none of it compared to the embarrassment of being forced to resign from her hard-won position at Camelot. She'd almost lost everything.

Ellie made her way through the bustling, marbled lobby to the VIP concierge desk. She held her composure seamlessly and tried to sort what she was building now from the cautionary tale that was Marcus.

Regret that she'd bought into his lies so deeply lapped like lava at the edges of her heart as she took her place among the well-dressed businessmen in line. Ellie told herself to center. Ripping open her old wounds didn't serve anyone tonight. That was her past, and this was her present.

Norah

"And now you know it all." Norah looked across the table and stirred her tea. The harsh fluorescent lights made her feel as if she were in an interrogation room on a bad cop drama.

"So—"

Bzzzzzzzzz. Her pager vibrated violently on the cafeteria table's smooth surface. Norah looked down at it, then back up apologetically.

"It's fine. I could use a second to"—her mother forced a stunned smile—"process all of this."

"Of course." Norah stood and walked to the window to return the call. A few minutes later, she was back in her seat, looking at the woman she'd spent her entire life trying to emulate struggle for the words to say all she felt. Norah knew she would have her mother's support no matter what she chose—just as she always had. The woman across from her was the mother she dreamed of one day being. In hindsight, maybe the fact that she had been a single mom was a blessing. Chances were, Norah thought sadistically, she would need her guidance in that area of life as well. Growing up, and watching her juggle it all, Norah had always sensed how hard it was but had never doubted she was her mother's number-one priority. In many ways, her mother always treated her like an aspiring equal. They even had a chant—"Team Norah and Evelyn, together forever, no matter what"—that they had recited until the rolled eyes and sarcasm stitched to puberty eventually killed the ritual. Regardless, the message stayed strong.

Some of Norah's best early memories were of waiting for her mom to walk through the door during what they called "picnic week"—her mother's code for pulling extra shifts in the postpartum ward during the seven days before payday. Her grandmother would pick her up from kindergarten every afternoon during those weeks, and the two would go back to the apartment to set the blanket table and plan a "surprise" meal for Mommy. Norah remembered how proud she'd felt on those nights when her mom walked through the door, eyes closed and guessing what they'd made. Would it be mac and cheese, PB and J, bald eagle, unicorn, manatee, noodles? She would always guess "wrong," until Norah and Gran proudly revealed the feast.

In hindsight, Norah now knew how exhausted her mother must have been and how torturous the precious picnic meal and the pre-bedtime game of Candy Land must have seemed with another extra shift on top of a twelve-hour day looming on the horizon. Even so, Norah had never felt it. She had never known she was part of a juggling act and never considered herself an obstacle.

Their picnics continued while her mother studied and sacrificed to become an OR nurse. Norah was in second grade by then, and oblivious to the fact that the elementary schools in her district were discontinuing all gifted-and-talented math and science programs because of funding issues. It would be years before Norah made the connection between the ice cream cone her grandmother bought her on the way to Destination Science practice and the time she spent with her tutor, studying what she later identified as fourth-grade math. She'd loved understanding division then, and still loved it now. The simple fact that every number was essentially a whole of its parts and could be broken down into various combinations fascinated her.

A year of picnics and savings later, they were living in a modest duplex in LA's best school district. Her fascination with math and science refined into a love of cells, and later cell division. There was no denying that microbiology and anatomy were her first passions, nor that her mother's sacrifices had delivered her to where she was today.

She closed her eyes, remembering her surprise at how many of her friends seemed to graduate from their mothers just as easily as they gave up their bows and digi-pets. She, of course, turned sullen in her own ways, quit the piano, and fabricated a million and one negatives about her mother to keep in step with her peers—most of whom either despised their parents or were newly experiencing divorced life—but she never truly understood the animosity they felt. Then again, maybe that was a perk of not having to struggle for independence. She suddenly had new clarity about why under-age drinking and smoking had held such little appeal to her as a teen. They didn't symbolize freedom and autonomy from authority to her. Of all of her friends, she was one of the few who could tell her mother the truth about where she was going on Saturday night.

She smiled internally, realizing how wise her mother had been not to make that an issue of control. Norah had had all the freedom she wanted, as long as she didn't violate their trust. The team's trust. Teenage Norah might not have had the words to express her grati-tude, but adult Norah had thanked her for her "liberal parenting" a thousand times.

Norah looked at her now, feeling her throat lock and the twenty-twenty hindsight that could never convey everything she felt for the woman who sat in front of her.

"So, you meant it when you said it was complicated." Her mother smiled but couldn't quite keep the shock out of her eyes. "Now isn't necessarily the time or place for me to tell you everything going through my mind, but I want you to know that I love you and I'm here for you."

"Thank you." Norah's phone vibrated in her pocket. "I still can't believe what I did. The regret is overwhelming at the moment. Regardless of the choices I make now, people I care about will be hurt."

Her mother reached across the table for her hand. "Everyone

ends up with regrets, Norah. The best advice I can give you in this situation is to look at all of your options and ask yourself which choices will leave you with regrets you can live with and which ones will leave you haunted. When you look back on your life, it's not about having no regrets; it's about having the right ones." She gently squeezed her daughter's hand. "Just don't forget that at the end of the day, you're still you. You're still the compassionate, giving person you were before all—"

Bzzzzzzzzz, bzzzzzzzzz, her pager interrupted mercilessly.

"Walk with me?" Norah said apologetically.

"And dedicated physician"—Evelyn grinned and stood, knowing their time was up—"that you were before all of this."

"Thank you. All I can say at the moment is that missing out on being a mother is not a regret I'm willing to have." Norah pursed her lips and looked down at her watch. "There's so much more to talk about. I'll call you tomorrow?"

"Okay, sweetheart." Evelyn hugged her quickly. "In the meantime, try to remember this isn't a circus act. Don't line up the conversations with Matt, Enrique, and the girls like flaming hoops waiting for you to catapult through them. Take some time to pause and reflect."

"You're right." Norah smiled drily. "The center ring might be preferable. This feels more like emergency triage. I might as well be trying to save one relationship in critical condition after another."

Her mother laughed, told her again she wasn't alone in this, and said goodbye as Norah walked down the hall into the only part of her future that was certain.

Ellie

$\mathcal{E}$llie silenced her buzzing phone as she approached the desk.

"Ms. Lindsay. It's a pleasure to see you tonight." The concierge smiled brightly.

"You as well, Evan."

"What can I do for you this evening?" he said eagerly, and typed her name into the touch screen on his desk.

"I believe my stylist made a delivery for a client who's staying in the penthouse."

"Of course." He typed her name again, and she knew he was looking for her room. "I show they were delivered at five o'clock this evening."

"Yes—promptly, I hope."

"Indeed. I've called security, and they will meet you at the private elevator. May I offer you an escort?"

"No, I am not going up just yet, but thank you. Please have the clothing sent up, and I will follow later this evening to make sure all is in order."

"Of course, Ms. Lindsay. As always, it is my pleasure to thank you and your parties for patronizing the Mandarin."

"Of course." Ellie nodded and tried to determine whether his appreciation was practiced or purchased, considering how many times she and her clients had stayed here. "The service never disappoints."

1 New Text—To—Patrick Grayson Cell
You should be getting a delivery shortly. It's a garment
bag from my stylist containing my clothes for the next
two days.

Ellie made her way back across the lobby and walked into Posh,
the sleek lounge attached to the Mandarin's world-famous restaurant. She ordered her usual and opened a report from the recruit-
ing department that had been waiting in her e-mail for the last two
days. It looked promising. She congratulated that team and then
e-mailed her head of scouting, gave him a budget, and asked him to
pick three supporting talents to vulture on *Life of Us*.

1 New Text—From—Patrick Grayson Cell
So these knickers aren't for me? I'd best take them off,
then. Your text just made my night, BTW.

Ellie smiled down at her phone. She'd tried so hard not to let him
in, but there was no denying it now.

1 New Text—To—Patrick Grayson Cell
Hot. Keep them on ;) I'll be up in half an hour or so.

1 New Text—From Patrick Grayson Cell-
And by that, I will admit that I'm into the Guinness
and was checking my phone obsessively, hoping you
would find a way.

1 New Text—To Patrick Grayson Cell-
I couldn't stay away. Turns out seeing you at the
top of a staircase suits me. This is me knowing it
won't be easy, and knowing that there are flights
left to climb.

And there were. She knew this as surely as she knew anything else. Regardless of their efforts, the short peace they'd experienced was already a fractured bubble. It would pop, and they would never be able to blow another one. The only question in her mind now was, when?

Leila

"Good job, Julia." Leila said, as she spooned another helping of black beans onto Clara's plate. "I really like how you used your napkin to wipe your chin without being asked."

"You're welcome, Mommy." Julia smiled, and a glob of avocado fell from her fork to the floor. Moments like these made Leila appreciate the dog. Her phone erupted in the Reba McEntire "Fancy" ringtone she'd recently assigned to her mother's ever-changing number. *Seriously?* Leila thought. *If you knew anything about my life, you'd know that now is the absolute worst time to call.* The hours between four and seven o'clock were her witching hours. For the most part, she felt like she was tapping into her reserves just to keep a smile in her tone and survive getting dinner on the table, the girls bathed, and powering through bedtime stories. Thank goodness Wes usually got home sometime in between their baths and night-lights, so she could clear the table and/or collapse in her chair.

"Mommy! I 'eed a 'dother one!"

"Speak kindly, please, and—"

"Mommy, I dropped my fork and have to go potty."

"That's fine, Clara. Use your napkin, and wash your hands when you're finished." Leila fished a clean spoon out of the drawer just as her phone erupted in the first five bars of Bruno Mars's "Just the Way You Are." She sandwiched it between her ear and shoulder and took Liam's bottle from the warmer.

"Hi! I was just calling to see how everything is going and how

Liam is. Thanks so much for tonight!" Kate sounded happy and refreshed. "I forgot how much fun it was to have dinner without . . . I mean, just the two of us."

"No worries! We're doing great. He had a blast playing with the girls. He's bathed, and I'm going to put him to bed in twenty minutes or so. I'll call you if he fusses." Julia stood up in her chair, and Leila snapped her fingers and pointed sternly down to the seat.

"Okay"—Kate hesitated—"and thank you again for tonight. I put his favorite blankie on the edge of the crib so it would be ready. He also likes you to pat his back."

"Mommy!"

"No problem." Leila shifted the phone to her other shoulder so she could wipe the drool trailing down Liam's chin. "Remind me how many ounces he takes at bedtime?"

"Six, but he's super-picky about the temperature. He likes it best when you take it out halfway through the warmer's cycle. Between thirty-two and thirty-eight seconds. You have to watch it, or it will get too hot or stay too cool and he won't drink it."

"Mommy, I didn't want to mess up the pretty point on Ms. Kate's toilet paper to wipe, so I solved the problem."

"Okay," Leila said into the phone. "I promise to call you if I have any trouble. Enjoy yourselves." She ended the call and turned to her daughter. "How did you solve the problem, Clara?"

"I used a towel."

"All done!" Julia squealed and threw her hands, spoon included, up into the air to wave the sign. "My I be 'cused?" She was out of her chair in a heartbeat and off to wash her hands.

"Which towel?"

"The white one. I thought it was a good choice because it looks like toilet paper and you know the poo-poo is all gone when it's only white. Then I hung it back up so Miss Kate won't have to find paper either!" Clara jumped down from her seat and danced. "Who helped? I did! Me, me, *meeeee*! I did!" Clara sang, dancing around the kitchen.

"Julia! Please don't use the white towel!" Leila called as she wiped Liam's face.

"I *woooooonnn't!*"

Here's your one chance, Fancy, don't let me down.

Leila's phone rang as she cleaned the bathroom, rocked Liam and the girls, read them stories, started *The Little Mermaid*, and scrubbed the avocado from Kate's perfectly pressed curtains.

Leila

*L*eila watched Wes's chest rise and fall. She was glad he seemed relaxed after a night out with his partners. She brushed her teeth and climbed into their comfy bed. She was just late enough to catch Patrick Grayson on *Goldberg*. She found the remote under the duvet and pressed PLAY. *Here's your one chance, Fancy, don't let me down.*

Not now. Leila rolled her eyes and silenced it. *I deserve to enjoy five minutes of nothing before I fall asleep and wake up to do it all again tomorrow.* She exhaled the negativity and put her phone on the nightstand. She laughed twice during the opening monologue and fell into a sleep that was as cathartic as it was temporary.

3 New Texts
Ellie Cell
BTW, I'm back at the Heartbreak Hotel.
Norah Cell
I'm sorry I didn't get a chance to return your call.
Thank you for the message. You're one of the reasons I know I can do this alone if it comes to that.
770-448-1999
U need to call ur mamma she got the cancer.

Cami

*C*ami leaned back in her chair and rolled her tense neck. Young voices bantered happily in the conference room next door, dotted by the bass drum of a band she didn't recognize. Today had gone well, but this position would be an adjustment, to say the least. They were all so young and distracted. She looked at the stacks of timetables and budgets on her desk and wondered what her twenty-three-year-old self would think of her now. What would Blane think? Would they be proud of her success, or would they be shocked that she was now the eye in the office that reviewed and critiqued the shots, and no longer the artist who took them?

Cami tapped the thin platinum Rolex on her wrist. Ten o'clock. Ironically, InFocus had given it to her as an achievement gift just last quarter. She turned her mind to the present, straightened the files, and packed to leave.

Just as she slid her computer into her satchel, a fist pounded on the wall, to the tune of "Shave and a Haircut."

"Hey, Clark! You want anything from Tokyo One? We're ordering sake and bentos in five," a male voice belted. What was the point of leaving her door open to seem approachable if they were just going to screech business through the stucco? She almost shouted an answer back but then thought of the precedent it would set and gathered her things to answer in person.

The conference table was littered with black-and-white stills and sepia copies. Daphne, a skeleton-esque redhead with oversize glasses and a spiked pixie, leaned against a corkboard full of pins and layouts. Cami gave her a nod and scanned the material. They had made little to no progress in the three hours since she'd last checked on them. "These ideas look promising. I look forward to seeing the direction you choose."

"Now you know why they need the sake." Daphne laughed.

"Dean's cool with the booze, in case you're thinking of ratting us out." Dylan, the reluctant note-taker from that morning's meeting laced his fingers behind his head and leaned back precariously in his chair. "Hell, he usually buys."

"Does he?" Cami raised her eyebrow at him. "Even when you've missed a deadline and are on borrowed time before you pitch the work?" She stalled long enough to make him look away. "I'm guessing not, but I will offer you an incentive. Impress me this week, and Friday's happy hour is on me. Have a good night." She shut the door behind her.

"You're such an ass hat, Dylan."

"Am I? You guys were the ones sucking up to the new warden. Twenty bucks says that hag hasn't shot anything real since menopause. Hell, she'll probably be asking where the darkroom is tomorrow."

Cami wanted to throw open the door and offer him directions to HR for his exit interview, but decided today wasn't the day.

Norah

Norah stood outside their suite with her key card poised over the lock. She'd sworn to herself that she wouldn't be in this space again before she had answers and decisions. Yet here she was, banking on a hot shower and a decent bed until a call or her alarm interrupted the little time she had left before her day began again. She told herself there was no reason to be a martyr in an on-call room when she could be getting decent rest in a prepaid Hilton bed. Her sleep would be tortured regardless of the thread count on the sheets.

She pushed the door open to the empty suite and flipped on the necessary lights. Everything looked eerily the same yet so different. Norah sat her bag on the bed and made her way to the bathroom to start the shower. The steam began to gather on the mirror as she stepped out of her scrubs. A minute later, her contacts were in their case and the hot water was pelting the tension knot between her shoulder blades. She twisted her neck, trying to concentrate on the release and not on the last time she stood in this bathroom with Enrique. He'd texted her earlier to ask if they could meet to talk, and she'd promised him some time tomorrow. She filled her lungs and sinuses with the steam and tried to ignore the suffocating panic that her secret would soon be public.

"Norah? Are you here?" Enrique's voice broke her concentration. Before she could respond, he was standing on the other side of the opaque glass.

"Hi," she said, and clenched her eyes shut. "I caught a break and thought I'd save myself from the OCR bunk." Norah turned off the water, glad he couldn't see her face at the moment.

"Good choice." His voice had an excited lift to it as she opened the door and he handed her a crisp towel. A new pang of guilt ripped through her when she saw how earnestly happy he looked to see her. "I actually came here looking for a few hours of peace myself. I didn't expect you, but I'm glad you're here."

"Me too." She softened and wrapped the towel around her.

"Are you okay, babe? You seem off, somehow." He stepped back and lifted himself up to sit on the granite countertop. "Have you talked to Matt? For what it's worth, I haven't slept since we fought. There just aren't words to say how sorry I am that I had to leave you."

"I'm fine." She looked into his worried eyes and lied to him for the first time. "It's just been an exceptionally long day."

"Then we sleep." He hopped down from the counter and gestured to the hallway. "Ladies first." Enrique grinned, and Norah smiled in spite of herself at the allusion he often made to their first night together. She walked a few paces in front of him, eyeing the bed and counting the seconds until she crashed into it. "Here." He fished through one of the dresser drawers and handed her one of his T-shirts. "So I won't be distracted."

"Good call." She tried to mirror his playful tone as she dropped the towel and slipped the well-worn tee over her head.

Enrique lifted the edge of the duvet, and Norah slid over to her side. "If we're going to explore this, then we need to spend some real nights together—dead tired and stressed to the limit included. You know I understand." He lay against her back and wrapped his arms around her. Norah sank first into the sensation of his warmth and second into the blissful escape that was three hours of sleep.

Ellie

"You're welcome, Ms. Lindsay. Sorry to trouble you for ID, but we can never be too careful," the large man said, as he punched the code and opened the door. For hotel security, he was refreshingly thorough. Less than a minute later, the elevator doors opened and Pat's bodyguard stood to greet her.

"Good evening." His expression was as monotone as his voice. *Please don't let him say, "Mr. Grayson is expecting you," like I'm some sort of escort*, she willed. Of course, he was bound by a contract so tight that leaking even the smallest amount of information about Pat's private affairs would send him free-falling into an entirely different tax bracket. There weren't many second chances at this level of private security.

"Thank you, Dominic." Ellie made a point of meeting his eyes and walking confidently toward the staircase to the master suite. A shiver of anxiety shot through her as she climbed the stairs. *Relax. You've picked this apart enough. It's time to trust yourself.*

As if on cue, or, rather, a heads-up from his security, Pat appeared on the top landing, beaming the way he must have as a child on Christmas morning.

"Ellie." He said and held out his hand. She glanced from it to the empty floor below. Pat frowned as he followed her eyes. "I know you're nervous, but we're as alone as we'll ever be now."

"I know." She smiled up at him, embarrassed that he was right.

"This is all a bit foreign to me. If we're being honest, I'm feeling naked at work."

"Let's go in." He grinned anxiously and found a place for his hand in the pocket of his jeans, before nodding toward the door to the suite. Steps later, they were standing silently in the elegant foyer, eyes locked together, each waiting for the other to speak. His disheveled hair told her he'd been on edge. Ellie started to ask if it was tomorrow's hellish schedule, their situation, or something altogether different, when he interrupted: "You'll have to forgive me this evening. Today's been somewhat of a roller coaster, and I feel as if I'm trying to get my sea legs again."

"I understand. It's been an exceptionally long day for both of us." She slipped her arms around his waist and felt him relax slightly. After all, she knew what it was like to cannonball back into the real world after a forced hiatus. "Should we sit?" she said, before realizing she was automatically shifting the balance of power between them.

"Of course. I'm, er . . . Sorry. I'm being very rude." He combed his fingers through his hair and gestured toward the plush leather sofas in the main living area. "Can I get you a drink?" he asked, walking quickly to the wet bar and lifting up a bottle of wine. She was about to comment that it was one of her favorites, when he said, "I made a request. It's the same vintage we shared the first night after I scared you on the balcony. Spoiler alert: I have it in cab sauv and pinot as well." She grinned, amused at his nervous shuffling, and slipped her feet out of her heels. "Look at me, rambling on and acting like a teenager who's somehow convinced the girl he likes to come to his house for the first time. You'd think my mum were listening just outside the door."

"I'm actually quite entertained." She smiled and tucked her legs sideways under her pencil skirt. Desire fanned through her abdomen as she watched him clip the foil and position the corkscrew. Even flustered, he looked effortlessly sexy. Was his inability to hide his nerves what she found so intriguing about him? He was so easy to read. She rubbed the aching arch of her foot and relaxed into the calm of the moment.

"So, watching me sweat amuses you?" He laughed and poured two glasses. "That bodes well, because I'm afraid we have some rather serious things to talk about this evening." Ellie whiplashed into his words, scrutinizing him for tells as he walked toward her. A voice inside her hissed, *I told you he was hiding something,* and she pushed away its resounding echoes that she should have known better, willing her expression not to enter stone-cold work mode. She needed to stay approachable enough to get the information she needed.

"You've got that look in your eye." Pat's face went from jovial to confused to hurt as he handed her a glass.

"If you're hiding something from me, you need to tell me now."

"So we're back to that? Seriously? Tell me you're not thinking this has to do with the bloody Scargate ordeal."

"Let's just say I'm hoping not." She unfolded her legs and straightened.

"Tell me your mind didn't go directly there when I said I wanted to talk to you about something serious." His pained eyes pierced hers, then looked down at his glass as he took a seat several inches from her. "You know it all, Ellie. No proposal and no sex. I thought, or hoped, rather, we were beyond all that—maybe not professionally, but as a couple, at least."

Tense silence hung in the air as she tried to center. What had she just let happen? Was she looking for a reason to push him away, rather than risk losing him?

"I'm sorry." She chastised herself for letting her fear get the best of her and reached for his hand. "My heart tells me we're past it, but my nerves are on hyper drive at the moment. I shouldn't have reacted that way." She knew now more than ever that trust would be their biggest obstacle if they chose to continue. He was quiet for a long moment.

"I can understand that." His voice softened, but he didn't take her hand. "I've been freaking out a bit up here, too. As much as I'd give anything to blame it on the Guinness or"—he shrugged and lifted his glass to hers—"the wine, I can't help but feel I owe you a brutally honest dialogue . . ." He hesitated, and she knew the conversation he wanted to have was beginning. "About where we go from here." He reached for his collar but then stopped and took her hand in both of his instead.

"What's on your mind, Pat? Just tell me. I can handle it."

"Simply put, I can't seem to shake the feeling that I'm cheating you out of what you deserve. Earlier, when I was alone in this beautiful suite, I was lying right here on the couch, thinking I'd give anything for a mini-fridge and a full-size bed at the Motel 6 if it meant we could walk down to the continental breakfast together the next morning like a normal couple. I can't stop thinking about what it means for you that we can't. Stale buffet pastries aside, I'm worried about what I might be taking from you." He forced a nervous laugh, then shook his head. "I thought, *What if she looks up when it's too late and wishes we had never happened?* Then I got the text you were coming, and all of that vanished for a moment." His dimples flared. "Honestly. I was grinning like a lovesick schoolboy and mooning over how I can't take my eyes off of you when we're in the same room." He paused, and she watched his expression grow more intense as he shoved his hand roughly through his hair, searching for the right words. "Ellie, what I'm trying to say is that I know how privileged I am that you're giving me the chance to be a part of your life." His eyes burned with an integrity unlike anything she'd ever seen before, as he pressed her hand against his pounding heart. "To complicate it. I feel like pulling you into all this is the most selfish thing I'll ever do."

"Pat, I . . ." She spoke before she had the words, then paused as the realization that she wanted be transparent with him washed over her. She didn't need the perfect words; she just needed the truth. "I wouldn't be here if I didn't think we had something special. Believe me when I say I know what I'm getting into and that I realize a future together comes with more real sacrifices than I've ever faced before." His heart pounded wildly under her palm. "I admit I hope we can explore it privately for as long as possible, but I know that's a crapshoot. On the one hand, I understand what being with you, publicly, means, and how drastically my life could change if we're discovered. On the other hand, I can't stop thinking about how incredibly my life has already changed and what it would be like now without you." Ellie closed her eyes and sank into the warmth that fluttered in her chest. "Without this."

If ever there were a time to give in, it was now. "Pat, this is me being as absolutely honest as I can be. I've never fallen for someone this quickly, much less this hard. It scares me. I'll admit I've been mercilessly critical of my feelings for you from the beginning, and I could list a hundred reasons why we shouldn't be together and how I could get hurt, but at the end of the day, whatever happens, I'm already changed. Before you, I was building a life for myself. With you, I'm finally beginning to see what it would mean to truly share it with someone." He raised her hand to his lips, and she smiled, relieved that she'd actually said the things she'd been poring over.

"This is all a first for me, too. " A flush touched his cheeks as he squeezed her hand. "I'm not saying I've never been in love before, but I've never asked another person to put so much at stake. Part of me wants nothing more than to shout—or tweet, for that matter— that I'm falling for a phenomenal woman. The better part of me wants to sweep you away somewhere we can make love for hours on end and talk until we have all the answers." He brushed the waves from his forehead in a frustrated second. "And at the same time, my head is screaming that that's ridiculous and that I can't possibly love you without hurting you. I keep thinking back to what Blythe and I went through after the world found out about us. The fishbowl we were already living in shrank to the size of an eyedropper in two seconds flat. It was hell." He stopped and searched her eyes. "I want so much more than that for you."

"Pat, this isn't the same scenario. That frenzy built for five years and broke during the height of the *Destiny* craze."

"But it is the same, Ellie. I feel like you have to know that no matter how quiet we manage to keep us, that could happen to you. Hell, you know as well as anyone that Blythe and I actually *were* platonic friends and roommates for the first two years. Even so, we didn't have a second of peace until the photos of us together off set stopped making big bucks. The rest, as you clearly know, is history." He rolled his eyes, and his voice trailed off.

Ellie mirrored the motion of his thumb with hers and tried to give his words the weight they deserved. She hadn't represented them at the time, but the incident was legendary in the PR world. A cast mate accidentally confirmed that Pat and Blythe's relationship had become romantic during a live Comic-Con panel promoting the second *Destiny* film. Their panicked faces, and garbled backpedaling became sound bites heard round the world.

"Pat, you've said it yourself that any relationship of yours—serious, inconsequential, or totally fictional—will always be a meal ticket for the paparazzi. Of course I'd rather not be hounded by the press, but I can handle it."

"I've no doubt you can, but that doesn't mean you should have to. It's like a crucible. Once you're in it, you're in. Even in your sleep." He pressed his hand into hers. "You're going to think I've gone absolutely mad, but I keep having the same nightmare over and over again. In it, it's the middle of the night, and we're both literally blinded and drowning in a sea of flashing bulbs. You're calling for help, but I can't get to you, no matter how hard I struggle. I always sink first, then wake up before I know what happens to you." He squeezed her hand, and she swallowed hard. Sadistic symphonies of clicking lenses had haunted her dreams since the night they slept on the pallet under the skylight. She resisted the temptation to turn the conversation and chose to be honest instead.

"I've been imagining something similar." She took his other hand. "In mine, I don't really see them; I just hear the shutters and the din of the approach." He nodded, and she forced a joke to break the tension in his face. "I wait until I'm at work to panic about the headlines."

"I can only imagine." He smiled briefly. "On that note, have you told anyone but the two friends?"

"No. Have you?"

"I told my mum tonight. I just couldn't keep it in any longer."

"And was she happy for you?"

"She was happy that I sounded happy, but concerned about you nonetheless."

"About me?" Ellie cocked her head. "Is it our professional relationship?"

"No." He laughed. "She was literally concerned about *you*. She simply can't fathom why anyone would choose to live in a glass cell voluntarily. She never would've chosen it for herself and hates being targeted when I'm in the news." He paused and Ellie saw the hurt on his face. "And then she said something that confirmed every fear that has been nagging at the back of my mind since our first night. It was everything I wanted to talk to you about tonight while there's still time."

"What did she say?" Ellie's predictions swarmed her mind as she stared into the cornflower blue of his eyes. *Please, Pat, be honest with me.*

"She said, 'Patrick, if you think you love her, let her go. You know what you're bringing her into. She still has the luxury of being on the fringes. Don't take that from her. Find someone who's already chosen this.'" Ellie winced from the phantom punch the words delivered as the oxygen drained from her lungs. "And the hardest part about it is, she's likely right. What kind of wretched person am I to ask you to make a sacrifice like that?" The anguish in his eyes burned into hers while everything she wanted to say threatened to come out in a garbled mess. How could she tell him that he would hurt her now regardless? That she'd been two steps ahead of him in the worry game the entire time and had strategies in place for them both if there was a fallout professionally? More urgent than that, how did she say she also came at a cost he shouldn't have to pay? He would want children one day. If she loved him, should she be the one to let go?

I agree. You deserve more than I can give. Let me end this now and give that to you the only way I can. There are realities neither of us can change. In the instant her lips formed the words, his elegant script on the last card burned into her mind. Remaining vulnerable was his choice as much as it was hers, and it was the only way this could work.

"Pat, I'm scared. I'm scared for the same reasons you are. I don't want to hurt you any more than you want to see me hurt. This is me making the words you wrote my own and accepting no relationship of mine will ever be simple either, and asking you to brave that with me. I can't think of a better promise to make to each other than to live those words and make them our anchor. I come with heavier stuff than you've seen so far, too, but I'd rather face all of those things with you than without you. I agree life in the spotlight is white hot and hard to understand, but I'm still choosing you. I'm choosing the man who brought down my walls and managed to date me in my own home, under house arrest no less. I'm choosing the man who makes me want to trust again and who makes me laugh when I need it most. Believe me, I know it won't be easy, but at the end of the day, no one's relationship is easy." She smiled and reached up to touch his cheek, delighted to watch the lines on his brow slowly fade as he pulled her closer.

"Ellie, I . . ." His eyes fluttered closed, and peace spread over his face. "I can't tell you how relieved I am to hear you say that. I knew I might lose you tonight, but I just couldn't live with myself if I didn't tell you everything and give you the chance to abandon ship before it was too late. I owed you that. You have to know I meant every word I wrote on those cards, and I want to live them with you. This is me"—his lips brushed hers—"promising."

Genuine. The word whispered through her mind, and she knew in an instant why she was so enchanted by him. He was simply who he was—no games and no spin. She looked into his eyes as if for the first time, struck by the sincerity and commitment shining back at her. That was it. It wasn't his charm or his sex appeal. It was his honesty. She was looking into everything missing in her life.

"I love you." She said the words to him for the first time and pressed her lips to his. Pat's face beamed as he slipped his hands into her hair, cupping her face.

"Ellie." He grazed his index fingers over the line of her jaw and down her throat. "I love you, too." It was a kiss more intimate than any they'd shared before, as fearless as it was comfortable. She slid her hands under the soft fabric of his shirt and up his sides, lingering deliciously over the ridges of his abdomen until he lifted his arms so she could push it over his head. She pulled his mouth back to hers, slowing the kiss and teasing her fingers down the muscles of his bare back, into the waistband of his jeans. He moaned softly, moving his lips to her neck while his fingers made quick work of the buttons on her blouse. Heat flared deep in her abdomen as he peeled the silk from her back, kissing and nibbling a line from her ear across the ridge of her shoulder. She buried her hands in his hair and relished the pulsing sensations coursing through her body. Ten more minutes of this, and she would climax before they made it to the bed. She'd never wanted a man so much. Ellie arched her chest closer to his as he ran his hands up her back and unclasped her bra, grazing slow circles around her nipples with his thumbs before slipping the lace from her shoulders and tossing it to the ground. One hand stroked her breast as the other trailed to her knee, inching the fitted black fabric of her skirt as far as it would go up her thigh. His face broke into a mischievous grin. "Your skirt's playing hard to get."

"I thought that was your game." Ellie laughed, and time stopped for a moment as two sets of blue eyes twinkled at each other.

"That laugh"—he pressed his forehead to hers and whispered—"just might be the most beautiful sound in my world." *This is me finding what I didn't know I'd been waiting for.* He took her in his arms and onto his lap. She slipped her legs around him, tingling at the warmth of her bare chest on his, and ran her fingers through his hair and down his back. He tilted his pelvis in a tantalizing rhythm, then stood. Ellie squeezed her legs more tightly around his waist as he boosted her up over the smooth denim and walked them, entwined, to the bed that was theirs for the night.

Leila

"*R*ahhhhhhhhhh." The monitor came to life, and Leila wrestled her mind into consciousness. "*Rahhhhhhhhhh, rahhhh, urrrrahhhh, ioooonta, ionta moooook, ionta.*" She tossed her leg over the side of the bed, listening to the quiet that followed and hoping she'd settled. Wes stretched beside her and yawned sleepily.

"Morning, beautiful." He looped his arm around her side, and she rubbed his head.

"Good morning."

"*Fwinkle, fwinkle all da tars.*"

"Julia's waking up. She sounds like she might be settling, but I'm not sure. Fingers crossed."

"That's right. You have something this morning." He pushed himself to sitting and shook his head. "I'm sorry. I know I should know, but I can't remember. Clara has school, and you're—"

"It's Bench Day."

"Oh, good. No, not good. I didn't mean that. I was just worried I might have forgotten your meeting at the university for a second. That's this week, too, right?"

Leila bristled, irritated he needed to be reminded of something so important. Friday's meeting could change the entire dynamic of their family, and it was barely on his radar? He was golfing with clients a week and a half from now and had reminded her three times already he needed the gloves he'd ordered from the pro shop picked up by Monday. "Because I've got the girls that morning."

"Thank you." Her voice was cold as she walked into the bathroom. "Torri will be here in forty-five minutes to sit with the girls until I get back." She looked at the clock and rolled her eyes. It was four fifteen; she was already running late. What was the point of their sharing an iCalendar if he ignored everything she posted? Friday's meeting was one thing, but Bench Day had been on repeat, with flagged reminders, for years.

"Are you mad, babe?"

"No." Leila pulled the French doors to the bathroom closed and dressed in silence. Wes left every morning at five thirty. She never asked him to go in later, and he never offered. He left when things were quiet, and he left when things were absolutely nuts. There had been so many mornings after the girls were born when she'd been up most of the night breastfeeding, or rocking, or tending illnesses, or all of the above, and wanted nothing more than to hear him offer to stay until seven to give her an hour of sleep or a quick shower, but she rarely asked. The few times she'd tried, he'd spent the next twenty minutes on the phone, arranging his late arrival, and the stress he'd radiated had made her feel too guilty to ask him to stay again, regardless of the situation.

At the end of the day, she wanted him to see the need—her need, the girls' needs—and want to fill it. She didn't want him to stay because she threw a fit, like so many wives she knew, and bullied him into it, or because they argued if he didn't; she wanted him to stay because he wanted to share her role, and ease her burden, for an hour when he saw her struggling. She wanted him to acknowledge how frantic things could get when he had both girls alone and then imagine the times she'd been sick when he left, or the times she'd been nursing a baby and simultaneously giving breathing treatments to a toddler with RSV. She wanted him to remember every time she told him not to miss work when her OB appointments conflicted, although they both knew it likely meant her getting lost in what she considered the most stressful and confusing area in all of LA, but she did it because she couldn't justify causing him more stress. Even at thirty-nine weeks, spotting, contracting, and worried about the decrease in Julia's movements, she had scrambled to find a sitter in case she was admitted and gone to the doctor alone. The list went on and on.

A pang of sadness struck her as she tied the laces of her gym shoes and reminded herself neither of them could save this morning. There wasn't time for a real conversation, and laying the groundwork for a fight wouldn't serve either of them, much less solve the problem. The doors opened, and Wes stepped tentatively into the bathroom, her phone in hand.

"Your phone is dead. Do you have the car charger?"

"Yes."

"You seem upset. Did I do something?"

"I'm not angry, Wes. I'm just frustrated. We can talk about it later."

"Um, okay. So, Torri will be here soon?"

"Yes, Wes. You're free as soon as she gets here. If Julia wakes up again, just start her on her breakfast. There's yogurt in the fridge, and she gets to pick a fruit. More than likely, I'll be back before they're awake." She tried and failed to keep the edge out of her voice. Was wanting to hear him thank her for having arranged a sitter so he could leave on schedule too much to ask? Was wanting him to acknowledge the empathy and importance behind their tradition on the bench unrealistic? And she was seriously considering a return to teaching? What would those mornings look like, based on this one?

She shook the snide comment from her lips. This wasn't some kind of tally game. She needed to wrap her mind around that before they talked and she came off as some sort of martyr.

Kate

Kate secured the last buckle on the harness and kissed Liam's smiling face. Today would be a beating, but she would deal. She would jog on, one foot in front of the other, to the bench. And when she got there, she would do what she'd done for Cami since the morning they'd heard: just be there. She trotted forward, visualizing the gaudy wrought-iron metal and sculpted wooden 'B' on the back of the bench her mother had donated in Blane's memory. Here she was, freshly embarrassed, eleven years later, about her family's lies and perjuries and the pain they had caused the Greens.

She picked up her pace, wondering how his family had forgiven hers for framing Blane for the accident and wondering how Cami was handling not being with them for the first time on the anniversary of his death. She might never know those answers, but she did know it mattered to Cami that she and the girls were there. Kate lengthened her stride, leading with the ball of her foot, as Cami had taught her, and trying unsuccessfully to accept what she could never change. She jogged on toward the twisted memory that was the bench, reliving the pain of Cameron's drug problems and the suicide attempt that left him alive yet mentally disabled and physically handicapped for life. Today wasn't about her. It couldn't be.

Cami

*C*ami sat uncomfortably against the edges of the intricately carved, gold-plated *B* that made up the middle of the bench. She ran near here several times a week but allowed herself to circle and stop only twice a year: on the anniversary of his death and on his birthday. Normally, she would be on her way to the airport afterward, to visit his family. Add another barb to being fired from InFocus. She never missed work, excepting this day, once a year. There was no way she could justify taking a personal day during her first week under Gatz and keep anyone's respect.

She stared across the street at the apartment they'd shared. After his funeral, those walls were her salvation and, in many ways, her prison. Everything was the same and different all at once. She still put her keys in the bowl on the table by the door and waited to hear his cheery hello. She constantly took two plates from the cupboard every evening before she remembered he wasn't coming home. No matter how many days passed, nothing felt right. The weeks flew by in the same blur as the funeral. She dressed for work, observed and shot her assignments in the studious silence expected of her apprentice role, took the same bus home, ate, and counted the minutes until she could climb into his side of the bed. The lingering smell of his Eternity aftershave on the sheets became her reward for making it through another twelve hours. Night after night she stared at the ceiling, unable to sleep, until suddenly it was the weekend.

Kate flew in every Friday, no matter how emphatically Cami

insisted she was fine. At first, she filled the hours with plans, dragging Cami from farmers' markets to art shows to concerts. Cami feigned interest for Kate's sake, but it was exhausting. The only bright side was that it led to sleep. Kate would roll a sleeping bag out beside Cami's side of the bed, just as she'd done every night for two weeks after the accident, and beside the twin bed in Blane's little sisters' room the night of the funeral. On those nights, Cami still stared at the ceiling cracks he'd planned to fix one day, but her eyelids ebbed and flowed in time with Kate's snores, growing heavier and heavier, until she slipped away from everything they'd never do.

The door across the street opened precisely on time, and she watched a thin young man in baggy pants push a wheelchair down the ramp. He stopped at the bottom, tucked the blanket around the girl's slight frame, and pointed at the bench. The girl untucked her gloved hand from the blanket and waved enthusiastically. Cami walked quickly across the street. She hadn't met everyone who'd stayed in the Love After Life housing, but she always made arrangements to meet the current residents of their apartment on the anniversary. Knowing the space that meant so much to them now helped others was cathartic to her. It kept Blane's memory alive and had let her manage to move out, even though she knew she'd never move on.

"You must be Ms. Clark." The young face, framed in a mess of brown curls, smiled back at her. "I'm Robert, and this is my fiancée, Savannah. We're so very grateful to finally meet you."

"Thank you." She shook his hand and looked down at the girl. "It's wonderful to meet you both as well."

"I'm sorry." The girl struggled to pull the mitten from her hand as Cami reached to greet her. "I know I look silly all bundled up, when it's just slightly more than balmy for Cali, but I get so cold."

Cami shook the icy fingers Savannah extended. "Not a problem." She smiled again and noticed the extra pair of gloves sticking out of the front pocket of the young man's T-shirt. "It looks like he takes good care of you."

"Temperature control." He smiled and gently rested his hands on her shoulders. "Just another way this transplant is going to help you finish kicking cancer's ass—I mean, butt. I, uh, I'm sorry. I didn't mean to cuss. Thank you again for creating this place. I just get—"

"You get excited. And cancer is an ass. No need to sugarcoat it on my account." Cami gave him a forgiving nod and turned her attention to the girl. "I hear you've made it to the top five on the transplant list."

"Yes." Savannah beamed. "And then they believe I will have finally beaten it and can move on with my life. Go back to classes." She reached up and patted Robert's hand. "Get married. Start really living again."

"That's wonderful. I'm happy for you."

"And I want to graduate and help you buy the last three apartments left in the building for Love After Life. Having a place to stay near the treatment center, that's an actual home and not a cheap motel, has made all the difference. Having Robert here has been priceless."

"Speaking of asses"—he laughed uncomfortably—"you've saved mine from logging another six months sleeping in a chair beside her bed. See, I won't leave her, and we can't afford the private room with the foldout."

"I'm glad." Cami's eyes pricked, and she knew she'd made the right choice with their apartment. "So glad." She looked down the street and saw three jogging figures drawing closer. The couple chatted happily about life after the transplant, Savannah's graduation, and their ongoing blog and Facebook campaign to raise awareness and support of the work Life After Love was doing. "It's our pleasure," she said during an awkward pause, then added, "Thank you for meeting me. I need to go now, but I'll be in touch soon."

"No, thank *you*. Again." Savannah smiled and then shivered. Robert shook Cami's hand a second time, before pushing the chair back up the ramp and into the apartment. Cami stood on the sidewalk a moment longer, fighting the molten lump that formed in her throat as they closed the door, then walked back to the bench to wait for Kate and the others.

1 New Text—From Ellie Cell
I'm sorry, but there's no possible way I can make it this morning. 911 is an understatement. Please know I would be there if it were at all possible to leave.

Cami reread the words, knowing something catastrophic must be brewing to make Ellie miss the tradition she herself had started, and suspecting Mr. Hollywood had something to do with it. She strapped her phone back into her armband and stared at the three figures approaching in the distance. She shook her head at the sloppy gaits that flanked Kate's graceful stride and tried to decide whether she loved or hated this tradition.

Ellie

Ellie's hand shook as she scrolled through the links from her source. She clicked on the first one and watched the fuzzy pixels slowly fill the screen. Pat's phone vibrated unremittingly for the third time in ten minutes against the charging dock beside the bed. He cocooned more deeply in the duvet, stirred by the sound but looking peaceful. Ellie watched the corners of his mouth twitch into a smile as his eyes blinked heavily, resisting consciousness. She wished she could extend his sleep knowing whatever he was dreaming about would be replaced by a nightmare in mere seconds as the harsh beams of exposure invaded the room.

Her phone vibrated again as the first pictures on her computer screen came into focus. Her eyes burned, begging to blink, as they bored into each image, shocked that this scenario had never occurred to her. She locked them on the last image. It was over.

> 1 New Text—From Jess Cell (6 attachments)
> The first 3 pics will hit in one hour. The next 3 at noon.
> Another source claims there are 9 total. I am trying
> to clean up the mess you hid from me and asking if
> there's anything else I need to know before I start
> calling producers.

Ellie rubbed her temples and tried to will herself to close the computer. E-mail after e-mail flashed over the pictures on her screen as her phone vibrated. She narrowed her ears on the commotion coming from downstairs and told herself to center. *Breathe. You knew this day would come. You knew you couldn't control the when or the how. You knew it from the second you let yourself fall. Look at him and remember what you're building together. Don't let anger and embarrassment cloud your perspective. You can and will handle this.*

Pat blinked himself awake and smiled at her. "Good morn—" He stopped and sat up quickly as her expression and the computer in her lap pulled him into reality. "What is it?"

"The cards." Her heart wrenched as she turned the screen to face him and watched his sleepy eyes grow wide with shock.

"The morning after." He dropped his head into his hands and shook his head. "When she walked in."

"Yes. They weren't on the stairs when I went up, but the lights were still there. I thought you moved them."

"I wish I had. I thought you did." His voice was hoarse as he set his jaw and stared at the screen in disbelief. "Of all the things. A shot of us naked might've been less intimate." He clenched his eyes shut and looped his arm around the small of her back. "I'm so sorry, Ellie."

She took a deep breath and reminded herself they were in this together. "There's more." She minimized the window and opened another. A picture of them lying on the chaise lounge, laughing, filled the screen. Pat's arms were around her, and she was touching his face. The next was of them kissing. "Stacie must have taken it from the office window."

The doorbell to the suite chimed and their phones vibrated in unison. This was it. Whatever their new normal would be, it started now. He covered her hand on the keyboard with his, letting his lips brush across her shoulder. She closed her eyes as he tilted her chin up to face him. The doorbell sounded again, and the intercom on the opposite wall buzzed to life.

"I can't decide whether to tell you I love you again or that I'm sorry again before they beat down the door."

"Just tell me we're in this together, no matter what happens. That's all I need."

"You and me." He kissed her softly and tucked her head onto his chest. "No matter what."

"Mr. Grayson?" Dominic's voice crackled over the speaker. "Your manager is downstairs and asked me to wake you. He says it's urgent."

"Let's hope he frisked Rick and Jess for weapons," Pat whispered into her hair, and she grinned in spite of her racing mind, awed again at the effect he had on her in moments like these.

"I love you." Ellie pulled him close one final time, knowing when they let go the storm would begin and wanting to remember everything they'd promised each other. "This doesn't change that." She closed her eyes and allowed herself a brief moment to grieve for the end of their bubble. "This is us," she whispered, "walking into the next part of our story." She opened her eyes, touched by the relief that spread over his face.

"Ellie." His eyes crinkled into a smile. "I . . ." A soft knock sounded on the bedroom door. "Love you," Pat whispered, and pressed his lips to hers one last time before the masses turned the page on their next chapter.

Kate

"I'm glad to see you running again," Norah said.

"Thank you," Kate answered, setting her pace and noticing how tired Norah looked. "I can't say it's something I'll ever truly enjoy, but it's helping. Ignoring the seven thousand excuses I seem to come up with every morning to skip it is the hardest part."

"Well, if you see me running outside any other day of the year, assume something is chasing me. " Leila puffed, and they all laughed. In the distance, Kate could make out Cami's frame crossing the street to the bench. She stood taller and corrected her gait.

"I want to like the treadmill, mostly for the air conditioning," Kate joked, "but it never clears my head. I feel like a hamster, just trudging along on a wheel, not really thinking about anything. Or running anything out." That was what Blane, and later Cami, had called it.

Kate tightened her grip on the stroller handles, thinking about her first real run. It had been on this very street, six months after the accident. She ignored the ping of her FitBit and let the memory of that dark afternoon sweep through her mind.

"What the hell is this, Kate? Why didn't you tell me you were using again?" Cami burst into the living room, where she was trying to rewind the mindless comedy they'd rented.

"I'm not *using*. They're temporary. Don't make a big deal about it."

"Uh, hello? My friend the recovering anorexic is stashing diet pills in her powder compact. That is the definition of a *big deal*."

"It's nothing! I just bought them to get through grad school finals and the holidays with my family so I can stand to eat." She punched the EJECT button angrily. "Why are you going through my things in the first place? What gives you the right to do that?"

"Why? What gives me the right? For the love of God, Kate, you show up thinner every Friday, wearing more layers to hide it. That's 'why' enough for me. I'm not exactly champing at the bit to bury another person I love because of her own stupidity."

"I told you, I'm fine. I'm just taking them for the next few weeks. You have no idea how much pressure I am under right now. Grad school, the internship—it's a lot, on top of flying here every week-end. And my grandmother says she won't pay next semester's tuition if I miss Thanksgiving. They're letting Cameron come home for a couple of days, and they want it to be special for him. You know how hard going home is under the best circumstances, much less these."

"Can you even hear yourself, Kate? I won't let you justify this. You bought the pills because you're stressed about grad school? Cut back. Graduate a semester later. Can't practice your recovery principles over the holidays? Go to a meeting. Beats the hell out of spending another Christmas on a feeding tube, doesn't it? Cruella won't pay for grad school? Get a loan. Want to work your anxiety out through your body? Start running. Damn it, Kate, it's time to move on from all that."

"Seriously? You want to talk about moving on? Like you're the expert in that area?" Kate flung her hands in the air. "Look around! You haven't done a thing but work since he died. I see it, Cami. The only things that change are your stacks of film and the layouts on your board. You haven't been home; you haven't been back to the track. Are you running at all anymore?"

"We're not talking about me! We're talking about you. Well, you and the pills you think you need to get through finals and a meal with your fucked-up family."

That was Kate's breaking point. She felt her cheeks turn crimson with rage as a hot tear spilled over her lashes. "No, Cami, *you* look around. You're worried about a few pills, when you live in a veritable shrine?" She stomped to the front door and yanked the Panther Track Coach windbreaker and Blane's faculty ID lanyard off the hooks. "*This* is what I'm worried about. He's gone, Cami. Keeping everything he ever touched exactly the same won't change that! *You* go to a meeting." Kate threw the jacket and badge to the floor, tears streaming down her face, and stormed outside down the steps to the street. When she came back hours later, they were back on the hooks and Cami was in bed. Her stomach lurched when she saw the sleeping bag rolled out in its usual spot. She'd planned to sleep on the couch to make a statement, but Cami had given her an olive branch she couldn't ignore. She washed her face and changed, guilt burning through her stomach, as she lay down on the peace offering that was the green Coleman sleeping bag.

"I'm sorry," Cami said quietly.

"I was a brat. I shouldn't have thrown his things."

"No." Cami sat up in the dim light. "You shouldn't have. I know they're just things. My head knows anyway. But for whatever reason, that logic isn't working. I can't seem to move them."

"I'm sorry." Kate sat up on the sleeping bag. "I never get that angry. I don't know what's wrong with me. I shouldn't push you like that."

"Nothing's wrong with you, Kate. You're just bottling everything. It's not healthy."

"I know it's not. But it's also not okay for me to lash out at you like that. It hasn't been that long. It's not about clearing closets and running with the team. Some days just breathing is enough. You'll know when it's right to start moving on."

"I tried to change the sheets tonight."

"And?" Kate looked up and saw a new pattern had replaced the Aztec squares and cobalt blue she'd been staring at for months from this angle.

"And all I can think about is getting them out of the laundry basket and putting them back on." Cami's hand moved to the edge of the fitted sheet, and Kate reached up to hold it. "I was lying here, envisioning a thousand reasons to justify putting them back on the bed. I've gotten up to smell them three times."

"They're in the basket, but you can't wash them." Kate squeezed her hand. "You see yourself loading them, and adding the soap, but actually doing it is a different ballgame."

"Exactly." Cami stared at her through the dim light. "But we can't live this way. Nothing will change if we do. Nothing can."

"My pills are your sheets." Kate closed her eyes and pictured the ones she'd bought and taken less than an hour ago. "You don't want to need them, but you do."

"For now." Cami looked away, toward the basket in the hallway.

"No, Cami. That's my point. You don't want to need them now or ever, but you do and you will. They're like a lifeline between what is and what was."

"I'll get help if you will," Cami whispered.

"Teach me to run?"

"Yes. We start tomorrow." Cami let go of her hand and lay back on the mattress. "Find me someone to talk to?"

"Done."

The stroller bumped over a patch of rough pavement and Liam's happy coo reminded her how far she and Cami had come in their journeys and how far they had left to go.

Norah

Norah put one foot in front of the other, wondering how Cami was really doing. Not being with his family today must be a brand of difficult all its own for her. She inhaled deeply, trying to alleviate the fatigue that whispered though her body. Tonight should be calmer. She would rent a room of her own and sleep. In the meantime, she would take some conscious time to decide what she wanted. If she'd learned anything over the last three months, it was that regret wore many faces.

They slowed to a walk just before the bench. "Fancy meeting you here." Norah smiled and tried to do justice to Ellie's annual line.

"You too." Cami's wry grin spoke volumes. "Training for the Warrior Princesses 5K again?"

"You know it," Kate and Leila chimed simultaneously.

"Let's go." Cami raised an eyebrow, stretched her neck, and began to trot.

Cami

*C*ami slowed her pace, hoping they knew she was equally appreciating and humoring them. She didn't exactly like having them here, but it definitely cut the pain. She looked over her shoulder at Kate, proud to see she was keeping form, and tried not to laugh at the others. Norah ran like a robot, one foot in front of the other, lost in thought. Leila ran sloppily, focused on her feet, like a true amateur, but with all the enthusiasm of a champion. Cami increased her speed at the beep of her Running Mate app and tried to imagine what Blane would say if he were jogging beside her right now.

Leila

Whew. Leila exhaled, ecstatic they'd finally made it to the bench. She could do this. One or two miles more to the café, and she could take her leave. Her shins ached, and her lungs were raw in the cold air. She was by no means an athlete, but she wasn't a couch bum, either. Considering that child care was her main motivation for hitting the gym these days, this run was a fitting penance.

At last, the warm smell of coffee hit her nose and cheered her on as she put one foot in front of the other toward the end. Leila looked in front of her and behind her, thinking how much they'd all juggled to be here today and wondering what had stopped Ellie. It must be something big. Her mind wandered to her dead phone, wishing she'd remembered to plug it in on the drive over and hoping her girls were still asleep, not needing her.

Kate

"I'm proud of you," Kate whispered into Cami's ear as she hugged her and said goodbye.

"Me too." She shrugged her shoulders. "Call me if Mommy Dearest and Mommy Dearest-er get to be too much. I know they'd love to see me," Cami said sarcastically, and arched her brows.

"Will do." Kate laughed and said goodbye to Norah as she took Liam back from her arms. She gave him a cuddle and a kiss before strapping him into the jogging stroller, thinking the coffee and croissants smelled divine but it simply wasn't fair to ask Liam to spend another hour in the stroller. Kate took a drink from her water bottle and watched as Leila hugged Norah and Cami in turn. Her tone was cheery, but something was off. Kate listened to her chipper goodbyes and watched her eyes linger on Norah. In many ways, Leila was both her easiest and her hardest friend to read. Nothing seemed to faze her. Kate often wished she could be more like her in that respect. She was always mystified by how easily Leila found joy in almost anything. Less than five minutes before, her face had lit up when she saw the marquee at Zac's advertising that it now offered iced decaf green tea. It didn't matter that she wouldn't be back for another year and didn't have time to stay and enjoy a glass this morning; she was simply happy just knowing it existed.

Kate smiled, thinking of how Cami had compared Leila to the Energizer bunny the first time they'd met. There was definitely a resemblance. Leila was a breed all her own. She hated confrontation but never shied away from stress or hard work. She met her challenges head-on and with a smile. Kate sometimes wondered if she was compensating for having survived the first eighteen years of her life and wondered why she couldn't do the same. Hers had been just as ugly in different ways, yet she continued to let it shadow her in the greener pastures that had come afterward.

"Are you ready?" Leila asked, glancing back at the signage on the chalkboard.

"Yes." Kate smiled and began to trot forward. A few hundred feet went by in silence. "This is probably too little too late, but are you okay? You seem a little off this morning."

"You're sweet to ask." Leila panted. "I'm fine." She grimaced again, and Kate slowed her pace.

"I think I've run enough today. Do you mind if we walk for a bit? I'm sorry. It won't bother me if you run ahead."

"I'm about done for today, too." Kate smiled graciously and settled into a walk, mentally subtracting the calories she wouldn't burn.

"Thanks." Leila blushed, and Kate knew she felt patronized.

"I can run anytime. Talking to you in person, on the other hand, is a rarer form of therapy."

"That's sweet, considering I feel like my own brand of crazy most of the time." Leila laughed and looked away. "So, how are you feeling about your mom's visit? Do you need anything?"

"I'm as ready as I'll ever be. That is, unless you have a sprawling estate and some polo ponies I can borrow for the weekend," Kate said, hoping to see her grin.

"I'll see what I can do, but we've just put ours out to foal. And you know how busy our villa in Venice is this time of year."

"Too touristy for her taste anyway," Kate joked, and they both laughed. Leila looked away again and briefly touched the corner of her eye with the sleeve of her shirt.

"I don't want to push, but are you sure you're okay? Want to stop in and talk a bit?"

"I wish I could, but I promised Torri I'd be back in time to take

Clara to school. Plus, my phone is dead. I need to get back to my car to charge it."

"Something's up. Give me the CliffsNotes version, then."

"It's nothing. I'm just extra anxious today. Wes and I had a less-than-stellar morning, and I feel bad about the way I handled things, or didn't handle them, rather. Do you ever have those moments with Ken when you try so hard to weigh the situation and not react emotionally but fail miserably?"

"Ha! Yes. And by that I mean I hold everything in until I lose my shit while he stands there calmly and tries not to make any sudden movements. Feel free to nominate me for wife of the year." Kate took another swig of water, happy to see her friend relax a bit. "So, what happened this morning?"

"Just that. Nothing and everything. I hired Torri to sit with the—sleeping—girls this morning so Wes wouldn't be stressed about going in late." Leila thrust her hands around the last word into a hybrid of air quotes and jazz hands. "Scratch that. So he could go in at the crack of dawn, as usual. Anyway, I had everything set for him to leave at five thirty, and the monitor went off. Julia settled almost instantly, but not before he asked what I had today." She paused. "He was racking his brain to remember and looked terrified that he might have to take care of them until I got back. I could see it on his face. He was panicking, trying to calculate how he could possibly spare an hour and a half and leave at six forty-five, much less seven o'clock. I know I sound incredibly selfish, but it triggered every fear I have about my interview Friday and going back to the university part-time. Bench Day is once a year. I schedule reminders on his calendar weeks in advance. I don't even care that we have to hire Torri. In fact, I feel blessed we can afford to. What I care about is that the girls and I are so far off of his priority radar that it doesn't even occur to him to go in one hour, instead of two, before normal time, one day a year." She exhaled and looked embarrassed.

"I get it. Believe me." Kate forced a smile. "If the arguments Ken and I have were a revolving door, division of labor would be on three out of four panels." *The other one would be sex*, Kate thought quietly.

"Us too. That's why I'm so anxious about Friday. What about today says our family dynamic is ready for me to even consider going back to work? Back to the job I love?" Kate watched Leila wipe the corner of her right eye again and noticed the left one, the one closest to her audience, was still focused straight ahead, dry and controlled. "Then I feel awful for wanting to risk what we already have. For even considering asking him and the girls to take this leap with me." She paused and added earnestly, "At the end of the day, I have to ask myself what right I have to make that decision for them. To ask them to make sacrifices to support me when I can't predict the outcome." Kate clenched her jaw at the pain in Leila's crystal blue eyes as they searched hers for an opinion. A tense moment passed as she struggled to put her thoughts into the right words. "I can't believe how ungrateful I sound. If my chief complaint in my marriage is that my husband works like a dog at a job he loves to provide a comfortable life for his family, I'm clearly out of sync with my priorities."

"No, you're not. You're exactly right. I know that sounds crazy, but you are. We make sacrifices for the people we truly love, and no matter how willingly we do so, we lose parts of ourselves in the process. It's the ultimate give-and-take, in a way. You believe in something bigger than yourself with someone, enough that love and commitment become synonymous with sacrifice and invest-ment, trusting all the while that they would do the same for you, until eventually this scary moment comes when you're faced with asking them to reciprocate, not because you think you deserve it but because you would do the same for them. And have done. It's not about gratitude, Leila. It's about finding a way to hold on to an important part of yourself. You love teaching, and trying to find a way to keep that in your life is anything but a selfish thing." Kate touched her arm. "It's a big part of who you are. I mean that."

"Thank you," Leila said quietly. "There's a lot of truth in what you just said. I'm so torn at the moment. Going back to the classroom would be amazing. I miss it more and more every day, but I need to make sure now is the right time for all of us, not just for me. I don't want to look up a semester from now and realize I jumped at an opportunity without weighing the realities. Wes and I have to be on the same page, or it will never work. I'll be running ragged, shuttling kids all over town and grading papers at stoplights, if we can't find a better balance." She shook her head and added. "That is, if the salary is even worth the complications. After I add three more pre-K days a week for the girls, I might owe money at the end of the month, instead of earning it."

Kate laughed and looked ahead, wishing she could find a way to spend more time in the studio. Before Ken and Liam, design had defined her. Design and her disease. She swallowed hard and tried to ignore the incessant jiggle of her thighs.

Norah

Norah blanched at the sensation of the bitter liquid on her tongue and pushed her mug discreetly to the side. Her eyes wandered again to the three framed pictures of Blane staggered on the wall behind Cami. The first was of him and his family standing in front of Wrigley Field. He was smiling from underneath a Cubs hat, with an arm around his grinning sisters. His dad's hand was on his shoulder, and his mom was ducking out from the other side, squeezed between them. Norah could all but feel the candid happiness coming off the print. The next picture was a gorgeous black-and-white of him and Cami on the jogging trail just after the proposal. Norah had seen this print a hundred times in Cami's living room, but it always had an entirely different level of poignancy here. To its side was a picture of Blane with Zac, the café's owner, and Cameron on graduation day. The red bricks and tall oaks of the university commons loomed elegantly in the background as they held their diplomas in the air. A collage of articles, recognition plaques, and photos hung below it, explaining the restaurant's affiliation with organ donation and the Love After Life house. Norah wasn't sure of Zac's current role in the foundation, but she knew he'd served on the board since the beginning and fed the patients and families staying there pro bono.

"And that's when I left them to it," Cami said, as she cut into her eggs Benedict. "They'll either come around or be fired. Dean, my new boss, told them as much in yesterday's staff meeting. As much as I'd like to replace them, I need to keep their vibe at least through the current project."

"Have you talked to Leila? She could give you tips on what makes that generation click."

"I should. I can't decide whether these kids are moronic because they're young or because Dean's let them get away with blowing budgets and deadlines. I was actually hoping to run some ideas past Ellie this morning. She seems to make good calls developing her associates."

"Did she say why she missed?"

"No, but I'll bet you breakfast Mr. Hollywood knows how to deliver a line." She grimaced and speared a tomato. "On second thought, maybe I've overestimated her judgment."

"Let's hope it's just breakfast in bed." Norah said and swallowed another spoonful of yogurt. "Call me a romantic, but she must see something serious in him. We know she wouldn't take this big a risk if she didn't." Norah's phone interrupted her words.

1 New Text—From Matt Cell
I land at LAX at 5:00 and catch the red-eye to Denver.
Can u meet me? I need to talk to you.

"Speaking of bad judgment, that was Matt." Norah said wanting and not wanting to tell her about the pregnancy. "We haven't spoken to each other since I packed my bag for the week." Cami arched an eyebrow and started to speak, when a petite middle-aged woman approached the table. Norah watched Cami's face shift from confusion to recognition to surprise.

"Fancy meeting you here." The woman beamed and put her arm around Cami's shoulders. "You couldn't be with us, so I came to be with you." The woman squeezed her again, then extended her hand to Norah. "I don't believe we've met. I'm Carolyn Greene, Blane's mom."

"Norah Merrit. It's nice to meet you, too." Norah looked from Cami's stunned expression to Blane's mother's kind smile.

"You're a doctor, an ob-gyn, right? I see your name on the Love After Life donor list." She laughed and added, "Cami mentions you, too, of course." Carolyn pulled out a chair and patted Cami's arm. Norah was instantly impressed by the woman's easy grace and charisma. "I'll never forget the sweet doctor who took care of me and my babies. Blane and his sisters were all born in the middle of the night. That's surely a calling if there ever was one."

"It definitely is," Norah said, noting the redness gathering in Cami's eyes, and engaged Carolyn in deeper conversation to buy her friend a few seconds. Norah felt the need to be Cami's advocate, as if she were a patient who needed a moment to process the situation without any other interested party in her ear. "And thank you for saying that. I always say you have to be borderline insane to love it enough to do it well," she added, to keep Carolyn's attention off Cami, and handed her a menu.

"So, what's Zac serving these days?" Carolyn said, glancing discreetly in Cami's direction. "I'm off carbs at the moment, or I'd go for the brioche French toast with Z sauce. You can't go wrong with browned butter and toffee, no matter how hard you try." She laughed, and Cami regained her composure enough to stammer only slightly through suggesting the farm-to-market omelet.

"That sounds good, but do you think I can beg them to slather the Z sauce on my egg whites?"

"For you? Anything," a cheery voice announced from behind them.

"Zac!" Carolyn stood and folded him into a motherly embrace planting a peck on his cheek.

"I'm glad you came," he said, and a silent moment passed between them. "Do you like the wall?"

"I do. I see you took my suggestion." Norah followed Cami's eyes to the picture of the three smiling boys on graduation day. "I'm proud of you for including Cameron. Blane would be, too."

"Thank you." Zac gestured to her seat and pulled out the chair on the opposite side.

"Do you remember Norah?" Cami asked, a little too quickly.

"Of course." He smiled and raised a finger to their waiter. "It's nice to see you again."

"You as well." Norah looked into his kind eyes, remembering the last time she and Matt had eaten here. He'd sat with them for a while, chatting about opening a third café in the arts district. Matt had criticized him about the high rent and hefty restaurant turnover rate in that area. She'd been embarrassed at his gruffness, expecting Zac to be offended. Instead, he had answered humbly that he was nervous about the location but proud to be in a position to take a gamble in the present economy.

"A carafe of mimosas and four glasses, please. Also, an order of the brioche French toast with extra Z sauce for Mrs. Greene." He winked across the table. "Thank you."

"Just three glasses." Norah smiled. "Unfortunately, I'll be leaving in a moment."

"Are you sure you can't stay?" Zac asked, grinning. "I'm buying."

"As much as I'd like to, I can't this time. I see my first patient at nine o'clock and need to grab a shower. But thank you."

"Give the lovely doctor a coupon, Zac!" Carolyn teased.

"I'm sure that can be arranged." He said affectionately and excused himself to the kitchen.

"I simply adore the tradition you ladies have." She continued, voice composed, but lingering her gaze on the pictures behind her head a beat too long. Norah watched her friend relax. "You'll have to tell the others I said hello. I phoned Zac last week, and we schemed this together. Family shouldn't be apart on days like these. Not that"—she paused, and her tone grew somber—"you girls aren't like family to Cami, but Gerri and I said that if she couldn't be with us today, someone from our family would be with her." She continued nervously. "'Would damn sure be with her,' if you want the direct quote." Cami and Zac laughed as the waiter approached with the tray of mimosas.

Norah thanked Zac for breakfast and said her goodbyes. As

the wet air hit her cheeks, she felt grateful to be leaving Cami in the company of people who loved her. No matter how stoic she managed to stay, today would always ring with regret and what-might-have-beens.

Norah's phone vibrated again in her pocket, and she took it out reluctantly.

1 New Text—From Matt Cell
We can meet somewhere in between Mercy and LAX.

She read the words, knowing that was as much of a concession as she would get from him.

New Text-To Matt Cell
I can meet you at Carlton's at 7:00.

1 New Text—From Matt Cell
Unless you get a call.

New Text-To Matt Cell
Yes, I am on call until next Sunday. I took an extra wk now in exchange for the wk after new year's bc you wanted to go skiing.

She typed the word *remember*, then deleted it and pressed SEND. Antagonizing him wouldn't help anyone. Fatigue and her own what-might-have-beens coursed through her head as she walked to her car.

Leila

Leila tapped her fingers on the steering wheel, willing the light to turn green. Her phone buzzed to life on the charger and she took relief in being connected again.. She swiped UNLOCK and scanned for messages from Torri or Wes. *Good*, she thought, only seeing a text from Ellie and a number she didn't recognize. The words from the unknown number popped from the screen as the light changed. *Cancer?* Leila eased into the intersection, wondering if the message was meant for her or if it was a mistake. At the next light, she typed a quick reply.

Reply to 1-770-448-1999
Who is this?

1 New Msg: From 1-770-448-1999
Tanya. I got a new number.

"Of course it is," Leila said to herself. She could hear Tanya and her step-father now, singing the same old chorus about how selfish she'd become since she'd left "home" and how above them she thought she was. Tanya was two years younger than she was, and the hero of the family in their mother's eyes. Despite having had her first baby at fifteen, she'd graduated high school and gotten a job as a night baker at a supermarket. Over time, she had become the assistant bakery manager. Leila respected how hard she worked and suspected it was Tanya who kept their mother and Randall in groceries when nicotine and lotto tickets overtook the food budget.

The light changed again as another text broke the silence. The rest of the message would have to wait. She would call after she took Clara to school and attempt to get to the bottom of it all. Her attention turned to weaving through the congestion as her mind stewed over her responsibilities and the room left on her plate.

Ellie

"You're going to need this before you go viral," Jess said coldly, and tossed her a phone. "Your contacts are already transferred."

"Thank you." Ellie nodded, knowing she would be furious, too, if she were in Jess's position. "Please sit. I owe you an apology." She gestured to a chair in front of the conference table. Jess looked down at her tablet and hit a few keys before grudgingly taking the seat.

"It's embarrassing, Ellison. I was vehemently adamant this was a hoax when I got the first call. 'Not possible,' I said, and told Nate to ignore it. Two hours later, I finally walk through the door of my apartment after a fifteen-hour day, and a source is e-mailing me pics of you and a client."

"As I said"—Ellie sat across from her—"I owe you an apology. Not telling you was clearly disrespectful of your time and the hours you've spent on his representation." Jess busied herself checking her phone as Ellie continued, "I want you to know that I planned to meet with you this morning to tell you Mr. Grayson and I were in the beginnings of a relationship. It's not something I anticipated, but it happened." Jess's jaw tightened, and Ellie lifted her tone to break the tension. "Clearly, that meeting is about twelve hours overdue."

"Clearly." Jess met her gaze.

"Again, I apologize. I feel you're an important asset to my firm, and I had no intention of disrespecting your position."

"You know how this makes me look. My name is the one on the line here. I'm the publicist of record on his account." Jess's voice was controlled, but her eyes were flaming. "Goldberg interviews him on the heels of a cheating scandal, and he leaves looking like the patron saint of good guys. Then, twelve hours later, it surfaces that he's been writing love notes to my boss? When this clears, all anyone who's anyone will know is that this went on right under my nose and Ellison Lindsay didn't trust me enough to tell me before it hit the press." Jess stared confidently into her eyes and drummed her fingers on the table. Ellie met her glare with a nod. What Jess wasn't saying spoke more loudly than what she was. She was worried this situation would tarnish her future in the industry and keep her from moving on from EP. Professionally, Ellie could easily milk that fear and keep Jess at the firm longer. She anticipated Jess would move on when the competition's offer was right, but in the meantime, she didn't want her jumping at the first thing that came along because she was afraid of stagnation. That wasn't necessarily in her best interest or Pat's.

"I realize your name is on the line. If you'd like to prepare a statement itemizing your involvement in these events, I'll gladly sign it and add an endorsement to your time here." Ellie studied her face. "We both know today will be a pressure cooker for all involved. I can tell you now that what you do from this minute on will be noted and remembered from the outside longer than anything you've done here before. Handle the fallout well, and watch the doors open." Ellie's new phone vibrated, and she pushed herself up from her seat. "I can promise you vultures are watching every move you make."

"Thank you," Jess said, and stood. "You should know I want to stay. And that I'm happy for you."

"I appreciate that." Ellie smiled and waited the necessary five seconds before adding, "Where are we regarding *Ellen*? Did you ask for Abe?"

"I did. Apparently, Mr. Grayson made quite the impression last time he was there."

"A positive one, I hope," Ellie said, trying to remember if they'd represented him at the time.

"Yes. I was ready to dance, but they were easy. It doesn't hurt that Ellen has been raving about *Life of Us* on her website and running a contest to send viewers with exceptional love stories to the premiere."

"That's good." Ellie's old phone rang, displaying an unknown number, and she silenced it. "Where do we stand with the other appearances?"

"They're salivating to get at him. Not surprisingly."

"Threaten to pull the interview if they won't accept the new script. I can call, if needed." The last five words left her mouth in tandem with the realization that her influence was laughable at the moment. A flush of embarrassment rose in her cheeks. She looked over Jess's shoulder through the glass into the bustling first floor of the penthouse. The rest of the PR team was hunkered over electronics, doing their best to steal discreet glances into the conference room. If the group fifty feet from her was this shaken, she shuddered to think about what was going on back in the office. "Call them in. We need to talk angles."

Jess nodded and stood. Ellie watched her leave the room, planning what she would say to the rest of her team and debating what the right spin would be from here. She'd predicted a hundred scenarios, involving everything from hidden agendas to pictures that Stacie or a telescopic lens could have snapped, but not once had she factored in the cards.

The team filed in, avoiding her eyes and busying themselves selecting seats and opening laptops. Jess motioned for them to sit, and Ellie watched them silence their phones and ready their devices to take notes. She filled her lungs and stepped to the head of the table. As if in unison, their heads snapped up from their screens and their eyes darted from one another's to hers. Fingers swiped and typed in a flurry of activity. Jess pressed her palm to her Bluetooth and shook her head.

"What is it?" Ellie asked, and fumbled over the unfamiliar icons on her new screen. Throats swallowed and mouths gaped around the table as strained eyes battled wordlessly over who would speak.

Activity behind the glass seemed to stop as a mural of faces turned their attention to the windows of the conference room.

"The cards just hit Twitter." Jess's words rang out in the silence. "And it crashed." Ellie steeled her gaze on the wall behind the table and curled her fingers into the palm of her hand. It was time to go to work.

Ellie

Ellie's heartbeat pounded in her ears, drowning out the sounds of the room. "I would like to say publicly that I value my privacy and that I intended to keep my relationship with Mr. Grayson separate from the firm. Unfortunately, because of the actions of an associate, that choice is not an option." She looked into each of their eyes. "Should any of you feel my involvement with Mr. Grayson compromises your ability to contribute to his representation, I will gladly assign you to another team"—she paused—"with a nod to your honesty and professionalism." She watched her words register on their faces, then added, "Should you choose to remain on Mr. Grayson's team, I will continue to accept nothing less than excellence. You're in this room because I, and Jess, believe you are among EP's best and because I trust you will continue to validate that opinion." A wave of nods circled the table. "Now, if you'll excuse us, I would like to speak to Jess privately." Ellie walked toward the door, followed by the staccato click of Jess's heels on the tile. She tried to ignore the dozen pairs of eyes watching her as she crossed the room. The office spaces occupied, she walked to the elevator and punched the private code. Jess stepped in and reached for the UP button as the doors closed.

"No. We don't need to go up. I just wanted to use the space."

"Of course." Jess posed her hand over her tablet to take notes. "It's a madhouse in there."

"And I plan to brief him when we finish. This way, I don't have to make two grand entrances." She watched her logic register on Jess' face. "We need to decide where we go from here. I'm thinking we take attention away from the cards and focus on the pictures. They're easier to spin."

"Ultimately, it's your decision. But I'd like to give you my honest opinion." Jess pursed her lips, unsure of whether to continue.

"Please do. I appreciate your honesty."

"Again, the decision is yours, but I've been analyzing our choices regarding this campaign. It's strongest when we let Mr. Grayson speak from his heart. Look at what he did on *Goldberg*. There were some rocky moments when they went on a tangent, but he spoke candidly and left with higher marks than we ever could have scripted. I say we let him tell the truth." She paused, and Ellie nodded pensively for her to continue. "Or as much of it, that is, as you would both like divulged."

Pat's entire campaign surged through Ellie's mind. Jess was right. From day one of his contract, he'd trumped every angle they'd created to promote him by lapsing into being himself. She nodded again, thinking of the interviews after he and Blythe Barrett separated. Her firm had worked hard to squelch the raging rumors that Blythe's affair had left him devastated and sparked a feud among the *Destiny* cast members. That alone was a difficult task not only because the rumors were true, but also because EP represented both stars. Blythe and another *Destiny* leading man began a romantic relationship while on tour representing the film at the European premieres as Pat, the director, and two other cast members attended premieres in Asia. Their split was anything but amicable, but both parties agreed to the spin. Blythe stuck strictly to the script and was lampooned as insincere and callous. Pat, on the other hand, let his nerves continually get the best of him on live camera and rarely stayed on script yet left the ordeal more popular than ever with fans. Ellie hadn't made the connection until now. Her concern at the time had been ensuring that the fires Blythe's reception created were extinguished.

"You're right." She exhaled sharply and shook her head. "We need to let him speak."

"I'll brief the rest of the team." Jess smiled briefly, before adding, "Discreetly, of course," and pressing the button to open the doors.

Ellie took a moment to focus. Right now, she needed to map out where they went from here professionally. Worst-case scenario, Pat left the building for the *Ellen* appearance and she waited out the paparazzi in the suite. She could do this. The elevator began to move before she reached for the UP button. A few seconds later, the doors opened and Pat was standing in front of her.

He ran his hand through his freshly styled hair. "I didn't hear from you, so I decided to come down. I wanted—I needed, rather—to make sure you were okay."

"Thank you." She was surprised by the quietness of her own voice. "Can we talk?" Ellie gestured to the sitting area across the foyer.

"Of course." His eyes flared nervously as he turned his body away from her. *No, it's not that,* she thought and softened her face.

"I'm sorry, Pat. I'm in work mode at the moment." Ellie reached for his hand. "I just need to talk to you."

"Thank God," he blurted, and then grinned and affected his best surfer accent. "I mean, that's cool."

"Cute." She smiled. "Can we sit now? The shoes my stylist sent are killing me." As they sat, she looked around the room to determine what members of his team had been here.

"We're alone. It's just Dominic now." He laughed. "Don't get me wrong. Rick was here, but he threw his fit and left. Not before he told me I was making the biggest mistake of my career since *Life of Us* and plopped the latest offer for the *Destiny* prequel on the coffee table."

"Something to fall back on," she said in a failed attempt to make him smile. "In all seriousness, I'm sorry. That couldn't have been easy. I know he's been with you from the beginning."

"Thank you," he said distractedly, and put his hand on her leg. "Soooooo, tell me about your morning. My manager can't be the only one raising Cain."

"Well, I missed Bench Day and Jess all but threw a phone at me. I'd say it went downhill from there."

"Until now, right?" He laughed and kissed her hand. *But I've come to realize I need to give the trust I expect from you.* The words were on her lips when he said, "Because I understand if today is your worst nightmare come true. I never wanted to put you in this position, and I know you never dreamed you'd be here."

"Yes. Today is epically difficult so far. And that's what I'd like to talk about with you." He squeezed her hand. "I've been doing a lot of thinking about you and us and your representation, and I've come to a conclusion."

"Ellie—"

She interrupted, "Please let me finish. I've come to the conclusion that I underestimate you."

"Underestimate? I don't understand."

"I mean that I continually predict the fallout of what you might say and script accordingly; then you surprise me by being authentic. I can't say that I regret those decisions, but I can say that I apologize. You deserve better."

"That's not necessary to say the least." The worried expression never left him as she continued.

"I'm serious, Pat." She said cupping his face in her palms. "It's important to me that you hear what I'm saying and give me your thoughts. I've underestimated who you are."

"I still can't say I'm following. Did I miss something?"

"No. I'm butchering what I'm trying to say. The sad truth is that the majority of what my firm—and me, by extension—does is invent or reinvent people. In your case, we handled situations, but there was never a moment when we needed to create a facade to trade on." She closed her eyes to gather her thoughts. "What I'm trying to say is that you have earned my trust in more ways than one. I look back over your representation and see that you're strongest when you're being yourself."

"Thank you. I think?" He squeezed her hand again.

"It's a compliment. I can assure you. Essentially, we need to decide what we want to tell the world about us and pick a direction. No script and no spin." Ellie looked into his shining eyes, knowing she'd been so focused on not letting her personal life bleed into her professional life that she'd done just the opposite. "I'm suggesting that from here on out, we decide together on what you will and won't talk about; then the firm will pass the questions along to the venues and you'll speak candidly."

"Sounds dangerous." He laughed, "Have you run this by my publicist? I think you might know her: five six–ish, blond, gorgeous . . ."

"We've met, and she approves this message," Ellie raised his hand to her lips as the mechanical ding of the elevator signaled Jess's arrival.

Cami

"That was kind of you," Cami said to Zac after Carolyn excused herself to the restroom.

"I wanted to warn you so you weren't caught off-guard, but she was adamant it be a surprise." He spun the specials menu absentmindedly between his fingers as he spoke.

"I meant expanding the picture of graduation to include Cameron. I know she's wanted that since we hung the cropped one of you and Blane years ago."

"Oh. I probably should have warned you about that as well. I can't say I ever thought we'd be sitting here like this the day she took it." He looked toward the restrooms.

"It's fine." She looked at her watch. "I'm just not quite as far down the road to forgiveness as you are." She shot an icy glance at the photo. "But maybe I will be one day." Zac reached for her hand, and she pulled it back, shaking her head. "I'm fine."

"Well, I'm not. Today is killing me." He tapped the specials card in a one-two rhythm on the table. "And I know it's even harder for you. Believe me when I say the last thing he said to me before they got on the Jet Ski, the accident, the lies after—hell, even the way the sky and the waves looked that day—all of it is running on a nonstop loop in my mind."

"I know." She looked down at her lap and swallowed the lump of lava in her throat. "Did you know they're in town to see Kate?"

"No." He slipped the card back into its wire holder and stood as

Carolyn made her way back to the table. "Listen, if you don't have plans tonight, join me for dinner. I don't want you to be alone." He looked from the wall to her and added. "You know he wouldn't want either one of us to be."

"Wouldn't want you to be what?" Carolyn's chipper tone was at once refreshing and out of place.

"Alone." Zac smiled, charm restored. "I'm trying to convince Cami to meet me for dinner tonight."

"Well"—she put one hand on his shoulder and the other on Cami's—"keep trying." The two exchanged a knowing look as Carolyn added, "I'd insist you take me, too, if I weren't flying out later this afternoon."

"Thank you for the offer. I'll consider it and let you know. As of now, my plan is to pull a double to wrap up a project, then go home and have a double."

"What I'm hearing is, you want a late reservation," Carolyn quipped to Zac and sat. Cami raised her eyebrows at the pair, noticing for the thousandth time that Carolyn's smile was identical to Blane's.

Kate

One avocado; half a banana; six, seven, eight, nine almonds to go. Kate counted the nuts she'd lined up on the countertop, then subtracted two for the half mile she'd walked with Leila. A salad plus five bites of chicken, and she would meet her goal for the day. The inquisition would arrive soon, and she needed to shower and change before Liam woke up. She walked into the bedroom, pleased with how the new throw pillows she'd sewn the night before popped on the white duvet. If hotel chic were a thing, that was her style. Creating complicated rooms and blending eclectic palettes was easy; pulling off simplicity was much harder. She paused, thinking that was, unfortunately, true in life as well.

Kate stopped to swallow the almond in her mouth before she walked into the bathroom. The last thing she needed right now was to look at herself while she ate. Kate's nerves flared and she tried to remember that she was enough.

Leila

"Some of us have to work and be moms, you know."

Leila gritted her teeth as Tanya continued to rail. *That was a low blow. I would have thought she would need to know me better to insult me that deeply.* "Can you at least get that rich husband of yours to pay for her to see a decent doctor? The ER doc took chest X-rays and said it looks like cancer. He might be wrong. You know they don't try as hard when you tell them you're a smoker. Daddy told her not to, but she was scared."

"Of course we'll help. I'll talk to Wes and we will try to help navigate the system."

"You'll try? God, you're more disgusting than I thought. Who the hell took care of you when you were sick?"

"I did. Who took care of you? Me again."

"Play the victim all you want, but you only got one family."

"That's very true," Leila said, before she could stop herself.

"You will never change! You are a selfish bitch and always have been!"

The conversation left her livid. She knew Tanya was scared and would be on Randall's side, regardless of the ways he controlled and manipulated their mother and of the abuse that Leila, more than the others, had suffered at his belt and temper. There was nothing Leila could say to open Tanya's eyes and, at the end of the day, she knew people accepted the love they thought they deserved. She needed to focus on that in lieu of replaying the ridiculously skewed conversation they'd had over and over again in her head. Yes, she was successful. Yes, she remembered where she came from. Yes, she would help her mother. She cringed as Tanya's last words echoed in her mind: *selfish bitch and always have been.* Her opinion shouldn't matter. But it did. Tanya thought she was callous. That was the last word in the world Leila wanted to describe her, but Tanya didn't know anything about her or how she lived her life, except for what she'd grown up hearing.

1 New Text— From Norah Cell
BTW, I met the 50-year-old version of you today.

Someone blessed and stressed? Leila thought, and hoped she hadn't done anything to embarrass Cami on the run. She thumbed through her texts again, thinking it took a simple glance at her phone to know who supported her. She stared at the text from Tanya and wondered if she was the sanest or the craziest person in the room. The people who were supposed to love her unconditionally, her biological family, treated her the worst, while the people who could exit her life at will, her friends and husband, continually stayed the longest and treated her the best. Of all the things she questioned about herself, the one thing she knew for sure was that she fostered every relationship in her life the same way. She closed her eyes for a second and tried to center her thoughts.

1 New Text—To Norah Cell
And I thought this day couldn't get any stranger.
You'll have to tell me the whole story soon.

1 New Text—From Norah Cell
It was Carolyn Greene, Blane's mother. She came into town to be with Cami. I hadn't met her before. She reminds me of you.

1 New Text—To Norah Cell
Thank you. I needed to hear something positive today.
I've always been impressed by her. I can only imagine
how strong she must be to handle things so graciously.

1 New Text—From Norah Cell
Sorry it's been a rough one. Let's talk tonight.

1 New Text—To Norah Cell
Sounds good. Miles to go before we sleep.

1 New Text—From Norah Cell
Exactly. Meeting Matt tonight on top of everything
else. I guess he's finally cooled down enough to talk.

Or he wants something, Leila thought as she read the words.

1 New Text—To Norah Cell
I'm sorry. I know that conversation won't be easy.

She looked from her phone to the clock to the cereal bowls still
on the table and couch full of laundry. Leila shook her head thinking about the changes looming in her own marriage and told herself
to take an inventory of what she didn't like and do better. Hard work
was hard work, and life was life. There were as many choices as there
were cycles.

Ellie

"You're sure this is what you kids want?" Dominic looked from Pat to her, with his hand poised to open the VIP entrance to the lobby. "I know this isn't exactly your first rodeo, Ms. Lindsay, but it's a whole new ballgame when it's you they want as much as the client."

"Yes." Ellie nodded. "The circus for the moment; the garage as much as possible from here on out."

"We're sure, friend." Pat clasped his hand on Dominic's shoulder, and Dominic raised his eyebrows with a shrug and pressed his hand to his Bluetooth. "Boss says we're still a go, boys. Get in flank formation seven for two targets—T-1: Mr. G.; T-2: Ms. Ellison Lindsay. Out the north doors, to the black Benz Sprinter." He looked at her with a wry grin. "You know the last diplomat's detail I served wasn't as much trouble as he is?"

"I guess it's good to be number one," Pat bantered, and reached for Ellie's hand as Dominic fired back, "And the soberest person at rehab still has a problem."

"I pay him extra for the jokes," Pat said to her, and held his hand to Dominic for a fist bump. The large man laughed, then turned instantly deadpan again as a voice crackled across the radio on his belt that the PD officers had cleared the sidewalks and were in place. Dominic opened the door and stepped into the foyer. Two hotel security guards standing outside the doors shook his hand, and the three exchanged words Ellie couldn't hear. She told herself to be strong in their decision as Pat leaned closer to her and whispered,

"This is us not only meeting the moment but owning it the only way we can."

"Indeed." She ran her thumb over his knuckles, still looking straight ahead. "What's waiting out there is terrifying, but I'd rather own it with you than let anyone but us put their spin on it first."

"Mr. Grayson, Ms. Lindsay." Dominic walked back to the door and gestured toward the lobby. "We're ready for you now." Ellie stepped over the threshold, reminding herself this was not the first, and would not be the last, difficult walk she'd ever take in public. The perfectly polished marble stretching across the lobby in front of her was no different than the slick, speckled laminate of the ICU; the green carpet of the funeral home; the shiny cherry wood of the stage at Sherri's graduation; the striped Orientals of her first pitch at Camelot; the metal steps of too many press conferences to count; the red carpets at a million events; the smooth aspen planks to cut the ribbon for Warrior Princesses; the topiary-dotted walkway leaving Cinque Terre; the Berber carpet of the bank that told her no and the paisley pattern of the one that financed year one of her firm; the ramp to ring the Stock Exchange bell when the company went public; the cracked concrete in front of the bench; the harried walk to podium after podium when the firm was recognized. She would approach this performance exactly the same way she had the others: by stepping out of the known and into the light, posture straight, eyes focused forward, face composed, faking what she felt or didn't feel as the moment dictated.

"Time to go live." She fixed her face into a relaxed smile and squeezed his hand. Guests in the lobby milled around, watching the activity with varying degrees of interest, as Pat's security officers moved in behind and beside them.

Dominic turned to face them, eyes on her, and said, "This is old hack for Mr. Destiny here, but you just keep your hand in his, and you both keep on keepin' your eyes on the back of my bald head until that car door closes." Ellie nodded, feeling the adrenaline rise into her chest as they took the first steps behind him. Across the room, additional security stood in front of the golden revolving door.

"Goodbye, gilded cage; hello, bright lights," Pat joked, through the smile she knew he was faking. His free hand darted quickly to his collar, then back to his side. The simple movement reminded her why she was walking into the lion's den.

"Don't fall harder than you're willing to crash." She held his hand more tightly and shot him her real smile—the one she'd felt cross her face more and more every day they had spent together. His stride broke momentarily, and a flush of color touched his cheeks. She pulsed his hand in hers in acknowledgment and returned her focus to the growing din of voices as they drew nearer to the door. Dominic stopped, and the pair of guards behind them closed ranks as the ones at the sides walked quickly to the first panel the door-man held open. They walked through single file as the lights and crowd on the other side went wild. Dominic barked a number into his mouthpiece and moved forward a step or two more quickly.

Walk. Ellie gaped unintentionally at the sea of flashing bulbs jockeying for position, then forced her eyes back to their normal shape and focused on the click of her heels as Dominic pushed the pane forward. Pat stepped in front of her, instinctively holding the door, and she broke her stride by a half step. She paused, covering the bobble on her heel with the habitual nod to politeness she used daily for doormen and drivers. Pat tightened his grip on her hand and mouthed the word *together* before taking the final step out of the door frame and toward the deafening roar of the crowd. A hand behind her held the pane as the white flashes in front of her seared her corneas and voices roared in scattered unison, blurring everything into a faceless landscape of jutting microphones, crouched cameras, and hanging booms. The echo of her full name tore through her eardrums as shouted questions and orders barked by police officers jumbled together in her mind. Adrenaline raced through her heart and pins of light stuck to her eyelids as she forced her feet to continue the one-two rhythm that would get her through this. Dominic's shape bobbed up and down in front of her as the blaze of bulbs and the furious clicking of shutters intensified. She lost Dominic's shape in the surge as the quickening pull of Pat's arm on hers led her forward.

"Ladies first" broke through her nerves, as a hand on her back told her she could pause. Static charges ripped across her eyes as the warm air of the cavernous space came into focus. She tucked her skirt and slid over the smooth leather until her arm touched the cool wooden panel of the door on the opposite side. Pat's hand followed behind, and she held it to her chest as the door closed. Her breath returned more quickly than her sight as her heart pounded into his freezing hand.

"You okay?" His eyes were wild.

"Yes. I . . . I . . . just need to catch my, my." She filled her lungs and tapped her tongue to the roof of her mouth to steady her racing pulse. "That was like nothing else I've ever done." She fought to steady the rise and fall of her chest. "I've been in the middle of my fair share of flashbulbs with clients, booed off stages, barraged with mics, but—"

"Shh . . . it's okay." He pressed his forehead to hers, and she fought to focus her eyes on his. "That was bloody intense," he whispered. "No amount of press time can prepare someone for what you just walked through." She blinked again as her eyes adjusted to the dim light of the vehicle and his face emerged. His eyes shone with a pride she hadn't expected. The icon on the privacy screen lit up, and the dark glass began to recede.

"Good work, kids." Dominic turned to face them from the front passenger seat. She noticed the dew on his brow and took a bit of comfort in the fact that what they'd just been through was stressful even for an industry veteran. "You're an old pro now, Ms. Lindsay. Nothin's quite like that first trial by fire." He gave her a nod as the screen began to rise again.

"Thank you," she said before it sealed. She looked down at Pat's hand, still laced between her fingers, and raised an eyebrow. "According to the Patrick Grayson fun facts I've collected, your freezing hand tells me you must be nervous."

"Nah." His face glowed with mischief. "It's just broken." She flushed, suddenly realizing how tightly she'd been holding it, and peeled her fingers from his.

"I'm sorry! I didn't realize how hard I—"

"Don't worry." He fanned and wiggled the fingers of his opposite hand. "It appears I have a spare." She shook her head and smiled in spite of herself as she reached for her computer case.

Cami

"Walk with me?" Carolyn offered her arm and gestured in the direction of the bench.

"Of course." Cami looped her arm awkwardly through the opening and began to walk.

"So, how are you really, dear?" Carolyn patted her wrist with motherly affection. "Leaving InFocus can't have been easy. I know how hard you worked to get to the top."

"It definitely wasn't. Then again, it also wasn't my choice." She looked away from a mother and daughter walking by in the opposite direction.

"Well, if I've learned one thing, it's that's pain is often opportunity in disguise. Either we learn to live around it or we learn to use it. I could see this being the beginning of something big for you. A new edge to your work." She blushed and added, "You know, Gerry keeps them all. We have an entire scrapbook of your spreads on the coffee table."

"That means a lot to me. Thank you." Cami smoothed her hair behind her jogging headband with her free hand, wondering if they realized she merely arranged photographs, rather than took them, these days. "And thank you for being here." Carolyn nodded and gave her arm a squeeze as the bench and the Life After Love house came into view.

"Don't be silly. It's nice to have a little time alone with you." She tensed and slowed her gait. "The next time I'll see you will likely be at Gracie's wedding. Goodness knows I'll be running ragged that weekend."

"It's hard to believe she's getting married," Cami said quietly, thinking she should be sitting with Blane at the ceremony, not lighting a candle with Zac in his memory.

"I know." She paused, and Cami felt her stiffen. "It feels like Allie's wedding was just yesterday, and it looks like Molly will be next. Her boyfriend, Tristan, took Gerry and me to dinner last week. He wants to ask her on Christmas Eve."

"That's wonderful." Cami forced enthusiasm as her hand went instinctively to her chest. Blane's ring dangled there on a long chain, out of sight but always with her.

"It is. He's a nice young man. You know he's graduating in May with a degree in social work? Such a servant's heart. He's moved back in with his parents for the time being, to save for their future. They won't have a lot in the way of luxuries, but they'll be happy." Carolyn rushed her words as the bench loomed twenty feet away.

"Shall we sit?" Cami asked, looking toward their old apartment and thinking she had the most when she had the least.

"Yes." She felt Carolyn's shudder, despite her best effort to hide it.

"Which is another reason I hoped we could talk." Cami watched a tear fall from each of Carolyn's eyes as she continued. "I . . . well, I wanted to ask you about . . ." She stopped and blotted her face with the sleeve of her shirt. A long moment passed as a hospice van pulled into one of the LAL ramps. "Let me start over. I want you to know we never intended this, but Tristan has requested on behalf of Molly to have grandmother's ring. He said he asked her early on in the relationship to describe her fantasy proposal, expense aside, and of everything she came up with, Eiffel Tower included, that was the most important to her. She . . . she feels like wearing it every day would honor the loved ones she's lost."

Cami's heart was on fire at the words. Not their ring. Anything but that. She'd gladly give Tristan a loan or have a replica made with a real diamond. Didn't Molly understand it wasn't about the object?

It was about linking your life to someone. No matter what the future held. She and Blane had done that. Cami opened her mouth, but the words wouldn't come. Carolyn's hand shook as she took Cami's arm again. "I want you to know we haven't said yes. In fact, we said it wasn't our choice. And I mean that. It's yours." Cami stared blankly ahead at the apartment. "Look at me, Cami." Carolyn begged. "The day Blane asked me for that ring was one of the happiest days of my life. I told him then that we would love you forever, right alongside him. And we meant it. No one but you, Gerry, and me will ever know about this conversation." She shifted her body so Cami had no choice but to look at her. "I mean that, Cami. Look at this." She pointed to the LAL building across the street. "I couldn't ask for a better expression of love for him and his memory than what you've created. He"—her voice cracked—"would be so proud of and humbled by everything you've done."

"I hope so." The words sounded foreign leaving Cami's mouth. The metal band riding the beats of her heart was more noticeable than ever. She knew she should give Carolyn the ring, let Molly love it for the rest of her life, but she couldn't. It. Was. The. Last. Thing. She. Had.

Leila

"Welcome back. You're listening to *Live with Lilly and Clive*. Social media is on fire over Pat Grayson and the continuing Scargate saga."

"On fire is right. The *Destiny* hunk is in even more hot water as pics of the steamy weekend he spent with new flame Ellison Lindsay circle the Web."

"So, let me get this straight, Lilly: just twenty-four hours after photos of him kissing Scarlett James—"

"Who is married—"

"Yes, kissing *Mrs.* Scarlett James in Aspen make worldwide head-lines, Grayson drops off the face of the planet and Scarlett has a mental breakdown. She lands in the loony bin, knocked up, and, well, at this point, we all know where he landed."

"That's right, Clive. It looks like Pat landed on his publicist"—she paused for laughter, before adding—"'s deck in Malibu."

Leila toggled to the next Hollywood Beat station on the XM radio list as she edged forward in the carpool lane. Another DJ chided, "Don't hate the player, man; hate the game. I've watched the whole interview twice now, and Goldberg calls him out on all the women he's been with, but the dude never bites. The opposite. He tells his fans he doesn't give away his body as often as he gives away his heart. Time to call a spade a spade, Mr. *Destiny*. You got some, and you got caught."

"Britain's own Patrick Grayson dominates entertainment news

once again as photos of love letters he wrote to a woman called Allison Lindsay go viral. More details expected later this afternoon, when he continues the American press tour for his latest film." Leila scrolled to the next channel thinking about what Ellie must be going through.

"I think it's safe to say women all over the country are swooning a little harder than usual over Pat Grayson after reading the intimate notes he left for the new lady in his life. We don't have all the details yet, but we do know Ellison Lindsay is one lucky girl!" Leila changed the station again.

"Awww, come on. You don't believe in whirlwind romances?" A giddy female voice countered her partner.

"That's just it, Cora. The dude's been all over TV and radio, fighting rumors he was engaged to Scarlett James; then it comes out he's been shacking up with his publicist, and the two practically skip down the stairs of the Mandarin together? Either this is the most blatant publicity stunt I've ever seen, or he really is that big of an idiot. I mean, just who is this knockout, anyway? She's a *publicist*. *His* publicist! Search her name on YouTube, and the first thing that comes up is the press conference she held for him after the Scargate scandal broke. How do we know she's not using him? At this point, no one has more to lose than she does!"

Leila rolled her eyes and scrolled again. "The Pink Ladies here, keeping you up to date on all the latest Hollywood buzz," a chipper voice announced. "If you haven't seen the photos of Pat Grayson getting cozy in Malibu this weekend, do yourselves a favor and get to our website, pronto!"

"You won't regret it," another voice talked over the first. "These pics are hot, hot, hot!"

"Somebody get Mama some ice!" a third voice laughed. "And the only thing hotter than the sunset smooching is what happened inside. Whew! Can we say *romance*?"

"With a capital *R*, Tish!"

"Who needs Hallmark when your boyfriend writes like this? My lady bits are tinglin' just reading these cards! Lord have mercy!" The three laughed again. "So, now that we know where he's been, let's get to the with who?"

"Who is right! The woman in the pictures is Ellison Lindsay. I Googled her, and it looks like she's pretty big-time herself. We're talking CEO big-time. Self-made, to boot."

The cars in front of Leila eased forward as the teachers began to load the younger classes first. She slanted the rearview mirror toward Julia, still sleeping peacefully in her car seat, then returned the radio to kid-friendly fare.

Kate

Kate ran the straightener through the bottom layer of her hair a final time, then reached for pomade to seal the ends. E! blared in the background, and she stopped to watch Ellie and Pat Grayson walk out of the Mandarin for the tenth time. Before Cami had introduced her to Ellie, Kate rarely watched entertainment news of any kind. Now she was fascinated by spin. She found herself picking the stories apart, looking for the grains of reality beneath the polished images and promotions with all the knowledge of an insider. The fact that even the most beautiful, successful, iconic people on the planet were flawed and required teams of support to maintain the illusion was an odd comfort to her. It reminded her perfection was fictional. She'd spent the better part of her life trying to achieve it, partly because she had equated it with love as a child and had come to feel safest when things seemed flawless.

Visions of perfectly trimmed Christmas trees she'd never touched and a Victorian dollhouse behind glass floated through her mind. No matter how ugly the fighting was the night before, her mother would appear downstairs the next morning, perfectly coiffed in tennis whites. Kate quickly learned she could gain her affection through a compliment and a smile, as long as she, too, was spotless, with every hair in place. She pictured her mother's nod of approval and controlled smile, before she shook her head and frowned at Cameron, slurping milk from his cereal bowl and wearing his pajamas until the last possible moment before school. Kate always waited to take her first spoonful until her mother had seen her, so as not to risk a drop of milk on her shirt or a crumb in her teeth. To a young Kate, the rules of life were simple. Image trumped everything. Being Mommy's little lady at the breakfast table earned a smile. Learning the piano meant she could play for the ladies during bridge, instead of going with the nanny.

Kate cringed as she thought about sitting straight as an arrow on the piano bench, determined to hit every key perfectly, while the women laughed and gossiped in hushed whispers at the elegant tables behind her. She left the bench assuming the pity in their eyes came from the G sharp and B flat she had missed. Her father's latest affair hit the papers the next day, followed by an indictment for insider trading. The resulting public scandals and divorce dominated her adolescence. She could control nothing except how the outside world saw her. So she did. She stamped a smile on her face, kept her hair perfect, and cinched in her school uniforms in the privacy of her closet.

Kate watched the lights go wild as Pat opened the car door for Ellie, and wondered if he saw the fear behind her friend's confident smile.

Ellie

"Also, I would like to video-conference with the Blythe Barrett team this afternoon. Please coordinate with Steven to arrange a time. Directives are in their inboxes." Ellie thanked her and ended the call before stepping into the viewing room. Pat's manager, Rick, and a woman she didn't recognize were the only two in the room. Rick looked her up and down with contempt as she took the seat opposite from him.

"Well, if it isn't the lady of the hour." He rolled his eyes and raised his glass in her direction as a young woman bustled into the room.

"May I offer you a beverage, Ms. Lindsay?"

"Mineral water, please," she answered coolly, as Rick rattled the ice in his empty glass and continued to shoot daggers in her direction. "Another bourbon?" The girl nodded and left as Ellen concluded her monologue and danced her way across the stage to the signature teal armchairs.

"You better hope this goes well. He was as freaked as I've ever seen him backstage."

"It will." Ellie met Rick's glare as her phone buzzed with an incoming text.

"Like I said, you'd better hope so. I don't know what kind of sick game you think you're playing, but that kid's worked too hard to have it all come crashing down because a pop tart and a cougar screwed him over and pissed off his fans." He narrowed his eyes at her, then laughed and slapped his knee. The sour bite of whiskey filled her nostrils. "On second thought, you may be the answer to all his problems." He laughed again and clapped his hands. "All this time, we've been panicked that this crap homo film would sink his rep with the soccer moms and teens who brought him this far. I mean, that's not exactly the demographic that's going to be cool with watching Lucas Lucien get it on with another man. Then he makes out with a teen queen and nails you in the same news cycle?" His voice rose an octave as he talked through his laughter. "It's genius, really! *Shhpew!*" he roared, mimicking a rocket blasting off with his hand. "Back on top! Pun intended! Cool again with the teens—thank you, Scarlett James—and their moms see you and think they have a shot at the fantasy!" He smirked. "Gotta say, I didn't know he had it in him!"

Ellie was speechless as she stared stone-faced at the monitor. The drunken idiot beside her was just that—drunk and idiotic. He may have touched a raw nerve, but she would not let his asinine commentary shatter what she knew was true. Even if she'd somehow missed this angle, Jess wouldn't have. Unless, of course, Jess was in on . . . No, that was her past and this was her present.

The young girl walked back into the room with Rick's next drink, and Ellie raised her hand to stop her. "Thank you, but he's clearly had enough." She steeled her eyes on his as the girl backed awkwardly through the doorway. "I will say this once, and once only, so listen up." She lowered her voice. "Today I will choose to overlook the drunken nonsense you just spewed. Understand I do this not because I think you're worth your keep as a manager but because I know you've been with Pat since the beginning and he balks at upper-level staff changes. That said, should I hear another word about your ridiculous seduction theory, I will know you're choosing to be replaced. I encourage you not to doubt my influence on him." She watched his eyes grow wider as he swallowed hard twice in succession. "You say I'm playing a *sick game* with his career? Welcome to the arena. Three will play, and one will lose. It won't be me, and it won't be Pat. I trust that's math you can do." Ellie left the room without looking back.

Cami

 ami surveyed the drafting room, pleased to see there were two fewer empty chairs than there had been the day before. Then again, it was half past ten. Her position, among other things, was different here, but work was work and remained a normalcy she could count on. Her computer blinked to life, and she scanned her e-mails before navigating to her home screen. Ellie's face, staring out from the headlines, surprised her. The picture was clearly a paparazzi shot, linear and flat, focused only enough to capture the two subjects in the frame. She stared at the pic for a moment, studying how straight Ellie's posture was as she walked just behind Pat and how tightly their hands were clasped together. Marilyn Monroe should have been glad there wasn't some untrained bozo with a telescopic lens in her day. Cami had worked hard to learn this craft. When she looked at her old stuff, just out of school and before, she saw talent developing. Now, any zit-faced kid with a knockoff Nikon could call himself a photographer. Selling your work to publications and magazines used to mean something. It meant you worked for art, if not for journalism. Granted, you had to be damn good to be profitable, but that's when you knew you'd made it. There was no art in this shot. It was a product of intrusive opportunity designed exclusively for profit.

A knock on her open door broke her focus. "Good morning, Ms. Clark," Dean stood smiling in the door frame. "I didn't peg you as the door's-always-open type."

"Um, good morning." She minimized the screen, surprised by the surge of nervous energy that coursed through her.

"I signed for this while you were out." He grinned and produced a bottle of scotch wrapped in a bright silver bow from behind his back. "I don't know who Ellie is"—he fingered the tag—"but she's got great taste in gifts. She and I should clearly be friends." He winked and walked to the chair in front of her desk, before taking a leisurely seat and putting the elegant bottle down in front of her.

"Sorry to disappoint, but she's taken at the moment." Cami strummed her fingers on the desk and picked up the bottle.

"That's nothing new. I hear all the good ones are."

"She's also not a scotch fan." Cami turned the label toward him and added, "An oldie but not necessarily a goodie."

"Ah, so you know your spirits?"

"Does that surprise you?" she countered, raising an eyebrow in mock insult.

"Everything and nothing surprises me about you, Clark." He laughed. "Stop by my office after work. I have the good stuff. We can toast your first week and you can tell me how you got the kids to cooperate." He pointed toward the drafting room. "The leads all but slept here last night, and four of the other six were back in this morning before nine."

"I promised them happy hour on me tomorrow if they impressed me today." Cami smiled slightly. "We'll see how they do."

"Happy hour." He cocked his head and held out one hand, then the other, palm up. "Not being fired." Then he smiled as he mimicked a scale moving up and down until it balanced. "Seems like a good incentive to me." He crossed one long leg over the other, and Cami noticed his calf muscles for the first time and wondered whether he was a runner.

"Exactly."

"Well, weed out the slackers as needed. I wouldn't mind carrying a little less overhead into the new year." He paused and grinned. "My new creative director is costing me a fortune."

"And worth her weight in gold." Cami said, as a ruckus from the drafting room burst through the wall. "Did I mention I charge double for babysitting?" Dean laughed jovially, and, for a brief second, she found herself present in this moment, on this path, away from the rain.

Ellie

*P*at stepped onto Ellen's stage, wearing a simple gray sport coat over the white button-down and dark jeans he'd worn that morning. The shirt was still open at the neck, and he wasn't wearing a tie. *Good call*, Ellie thought, thankful he looked relaxed and casual, instead of ready for court. The audience roared as he waved and crossed the stage. Ellie studied his fluid, confident gait, trying to gauge his nerves. This had to go well if they were to steer the tide of public opinion decidedly in their favor. If he goofed, she would be the laughingstock of her profession by lunch.

The audience continued to cheer as Ellen hugged Pat and a PA signaled for them to sit.

"What a fantastic welcome." He gestured to the crowd. "Thank you." They clapped again, and a trio of voices shouted, "We love you!" followed by laughter as the words echoed over the quieting crowd.

"I love you, too," he joked, and grinned as the women cheered.

"I hear you've been sayin' that a lot lately." Ellen laughed, and the audience settled to attention.

"Yeah... according to the papers it's becoming a problem." Pat's voice was cheery edging on nervous. "I love you, too, Ellen."

"Everybody does. I'm adorable," she wisecracked to more applause. "In all seriousness, we're thrilled to have you back. I know it's been quite a ride for you over the last few days."

"Indeed. And thank you."

"So, basically, you're here to talk about love." Ellen pretended to look at her notes and a wave of brief laughter swept through the audience. "Your film *Life of Us*, which my audience saw in a private screening earlier today"—she paused as the audience applauded again—"is simply phenomenal. Isn't that right, ladies? And Sam?" The camera panned to a man in the audience wearing a T-shirt proclaiming that this was his ninetieth taping. "I call it the greatest love story of the year. How did it feel to be part of something like that?"

"It was extraordinary, to say the least. And thank you for giving it such a rousing endorsement. From the second I read the script, I knew I had to be part of it. I remember telling my mum that if I did only one more film in my career, I wanted it to be this one. The work itself is such a raw depiction of what true love really is. . . ." He paused and took a sip from his mug. "And of course I couldn't pass up the chance to freeze my arse off and whiz in a porta-potty somewhere north of Toronto for half a year." Ellie relaxed slightly as the audience clapped enthusiastically.

"What touched me most is the unimaginable grief your character conveys as he's recording the video diaries. I saw it at Cannes and was totally that person texting Portia through the entire film. I couldn't go another second not saying everything I've said to her a thousand times just one more time."

"Wow, that's quite a testament to the film." He ran his hand through his hair. "I know exactly what you mean, though. I've always fancied myself as genuine, with no problem telling my family and friends how I feel about them, if that makes any sense. Then I read this script and I realized Roland, my character, is not only the living epitome of a man in love with his spouse and kids but also the epitome of loss. In particular, the scene when he apologizes to his husband about falling in love with him in the first place and says he would never have asked him out if he'd known he would die before forty, to save him the pain, to give him a chance at a happily ever after, struck me."

"So now, after losing yourself in this story, would you say the old adage that it's better to have loved and lost than never to have loved at all is true?"

"That's a good question. You watch him grieve and struggle with leaving his loved ones behind, and you realize grief is love's hidden price tag. To love anyone means to risk losing them." He shifted in his seat and looked out at the crowd. "Or having them stalked and exploited in my case."

"Ah, the elephant in the room." Ellen took the cue, and Ellie turned her attention to the audience. They were invested. Good. The now-infamous picture of her and Pat on the deck chair illuminated the screen behind them. Ellie felt as if she were looking at another person as she stared at the woman in the photo. She looked so unguarded and happy.

"You know what I see when I look at this picture? I see happiness. Look at you two. You're throwing your heads back, laughing like little kids. It's beautiful, and private."

"Thank you." He stared up at the image, and Ellie watched his mouth curve into a smile. "She's amazing." His eyes crinkled as he blushed slightly, and a chorus of *oooh*s swept over the audience.

"By now, half the world knows she's your publicist. Is that how you met?"

"Yes." His hand touched his collar and then found its place on his knee. "We've worked together for the last two years and recently, very recently"—Ellie flushed alongside him—"started dating."

"Dating? That looks more like falling in love to me." Ellen pointed to the picture and an expectant silence hung in the air.

"From the moment I first laid eyes on her." The audience gasped and Ellie stared speechless at the monitor, running their first meeting through her mind. She had been impressed with his manners and unassuming nature, but business and securing him as a client had been the goal of the day. And his eyes. She suddenly remembered noticing how blue and earnest they were when he shook her hand. "It was a standard meeting, until she walked in and my world practically stopped. And it may *actually* stop today considering I haven't told her any of this." The crowd roared.

"I'd say that's a definite possibility." Ellen laughed and then leaned in conspiringly. "Tell us more."

"Ellie was like confidence in motion. I remember looking up from a stack of legal papers and literally losing my breath. I stammered and joked my way through the meeting, trying not to stare at her. I'm sure she thought I was denser than pavement." The audience snickered. "Nonetheless, she agreed to represent me. I didn't often work with her directly at the beginning, but something as simple as seeing her electronic signature on the schedules my manager passed on made me smile, just picturing her, and then remind myself she was light years out of my league." Ellie's blood rose in her cheeks again. "But when we were together at premieres and the like, I made sure to trip over my words—you know, for old times' sake." He grinned as Ellen and the audience laughed.

"Well, it looks like it's working out." Ellen smiled and gestured to the picture on the screen. "I, for one, am happy for you both. You've been a friend of mine and a friend of the show for several years now, and I can say you've always been nothing but a gentleman onstage and off." The crowd applauded, and Ellen reached behind her chair. "That's why I had a little something made for you," she said, as she handed him a white bag erupting with aqua-colored tissue paper.

"It looks too big to be knickers this time," he said, as he pulled the tissue from the bag. The audience laughed as he held up a *Brady Bunch*–inspired diary and a padlock with Ellen's face on the dial. "How very, um, timely." Pat laughed and reached to embrace Ellen. "Maybe I'll use this to leave her notes from now on."

"You do that!" They hugged again. "In all seriousness, I wish you the best. The next time you're here, I predict we'll be raising a glass to *Life of Us*, the little movie that could." Ellen raised her mug.

"To love." Pat smiled and met her toast.

Ellie's phone vibrated in her hand as tried to grasp the surreal-ness of everything he'd said.

1 New Msg: Leila Cell
Hi, friend. I know you must be swamped but wanted to
say I saw the balcony pics and you look—quite simply—
happy. I know what your privacy means to you and can
only imagine how nervous you must be watching this
all unfold in front of the world. Anyone who can put
that smile on your face likely knows what a blessing it
is to earn your trust.

Ellie shook her head, impressed again that Leila always seemed
to know what they all needed to hear.

Reply—To Leila Cell
Thank you for the vote of confidence. It's been a roller
coaster.

Can't wait to fill you in, Ellie thought but didn't finish typing, as
Rick's loud voice coming down the hall caught her attention.

"You're not making any sense, Rick." Ellie heard the stress in Pat's
voice and wanted to step in, but she also knew where this was going
and thought it best to give Rick just enough rope to hang himself.
He had everything to lose and was trying to point the firing squad
toward her.

"What I'm trying to say is, she's using you, bro." Rick lowered his
voice as they approached the door. "Take your blinders off. Ellison
Lindsay doesn't care about anything but her firm. You need to wake
up and see that before it's too late and she has you doubting the
people who've been with you from the beginning. I may be an asshole, but I'm the only asshole who gives a shit about you. Remember
that."

Ellie stepped away from the door when she heard retreat-
ing footsteps and a hand on the knob. She turned her back
to it and put her phone to her ear, muttering a few nonde-
script sentences into the mouthpiece as the door opened. Pat

stepped in, and she turned around, saying goodbye to her phantom caller.

"Ellie." He looked surprised, and his eyes darted toward the hall. Part of her wanted to speak and ease the tension, but a bigger part wanted to memorize what he looked like when he was hiding something that might upset her. "I'm surprised to see you in here." He looked behind him nervously. "Happy, mind you, but surprised. Rick said he just left you in the viewing room."

"Um, yes. Things got a bit heated in there, and I needed to make a call." His eyes searched hers, and she watched his shoulders fall.

"Do I want to know what happened?"

"It's not important." Ellie took a step toward him. "All in a day's work, as far as I'm concerned." She wrapped her arms around him and let her cheek rest briefly on his chest.

He bent to smell her hair and pressed her closer. "Thank you. I needed this," he whispered.

"I think I did, too." She looked up at him and added, "You did great out there, by the way. I was . . ." Her words left her for a moment as she realized she was proud of him. "I was proud of you. I'm not used to saying that to—"

"To clients?" His face was a mixture of amusement and disappointment.

"I was going to say 'to men.'" Ellie couldn't fight the grin that crossed her face as he smiled down at her. A knock on the door interrupted the moment. Pat opened it as a gracious PA handed him another white bag stuffed with aqua tissue paper.

"Mr. Grayson. Hello. My name is Theo." He flashed his badge. "This is for Ms. Lindsay."

"Splendid. Thank you." He closed the door politely and held the bag out to her. "It appears you have fans as well."

"Don't look so surprised." She raised an eyebrow and took the bag. The tag read simply: "Ellison,

Sometimes life changes in a flash. Use these if the spotlight gets so bright it threatens to block out the beauty that's right in front of you. This is me wishing you a life of love and laughter. Yours, Ellen."

She reached into the bag and fished out a black sunglasses case emblazoned with the *Ellen* logo. Pat shook his head and smiled.

"We're in for it now," he said, and pulled her close.

Norah

"Dr. Merrit?" Norah looked up from the chart on her desk to see Kelsey, the receptionist, standing in the doorway. "There's a Dr. Orlando here to see you. I told him the office is closed for lunch from twelve to one thirty, but he says you're expecting him for a consult."

"Yes." She straightened. "Show him back, please." Norah felt a rush of adrenaline rise into her chest. This was the first time they'd been together in public since the conference. A moment later, Enrique stood in the door frame. "Thank you." Norah smiled and nodded to dismiss Kelsey before standing to shake his offered hand. "Dr. Orlando."

"Dr. Meritt." He pulled the door shut behind him and smiled. His teeth were bright against his tanned skin and the pastel yellow of his shirt. He looked crisp and tailored, as always. "Thank you for meeting me."

"Of course." Her heart thumped a little harder as she gestured to the leather chairs in front of her desk and sat in the one closest to her. He took the other and reached for her hand.

"Finally, a chance to talk." He squeezed gently. "I feel like there's so much to tell you and so little time."

"I know that feeling well." She shook her head at the irony.

"I've been doing quite a bit of soul searching over the last week." His dark brown eyes looked confident and jittery all at once. "And I've come to an important decision." He glanced at the clock behind her, before continuing, "I've decided to stop merely going through the motions of my life. I'm so tired of rolling out of bed and doing exactly the same thing every day. The same exams, the same surgeries, the same questions. Day after day, it's always the same. At work, all I think about is dreading going home. I love my kids, but my marriage is over. Every night I walk in thirty minutes before they go to bed and play ten minutes of Just Dance, read a story or two, and then sit on the couch, watching ESPN, while Deanna stares at Facebook on her phone and falls asleep. I didn't even know how miserable things had gotten until we reconnected at the conference. For the first time in longer than I can remember, I felt like myself. All the reasons why I chose to be an ob-gyn came flooding back, and I realized that somewhere along the way, I traded my passion for a paycheck. You knew me then. You know how on fire I was for women's medicine. That person wouldn't even recognize me now."

"So, you're not happy in private practice?" Norah was confused. Sure, the exams could be monotonous, but her days were anything but boring.

"What I'm trying to say is that I don't feel *alive* anymore, Norah." He squared his body with hers and put his hands on her shoulders. "Except when I'm with you."

"Enrique, I—"

His eyes were intense as he interrupted her. "Please, Norah, let me finish. I realize now how lost I've been. Because of you. That night, the first night, opened my eyes. Since then, when I'm at home, you're all I think about. Being with you, holding you, wanting to know about your day." He stroked her arm gently. "I know what I want now. I want you. I want to start a life together. And I want to get back into the mission field." His eyes burned with intensity as a wave of nausea crept into her throat.

"What about your kids?" The words hung heavily in the air as he shook his head.

"They'll be part of it, of course. But I want to start over. With you." He moved his hands to her face and kissed her. "Do it right this time." His voice was little more than a murmur. Hot pokers pricked the backs of her eyes as a million different scenarios thrashed through her brain.

"I'm pregnant," she whispered, looking down, and pulled the ultrasound film from her lab coat. The shock registered on his face as he stared at the image. She knew he was doing the calculation. She talked on, trying to anticipate the painful questions that were bound to come. "We both know the odds that it's yours are miniscule, but there's still a chance."

"Have you told him yet?" He looked up from the ultrasound.

"No."

"It's still early," he whispered. "You have time." A shudder ran up her neck at the implication.

"Yes." She matched the emotional distance in his tone. "I still have time to decide." *What's right for us,* Norah continued in her mind, knowing that at that moment the concept of the word *us* was irrevocably changed.

Kate

1 New Video Msg: Ken Cell

Kate raised a surprised eyebrow at the frozen image of her mother's perfectly coiffed head on the body armor of an Imperial Storm Trooper and pressed PLAY. Darth Vader's march blared from her phone as the figure stomped forward before looking side to side, then bursting into the macarena. Kate laughed and typed a reply.

1 New Text—To Ken Cell
LOL! So true. Of course, she'd never wear white after Labor Day.

1 New Text—From Ken Cell
Scandalous. BTW, she thinks we sent a car. Just smile and nod and thank Ellie later. She knew you'd say no and asked me a wk ago if she could send one of the firm's drivers.

Kate smiled at Ellie's thoughtfulness, recalling her mother's visit to attend their engagement party four years before. The scene had become an inside joke between her and the girls. Kate chuckled as she pictured walking into the living room to find Cami, red-faced and speechless with laughter, as Ken innocently recounted the frantic call from the airport he'd just received, demanding to know where the car was. Ken looked confused; he'd told Kate's mother there should be plenty queued up outside the doors—just follow the signs toward ground transportation. A fresh roar from Cami made Kate laugh so hard that her mascara ran as tears rolled down her cheeks and she squeezed out, "A *cab*! He told my mother to take a *cab*!"

She giggled again at the memory and at the thousand times after Ken had pointed at a cab and asked, "Is that our car?" The speaker box by the front door buzzed. They were here. Kate took in her spotless apartment and sucked in her stomach as she walked by the mirror in the entryway toward the door.

Kate pressed the button and gave the front desk permission to send up the firing squad. *Breathe. Reflections in glass are just that— reflections. They say nothing about the real you—the beautiful you. Only actions can do that.* She released the button, then frantically darted back to the love seat to angle the first and last pillow to ninety degrees. The look needed depth. Kate walked back to the door and listened for the footsteps, humming the Vader theme in her head.

Cami

1 New Msg: From—Zac Cell
Seeing you made today infinitely easier. This is me
taking Carolyn's advice and officially pestering you
about dinner. I think aged steaks and older scotch are
order. No one wants you to be alone.

Cami read the words on the screen again. She didn't trust herself
to go. Zac could never be safe.

Leila

"Look, Mommy!" Clara scrambled into her car seat, waving a candy-apple-red flyer that read BRING YOUR DADDY TO SCHOOL DAY! "The daddies get to come to school *and* sit with us at morning meeting *and* have a special muffin after!"

"That's wonderful, sweetheart." Leila noted the date, two weeks away, knowing it didn't really matter. "Get strapped in, please. What was your favorite part of school today?"

"Can Daddy *puh-lease* come?"

"I know he'll want to." Leila forced a chipper tone as she careened her neck to make sure the car seat buckle was secured correctly. She could already see the guilty look cross Wes's face as Clara told him the news. She promised herself that even though the flyer made the conversation that loomed between them that night more timely than ever, she wouldn't use it against him. It wasn't about being right. It was about changing their dynamic. She wanted him to want to be there for them, to adjust his knee-jerk reaction from an instant "no" to one of consideration.

"We'll tell him tonight. Right, Mommy?"

"Right." Leila's phone buzzed as she eased forward another few inches in line.

1 New Text—Tanya Cell
Mamma says forget about it. She don't want u comein' to help just cuz she's dying. She wants u to come bc u want to.

Clara waved the flyer in Julia's face, and she jolted awake and grabbed it, tearing the corner.

"No! That's not okay, Sister! That was for Daddy!" Julia screamed, and Clara began to cry. "Mommy! She tore it!"

"*Rahhhhhhhhhh!*" The sound twisted the tension knot between Leila's shoulder blades impossibly tighter.

"Mommy!" Julia screamed over the cry.

"I love you both very much," she said, and sucked in a deep breath as the line began to move. "Clara, when you chose to put your flyer that close to Sister, you chose to risk her tearing it. You know she is still learning to be gentle. Julia, Mommy needs you to stop crying and promise to be more respectful of Sister's things." She pulled out into traffic, wary of the merging cyclists, and wishing they would designate a bike lane on this street. "I think the reason you waved it in Clara's face was that you were excited to tell her about the fun day. Let's all take a breath and refocus on that. Clara, would you like to hear about the super-fun day coming up at Sister's school?"

"Tell me! Tell me!"

"Speak kindly, Clara. '*Please* tell me.'" Leila corrected, scanning the traffic and trying to remember if she'd taken her birth control pill that morning.

Kate

*K*ate plastered a smile on her face and opened the door. There stood her mother, Regina, dressed head to toe in beige silk. Her hair was swept high on her head, and an Hermès scarf fell in soft folds over the gorgeous fabric. Her thin mouth was pressed into a tight line as she looked through Kate and into the apartment. Her grandmother Carmine's face remained stern, frozen via a look of disappointment and surgical handiwork.

"Hello! Come in!" Kate said stepping backward as her grandmother raised an eyebrow at the apothecary table Kate had repurposed as an entry piece. "How was your flight?"

"Would you have me give this to you now or just throw it anywhere?" Carmine snapped, and held out a black handbag.

"I'll take it." Kate looked down, then smiled at her and reached for her mother's bag as well. "No need for grand entryways here."

"Clearly not." The comment hung in the air as Kate invited them into the living room to sit and excused herself to get the tea tray she'd prepared. *This visit is off to the usual fine start,* she thought, and rolled her eyes at the remaining three almonds on the counter. *Not now. I'll eat them later, when it's calm,* she lied, and balanced the tray carefully on her arm.

"Katherine? The baby is crying. Is anyone going to get him?"

"Yes, Mother," Kate said, and hurried back into the living room to set the tray on the coffee table. "I'll be right in with him." She smiled and hurried down the hallway to Liam's room. The unmistakable odor of fresh feces hit her nose three feet from the door.

"Katherine, darling, you've forgotten the lemon. Your grandmother takes her tea with fresh citrus."

"I'll be right there," she said over her shoulder, and opened Liam's door. The acrid smell permeated the air as she pulled the door closed quickly behind her. *Please don't be a blowout*, she thought, as she peered into his crib. *Not today.*

"Hi, sweet boy," she cooed, and picked him up, tucking the blanket around him to avoid dripping the mustard-ish grainy liquid oozing down his leg onto the rug as she laid him on the changing table. "Shh . . . it's okay. We'll fix it," Kate whispered, stretching the neck of Liam's onesie wider so she could slip it over his head without smearing the poop onto his hair.

"Katherine, did you hear me?" The door opened, and her mother gasped. "Katherine! What on earth? Why is he covered in his own filth? That's it. I am putting my foot down. You will hire a nanny this week—someone qualified to take care of a child. This is absolutely unacceptable."

"Mother." Liam's face turned red as he wailed more loudly at the harsh, unfamiliar voice. "It happens. I'm cleaning him, and he'll be fine. Shh . . . shh . . . it's okay, we're almost done. Just a little bit more," she whispered, and smiled down at him while her blood boiled and her mother's eyes bored into the back of her head.

"Regina?" She heard her grandmother approaching. "Regina? What in heaven's name is going on in . . ." Kate clenched her eyes at the sound of her grandmother's gasp and closed the Velcro on the new diaper. "And the smell? It's absolutely putrid, Katherine."

"Liam woke up with a dirty diaper, and I've changed it. Now I'm going to dress him, then throw the blanket and crib sheet into the wash. It's completely normal, and nothing I can't handle." She fought the quiver in her voice as two cold stares and one raised eyebrow sliced through her confidence.

"Again with that awful nickname?" Her grandmother tsked at her mother. "Unacceptable. Regina, I believe we've discussed this."

"I've put my foot down," Regina said to her mother. "She's getting some help with William. No daughter of mine is wasting her life as little more than a chambermaid." She turned on her heel and walked down the hall.

"I trust you'll rejoin us when he's decent?" her grandmother added, before shutting the door and following her daughter.

"Of course." Kate held him a little more tightly and pressed a soft kiss onto the top of his head. Who was she kidding? He deserved so much better. Liam snuggled into her neck, and she took a breath so deep, her rib cage felt concave. Holding it until her chest burned, she turned the rocker toward the wall with her hip, knowing her mother would be mortified at the idea of her breastfeeding, and sank into the overstuffed cushion. Liam latched hungrily, and his little muscles began to relax. Kate stared into her son's crystal-blue eyes as he suckled and smiled up at her, trying to remember she was not her mother or grandmother. Their sins would not be hers.

Norah

The red letters of the EXIT sign peeked though the sheer panels separating the lounge from the main dining area. Norah looked at the sign, blurred but recognizable behind the opaque glass, and thought it a fitting mirror for the conversation she and Matt were about to have.

Laughter split the air, and her attention turned to a young couple adjacent to her. They were seated side by side, lingering over a carafe of house wine, oblivious to the computer cases and blazers draped over the chairs on the opposite side of the table. Norah sipped her Perrier and watched as the girl took his hand in a practiced motion beneath the tablecloth. She and Matt didn't reach for each other anymore. Not like that, anyway. The couple laughed again, and she studied the tablecloth to avoid staring. Maybe it was the veiled metaphor of the sign or the infectious joy of the couple beside her, but Norah closed her eyes and let her earliest memory of feeling that unguarded with Matt fill her thoughts.

They'd sat in a restaurant lounge like this one, having ditched their double date with Leila and Wes at the avant-garde film showcase one movie in, and toasted to being "film-festival dropouts." She remembered the butterflies in her stomach as one conversation cascaded into another and flowed so effortlessly that time melted away. It felt like minutes, not hours, had passed when they realized the lights were full strength and the waitstaff was sweeping the floor around their table. She recalled feeling somewhat embarrassed but mostly exhilarated as they stepped out of the closed restaurant onto the sidewalk, grinning, arm in arm. Matt had been so happy then as he chatted about earning his first solo lead on a case and listened to her describe the surgical marathon that was her time in India and how much she had learned about medicine's dual role in humanity.

It was painful to remember that young couple walking aimlessly through the arts district with nowhere and everywhere to go. She kissed her future husband for the first time that night. Norah would never forget the glow of the streetlight behind them as he smiled, stretching the anticipation, before gingerly taking her lips and parting them with his own. It was the best kiss of her life. The sensation of sinking into the tender rhythm and the flash of heat that coursed through her body stayed with her long after they meandered farther down the street and squeezed into a patio table next to Wes and Leila at the Blue Note.

The EXIT sign. *Of course*, Norah thought, looking up at the panel again and clenching her jaw at the bittersweet memory of the story Matt told them that night.

"All hail!" Wes announced boisterously, and clasped Matt on the back. "The defectors have arrived!" Norah remembered Leila's loud giggle and pronouncement that if ripping her dear friend away—likely by her own free will—from So-and-So's best work was the worst thing Matt had ever done, he still had permission to date her. Norah laughed, saying she already knew about his wife and six kids in another state, to which Wes jibed that was nothing compared with his pesky crack problem.

The teasing went on from there, until Matt raised his hands in the air and said, "Okay, I confess! Norah, you deserve to know the truth. For the small fee of one more pint, I will regale the court with my complete criminal record." A round of Shiners later, Matt had them in stitches as he told them he'd gotten suspended in high school after organizing a prank in which seniors ducked out of the homecoming dance one by one to paint the letter *s* in front of, and the letters U and P behind, every EXIT sign in the school. "Using the school colors, of course." The memory of laughing until her side hurt twisted the knot of guilt in Norah's gut like a vise. "And did I mention we were the Trojans?"

Was there a road back to who they were then? Did she want there to be?

"Thanks—I see my wife." Norah blinked back into reality at the sound of Matt's terse voice behind her. She looked over her shoulder at the hostess stand and met his eyes. He gave a compulsory nod in her direction and she tried to quell her nerves.

"Hello."

"Sorry I'm late. Traffic."

"Not a problem," Norah said clinically. The tension pulsed like static as silence stretched between them. Matt busied himself unbuttoning his suit jacket and fishing his phone from his pocket. At last, a waitress mercifully approached to take his order.

"Good evening, sir!" Her overly chipper tone grated on Norah's ears. "Sorry to keep you waiting. May I get you a cocktail?"

"I'd like to see your scotch list."

"Sure! It's right here." She bent over his arm and flipped the menu. "On the other side of the wine menu! See?" The busty girl batted her eyelashes at him, and Norah pressed closer against the cool metal back of her chair. She looked across the table at Matt, trying to see him as she had that night so long ago. Physically, he wasn't all that different. There was a touch of gray in his black hair, and deeper creases in his brow, but he was still fit and trim. It was easy to see him as the girl did—a clean-cut man in an expensive suit who thought nothing of ordering a $40 pour of scotch.

"Excellent choice, sir! I'll have that right out." The girl sauntered off, then turned on her heel abruptly. "Anything else for you, ma'am? A glass of wine, maybe, or a—"

"No. She's headed back to work." He answered, steely with contempt, and pointed to Norah's scrubs, barely acknowledging the girl's bumbled apology and offer to bring more mineral water.

Norah nodded distractedly, trying to look past the disdain in his eyes and find the twinkle she had once found infectious.

Another stretch of edgy silence passed as they stared at each other. Matt spoke first, as she knew he would, and she braced herself for what was likely the opening argument he'd been refining for days. "Whatever you do, don't say you're sorry." He drummed his fingers on the table. "I can handle anything but that."

"Understood," Norah said, refusing to flinch at his words, "and I'll ask you to do the same."

"Me?" He raised his eyebrows. "As if I'm the one who did this to us?" Norah was dumbfounded. She expected him to blame her monumentally, but the fact that he was completely denying his role in their problems infuriated her.

"I think we're both responsible for this."

"That's ridiculous, Norah. *You* cheated. You realize that, right? The vows we took? Destroyed. By you."

"By us." She kept her voice low. "By us, Matt."

"No. Not by me, at least. I followed an urge. I took a colleague who's flirted with me for years home for a night or two. That's it. It happened after I found out about you."

"I don't see the difference. Reactionarily or not, you slept with someone else, just like I did. And that's not even to say that—"

"You don't see the difference? You had an affair, Norah! A full-blown affair! You screwed him often enough that you rented a room together!"

"And you," she hissed, "took another woman to our home. I don't understand what you're trying to prove, Matt. This isn't like trying to win a case. There are no winners here. We both did something terrible." He opened his mouth to respond, then paused as the waitress approached with his drink.

"Are you ready to order? Or do you need another minute?"

"I'll have the tenderloin, rare. With the asparagus. Thank you."

"Perfect pairing!" She swept the untouched menu off of the table. "And for you, ma'am?"

"Nothing for me, thanks." Another server passed their table, and the smell of shallots and trout singed her nostrils.

"Well, I'm yours all night if you change your mind!"

"Thank you." Norah said absently and swallowed against the nausea as the girl walked away.

"There's a huge difference, Norah. What you did is a totally different animal. You had a relationship with someone else. And what hurts the most, what keeps me up at night, is that I don't know how much further you plan to take it. Are you staying with him? Are you leaving me? It's like I'm sitting here, looking at my wife, but she's not my wife." The pain in his eyes cut like a knife. "Don't get me wrong—I knew things were bad—but I never expected this."

"I know. I didn't either. In a way, I still can't believe we're sitting here having this conversation. I don't know how things got this far."

"You didn't answer my question. I want to know if you're still seeing him. If you've seen him since you left." He wanted something. Norah scowled across the table at the sudden realization. She knew that face. This was their pattern and everything that had led them here. He wanted something and would continue his emotional assault until he got it.

"You always did know how to manipulate me." She sucked a deep breath through her nose. "You don't care if I've seen him. You're just using that as a platform to put me on the defensive so we don't talk about What's-Her-Name and the little romp you enjoyed. You want me to feel too guilty to bring her up so you can ask for what you really want. What is it? Just tell me."

"Fine." He swirled the amber liquid in his glass. "I'm beyond angry at you, Norah. And what's worse is that we're running out of time to make decisions."

"Decisions?" The word was more loaded than he could possibly know.

"Yes. I will have to start answering questions soon."

"Questions from whom?"

"My family, for one."

"Have you told th—"

"One absolutely gorgeous tenderloin cooked rare, just like you ordered!" The waitress smiled underneath a fresh layer of lip gloss. "I hope you don't mind, but I had the chef add a side of our signature hollandaise sauce to the asparagus. It's delish."

"Sounds good. Thank you."

"My pleasure! Just let me know if you need another Macallan or anything else at all!" She giggled and shrugged. "You too, ma'am."

"Thanks." Norah replied, keeping her eyes on Matt. "Have you told them?" If he had, there would be no going forward from this. She was already the antithesis of everything his family thought a wife and prospective mother should be. Knowing about the affair would only give them official grounds to yell out loud that they'd told him so, versus in the hushed whispers they currently used.

"Of course not. Do you think I want them celebrating in the streets?"

"No." She clenched her fingers around the flesh of her thigh. "At least, I hope not." God, he knew how to hurt her. "I don't know if we can fix this, but I do know that we need time to decide before the world weighs in."

"Don't tell me you haven't told anyone. I know Leila knows."

"I haven't told anyone but the girls and my mom." She took a sip of Perrier to push the bile from her throat. "That's a little different. You know how your family feels about me. What I meant to say is that I think we need time before critical audiences weigh in."

"You mean critical against you, right? Matt haters, step on up." His eyes were piercing. "I can all but hear Ellie and Cami now." He shook his head and glared at her. "And I thought the earful I got from Wes was bad."

"Wes?"

"Yeah, I called him when I found out, and we went for a drink. Let's just say he said some things that were way out of line and we haven't talked since. Then again, Leila's always had him by the balls, and we both know where that loyalty lies."

"Loyalty? It's not about picking sides, Matt. The last thing we want is to drag the people we love into the middle of all this before we know what we want. They don't get a vote." He raised a shoulder, and Norah knew the abruptness of what she'd just said surprised him. "Understand I'm not trying to deny the reality of what we've done, but I want to deal with it on our terms. I hate the idea of being forced into a decision, just to save face because other people are expecting a verdict."

The thought of this dinner and this conversation being the end of their relationship sent a shudder through her soul. She could accept that they might not ultimately survive this, but the thought that giving up before they even tried to treat the problem was a viable option to him made her pulse race. Norah set her jaw and looked into his eyes.

"I agree. I admit I botched the beginning of this conversation because I was angry. But it feels like we're running out of time before we have to say something. I just can't sit with my family, next to you, and lie while we toast my parents' fortieth anniversary." He searched her eyes, and Norah knew what he wanted. "It's just not right."

"You still want me to go to the party with you."

"Yes." He tapped his fingers on the table and softened his face. "I want to buy us some time. If I go alone, they'll only start digging harder." He checked his watch. "Assuming you can take off for two days, that is."

"The date has been on my calendar since your sister sent the invitation." Norah paused and added a stab of her own. "It's why I traded call duty last weekend to be off next."

"Don't get me wrong. Going with you might be just as painful as going solo." Matt sliced into his steak against the grain, and Norah watched the flesh bleed. "I want us to go together only if you think we can pull it off and act like a normal couple for a weekend."

Norah knew what he wanted to hear. Of course they could make small talk and blend in. That didn't make them normal. It made them subpar. She looked into the face she no longer knew and asked herself whether their definitions of normalcy would ever be the same. Infidelity aside, the tension in the air between them *was* their normal. He was always angry at her, and she was always on the defensive. All couples fought, but not all couples failed.

"Well? Can we table this for a few days until after I get back from New Hampshire?" The nervous undertone in his voice surprised her. "And if you can't—if you're in love with him—I need to know what you want me to tell my family."

"We'll go together," she said, aware of the veiled threat in his words. "Your family doesn't have to know how hard we're struggling," Norah began dreading the weekend the moment the sentence left her mouth. "But I think we need to make sure we're both in agreement about a few things before we go."

"Of course." He said looking at his watch.

"I think it's important we spend the next week apart, thinking about what we want and"—her pulse raced as Ellie's signature words left her lips—"where we go from here."

"Are you saying you want another week to play with him?"

"No."

"Then what are you saying?"

"I'm saying that I want us both to take a hard look at ourselves. At who we are right now and who we want to be."

"You mean who we are together, right?" His eyes were harder than she'd ever seen them. "Because I can tell you I don't like who I am in this marriage right now."

"I meant as people. As people who want to do better together. I'm suggesting we go to your parents' party, keep our problems private, and agree to start seeing a counselor."

"And if we fail?" He signaled across the room for the check.

"Then we fail." Norah's eye twitched, and she looked away. "But we can say we tried everything."

Leila

Leila sat on the couch across from Wes and reminded herself that communication, not winning, was the goal. He rubbed his right eye and loosened his tie. He was tired, no doubt more from the stress of the day than from worrying about their spat that morning.

"I'm sorry I upset you. That wasn't my intention when I said it."

"I get that." She shook her head. "I know you didn't mean to be hurtful. I'm not asking you to apologize. I'm asking you to understand that this morning scared me. It was a glimpse into what our dynamic might look like if I take the teaching position. I'm asking you to look at this with me and say either, 'Yes, I can commit to supporting this family in fill-in-the-blank way' or, 'No, it's not a good time to try to make this change, because of how it will affect me—meaning Wes—and the girls.' I'm asking you to understand that right now I feel like this family's anchor. I am trying so hard to be everything the girls need and everything you need that I'm drowning keeping everyone else afloat."

She swallowed the anger on the tip of her tongue and forced the image of Wes proposing to the front of her mind. That night, when she said yes, she made a conscious point to memorize the euphoria of her love for the man in front of her and promised herself that, if she would picture that moment and cling to it when she needed to, at stressful times when things were hard and lashing out would be the easiest choice, they could survive anything. "What I'm trying to say is that I'm overwhelmed and worried about adding more to my plate when it feels so full already. And the last thing I want to do is to come across as ungrateful for how hard you already work for this family. I hope you know that's never lost on me. I'm able to stay home with the girls, without worrying about how we're going to buy groceries or pay for extras like preschool and dance class, because of how hard you work. I try to make a point to acknowledge it every day."

"I know that, beautiful. You never make me feel like the things I do are taken for granted. I know you want me to be here more. And believe me, I want to. I want to be able to say that every Tuesday I'm taking off at four o'clock to pick up the girls and go on a daddy-daughter date. I want to be the dad who can coach the soccer team, who doesn't see a flyer for a preschool event and know that will be hell to juggle. I see my managers and the brokers clocking in at nine and out at five every day, and part of me envies them. I think, *That's what my kids deserve, too.* Then, the next morning, the same guys are the ones in my office asking what they need to do to get promoted and why they're not moving any further up the ladder." He rubbed his temple, and Leila knew he was dehydrated. "I'm listening," she said, and walked into the kitchen to get them both some water.

"And the truth is, I can't be both. I can't stay as VP and clear five hundred K a year and be the room dad." His words and the stress on his face made her heart ache as she handed him the glass and a B_{12}. "And then I think, *What's wrong with me?* I should just look at you and say, 'Take the job. We'll make it happen.'"

"And I appreciate that you want to. I know you do, Wes. But what I'm saying is, it's more important that we're honest about what more you can actually give. Not what you want to give. What I'm hearing is that you want to be there more for the girls than you are. I say we start by finding a solution to that. We both know you see them for less than two hours a day and some days not at all. I don't love it, but that's their version of normal. I don't want you to beat yourself up about not being the dad who coaches soccer and is at the dinner table every night. It's not about being there for everything. It's just about consistency. I think we start by finding a better constant for them."

"Agreed. I need to do better. I will do better. For you and for them."

"Not for me, Wes. I'm fine. We're fine. It's just something we have to work through." He put his hand on her shoulder, and she shrugged it off. They both knew she hated to be touched when there was tension between them. "Of the unknowns on the horizon, you and I aren't one of them. I had a call from Tanya today. They think my mom has cancer."

He looked at her the way he might have looked at someone who'd just said her 107-year-old grandmother had passed away. It was the sort of somberness that came when the nature of the death made sense.

"I'm so sorry to hear that." His voice was more sincere than his face. "How are you?"

"Sad." Leila closed her eyes briefly. "Sad even though I always knew it would end this way, and sad because now it's really too late for things ever to change."

"I know." He reached for her again, and she shied away.

Kate

*T*hank *God he was finally home.* Kate thought as she listened to Ken making polite small talk with her mother in the living room. Considering Liam had finished his bottle of formula ten minutes earlier, being alone with him in the nursery now qualified as hiding more than feeding. She couldn't make out her grandmother's words but trusted they were critical.

She kissed Liam and pushed herself up from the rocker. Her phone sang "Soul Sister" by Train, the text tone she'd assigned to Cami, and she swiped the screen.

1 New Text—Cami Cell
How goes it with Mommy Dearest?

Reply—To Cami Cell
As expected. She found the wire hangers.

1 New Text—Cami Cell
Guess who's coming to dinner? I'm around the corner.

Reply—To Cami Cell
Seriously? That would be awesome.

Kate beamed at the screen and walked down the hall to the living room.

"Kenneth stepped into the kitchen for a moment," her mother gloated. "We could smell the fish beginning to dry."

"Of course." Kate said and shifted Liam to her hip. "I'll just duck in and see if he needs any help." She couldn't help but chuckle as she pushed through the swinging French door and added over her shoulder, "And I'll need to set another place at the table. Camille is joining us for dinner. I'm sure you remember her from—"

"From school," her mother finished, with a warning stare that Blane and the trial were not to be mentioned. "She and Katherine were roommates, Mother."

"Oh, I remember Camille." She paused, then added under her breath, "No matter how hard I try to forget."

Kate entered the kitchen, happy to see Ken with a corkscrew in his hand.

"Smooth." He laughed. "Were they thrilled *Camille from school*"—he mimicked her mother's exaggerated vowels and raised his pinkie—"will be joining us?"

"Naturally." She grinned and homed in on the bottle next to him. "Oh, good, there's wine."

"Not that one." He laughed. "That one is quote-unquote 'breathing.' Your mother had it delivered."

"Damn."

"This one, however"—he produced her favorite cheap bottle from behind his back—"clearly needs mouth-to-mouth." Ken took a playful slug and passed the bottle to her. Kate laughed and pulled him toward her. Liam cooed, and she kissed them both.

"Katherine." Her mother opened the door with a grunt, then cleared her throat disapprovingly. "Someone is at the door, and they were not buzzed in. Perhaps you should ask your husband to open it."

"My pleasure." Ken kissed Kate again and took Liam. "Little Man and I will investigate." Kate smiled at his drawl. It was always more pronounced after a little vino, and even more so in front of her mother. His heritage had been his best-kept secret in the beginning.

In many ways, the early days of their friendship, before they became a couple, were still her favorite. They met on a job site, about a year after she finished grad school. He was just starting to make a name for himself as an architect, and she was leading her first design project. Normally, their paths wouldn't have crossed, but she wanted to have exact measurements to ensure a salvage display she was planning wouldn't overly dominate the space. She remembered his Southern accent on her voice mail, saying it was an unorthodox request and non-union to allow it, but that he would make an exception for someone determined enough to leave him sixteen messages. Something about his voice told her he would be good-looking, and she was anything but disappointed. She remembered how at once perfectly at home and perfectly out of place he looked standing in his hard hat and white polo among the debris. She'd noticed the contrast between his tanned, athletic arms and the white fabric immediately.

"Ken Stone. Pleasure to meet you." He flashed a perfect white smile and handed her a bright orange hard hat. "I'm going to have to ask you to put this on."

"Of course." She took the hat, trying to pretend it was something she'd done often, not for the first time in her life. In her messages, she'd implied other architects often let her tour the framework of the buildings she would later design.

"It's backward, ma'am." He grinned and she confessed this was her first time on a construction site. That was where it all began. A year later, he took her home to meet his family, and she understood why he'd been so guarded about where he came from. To say the house and the grounds were immense would be the understatement of the year. It wasn't that he'd been secretive about his family's wealth—more that he'd been vague about the degree. He told her his grandfather Glen Stone had opened a construction company when he returned from World War II and spent his life growing it into a successful small business. It wasn't glamorous, but he fought hard to build a reputation and to be the best of the best in his league.

Glen Stone was adamant about a lot of things in life, but none so much as that his son would go to college—kicking and screaming, if necessary.

After a year spent majoring in "skirts and suds" at Ole Miss, Ken Sr. returned triumphantly to join the family business. One afternoon, a backhoe driver accidentally pressed the DROP and SWIVEL switches simultaneously, spewing the contents of his granite load all over the crew on the ground. Miraculously, no one sustained more than a few cuts and bruises. A week later, another seasoned driver accidentally flipped the transmission override on a forklift and spun the tires bald trying to back the machine onto a trailer. Ken Sr., frustrated with the expensive repair and inevitable goading from his father, picked up a piece of plywood and sketched the control plate of each machine on the job site. He worked into the night, fashioning switchplates labeled LOAD, REVERSE, and DRIVE out of particleboard, and attached them to each machine. Placed over the controls, only the needed buttons and switches for each function were accessible, preventing the operator from pressing more than one command at a time. The men balked loudly, and his grandfather equated the idea with putting training wheels on a motorcycle, but Ken Sr. stuck to his guns and watched with pride as the plates proved themselves in the quarterly books when incidentals and damages declined and profit margins increased.

A few thousand buckets of sweat and a patent later, the switchplates were picked up as standard install on large machinery across the state and later the country. Kate remembered hearing the story a dozen dates into their relationship over ouzo and buy-one-get-one gyros at the Greek place they still frequented. When Ken took her to meet his parents, his dad greeted her with a bear hug and a warm pronouncement that Ken had undersold how pretty she was. Kate often teased that he and Ken were doppelgängers decades apart. Both had nearly identical ash-blond hair, emerald eyes, and lean builds. They boarded the family plane the next morning and flew into a small airport in Baton Rouge.

"When you asked if I wanted to go to a crayfish fest and meet your family over some beers, this isn't exactly what I had in mind. I—"

"You had no idea. I know. I didn't want you to. It's not that I didn't trust you; it's just that I've been used in the past. Including by Karly."

"As in your ex-fiancée Karly?"

"Yes. My dad hired a PI and found out she'd been following me for months before we met in what I believed was a chance encounter. She knew exactly who I was and what I was worth. From then on, I swore if I ever fell in love again, it would be with someone who didn't care whether I was a custodian or the heir to all of this. That's when I started taking girls to RudyDogs on first dates and telling them I worked in construction."

"You never took me to Rudy's." She grinned.

"Didn't have to," he said mischievously. "I knew my heart was yours to break the second you laughed at me underneath that backward hard hat."

Kate fell in love with him a little more on that trip, in large part because she realized how open she felt around him. No one but the girls knew more about her, much less about the perjury at Cameron's trial, the feeding tubes, the pills, and the bullet that had shaped her into who she was, than he did.

Two months later, Kate took him to meet her family at the beach house for the Fourth of July. No amount of warning could have prepared "the boy from the job site" as they called him for the icy reception he received. Kate's family would never care how much money Ken had. It mattered simply that it wasn't the right kind. Every second she spent with him and his family redefined her definition of wealth. They were so simple and unassuming. Their lives were everything a name and a heritage should be. It was no longer about what parties you were and weren't invited to, or how often you vacationed; it was about day-to-day stability. Ken managed his trust and their salaries tirelessly. The truth was, they had enough in savings to buy their dream home tomorrow. They lived in the apartment because she loved it. It felt cozy and personable. She'd grown up in thirteen rooms, surrounded by perfection and empty space. She wanted anything but that for Liam.

"Katherine," her mother snapped. "Are you even listening to me?"

"Yes. Of course." Kate flinched back into reality as her mother's fingers bored into her arm.

"Not a word. Are we clear?"

"She won't. Cami never talks about it."

Ellie

"Hi, Ellison, it's Blythe Barrett. I spoke to Pat earlier, but I wanted to tell you, too. He looks so happy in the pictures, and that makes me happy. I want you to know I planned to tweet I was thrilled for both of you, before the team suggested it. He's a good guy—complicated, but aren't we all? I still hate that I broke his heart. That was complicated, too, and I'll always be grateful that you fixed it when half the world wanted to see me hanged. Let me know if I can do anything else for either of you."

Ellie saved the voice mail and signaled *one minute* to Jess with her finger.

"Good evening, Ms. Lindsay. This is Leon, director of security for Emerald Bay. I'm calling about the break-in. I've terminated the men who were on watch when it happened, and we are working closely with LAPD to find the intruder. Sincerest apologies. This is my personal line. I'll be available to you all night if you would like any further information."

Ellie's heart skipped a beat at the words.

"Do you know anything about a break-in at my home?" She asked refusing to allow any emotion into her tone.

"Yes. That's why I came in while you were on the phone. The intruder entered through the balcony landing sometime last night or early this morning. The lower floor was ransacked, along with your bedroom, but nothing of value is missing. The office door sustained some damage, but they weren't able to open it."

"Thank you. Keep me posted if there's anything else I need to know."

"Of course." Jess frowned. "I've also spoken with Blythe Barrett's team. She will be sending a congratulatory tweet to you and Mr. Grayson this afternoon."

"Good call. Anything else?"

"Yes. I have two confirmed sources saying Josh Kray is shopping for private PR. The Spec is apparently splitting at the end of the month."

"Are you positive?" Signing Josh Kray would be a coup, Ellie thought. The rest of the group were glorified backup singers in comparison with his talent.

"The sources seem to be."

"Ask Alicia Preston to get me a meeting." Ellie gathered her briefcase and handbag.

"I already have. He and his manager can meet tomorrow morning. We will be their first interview."

"Tell Sylvia to rearrange my calendar."

Jess raised an eyebrow. "I thought you were going to New York for the premiere with Mr. Grayson. I can run the meeting."

"I've no doubt you can." Ellie said, knowing Jess was more than capable of wooing him, but not wanting to give her more power than she already had. "But I think my presence would make the statement we're after."

The intercom buzzed. "Ms. Lindsay, your car is here."

"Thank you, Leslie. Have security sweep and clear the garage, please," Ellie answered, keeping her eyes on Jess. "And I would like for you to be there. You'll be the lead on his rep. Reassign two other clients as you see fit. I trust you."

"Of course." She said curtly.

"Thank you." The only thing Ellie had less time for than stroking Jess's ego was finding her replacement. "I would like for you to make time to meet with Rebecca in finance on Monday. They have your bonus package ready," She lied, making a mental note to place that call. "I think you'll be very pleased."

Jess nodded and thanked her, disappointment oozing from behind her controlled expression. "I'll spearhead the meeting to sign; then his campaign will be yours entirely."

"Define *entirely*."

"Your baby. Staff of your choosing, et cetera." Ellie pulled her blazer from the coatrack by the door and draped it over her arm. "Think of it as grooming for something bigger."

Cami

"*D*arling, I need to tell you something in all honesty. Now, I don't mean to be harsh . . ." *But you will be. You have been all night*, Cami thought, and watched Kate rest her fork on the edge of her plate without taking a bite.

"It's about the gallery. I've brought a more suitable outfit for William to wear than what he has on in the photos you've sent. It's not that yours were in bad taste, necessarily; it's just that those settings, under those lights, won't coordinate with the ones on the wall."

"You know we need him in whites," Grandma Dearest added.

"Why don't you and he come out next weekend, and I can arrange a garden shoot of sorts? Of course, it will be just William. I know you won't want to be photographed until you've toned up a bit, but at least I'll have a nice portrait of him in time for my next event."

"If you send the outfit, perhaps Cami could snap a few on the beach one Saturday," Ken said, as he reached for another roll. "Might be a nice afternoon for them."

"I'm sure we can find a garden somewhere," Kate offered.

"With all due respect to Camille"—Regina said coldly in her direction—"I had something a little more *professional* in mind. No offense."

"None taken," Cami smiled broadly. "*Time* magazine will print anyone these days." Despite Ken's snicker, Cami felt instantly guilty watching Kate shift in her seat.

"That's not to say Katherine can't use your services as she sees fit."

"Why don't I go start the coffee?" Ken stood, and Kate reached for the last of the wine.

"Thank you, Kenneth. I forget there's no one in the kitchen."

"Such a waste," Regina added. "Perhaps you can find a nanny who cooks."

"No nannies for us." He clasped Kate's shoulder. "We're doing just fine. Right, babe?" Kate looked stressed to kill as she patted his hand. The truth was, Cami would rather have been anywhere else tonight than sitting across from the two women she considered the worst of humanity. She had come because she hoped her presence would redirect some of their assault away from Kate. They usually circled her like sharks in chum-filled water, but something was different tonight.

"Right." Kate put her hand on Ken's. "We're fine, Mother."

"A little overwhelmed, maybe, but who isn't with a new baby?" Ken said, with a guarded smile and a squeeze of Kate's shoulder. "Remind me, Regina: Do you take cream or sugar?"

"*Fine*?" Carmine said. "That's not exactly how I would describe what we've seen this afternoon."

"*Surviving* might be more apt terminology," Regina said firmly.

"With all due respect"—Cami used her calmest voice to clone their words—"how much time have you spent around new mothers and their babies?"

"Enough to know Katherine is struggling." Regina grimaced.

"Struggling how? Because she and Liam aren't company-ready at every single moment? Because there's no nanny to take him when he's inconvenient to adult conversation?"

"You're out of line, Camille. Please don't make me be uncivil."

"What I'm asking is, would you be sitting here demeaning your daughter less if she were making small talk and someone else was soothing your grandson in his nursery?" Cami looked directly at Kate. "Not that it matters to me. She knows where I'll be—for both versions."

"Fine. I said don't make me be uncivil, but you've given me no choice. The child sleeps in his own filth until he screams, and rarely has more than a third of his mother's attention because she has—for reasons far beyond me—burdened herself with the rest of the household duties. My grandson deserves someone devoted solely to tending to him. It's quite selfish, really, and I won't st—"

The anger rose in Cami's throat as she watched Kate shrivel under the words as if they were a whip. It was Cameron's trial all over again.

"That. Is. Enough!" Cami's temper erupted out of her mouth in a fury of words that seemed to completely bypass her brain. "Don't make you be *uncivil*? What the hell would it look like if you weren't? Can't you see what you're doing to her? Or do you just not care? Isn't one shattered life on your conscience enough? Or does Cameron not matter either?"

"What gives you the right to speak to me like that in her home?"

"Fine!" Ken slammed his hand down on the table in the first hint of temper Cami had ever seen in him. "Cami may not have the right, but I certainly do. You are in *our* home!" He looked at the baby and lowered his voice. "I want you to listen closely to what I'm about to say, because I don't plan to repeat it. I may never understand why you are so intent on spending every second you're with us being critical and turning your nose up at our lives, but if you continue, you will no longer be welcome. In this home. Ever. Can't you see what your words are doing to her? Can't you see they haunt her?"

"Sit down, Ken." Kate's voice shook as she stood. "He's right, Mother. They both are. This is what you do. It's what you've always done. You pick and pick until the tiniest flaw bleeds like a war wound. I always thought it was me. That I wasn't good enough. But it was never me. There wasn't ever anything wrong with me." Her voice cracked. "It was you, Mother. It was always you. You hurt everyone around you, just like your mother before you." Angry tears rolled down her cheeks. "It stops here. With me and with Liam." Cami stared at Kate, astonished, as she handed the baby to Ken. "Excuse me while I call my mother a cab."

Norah

1 New Text—To Dr. Orlando, Cell
I know it's late, but can you meet me in the room? It's important.

Reply—From Dr. Orlando, Cell
Yes. I'm already there.

Norah read his response and slid the key card into the slot. She had to end it tonight.

"How was your night?" He walked to her and took her coat. "All things considered, you've achieved the perfect storm of a call week," he leaned forward and kissed her forehead. It was warm and lovely and wrong. "I've done a lot of thinking today," Enrique whispered, and cupped her face in his hands.

"About us?" She let herself sink into his palm for just a moment.

"About everything." He tilted her chin up and looked into her eyes. "When I left your office, I cleared my schedule for the rest of the day and just started walking the hill district. I must have walked ten miles back and forth, thinking about everything. I know what I want, but, more important, I want to know what you want."

"That's not fair." She whispered. "You can't say what you said in my office, leave things that way, have an epiphany, and expect me to answer that question. It's not that simple."

"I know. It's not simple for either one of us. I'm not suggesting it is." He grazed her cheek with his thumb. "Just hear me out. Can you do that?" Norah bobbed her head, hating what she had to say. "Knowing where I want to be in my practice isn't the only epiphany I've had recently. I've also come to realize that I am an idiot."

"Idiot?"

"Yes." He smirked. "I should've realized it two months and one conference ago, but I was afraid. I was afraid of making a change because of what it might do to Deanna and the kids but now I realize staying stagnant is just as detrimental to them. I am making changes in my life regardless of your answer to my next question."

"Enrique, don't." She hung her head. "I'm in no place to—"

"Shh." His face was bright and hopeful. "It doesn't have to be now. I want you to know today is my last day as an idiot. I was an idiot to let you go the first time, all those years ago in Mumbai, I was an idiot to leave you vomiting in this room, and an even bigger idiot in your office this morning." He pressed his forehead closer to hers. "I was scared it was the end. Have you ever taken a breath that was so pure it made you realize you'd been suffocating?"

"I think we both have." Norah wiped the tear that fell from her lashes.

"That's how I feel with you. I know it doesn't make up for everything I've done, but I'm asking you." Norah sniffed back her emotions as he knelt. "I'm asking you to see the person I am right now, the broken me who wants to be more than he is. I'm asking you to accept the person who wants to do that, with you. Not with the Mumbai version of you. With the guarded you. I want the Norah who's holding my hand right now." He pressed his lips to her fingertips. "I'm asking you to love the imperfect man in front of you, and the road that brought him here, and to know he'll do the same for you." He produced a polished amber box from the pocket of his suit. "I'm asking you to swim upstream with me today, tomorrow, and forever. And promising I'll never let go."

Norah's head swarmed with mixed emotion as she struggled to form the words to tell him it wasn't right.

"And if it's this hard say *no*, that should tell you something." He stood and wrapped his arms around her. "Like I said, it doesn't have to be now. I'll wait."

Ellie

"And those were her last words to me," Ellie said, pressing her back into Pat's chest as he massaged the tense muscles of her right shoulder under the bubbling water of the nightly bath that was becoming their ritual. "I held her hand and smoothed her hair until the end and didn't let go until five hours after she was gone. My point is, I knew her well enough to know she'd thought about those words for a long time. She was charging me with a mission." Ellie turned to face him. "I think she wanted me to be her legacy and was afraid I'd shut out the rest of the world because I was in pain."

"It sounds like she was giving you her blessing to move on with your life." Pat said softly and Ellie knew he was thinking about his grandfather and the closure that would never be.

"And that's how we spent her last night together." Ellie took a deep breath and then a deeper one. "The week before that, when we knew it was the end, the nurses connected a VCR to the television in her room." She shook her head. "It all seems so old-school now." They shared a smile that seemed slightly wrong. "We watched Sherri's favorite movies on a loop. I snuggled in next to her and pressed PAUSE every time she dozed off. The meds made her so tired, but she always seemed to wake up at ninety-minute intervals and say she was glad she hadn't missed whichever part, and I'd press PLAY."

"Is that why *Ghost* is in your DVD player upstairs?" He blushed, then rushed to add, "It's not as if I were snooping. I was under house arrest on that floor and wanting to watch Netflix. I may be the last person in the free world who doesn't know how he met the mother."

"Agreed." She laughed, loving his smile at that moment. "That was the movie we watched the most. I turn it on sometimes and just sit there until one of her favorite scenes comes on. I can feel her then, and it reminds me of who she wanted me to be and that neuroblastoma doesn't have to be her legacy. It's when the pain is finally bearable."

"Go love." Pat repeated Sherri's last words. "She could have said 'live,' but she said 'love.' It's beautiful." He kissed Ellie's neck and traced the line of her thigh with his finger. "Makes me think of the film. About the last scene, when Roland tries to choke out his final 'I love you' to his husband but can't."

"And then smiles peacefully, confident that he knows and comforted that what he left behind speaks for itself. I think that's about legacy, too."

"You're spot-on," he said, and Ellie felt him smile behind her. "Life doesn't get better than that."

"You're right." She moved his hand farther up her thigh. "Life is this crazy combination of love and risk and loss; then, just when you think you have it figured out, it throws you a curveball."

"Exactly. Recent events—the film, you and me, Roland's story— have me thinking about what I want my legacy to be. What I want people to say at my funeral."

"And?"

"And I know that I don't know. I also know that I don't want *Destiny* to be the most important thing I ever did." Ellie turned to look up at him, wanting to tell him it wouldn't be but knowing that would always be a big part of his public identity, a tagline he'd never outshine. "When I did the interview with *Actors Studio* during the Cannes screening, they asked me what kept me straight after coming to fame young. It's simplistic, but my mind immediately flashed to the first limo that was sent just for me. Not for a director or for a cast appearance, but just for me. I remember sitting there, impossibly alone, and realizing, for the first time, that fame was a sort of power all its own, an animal separate from money or class. I knew then that I wanted to influence more than a rolled-sleeve trend or the bloody cologne market. I told myself I owed it to every dreamer out there trying to buck the word *can't* to use it to do something good and meaningful. That's why I started the charity in my grandfather's name then, and why I want *Life of Us* to be successful now. All of my work before it, the love and loss in between, living under a microscope, launched my career and defined my first twenty-nine years, but I want the next thirty to be about more. I want them to be so authentic that I never have to question whether the twenty-two-year-old in the limo would be proud of his legacy." His eyes crinkled as he smiled and said, "This is me charging him to go live it."

Ellie grinned, the warmth of all she felt for him washing over her as she ran her hand up his neck and into his hair, releasing the pain their tomorrows together might hold in favor of the joys, and knowing they had taught each other one of life's irrevocable truths about love.

Leila

1 New Text—From Tanya Cell
It's what she wants. Will u.

Reply—To Tanya Cell
Yes, but . . .
Yes, as long as I can be back by . . .
Yes, is 11:00 an option? I have to . . .

Leila read the options on the screen and saw everything she didn't want to be.

Reply—To Tanya Cell
Yes. I think seeing the hospice counselor could be good for both of us. Please tell me when.

Leila looked into the mirror and told herself she would live the expectations she had for those around her. Last night's conversation had proved that she wasn't doing that. She'd asked Wes to take a hard look at the whys of what he felt he couldn't give and compromise. This was her why. It wasn't that her mother and Tanya invested any time in her life or deserved any of her time in return; it was that she wanted to live with grace. She was making mistake after mistake after mistake with Julia and Clara and Wes, and trying every day to do better. She wanted to text Tanya and say if their mother had died the previous week, her girls wouldn't have noticed any difference in their lives. She wanted to type that they didn't know her enough to miss her, but she didn't. The simple reason was that she didn't have the courage to turn her back and be what they already thought she was.

"Dr. Oliver, they're ready for you now."

"Thank you, Sarah." Leila smiled back at one of her favorite former undergrads, proud to see she'd become a TA and was still pursuing the humanities postgrad. "And if I don't see you on the way out—"

"Never stop reaching for the ring." Sarah smiled and recited the words Leila used to close every class. "You taught me well."

Cami

Molly,

Congratulations on your engagement. I hope your grand-mother's ring made the moment everything you'd hoped for. It feels right to pass your brother's words on along with it. When Blane asked me to marry him, he said, "To me, saying, 'I do' is saying, 'I will.' It is saying, 'I will love you. I will for-give you. I will support you. Always. Do me the extraordi-nary honor of promising me the same, Say you'll run with me headfirst into the rest of our lives together, rain be damned.'" That's my wish for you and Tristan.

Love,

Cami

Cami squeezed the ring to her heart one last time and slipped it, chain and all, into the box addressed to Carolyn. This was the first time she'd shared his words with anyone.

1 New Text—To Carolyn Greene Cell
You should be receiving a secure delivery from me tomorrow. Please pass on the note to Molly when it's appropriate.

Reply—From Carolyn Greene Cell
Thank you, darling. I hope you know how much this

will mean to them. And that you're still part of this family. Stuck with us!

Cami nodded down at the screen and stepped out of her office. The messenger's polite thanks landed on deaf ears as he took the box from her. She nodded and turned on her heel toward the conference room. Watching him walk away would be too painful.

Norah

Norah pulled the chart from the wall and began scanning the pertinent new-patient info. She didn't see many cases like these. Norah mentally checked off the labs and histories she would need and stepped into the room. "Hello, I'm Dr. Merrit." She smiled warmly at the woman on the table. "It's nice to meet—"

Norah stopped in her tracks midsentence as the name *Orlando, Deanna H.* leaped off the chart.

Leila

Leila checked the rush that came from being back on campus, along with her ego, and finished what she'd come to say. "And those factors, ladies and gentleman, are why I can assure you education will always be my passion, and that no time away from the classroom will ever change that." She paused, taking in the distinguished faces in front of her. "But I cannot accept the position you're offering. Not at this time." A hushed whisper seemed to circle the table. "However, I hope you will consider me in the future and know I will serve the students of UCLA with just as much dedication as I did before." Leila gritted her teeth and stood. "Thank you for your time." She slid clumsily out of the chair, banging her knee on the table in the process, just as she'd done countless times behind her desk.

"A moment, please." Dr. Allen, the department head, said, and Leila nodded, shifting her weight from one foot to the other, looking awkwardly from wall to ceiling, as they whispered behind the fictitious curtain. "Sit, please." He scribbled something on a legal pad and passed it down the row. Leila watched the heads nod with varying degrees of hesitation. "What if we offered you a split—two Tuesday-Thursday grad classes: Lit Crit 6778; one day on campus; and one webcast?"

Leila stared at him, exuberance at the possibility barreling its way from her toes to her heartstrings. She knew 6778 was a manageable grading load, and one day on campus could be doable with some tweaking to the girls' schedules. *Clarify before you get carried away.* The logical thought tempered her excitement as she asked, "Let me make sure I understand correctly. I would alternate? Teach two sections on campus and two sections online?"

"Yes. The Thursday lectures can be uploaded at any time of your choosing. Understand this is an offer we will need to reevaluate based on performance, but in my opinion, you're the best of the best. The next crop of doctoral students have spoken, and they want you back."

"And," the university president chuckled, "it's in all of our best interest that they stay and pay."

Leila's chest was bursting as she accepted and shook hands all around, feeling as if a part of herself she'd loved but lost somewhere along the way had just stepped into the spotlight and offered her a hand. Twenty minutes later, she sat in the front seat of her car and called Wes, beaming more brightly as he congratulated her and listened to her recount her refusal and the unexpected counteroffer.

"That's awesome news, beautiful." His voice swelled with a mix of pride and a tinge of relief as she explained the flexibility. "I knew they'd find a way to bring you back. I'm so proud of you. You should see if Torri can come until I get home, and go out and celebrate with the girls."

"Thanks, babe." She smiled into the rearview mirror.

"Listen, I'm walking into a meeting. Let me know about tonight."

"No worries. Love you."

"Love you, too."

1 New Group Text—To Sister Friends
(Norah Cell, Kate Cell, Ellie Cell, Cami Cell)
Hi! I walked into my interview to turn it down, and they offered me a compromise. It will take some juggling, but I am so excited to get back in the classroom! Anyone free to celebrate tonight?

Reply—From Kate Cell
What?!?! That's awesome! I am so so proud of you! I can leave when Ken gets home. Just let me know the plan.

Reply—From Ellie Cell
Well done! Getting anywhere around the press right now is an odyssey. I'm at the Mandarin with Pat until my place is more secure. It's lame, but you're welcome to come watch the *Life of Us* premiere with me in the penthouse. It's live from NYC at 7:00.

Reply—From Cami Cell
Famous-people problems. Can you see me rolling my eyes from here? I'll be there . . . assuming the tab is on Mr. Hollywood. LOL.

Reply—From Ellie
Cute :) See you at 7:00.

Reply—From Leila
Sounds great! So excited!

Ellie

"So he signed with you?" Pat said, and Ellie grinned, listening to his hairstylist fuss at him not to move.

"It took some convincing, but yes. Camelot had his ear, too."

"That's fantastic news."

"Where are you?"

"Getting ready to get out of the car. Salvador is trying his damnedest to make me bald before I touch the carpet."

Ellie laughed, then blushed as she noticed the girls' conversation had dropped to a whisper while they strained to hear. "I'm sorry I'm not there to walk with you, but I appreciate your understanding how huge this was for me and the firm." She shook her head at them and closed the sliding door to the penthouse office.

"Of course." He lowered his voice as if someone were listening. "It was important, and I want you to know I realize being together means there will be times we'll be apart. Location for me, LA or NYC for you. They're tapping me that I'm next. Are you watching?"

"Yes. I'm in the suite with the girls."

"Nice." He laughed. "Tell them I won't be happy until there's a pillow fight or the like."

Ellie smiled. "Listen, you know I can't control what the mics on the carpet ask."

"And don't call boys."

"In all seriousness, Pat, don't feel like you have to defend us. They can't do much with a smile and a 'no comment.'"

"I won't." His words were barely audible as the din of the crowd filled her ear. She glanced at the television in the other room and watched the lights go wild as he touched his phone to his lips. "See, you made it after all."

"Clever." She laughed. "Now hang up and let me watch." The noise was thunderous as she added, amid the laughter in the other room, "And I love you."

"I luff—"

The garbled syllable drowned in the din. Ellie clicked the END button as the signal waned, and wiped the grin from her face before she joined the girls.

"Oh, good." Leila giggled and scooted closer to Norah so she could sit. "I was worried you'd miss his first interview." Ellie squeezed her thigh affectionately and waited to see which mic it would be.

"That looks like hell on Earth," Cami said, as flashbulbs filled the screen and people holding mics lunged over the velvet ropes, screaming at the actors.

"That's a midsize premiere for you." Ellie reached for her wineglass. The three camera feeds turned to Pat as he scribbled his name on the outstretched programs and posters, many of them *Destiny* related, before stopping in front of the *Scene It!* mic. A tanned blonde in a flowing yellow dress turned to face the camera.

"Congratulations on the film. It's fantastic."

"Thank you." Ellie watched his eyes dart nervously to the side.

"Rumors are the film will get a Golden Globe nomination for Best Picture next week. Are you hoping for a Best Actor nomination as well?"

He moved to the left as part of Dominic's frame came into view on the slight right. "I'd be lying if I said I wouldn't be thrilled, but just being a part of this amazing film and working with such a phenomenal director is prize enough." He thanked her and moved on to the next reporter.

"The man of the hour has arrived!"

"If you say so." Pat shook his hand and smiled.

"How does it feel to be standing here promoting a film that's so different from your norm?"

"It feels fantastic. I've never believed in a project more."

"Do you think some of the attention it's receiving is from people who don't believe you can be more than Lucas Lucien? Do you think they're banking on you to fail so they can laugh?"

"That's interesting." Pat said and stepped forward. "You might be onto something—"

"Where's Ellison Lindsay tonight? Was that her on the phone?" a voice interrupted from over the rope.

"It was." Pat ran his hand through his hair, and Ellie cringed.

"I should have been there. He looks nervous."

"If you get the Globe nod, will you attend without Ellison?"

"Why would I do that?"

"Publicists and agents aren't allowed," Ellie explained, in time with the reporter.

"No." Pat shifted, as if trying to decide which camera to address. "The film is about loving who's right for you, regardless of rules or popular opinion. It wouldn't seem right to go without the person I love."

"Wow," Kate said, and Ellie counted the grapes remaining on her plate. Seven fewer than when she'd taken the call. Ellie watched Pat and his entourage shuffle forward, grateful the red-carpet portion of the evening was almost behind them. The camera angle shifted to the glitzy entrance and high-profile guests posing in front of the sponsored backdrops. It cut back to the velvet ropes as the network voices began to narrate. "That about does it for us on the red carpet. Let's take one more look as the man of the evening, Patrick Grayson, makes his way to the front for a few pictures with the rest of the cast."

"Would you say this moment, tonight, is his destiny?"

"I don't know, Chris." The woman's sugary voice irritated Ellie's ears. "But I'll say it's definitely a game-changer." The crowd behind them erupted in applause. "Wait." She pulled her lips impossibly wider around her blazing white teeth. "I'm being told Pat Grayson has turned back. "Yes." The camera cut back to the carpet. "Let's go to Jenny on the ground."

"Yes, Chris," Jenny screamed over the noise. "There's quite the uproar down here. It appears Patrick Grayson was posing with the cast, when a special fan caught his eye." The camera feed flashed again to Pat, chatting and shaking hands with a young girl in a wheelchair wearing a TEAM LUCAS bandanna over her shaved head. Behind her, a burly man held a sign that read DESTINY IS A CHOICE. CANCER IS NOT.

"You can't buy publicity like that," Cami joked, as Ellie's phone buzzed on her lap. She kept her eyes on the screen, watching Dominic step to the side as Pat ducked under the rope and bent down beside the girl to pose for a picture. The cameras homed in on the flashes in the crowd. The word *authenticity* lapped at Ellie's mind as the man flipped the sign to the opposite side. The words PRAY THE GAY AWAY seared her eyes as a deafening shot split the air and Pat crumpled forward into a heap, blanketed seconds later by Dominic. Shaky images of running feet, carpet, and pavement dotted the panicked audio feed as the camera teams ran while the lenses above zoomed in shamelessly on the pool of blood oozing in maroon semicircles onto the carpet beneath Pat's figure. His eyes darted wildly from side to side as a police officer knelt beside him, radio in hand.

Noooooooooooo! Ellie screamed inside her head, at a decibel she didn't know was possible, as the group behind the rope began to chant, "Pray. It. A. Way. Destiny. Is. A. Choice."

Norah

Norah gaped at the television in disbelief, then blinked herself into reality. Ellie stared ahead at the rapidly changing images, her mouth shaping a silent word, as her phone buzzed incessantly. Norah reached down and gently pried her hand open, one white knuckle at a time. Terror and shock aside, decisions had to be made.

"Give it to me," Cami said, standing.

"It's Jess," Norah read the screen as she handed it over. Cami nodded and crossed the room before answering it.

"He's not dead." The harshest whisper left Ellie's lips as the EMTs loaded the stretcher into the ambulance. "He's not dead."

"It's going to be okay." Leila's panicked eyes met Norah's as she put a shaky arm around Ellie's shoulders.

The chime of a doorbell split the tension in the air like a meat cleaver. The sound was as pitifully out of place as it was intrusive.

"I'll, um, get it," Kate mumbled, and stood.

"Turn off the TV on your way, please." Norah kept her tone calm and steady, as if she were talking to the OR team in the midst of emergency surgery. "What do you want, Ellie?" She knelt in front of her friend and took her hand: "Tell me what you want the next step to be." Ellie's eyes seemed to snap back to life as she shook her head and straightened.

"I need to talk to Jess."

"Cami has her on the phone."

"Find out where he is"—her voice cracked—"which hospital, and tell her to get me there."

Continued in *The Act*, Book Two of the *Circus of Women* series. Subscribe to Nicole's newsletter at NicoleWaggonerAuthor.com to read the first two chapters now!

Acknowledgments

I often joke that this series exists because I moved to Oklahoma and missed my girlfriends so much that I made up five imaginary friends. That is a lie. It exists because I had teachers like Mrs. Griffin, Mr. Grady, Mr. Bracheen, Mrs. Williams, Dr. Fly, Mr. Singleton, and many many others whom I wish I had space to name, who believed in me and taught me that in education there was promise.

Thank you to the friends and family who provided support, talked plotlines, read, and grew these characters with me. Thank you to my husband, Mike, for being my unwavering champion. I'm still glad I opened the door. Thank you to my children, Noah and Maya. You remind me every day that love is a verb. Thank you to Jillan Hanel for W3s and for giving my dream your precious free time. You kept my finger off of the delete button more than twice! Thank you to Holly for being my person and to Jen who believes *all* the books should start in cars. Thank you to my Beth. Thank you to Keith and Diane Boone, Joe Pool, and Linda Harker for being the hands and feet of the church. Your leadership inspires me to strive to be Christ-like in all I do. Thank you to Carol Thompson and family for allowing me the honor of using Blane's likeness and spirit. He will always have our hearts and we will always have dragonflies. Thank you to Dale Ehmer, D'Andra Moody, and "Nurse Jackie" who saw me through ultimate joys and devastating loss. You are the epitome of excellence in women's care. Thank you to Brooke Warner for your vision and your faith in the stories we tell. Thank you to Sharon

Bially at BookSavvy PR for loving Kate with me—*la publicité est également très appréciée. Nous en font peut-être de trop, mais nous la faisons si bien.* Thank you to celebrities like Michael Bublé, Oprah Winfrey, Ellen DeGeneres, Maya Angelou, Taylor Swift, and Neil Patrick Harris who give more than they get and who remind us all that being ourselves is a gift and that gifts are meant to be shared.

About the Author

Nicole **Waggoner** is author of the Circus of Women series. In addition, Nicole is a decorated teacher with 12 years' experience teaching upper level English and Literary Criticism courses. She is proud to call her husband, Mike, and children, Noah and Maya, her biggest fans. The other loves of her life include green tea, great conversation over vino, all things theater, water and sand, women's health, and a fanatical commitment to live her belief that love is a verb to be paid forward.

SELECTED TITLES FROM SHE WRITES PRESS

She Writes Press is an independent publishing company
founded to serve women writers everywhere.
Visit us at www.shewritespress.com.

Stella Rose by Tammy Flanders Hetrick
$16.95, 978-1-63152-921-4
When her dying best friend asks her to take care of her sixteen-year-old daughter, Abby says yes—but as she grapples with raising a grieving teenager, she realizes she didn't know her best friend as well as she thought she did.

Shelter Us by Laura Diamond
$16.95, 978-1-63152-970-2
Lawyer-turned-stay-at-home-mom Sarah Shaw is still struggling to find a steady happiness after the death of her infant daughter when she meets a young homeless mother and toddler she can't get out of her mind—and becomes determined to rescue them.

Play for Me by Céline Keating
$16.95, 978-1-63152-972-6
Middle-aged Lily impulsively joins a touring folk-rock band, leaving her job and marriage behind in an attempt to find a second chance at life, passion, and art.

Again and Again by Ellen Bravo
$16.95, 978-1-63152-939-9
When the man who raped her roommate in college becomes a Senate candidate, women's rights leader Deborah Borenstein must make a choice—one that could determine control of the Senate, the course of a friendship, and the fate of a marriage.

A Tight Grip: A Novel about Golf, Love Affairs, and Women of a Certain Age by Kay Rae Chomic $16.95, 978-1-938314-76-6
As forty-six-year-old golfer Jane "Par" Parker prepares for her next tournament, she experiences a chain of events that force her to reevaluate her life.

Things Unsaid by Diana Y. Paul
$16.95, 978-1-63152-812-5
A family saga of three generations fighting over money and obligation—and a tale of survival, resilience, and recovery.